ASSHOLES
TO
ANGELS

*A Change of Mind in the
Workplace (and the World)*

T.E. Corner

BALBOA.PRESS
A DIVISION OF HAY HOUSE

Balboa Press books may be ordered through booksellers or by contacting:

Balboa Press
A Division of Hay House
1663 Liberty Drive
Bloomington, IN 47403
www.balboapress.com
844-682-1282

Because of the dynamic nature of the Internet, any web addresses or links contained in this book may have changed since publication and may no longer be valid. The views expressed in this work are solely those of the author and do not necessarily reflect the views of the publisher, and the publisher hereby disclaims any responsibility for them.

The author of this book does not dispense medical advice or prescribe the use of any technique as a form of treatment for physical, emotional, or medical problems without the advice of a physician, either directly or indirectly. The intent of the author is only to offer information of a general nature to help you in your quest for emotional and spiritual well-being. In the event you use any of the information in this book for yourself, which is your constitutional right, the author and the publisher assume no responsibility for your actions.

Any people depicted in stock imagery provided by Getty Images are models, and such images are being used for illustrative purposes only. Certain stock imagery © Getty Images.

Print information available on the last page.

ISBN: 978-1-9822-6998-2 (sc)
ISBN: 978-1-9822-7000-1 (hc)
ISBN: 978-1-9822-6999-9 (e)

Library of Congress Control Number: 2021911844

Balboa Press rev. date: 06/15/2021

My hope and goal is to spark new intellectual capital by sharing ideas positioned at an angle to conventional thought—in short, to publish books that disturb the present in the service of a better future.

—*Warren Bennis*

To my colleagues, peers, and business acquaintances who supported me over the years and saw through the bullshit while remaining honorable and true to themselves and their peers.

For my parents and grandparents, thank you for your love, guidance, belief, and instilling a virtuous way of life.

For my wife, who keeps me grounded and has been very patient through many ups and downs while holding fast to love and faith.

Contents

Prologue xi
Preface xv

Birth... 1
Chrysalis—Our Metamorphosis 3
Playground 7
The Fight 17
Champions without a Leader 23
Time is Killing Me 29
New Hire 37
Welcome to the Nightmare...51
I.T.S. to Succeed..57
The Teacher Left the Classroom 71
Asshole's Fable—The Manager Who Cried Wolf 81
On the Shoulders of Giants..97
Addict—Mindlessness Man 113
Encounter with a Buddhist Monk...................................125
Names before Numbers—The Moment I Realized I Was
       Working for an Idiot..137
Mediocre Management Massacre 151
Coaching is about Behaviors, Not Outcomes 161
You've Got to Play the Game...169
You Must Prove that You are the Right Person for the Job..........183
Love Calls, but Hate Would Have You Stay 197
Pain is a Wrong Perspective..203
No Risks in the Absence of Fear 213
Walk Away from the Other 97 Percent! 219
Imposters and Posers..229
Fu★k Success 237
Gradually and then Suddenly 247

The Sun Also Rises 269
I Healed 277
Blackballed 287
Jumping Back into the Toxic Soup 299
I'm a Frog 309
Final 325
Chrysalis or Sarcophagus? 331
What's Right? 341

Suggested Reading 347
About the Author 349

Prologue

For this world is the symbol of punishment, and all
the laws that seem to govern it are the laws of death.
Children are born into it through pain and in pain.
Their growth is attended by suffering, and they learn
of sorrow and separation and death. Their minds
seem to be trapped in their brain, and its powers to
decline if their bodies are hurt. They seem to love,
yet they desert and are deserted. They appear to
lose what they love, the most insane belief of all.

—*A Course in Miracles*

Welcome to *Assholes to Angels*. You are about to embark on a journey about life and work. Although this is being written as a work of fiction, the story is based on actual events. The protagonist in the story is based on a nonfictional individual, as are all the supporting characters throughout the story.

The initial chapters touch on a jagged recollection of childhood experiences from the perspective of Wayne Renroc, the story's protagonist. This preamble lays the groundwork for Wayne's life and career bleeding out the many parallels between human behavior in childhood and adult years, specifically in the working world.

We carry all our past experiences into the present moment, and they define who we are and how we behave. At the end of the day, this story's intent is to call out the disconnects in the workplace to lay the foundation for a better, more loving work experience.

The title aptly reflects the raw feelings, emotions, and experiences in the workplace and in life. The cover art, as with the book's title, were visualized during a morning meditation while gazing at a statue of the Buddha. As I was focusing on the Buddha's face, an angel emerged before my eyes, interrupting my meditation. When I looked at similar sculptures and images of the Buddha, an angel emerged in each of them as well.

Looking at photos of my daughters on the bulletin board of my office, I saw the same angel. When I focused on the Buddha's face, the Urna, bindi, or third eye formed the angel's head. The eyebrows formed the angel's wings. The nose formed the angel's gown or dress. It was in that moment when the angel came to life.

We are all angelic beings, but as life's experiences unfold, fear and the ego sink their claws in deep, and we gradually lose sight of our angelic ways. If we take the time to break through the harsh exterior of our ego, we can awaken our angel from deep within once again. This angel has always been there and will remain regardless of our mood, disposition, or chapter in life—no matter how upset or angry we become, no matter how happy and peaceful we are. Our angelic source is the only constant. It keeps us engaged and aligned despite the turmoil, despair, or suffering we experience while on our journey.

Whenever you feel anger, hatred, judgment, jealousy, or any other fear-based emotion toward someone, look closely into that person's eyes. You will see an angel before your very eyes. Next, ask yourself what you are truly upset about. Whenever we feel anger, it is not with the person, event, or thing, but rather our thoughts about the person, event, or thing.

Most people spend their lives "asleep at the wheel," living unconsciously. They feed the monster, or ego, with the illusion of fear, death, and dread. Most people never awaken from this dream, or, more aptly stated, nightmare.

Losing sight of their angelic ways, they gradually start acting like assholes believing they must fight and protect their image, their things, their titles, and everything that defines them. This is a product of the ego and fear. If we find the strength to reveal our angelic ways by allowing them to shine brightly once again, our lives will change because our perspective of the world has changed.

Thank you for joining me on the journey. I wish you love, laughter, and abundance.

Preface

This book is a bit more explicit than prior writings with a decent sprinkling of profanity throughout, which is intended to capture the raw feelings and the energy of frustration, dysfunction, and toxicity in the workplace through Wayne Renroc, the protagonist of the story.

It is a story whose time has come. A story told from the perspective of a regular guy who, through hard, honest work and dedication built a remarkably successful career as a leader with a national insurance company. This story captures the disconnect, the dysfunction, the bullshit, and the bullying that is rampant in an increasingly toxic workplace and world. Although writing this story began prior to 2020, it speaks loudly to the hatred, disconnect, and dysfunction that has recently unfolded in the world.

It calls out atrocities in the workplace that can easily be attributable to ineffective and ignorant upper management, which is rampant at most, but not all, companies. It brings to the surface the breakdown between effectively balancing and nurturing people and profits or names and numbers. Many companies and managers fail because of their ignorance of, and lack of love for, the names— the employees. Despite management's and leadership's knowledge, expertise, and track record of experience, although an admirable trait, their obsession with the numbers and efficiency alone proves to be a weakness. When focusing only on the numbers and neglecting the names—employees—eventually dysfunction and toxicity find their way into the workplace, and the world.

Add the many failed attempts at this mysterious, unicorn-like "work-life balance" to the picture, and it turns it into a work-work balance, leaving little time for life and loved ones. This ticking time bomb of stress and angst at the hands of self-serving and mindless management leads to burnout, sickness, and a miserable work experience for many.

At the end of the day, when all is said and done, the legacy these self-serving managers leave behind from their reign of terror will not be hailed as the work of true leaders. It will not be the stuff that books are written about except, of course, a book like this one.

The opinions reflected in this book are based on actual experiences and events, representing the voice and perspective of the author. Although, it is also intended to give a voice to fellow colleagues who felt similar frustrations as he did. The names, places, and titles have been changed to protect people's privacy.

This story is a narrative of sorts drawing out the parallels between the playground during childhood and work during adulthood. The corporate world is the playground of our adult years, and the childish behaviors from the playground of our youth persist long into our adult years.

Before you turn the page, I will leave you with this little nugget.

> The system is so flawed that you can't get rid of mediocre management. Here's an example: Let's say I inherit a nice vineyard on beautiful land. Six months later I want to sell it, because it's not making any money. But I've got a problem: the guy who manages the vineyard is never there. He's playing golf all day. But he won't give up his job running the vineyard. And he won't let anybody look at the vineyard because he doesn't want to see it sold. You might say to me, "What are you, crazy? Get the police, kick him out!" But that's the trouble with public companies: you can't do it without a very difficult fight.
>
> … it is very hard to get rid of a CEO even if he or she is doing a terrible job. Often CEOs get that top job because they're like the guy in college who was the head of the fraternity. He wasn't the smartest guy,

but he was the best social guy and a very likable guy, and so he moved up through the ranks.

—Carl Icahn (*Money: Master the Game,* Robbins (2016))

Enjoy what lies ahead!

 # Birth

What is not love is always fear and nothing else.

—*A Course in Miracles*

Wayne sat at the kitchen table lost in his thoughts. His left forearm gently rested on the tabletop with his fingers gently wrapped around the handle of his favorite coffee mug. He lifted the warm cup of coffee to his lips to take a sip while his thoughts romped around the mosh-pit of his mind.

Life and death, birth and rebirth. The sun never sets on our lives—rather, the world rotates while revolving around the sun, giving the illusion of the sun setting. Just as the sun never sets, our lives never end. Birth is like the sunrise, as death is like the sunset. Although birth seems new and marks a new beginning, in truth, it is a continuation of what has always been.

At birth, we enter a world unknown. The place we came from has been long forgotten by everyone who is already here despite manifesting from the same source. The miracle of birth is just that: a miracle!

We grow inside our mother's womb for nearly one year. Through the umbilical cord, we are fed oxygenated, nutrient-rich blood, allowing us to grow an astronomical five thousand times larger.

By the time we are born, the two cells that united have become two hundred million cells, and those millions of cells weigh six billion times more than the fertilized egg. This astounding growth occurs after spending over nine months in our mother's womb with no exposure to light, no exposure to air, and no exposure to sound other than what is sensed through the vibrational energy from the sound of the outside world.

From birth to early adulthood—approximately eighteen years—we grow a measly three and a half times larger than our height at birth. Growing from one-and-a-half feet to nearly six feet tall seems astounding, but it pales in comparison to the herculean thousandfold growth we experience in our mother's womb from conception to birth.

Life itself is inexplicable and inevitable, as is death. Does anyone truly know how life happens, how we exist? Although there are medical explanations for life, no one can explain what gives us life, the force that beats our hearts and powers our brains. What gives our bodies the power to live, to think, and to do all the miraculous things we do?

Our births introduce us to the miracle of human life. As far as we know, birth is the first time we are introduced to fear and suffering. The experience of birth is quite violent. It is no wonder we cry when we are born. This just might be the first time we learn to breathe on our own through our lungs. Coming from darkness, our eyes are exposed to a bright new world for the first time. We hear sounds, crisper and louder than when we were protected while inside our mother's womb.

Time does not exist for a fetus or a baby, or a young child. When we are taught the concept of time, often from the wrong perspective of fear and death, it ends up killing us—stress, anxiety, deadlines, and tardiness. When a baby is born, the doctor takes note of the time of his or her arrival. Then we are cut away from the only life source we knew up to that point. All our experiences were through an intimate connection to our mother, picking up the energy and vibrations from her and from the outside world.

Sadly, for most people, this is the beginning of the end, because many people base everything they do in their lives on the concept of time and the ego. Time and ego are things that we celebrate, things that introduce us to the concept of individuality or separateness. But they are what divide us, causing hatred and war.

We are all angels born into a world of fear and suffering. This fear and suffering clouds our true angelic ways, and many of us build what we believe are protective outer shells to keep us safe from harm, from our fears. Our fears are products of our egos as they slowly change our perspective of ourselves, other people, and the world.

Welcome to life?

Chrysalis—Our Metamorphosis

It's a little more like the image of a caterpillar
enclosing itself in a cocoon in order to go through the
metamorphosis ... We're talking about a metamorphosis.
We're talking about going from a caterpillar to a butterfly.
We're talking about how to become a butterfly.

—Ram Dass

Wayne was still sitting at the kitchen table lost in his thoughts. In less than an hour, it would be time to take his youngest daughter, Chloe, to kindergarten for the day. "Hey, sweetie! Can you make sure you go to the potty, brush your teeth, and get your shoes on?" he chirped.

"I already brushed my teeth," came Chloe's loving reply.

"Okay. Great job! Please make sure you go potty and get your shoes on."

"Okay."

Wayne smiled and gave Chloe a hug and a kiss on her forehead. She ran into her room to get her shoes on and her backpack ready for the day while Wayne lost himself again in his thoughts about how some people can be so angelic while others can be complete assholes—sort of like an ugly caterpillar versus a beautiful butterfly.

Caterpillars are miracles of nature, he thought to himself. *They mysteriously transform from delicate and often somewhat grotesque-looking creatures into beings of beauty with wings that allow them to soar into the heavens above.*

But they must undergo a metamorphosis though. It's their nature. It's an ugly, multilegged, furry, worm-looking creature that creeps along a branch, feasting on delicate green leaves to store away energy in preparation for a miraculous transformation. Like a bear feasting for hibernation, the caterpillar feasts for its metamorphosis.

Once the feast ends, this tiny, unsightly creature will begin the process of encasing itself in a shell by securely fastening itself to a branch or leaf. This chrysalis will keep the caterpillar safe while it undergoes a metamorphosis in which it literally turns to liquid mush safely encased inside the chrysalis. The caterpillar appears to melt, changing from a solid creature into a liquid caterpillar. To be successful, the shell of the chrysalis must be secure enough to encase the soon-to-be butterfly. Equally important, the chrysalis must prevent threats from entering, which could jeopardize the butterfly's emergence, possibly ending in tragedy.

Like the caterpillar, we humans slowly creep along on life's journey, receiving nourishment and gathering experiences, all of which define who we become. Along the journey, we often weave an outer shell to keep us safe from our perceived fears. The ego is akin to a caterpillar's chrysalis. We spin this outer ego shell, layer upon layer, to keep us safe from harm as we undergo a transformation, a metamorphosis, turning us into fear-based beings who often act like assholes rather than the angels we are intended to be.

Unfortunately, we often spin this outer shell from a foundation of fear, tragic experiences, and negative memories until this shell becomes our burden. Shedding our past hurts and tragedies proves exceedingly difficult as we allow our past to hold us hostage from growth. This resistance wraps around us, suffocating us and preventing us from fulfilling our true intention of spreading our wings to soar in the heavens above like a beautiful butterfly.

Our emotions and thoughts are analogous to the tiny threads spun, which create the caterpillar's chrysalis. The chrysalis is intended to surround the caterpillar, keeping it safe from any threats. With the chrysalis properly spun, the caterpillar successfully undergoes a metamorphosis, allowing it to emerge as a beautiful butterfly. When our thoughts and emotions emerge from a place of positivity and love, we are all but guaranteed to live a life of beauty, just like the beautiful butterfly emerging from its chrysalis.

However, if our mind and thoughts are resistant, laden with fear, anger, hatred, self-doubt, ridicule, and judgment, our chrysalis may very well end up becoming our very own sarcophagus.

Our minds—conscious, subconscious, pain body, id, ego, or however you refer to the human mind—spin a chrysalis of experiences intended to keep us safe. If we experience a shift from a place of love, safety, and acceptance to one of fear, anger, defensiveness, or attack, which can be the result of an unloving and unsafe environment or traumatic experiences, we begin to weave what we falsely believe is a protective barrier around ourselves that seems to keep us safe from future harm. The longer we allow this outer shell to grow, the more unlikely it is that we will emerge to see the light.

Like a beautiful butterfly, we are intended to emerge from the chrysalis and spread our wings after undergoing a miraculous metamorphosis, but not everyone does. Consider for a moment a caterpillar spinning a chrysalis that is paper thin. Because of inferior construction, threats from the outside world introduce harm and potential disaster, ultimately resulting in the demise of the caterpillar. However, if a caterpillar spins a chrysalis that is too thick, shutting everything out, ultimately the butterfly does not emerge. The intended protection of the chrysalis becomes the butterfly's very own sarcophagus.

The good news is that this scenario of disaster has not been witnessed in nature—although, it is intriguing to ponder what would occur if the caterpillar's chrysalis was damaged or flawed because of the negative influences of the environment, which then could ultimately lead to its demise. But, then again, maybe they never make it to the point at which they even have an opportunity to spin a chrysalis.

What do caterpillars and butterflies have to do with business and the working world? Well, everything! Even though humans are very resilient, we are all subjects of our environment and our mind-set. Depending on our individual perspective, experiences, and environment, our life or career may never transform into one of beauty. We all have a choice and can change our lives and career for the better if we allow it to happen and believe it can happen.

For many, their suffering is so strong that their lives are spent in a constant struggle to find experiences of enjoyment and fulfillment, which are often fleeting. The more we fight to break free, the more suffering it creates. This continual resistance prevents a life of ease and joy from emerging. Deep down, the beautiful butterfly hidden inside is dying, and the world may never experience its true beauty.

How many people weave a confident and strong exterior, but deep down, they are suffering and slowly dying?

Words to Live By

Some will read this story about Wayne Renroc, dismiss it as absurd, and go about their day. Others just might have no idea what any of this means and cannot relate to Wayne's struggles. And there are those who will read Wayne's plight, and it will resonate with them and possibly transform their lives. Maybe, just maybe, they will awaken and spread their wings like a beautiful butterfly sharing its miracle of love with the world.

chrys·a·lis /ˈkrisələs/ noun
noun: chrysalis; plural noun: chrysalises
- a quiescent insect pupa, especially of a butterfly or moth.
- the hard-outer case enclosing a chrysalis.
  a transitional state. "she emerged from the chrysalis of self-conscious adolescence"
  (https://www.google.com/search?q=chrysalis)

Definition of *chrysalis*

1. a: a pupa of a butterfly
   broadly: an insect pupa
   b: the hardened outer protective layer of a pupa

2. a protecting covering: a sheltered state or stage of being or growth
   (*https://www.merriam-webster.com/dictionary/chrysalis*)

 Playground

It's called a playground, but it's nearer
to a battlefield. It can be brutal.

—*Keith Richards*

Wayne's daydream continued, and he found himself reminiscing about his days as a youngster in middle school.

The warm afternoon air caressed their cheeks as Wayne and his friends sauntered outside. He was feeling quite sluggish after inhaling a peanut butter and jelly sandwich and potato chip lunch washed down with chocolate milk followed by a Tastycake Butterscotch Krimpet.

"Ah man, this sucks! I can't see," Wayne's friend Will quipped, rubbing his eyes. The sudden exposure to the bright rays of sunlight beaming down to earth felt like a laser scorching his eyes in the quick eight-seconds it took to reach earth from ninety-three million miles away.

"This happens every day, and you're still surprised by it?" their friend Steve taunted.

"Screw you! I'm gonna kick your ass!" Will retorted.

"Whatever, loser! How in the world are you going to kick my ass when you can't even see?" Steve punched Will in the upper arm as hard as he could. The perfect spot between the shoulder and bicep hitting bone, which hurt like hell. He ran off laughing.

"Ow! That friggin' hurt. You jerk!" Will roared, taking off after Steve in hot pursuit.

The afternoon sunshine accompanied by the fresh spring air awakened their senses. A buzz of energy began pumping through their veins as they jokingly berated one another on the playground. This was exactly what they needed after a lunch of high-fatigue foods preceded by a sedentary morning sitting in class, which felt more like an eternity.

This momentary reprieve from their desks was the best part of the day, other than the final bell signaling the end of the school day. Smiles were plastered across their faces as they grasped onto the joy of the moment. Their goofing-off rapidly heated up into a frenzy of excitement in the afternoon sun. Hot days of summer crept into the backs of their minds as they fantasized about their summer break, which was just around the corner.

Although a flash in time, this moment would remain a permanent fixture in their minds, reminding them of the carefree days of their youth.

For the past few weeks, they had gathered for recess on the lower parking lot of the school while the athletic fields were aerated and seeded in preparation for baseball and soccer season. It really did not matter to them. They always found something fun to do no matter where they were or what was going on.

Standing at the edge of the parking lot, Wayne and his friends spread their arms wide while delicately balancing on the curb as though they were soaring like an eagle. One fatal slip in the wrong direction and they would tumble down the hill of stones and rocks, careening toward the trolley tracks.

The local trolley rumbled by about every twenty minutes or so. It was on schedule and arriving soon at the next stop, Woodland Avenue. Off in the distance, they could hear it approaching. The faster the trolley sped along, the faster the rhythm of the solid-steel crane wheels sounded as they pounded across the seams in the tracks. Approaching the Woodland Avenue stop, the trolley's pace slowed, followed by the rhythm of the wheels: *click clack click clack click clack … click … clack … click … clack … … click … …. clack … … click … …. … clack … … …click.*

The force of the trolley created a tremor that emerged from the earth's surface. Vibrating through their Nike sneakers into their feet and up their legs, it rattled their bones. *Clang!* They heard a loud crash, sounding like someone smashed a Rawlings aluminum baseball bat against a flagpole.

"Holy crap! What the hell was that?" Steve blurted out.

"Dude, that was Kevin. He threw a rock at the trolley!" They cringed and turned their heads to look in the direction of the teachers who were monitoring recess. They grasped onto the hope that the teachers did not hear the earth-shattering crash of the rock smashing against the rooftop of the trolley.

"Oh man! The trolley's slowing down!" Will shrieked. "Dude, it's stopping! We're screwed."

"Naah! It's just slowing down at Woodland Avenue," Wayne commented.

Wayne and his friends watched it come to a complete stop when the doors sprang open. They held their breath as they stood nervously in silence, waiting for the trolley conductor to come over and beat the crap out of them. When a figure emerged from the trolley, Wayne and his friends prayed it was not the conductor. Someone exited the trolley. He planted both feet firmly on the ground, turned his head, and looked in their direction. Then he began walking toward them.

"Oh shit! Is that the conductor?" Wayne shrieked, fearing their worst nightmares were about to come true.

"Crap! He's coming over here. Kevin, why'd you throw the rock? You asshole!" Steve shouted, but Kevin was long gone. He had run off while Wayne and his friends stood there like knuckleheads, watching everything unfold.

If this guy came over, he would most likely accuse Wayne and his friends of a crime they did not commit. Even if this guy tracked Kevin down, he sure as heck was not going to fess up and admit to his misdeed.

Still trying to make out whether it was the conductor, they stood there in a trance. Luckily, the man walked away, and the trolley cruised off into the horizon.

"Holy crap!" Steve sighed. "I thought he was coming over here."

Once the trolley cruised out of sight in the background, off in the distance, about a block away, they spied the local 7-Eleven convenience store. They often fantasized about skipping out on recess, jumping across the tracks, and making a run for 7-Eleven to get some candy and a Cherry Slurpee. It was too risky though. Fearing they would get caught, they never riled up the courage to execute their daring escape despite the burnouts doing it all the time.

Danger lurked on the tracks, where badasses and tough guys hung out. The trolley tracks had this strange allure of danger mixed with the fear of getting busted by the cops. But there was something even worse than being busted by the cops. That was getting caught by the burnouts, on their turf!

Decked out in AC/DC and Black Sabbath concert shirts, they puffed on Marlboro Red cigarettes and made out with their girlfriends adorned in leather jackets. It was very reminiscent of a scene out of the movie *Grease* with the T-Birds, Kenickie and Danny Zuko, and the Pink Ladies, Rizzo and Sandy. Although it was more intense, like *The Outsiders*, with Dallas Winston and Cherry Valance mired with *Freddy Krueger* nightmares lurking on the tracks.

The mystery of the trolley tracks still tugged at their curiosity, distracting them from Kevin's recent antics, which had nearly landed Wayne and his friends in a heap of trouble. Regardless, it felt good to be among friends, running around and goofing off without a care in the world, even despite knuckleheads like Kevin who always tried to ruin their day. They wished the fun on the playground would last forever, but it unfortunately came to an end. And it was not with the usual ring of a school bell.

On this particular day, Wayne was about to get his bell rung when this kid Trevor rudely interrupted Wayne's fun. Trevor was an upperclassman, a friend of Kevin's, and trouble followed him everywhere.

Trevor stopped Wayne in his tracks, separating him from his friends. "Hey, I heard what you said about my mom! You better apologize, or I swear to God I'm going to kick your ass!"

Easily a foot taller than Wayne, Trevor towered over him like a dark cloud slowly creeping in to overwhelm a small town. This impending storm of Trevor infiltrated Wayne's afternoon with no opportunity for escape. Then a sudden flash of lightning crashed from the heavens above, hurtling toward earth. Wayne cringed in anticipation of the loud *crack* of thunder in the form of Trevor's fist crashing into his skull.

Time stood still. Trevor crept closer. Wayne's fear intensified. Trevor's nose inched closer to Wayne's face. Wayne was unable to avoid the constellation of pimples scattered across Trevor's cheeks, forehead, and nose. This grotesque close-up of Trevor's complexion was quite horrifying, eliciting fear of an entirely different sort.

In a strange turn of events, Wayne happily welcomed the idea of Trevor beating the daylight out of him. This was a far better alternative than being showered in infectious pus from one of Trevor's pimples.

Trevor was so close to Wayne's face, he could visibly see the pus awaiting its release. And all that separated Wayne from this infectious yellow pus was a paper-thin layer of skin. It could very easily burst under the intense pressure, squirt through the air, and land in Wayne's eyes blinding him! Yecch! His nightmare worsened when he envisioned it flying into his mouth!

The closer Trevor crept in, the faster Wayne's heart pounded. Nausea and fear jockeyed for position while the palms of Wayne's hands became damp with perspiration. He was not sure if he was going to barf in Trevor's face, burst out in tears, piss in his pants, or maybe a combination of all three.

Wayne cringed and took a nervous gulp. His eyelids slowly slid shut, and he prayed that Trevor would disappear. Images of Mr. Creosote from Monty Python's movie *The Meaning of Life* entered the plotline of what Wayne imagined could happen to him.

Having recently watched the movie with his brother the weekend before, a scene flashed through his mind. Mr. Creosote, who is a morbidly obese middle-aged man, dines at a French restaurant. His entrance into the restaurant is accompanied by ominous music followed by a short dialogue with the maître d' (played by John Cleese).

Maître d': Ah, good afternoon, sir, and how are we today?
Mr. Creosote: Better.
Maître d': Better?
Mr. Creosote: Better get a bucket—I'm gonna vomit.

Mr. Creosote is then escorted to his table. Once seated, he starts to projectile vomit, failing to hit the bucket he had requested a moment before. The floor quickly becomes covered in vomit, and so do the cleaning woman and the maître d's trousers. Mr. Creosote listens patiently while the maître d' recites highlights of the evening's menu; after vomiting on the menu held open right in front of him by the maître d', he orders everything off the menu and six bottles of Château Latour 1945, a double magnum of champagne, and half a dozen cases of beer. He finishes all of it, vomiting profusely all over himself, his table, and the other diners, many of whom leave in disgust. Finally, after being persuaded by the maître d' to eat a "wafer-thin mint," he explodes in a tsunami of innards and partially digested food.

Wayne feared a similar scene was about to transpire on the playground, but he would be the one profusely vomiting all over the place. This experience would surely scar him for life, and it would not be from Trevor's fists pounding on his face. Catching his breath, Wayne reopened his eyes to regain his composure and bearings. Summoning the courage, he timidly replied with a meek, "What?"

Trevor blurted, "What did you say about my mom?"

"Nothing?" he sheepishly answered as his voice faded off in a whimper.

"You better apologize!" Trevor continued his taunt.

Standing motionless, paralyzed with fear, Wayne played out scenario after scenario in his mind regarding his fate. *Do I run, risking humiliation and everyone laughing at me for being a coward, or do I stay here and take a beating like a man?*

He feared the end, his end, was imminent. This giant was about to squeeze the life out of him. *Could this really be the end? Is it all over for me? I haven't had a chance to do anything: my first kiss, my first love, my first beer.* He wished for it all to go away, hoping this was just a bad dream.

Trevor glanced over his shoulder toward his friends who were in the background, watching the scene unfold. With a sinister laugh, Trevor shoved Wayne in the chest with both hands. Feeling as though Jean Claude van Damme had just thrust his fists through his chest cavity, Wayne stumbled backward, trying to catch his balance.

"Today's your lucky day!" Trevor said with an evil grin and a chuckle. "You better not piss me off!" He walked away to claim his next victim on the playground.

What the heck was that? Wayne thought to himself. Still in a state of shock, he floated over to his friends. "Hey did you see that? That asshole Trevor jumped in my face accusing me of saying something about his mom." Wayne shuddered from the shock. "He said he was going to beat the shit out of me if I didn't apologize."

Will laughed. "He's been doing that all week at recess. He thinks it's cool, but he's just a big jackass."

"Thanks. That makes me feel a little better. He scared the crap out of me! I almost pissed my pants. I thought I was dead."

"Don't sweat it. He did the same thing to me yesterday. I told him to go screw himself," Will added.

The bell rang, signaling the end of lunch break, which was far better than the end of his existence! It was time to head back to class. Wayne was saved!

The incident on the playground was one of the first times Wayne realized the veil of safety from his parents was not always going to be there to protect him. Despite a fair share of arguments and scuffles with his brothers, even a few of them escalating to bloodshed, his parents were always there to keep the peace.

A new reality was revealed, one for which he was not prepared. Not only did he have to contend with his brothers, but he was now contending with other kids on the playground of life. The safety and protection provided by his parents was now substituted by the protection from other adults, teachers and coaches, whose focus was not solely on him but on dozens of other kids as well. He was fading into the background among the fray.

Adjusting to this new reality that a teacher's protection would not be enough to keep him safe, he quickly learned to fend for himself. Plus, it did not sit well with him having to plead his case against the Trevors of the world, while grasping onto a pipe dream that a teacher would see through their lies and bullshit. These unexpected experiences gradually changed his perspective of the world for the worse. His eyes were opened to a new reality which was a growing world of assholes—Trevors.

———◆———

It felt as though his experience on the playground was a lifetime ago and whenever he relived that experience, he chuckled at the absurdity and irony of it all. Now a grown adult with a family and career, Wayne was astonished and embarrassed by the behavior of so-called professionals in the corporate world, which was not a far cry from his days on the playground while in middle school.

It was one of those things that people accepted, but Wayne was perplexed by this behavior and questioned it. He wondered how it was possible that knuckleheads like Trevor and Kevin from his middle school days got away with the stunts they pulled. How could these jokers get what they wanted out of life by doing the opposite of what Wayne was taught, which was to be honest, to be fair, and to treat others with dignity and respect?

Why did it seem as though the kids who were honest and nice were picked on and made fun of? Kids like Trevor and Kevin treated people like crap while twisting words, misrepresenting themselves, and manipulating stories into their favor so they could get what they wanted.

The more this occurred the more he wrestled with the idea of going down that same path, but deep down, Wayne knew it would not feel right. Plus, his parents would not put up with that type of behavior anyway. The incident on the playground left him feeling as though he did not have much control over the world around him. It was this kid Trevor's word against Wayne's. Since he was much bigger than Wayne, Trevor could simply intimidate him and get away with practically whatever he wanted.

Wayne would come to learn that this scenario was not segregated to the playground and unfortunately carried over into adulthood and the workplace. This was not the first time he had to deal with an asshole at school, and it would not be the last. Like a plague overwhelming a town, it would spread into his work life as an adult.

His newfound realization was that there were people in the world who would do whatever it took to win and get what they wanted via the wrong means, by being an asshole, a jerk, and leaving a trail of hurt and devastation in their wake. A downright disappointment, this would test his gumption and personal beliefs.

Although we all are angels, many of us fall victim to the ego and the illusion of fear so that we unintentionally, or unconsciously, morph into assholes under the guise of protecting ourselves, keeping ourselves safe, and winning at all costs. This story is a *Return to Love* (Marianne Williamson). It is a return to our angelic ways in life and the workplace. It is a path toward happiness via a calm and modest life rather than a life of constant unrest.

Words to Live By

When you find yourself in a state of anger or upset, pause, and ask yourself what you are angry or upset about. Then ask yourself, "What am I really angry or upset about?"

You cannot be angry at someone, but you can become angry and upset based on your perspective of an event or person. It is impossible to be angry or upset at someone or an event. When you awaken to the reality that you are angry and upset at your thoughts, or perspective, of the person or event, then your life will change for the better.

Asshole Definition

"a stupid, irritating, or contemptible person" (Apple dictionary)

"an irritating or contemptible person" (Google definition)

"a stupid, mean, or contemptible person" (dictionary.com)

"a usually vulgar: a stupid, annoying, or detestable person; b usually vulgar: the least attractive or desirable part or area—used in phrases like asshole of the world" (*Merriam-Webster.com*)

Angel Definition

"a person of exemplary conduct or virtue" (iMac pages dictionary)

"a person who is like an angel (as in looks or behavior)" (*Merriam-Webster*)

"a person having qualities generally attributed to an angel, as beauty, purity, or kindliness" (dictionary.com)

👊 The Fight

> I do believe that, where there is only a choice between
> cowardice and violence, I would advise violence ...
> But I believe that nonviolence is infinitely superior to
> violence, forgiveness is more manly than punishment.
>
> —*Mahatma Gandhi*

Summer 1983 on a beautiful Saturday afternoon, Wayne and his brother, Matt, sauntered back home after spending the day hanging out at the local pizza shop, goofing off and playing video games. They split their time between New London Pizza and Drexel Hill Pizza, also known as "Greasy Greg's," for the obnoxiously greasy pizza. The pizza shop they spent their time at depended on which one had the hot video game at the time: Pac Man at New London Pizza, Centipede and Galaxian at Greasy Greg's. Occasionally, they would divert their plans and end up at Hartnett's Five and Ten store to play Asteroids or Donkey Kong.

The haze of grease in Greasy Greg's pizza shop was so dense their eyes burned upon entering. The smell of grease was so thick it sank deep into their hair and the fibers of their clothes. They hung out as long as possible until the feeling of nausea kicked in, signaling their time to go.

When the time came to leave, they somehow found a way to pry their faces away from the screen and peel their fingers off the joystick. Running out of quarters made the decision to leave much easier. After quickly refilling their sodas, they meandered out of the pizza shop. Shoving the glass door open, they stepped outside. Emerging from under the store canopy, they were greeted by the bright afternoon sunlight, reminding them of the beautiful Saturday afternoon that awaited them.

An overindulgence in junk food, soda, and candy made the journey home a slow one. On their lazy trudge home, they moseyed down the hill on Harwicke Road. Upon reaching the end of the block, they cautiously scanned Powell Road for any cars zipping around the bend. They looked left, then right, and then left again to make sure the coast was clear. As though hit with a swift kick in the butt, they jumped into Powell Road in a sprint toward the other side.

Wayne held his left hand outstretched, grasping onto his cup of soda in a lame attempt to avoid spilling the precious nectar of happiness. For any onlookers, it looked as though he was holding a cup of nuclear waste while frantically running to clear it safely away from nearby civilians. Upon reaching the other side of Powell Road, they hopped onto the sidewalk and continued their journey home on Harwicke Road, sipping their sodas and laughing with one another.

Suddenly, Wayne heard his name echo through the afternoon air. Initially, he paid no attention to it. They continued their stroll home until he heard his name again. A nagging curiosity tugged at him, so he glanced over his shoulder to find out who was shouting his name.

"Wayne, I think that kid is calling you," Matt said.

"Oh crap! Just keep on walking," Wayne emphatically demanded.

"Why? Who is it?"

"It's this kid Mitch from school. He's a total jerk, so keep walking. I don't want to hang out with him."

"All right. If you say so." Matt rolled his eyes.

They continued their walk home, maintaining their gaze straight ahead, doing their best to ignore the wails from this kid. Then it stopped.

"Thank God! I think he's gone!" Wayne exclaimed.

"Dude, no he's not!" Matt announced.

"What?" Wayne looked back, "Oh shit! He's running toward us."

This kid was relentless. If it were anyone else, Wayne would not care, but this kid, Mitch, was a notorious troublemaker. Everywhere he went, bad news followed. Wayne wanted nothing to do with him.

"Hey, Wayne!" Mitch caught up with them. "What are you guys doing? Who's this? Where are you going?" The interrogation began.

"Hey, Mitch. What's up?" Wayne replied.

Deep down, Wayne wanted to tell this kid to screw off, but at the same time, he did not want to be rude or cause any trouble. So, they allowed him to walk with them, hoping that he would eventually peel off and go on his way.

"Were you hanging out at New London?"

"Nope. Greasy Greg's. What's up with you?" Wayne replied.

"That place sucks!"

"Whatever, Mitch," Wayne replied. "Idiot," he mumbled under his breath.

"Dude, I could beat you at any of those games. Where are you going now?"

"Home," Wayne replied while they walked along the sidewalk.

Mitch kept pace with them, straddling the curb with his left foot on the curb and his other foot stepping into the street, making it appear as though he had an awful hitch in his walk.

"Why? Who's this guy?" Mitch ignorantly asked. "Let's go to New London Pizza and play Pac Man."

"This is my brother."

"Hey," Matt said.

"What's your name?" Mitch continued harassing them. Still straddling the curb, he approached a tree in the middle of the block between the sidewalk and curb. Wayne hoped Mitch would walk into the tree and smash his forehead against the gray bark of the oak tree, knocking him unconscious. Unfortunately, Mitch avoided the tree by jumping into the street and maneuvering around it.

"Matt," Wayne's brother replied.

"Oh. Hey, Matt," Mitch replied. "Why won't your brother play me at Pac Man? Is he afraid? Does he need you around to protect him?"

They did their best to endure Mitch's verbal assault, hoping they would soon be home, where they could ditch him. If they could just make it to Alford Road, they would almost be home.

"No, like I said, we're heading home," Wayne said in annoyance.

As they turned left onto Alford Road, a car approached, headed in their direction, but Mitch didn't budge. He just kept straddling the curb and the street. The car laid on the horn for Mitch to get out of the road. *Beep! Beeeeep!*

Mitch looked up and gave the driver the middle finger. "Up yours!" he roared as the car passed them by.

"You're an asshole, Mitch," Wayne said in annoyance.

"Whatever, Wayne! What are you going to do about it anyway?" Mitch taunted him. "So, are you afraid to play me at Pac Man?" he continued.

On this day, for whatever reason, Mitch was determined to rattle their cages. It became noticeably clear that he wasn't going anywhere unless he was forced to.

"No," Wayne calmly replied.

"Then why are you going home? Is your mommy calling you?"

"I told you. We have to get home," Wayne said, quickly losing his patience.

"Come on, Wayne. Just ignore him. Let's go," Matt said, sensing Wayne's irritation.

"I'll see you at school on Monday, Mitch. See ya," Wayne said as he kept walking.

"Where are you going? Oh, I get it! You need your brother to protect you!" Mitch walked toward Wayne, stepping into his path.

"No, I am just heading home," Wayne said in a matter-of-fact tone.

"Why? Whatever! I can't wait to tell everyone at school that you're chicken-shit and afraid to play me at stupid Pac Man!" He crept closer.

Butterflies began fluttering around Wayne's stomach in a chaotic frenzy of adrenaline. The patience he had displayed was running low, soon to be replaced by anger, which would quickly boil into rage. His body began to tremble. Deep down, he wanted to put Mitch's head through a wall, but he really did not want to fight. So, he did his best to keep his cool until the shithead punk lunged at Wayne with his fist!

Fortunately, Wayne dodged the attack. He bobbed backward, avoiding Mitch's fist as it floated past his jaw. The only impact he felt was from the cool breeze caused by Mitch's fist flying. Wayne instinctively struck back with a left hook to Mitch's temple. Mitch immediately fell, crumpling to the ground like a sack of potatoes.

"Get up! Come on you piece of shit! Let's go!" Wayne roared while Mitch rolled up in the fetal position, awaiting an ass-whooping.

Immediately upon seeing Mitch crumple to the asphalt, without hesitation, he stepped over top of him, like Muhammad Ali standing victorious over Sonny Liston, about to rain down fists of fury upon his face, cutting him open and letting his blood spill onto Alford Road.

For the briefest moment, visions flashed through Wayne's mind of beating Mitch unconscious until his face was painted a Navajo red in his own blood. Fortunately for Mitch, something told Wayne that this was not the right thing to do and he should walk away. Instead of putting his foot through Mitch's face, Wayne walked away.

"Holy shit, dude! That was awesome!" his brother said in amazement. "You knocked him out with one punch! Who does that?"

"Yeah," Wayne muttered and walked home.

"Wait up! Don't leave me here with him." Matt jogged over to catch up with his brother.

Wayne said nothing. They commenced their walk home, once again. Wayne trudged up the tiny driveway approaching their home. He thrust his right hand forward, grabbed the brass handle of the screen door, and flung it open. The paint around the frame was peeling: it was desperately in need of a fresh coat of paint. The hinges creaked when opened. The screen even had a big hole in it from Wayne's many attempts at opening it with his foot.

The tension spring on the door slowed it down upon opening to prevent it from flying off the hinges. Wayne stepped onto the porch. The door immediately reversed direction, slamming closed behind him with a loud *crack!* The sound of the screen door slamming shut echoed through the neighborhood like a gunshot, shattering the afternoon air. Flakes of paint jumped off the door frame. The door nearly took off his brother's face, as he was a couple of steps behind him.

"Dude! Stop. Are you trying to kill me?" Matt wailed.

Ignoring his brother, Wayne opened the front door and walked into the living room, leaving the door wide open for his brother to enter. Wayne fell to his knees and began to sob. Gasping for air, he moaned. Matt came running over.

"What's wrong? Why are you crying?"

"I'm sorry. I didn't want that to happen. I didn't want to fight!"

"Yeah, but he started it. You had no other choice."

"I know, but I didn't want that to happen."

His brother placed his hand on Wayne's shoulder. "It's okay, Wayne. You did what you had to in the moment. He's never going to mess with you again. Don't worry about it."

"I wanted to walk away, but that asshole kept taunting me."

"Yep. He wouldn't stop. Dude, he threw the first punch! He got what was coming to him. Screw him! Your only option was to fight!" Matt exclaimed.

"Yeah, I guess so."

The following week at school, everyone asked Mitch about the shiner on his face. He made up his own story, denying what really happened. In the meantime, Wayne wanted to tell all his classmates about the fight but knew it wouldn't do him any good, so he kept it to himself. He felt proud for sticking up for himself, proving to himself that he was strong enough to stand on his own.

Words to Live By

Stand up for yourself in life and the workplace from a platform of love and strength, rather than fear, anger, and victimization.

Champions without a Leader

Winners focus on winning; losers focus on winners.

—*Unknown*

Spit flew from their coach's mouth on a cool March afternoon in the spring of 1987. He roared at the players, commanding them to run another drill. They ran lap after lap and pushed through hundreds of push-ups, sit-ups, and suicides, executing one play after another—all under the direction of a coach who only knew how to coach and lead a team by pounding his chest, roaring commands onto the field, and throwing his clipboard in frustration.

This was Wayne's senior year of high school. He and his teammates were growing tired of their losing ways. They were talented, but their coach could not get them to come together to win a game. Their coach did his best, but clearly there was something amiss, and it certainly was not due to a lack of talent on the team. They had some of the best players in the league, consisting of three all-state honorees—a midfielder, an attackman, and a goalie—and an All-American attackman. This team was stacked but destined for failure.

The problem was the team had a coach who ruled with an iron fist rather than lead, coach, and guide these young players. Hoping to win the team over through intimidation, he roared commands and ran them until their lungs burned and their legs could no longer carry them.

It can be a difficult task to earn the respect of a high school kid, but not impossible. A true leader recognizes that although he may not experience immediate results, by understanding the players, the game, and what it takes to be a champion, his efforts will pay

23

off. Real leaders understand they are planting seeds for a lifetime of success and victories, while tyrants leave a trail of devastation behind them and plant the seeds of fear and failure.

Their head coach lacked sufficient knowledge of the game he had been hired to coach, and the players knew it! Practices ended up being an exercise in frustration and futility for both the coach and team. He had lost them.

The more he roared, hoping to scare Wayne and his teammates into respecting him, the further they drifted. Practices were a farce; scrimmages and games were a joke. The prior season was an utter embarrassment for Wayne, his teammates, their parents, and the school.

Despite these setbacks, there was one thing this group of young leaders embraced that made all the difference in the world. This one thing was a deep-seated belief in themselves and one another. It was clear their coach was not going to lead them to victory, and these youngsters recognized they were set up for failure. Not being in a position of authority to implement change left Wayne and his teammates feeling hopeless. Realizing they could not rely on their coach to get things done, they had no leverage to make any changes. So, instead, they came together as one to find a way to succeed despite the loser leadership from their coach.

At that time, in the late eighties, the sport of lacrosse was relatively unknown. The kids who played the sport did so out of a pure love of and passion for the game. When speaking with any of the players, you heard it in their voices, saw it in their eyes, and felt it in their presence.

Although the team had a coach, they were without a leader. When a coach leads with fear and anger rather than an intense desire for victory built upon the foundation of love, he or she runs the risk of failure, failure as a coach, failure as a leader, and failure as a team. This will ultimately lead to devastation and defeat.

Wayne and his teammates were aware that their coach's approach and playbook were destined for failure. Despite the urging from the players and Wayne, the team captain, along with the increasing pressure from their mounting losses, the coach did not seem too interested in making the appropriate adjustments, or he just didn't know how to do so to improve the team.

Because of their relentless winning attitude and championship mind-set, they came together, exhibiting admirable leadership traits in a situation that grossly lacked any semblance of leadership. Wayne and his teammates called a private team meeting to figure out how they could come together to fix the mess and find a way to start winning. They decided the names of the plays would remain the same, but the plays and execution would change. The true test of their new play calling could only be vetted on the field of play during their next game.

Upon winning the opening face-off, their All-State midfielder sprinted down the field, settled at the top of the box, and worked the ball around the horn to Skyler, their All-American attackman, who cruised behind the crease.

Their coach barked a play onto the field. Skyler looked in the direction of their coach on the sidelines and called the play to his teammates but with an audible. Like Peyton Manning calling an audible, "Omaha! Omaha!" Skyler roared, "Cougar! Cougar!"

He pressed the defender into the crease up against the back of the goal, cut left around the edge of the crease, and reversed direction, toeing the line of the crease and forcing his defender backward nearly stumbling over the back of the goal. The midfielders shifted position, setting a pick for Wayne. Wayne broke free, and Skyler zipped a pass to him. Alex, their All-State attackman, popped away from his defender when Wayne passed the ball to Alex for a quick stick and a goal!

The fans roared in excitement. The players celebrated. They knew they had found their secret to winning. "Cougar! Cougar!" echoed in their ears, and the team found a way to win. They did so without their coach's awareness of the change and without disrupting the status quo. They found their recipe for victory despite poor leadership from their coach.

The *Cougar! Cougar!* audible and new playbook was executed discreetly by Wayne and his teammates in a trusting collaboration. The team began scoring more goals per game and were defeating opponents they were not supposed to beat. The victories piled up as they climbed their way to the top of the Central League, while the bleachers piled up with more and more fans.

As they won game after game, the league took notice of Springfield's victorious ways. Now with a winning record, there was not much their coach could do about the team's disregard of his methods and ineffective play calling. His only choice was to ride the wave of success, which in effect made him look like the hero.

To say it was amazing watching Wayne and his teammates come together as one cohesive unit to win the state championship in lacrosse would be an understatement. They turned a lost season and a loser coach into a legendary season and a leadership lesson for the record books.

Because of a deep belief in one another, an unrelenting winning attitude, and a championship mind-set, a group of young men displayed true sportsmanship and leadership skills many executives can only hope to replicate.

The experiences from Wayne's youth would not be the first time, nor the last, that he dealt with confrontation and loser leadership. Nearly thirty years later, after his middle school and high school experiences were long behind him, Wayne had established a successful career in the financial services industry. Working for a national insurance company, Pigeon Financial, he encountered remarkably similar scenarios to those that befell him during his days on the playground and as a leader on a championship lacrosse team in high school.

Once again, he and his teammates were dealing with a similar scenario to the one on the field during his youth. He experienced executives who didn't understand the business or were too far removed, executive management who did not care to invest the time to understand their employees, who made too many wrong decisions or were unwilling to set their ego aside to listen to the voices within the organization.

Sadly, in a similar twist of fate, just like in his days in high school when Wayne and his teammates took things into their own hands because of loser leadership, he found himself doing the same thing three decades later. Because of an unrelenting desire to win, Wayne and his teammates came together in a trusted collaboration to ensure Pigeon Financial's success. This group of professionals came together when leadership had failed them. They ensured the company was victorious and despite the odds quickly became one of the industry's leading fixed indexed annuity carriers. They were beating competitors they should not have been beating and winning when others did not think they should have ever been on the field. Wayne and his teammates turned loser leadership into a winner despite a growing dysfunction among executive management.

Words to Live By

Attract honor, respect, and dignity for yourself as a leader and for your players, your people. Just because someone is in a position of power and authority does not make it okay for them to act like a tyrant. True leaders lead with and through love—love of themselves, love of their people, and love of the process.

🕐 Time is Killing Me

Delay does not matter in eternity, but it is tragic in time.

—A Course in Miracles

Wayne could not find a legitimate reason why he awoke every day feeling anxious and stressed, other than the usual worry over being late—late for work, late for school, late for an appointment, missing a deadline, wasting time, and so on. Even as a young man, he recalled being stressed about being late for school and missing a deadline for an assignment or lacrosse practice. It felt like time was killing him.

Now many years since the days of his youth, Wayne had a family of his own. "Life would be considerably easier if we did not always have to be somewhere on time," he mumbled to himself as he was getting his daughters ready for their day. "Hey, sweetie, time to get up."

"Daaad, I don't want to get up," Kylie, his nine-year-old daughter, whined.

"Chloe, make sure you brush your teeth."

"Ugh. Okay," Chloe replied.

"Abby, do you have your tennis racquet?"

"Yes, leave me alone!" Abby, his eleven-year-old daughter, screamed.

His wife usually took care of the morning routine with the kids, but today, Wayne was filling in for her and doing his best not to feel overwhelmed. He barked commands at his kids, "Are you dressed? Did you eat breakfast? Did you brush your teeth? Don't forget to pack your lunch. What about sunscreen? You must put sunscreen on. It's going to be hot today! Make sure you have your water bottle … Okay, let's head to the car."

"I'm going, Dad!" Abby retorted.

"Thanks," he replied.

Getting the kids to camp on time was a big mission, which seemed more like a mission impossible. Adding to the tension, he had an appointment immediately afterward, which did not make his morning any less stressful!

The more his daughters grumbled in response to his requests, the more his impatience grew. His blood pressure was coming to a boil. Then something hit him. Pausing, he mumbled to himself, "Shit. Time is killing me!"

He pondered what he had just said. "Could time really be killing me?" he mumbled again.

Impatience crept in with mounting angst over his fear of not getting the girls to camp on time.

I am freaking out over something that really doesn't matter in the grand scheme of things. The kids will get dressed, they will eat, they will brush their teeth at their own pace, not mine. They always have and always will. His thoughts romped around the mosh-pit of his mind.

This apparent feeling of angst, which morphed into stress, led to impatience, and ultimately became anger, was killing him. His kids were upset because of his growing impatience, and it was all because of time! Time hovered over his head like a dark cloud of death pouring down in a storm of impatience, engulfing him. The tone of his voice suddenly shifted from love and patience to irritation and frustration.

"How is this possible? How in the world can I shift from blissed to pissed?" he mumbled. "Is it really because of time?" He envisioned pulling up to camp late, and the camp counselors giving him the evil eye as they held their hands on their hips, expressing their impatience with him and disapproval of his tardiness—the same tardiness that will, somehow, magically change his demeanor, causing him to grow exceedingly impatient with his daughters.

He played a dialogue in is head regarding the lecture he imagined he would receive from the camp counselor. He envisioned the tongue lashing his wife would give him. His angst mounted. Of course, none of this would transpire. Even if it did, it was never quite as tragic as he envisioned it to be. This was simply a dreadful dialogue that he fabricated in his mind, something that was as far from the truth as possible.

Grasping a final thread of patience, he made sure each of his kids had her backpack, sunblock, water bottle, and snack. "Let's go! Get in the car. We have to go, or we're gonna be late!"

"Fine!" Abby replied.

"Geez, Dad. I'm going," Kylie moaned. "Gosh!"

He jumped into the front seat of the car. "Let's go. Shut the door. Chloe, get your seat belt buckled," he implored. "Abby!"

"What!" Abby replied.

"Help her get buckled!"

"Okay!"

In a mad rush, he flew down the driveway, turned left onto the street, and sped around the bend in the road. Navigating the s-curve in the road, he headed toward Route 252 and came to a dead stop! He was stranded behind a line of cars waiting to merge into traffic. Argh! He slowly crept along while scanning the traffic up ahead for a gap between cars so he could nose his way into traffic, but there was no room to be found. The line of cars crept along, practically kissing the bumper of the car in front, preventing anyone from merging into traffic. "Oh my gosh!"

"What, Daddy?" Kylie asked.

"Oh, nothing. I am just amazed by all this traffic. No one's letting anyone in. This is crazy!"

"Oh, Daddy, don't worry. Someone will let you in," she replied.

"Yeah, you're right. Thanks, sweetie!"

He continued to gaze at the commuters behind the wheels of their cars, watching them swerve in and out of traffic, trying not to be late. Horns blared at fellow citizens, all because they needed to be somewhere on time! Unbeknownst to them, time was killing all of them. The culprit of their irrational behavior was time! Their growing impatience was feeding their impudence and unfortunately, in a few instances, road rage!

Why? All because they were going to be late! Because people needed to be somewhere on time—work, the office, school, an appointment, a meeting, a date, happy hour, and so on. Believing they are going to be late magically incites a dialogue in their head, feeding the frenzy in the mosh-pit of their minds. This leads to impatience, ignorance, frustration, and often rage. All because of time! What's the worst that could happen if, with a smile and a wave, they allowed one car to merge into traffic? Is it really going to make them late for work? Probably not! Is the world going to end? Nope! But tell that to the guy or gal who is late for work. Their angst fuels irrational thoughts leading to irrational behavior, and they often attack.

Drivers continued hugging the bumper of the car in front of them while maintaining their gaze straight ahead, laser focused on their destination. The irony of this insane ritual is that most of these people were literally in a mad rush to go somewhere that they despise—work! All of this because of time. People were angry because of time! They were rude to fellow citizens because of time!

He laughed to himself, observing all these normally nice people who seemed dead set on preventing fellow citizens from merging into traffic. Engines revved at red lights. Vehicles roared ahead from zero to thirty-five in under six seconds just to beat other commuters to the next traffic light. Hands waved, heads shook, and fists pounded on steering wheels while vulgarities roared in this insane ritual to be repeated morning and night, day after day, continuously.

What began as a beautiful, sun-filled warm summer morning had turned into a hyperactive, angst- and anger-filled morning commute. Fortunately for Wayne, on this day, he had planned on leaving an extra twenty-minute cushion of time. This made his commute an easy one and provided him with a different perspective, allowing him to see things through a different lens and opening him up to the revelation that time was killing everyone, but it did not have to be this way.

Cruising down the road, Wayne continued to witness the frenetic activity around him until finally they arrived at camp. He cut the wheel, slipping neatly into the car line with other parents waiting to drop off their kids at camp. *I will no longer allow time to kill me*, he thought as he stopped the car and put it into park at the drop-off area.

In a Keystone Cops routine, he jumped out of the driver's seat and scrambled around to the passenger side of the car, trying to direct each of his daughters to the appropriate counselor in under sixty seconds. The pressure mounted, and the camp counselors began waving at him to move ahead so the other cars in line could drop off their kids next. Time was killing him. He had to move quickly.

After safely getting his kids out of the car and to camp on time, he jumped back into the car to immediately head to his appointment. He zipped through the parking lot and flew down the roadway toward Newtown Street Road to sit in traffic, again! Cars still zipped in and out of lanes, hugging the bumper of the car in front of them, preventing fellow commuters from merging. "Here we go again," he laughed.

We have become slightly insane because of timeliness and tardiness. We must be at work on time at nine o'clock. We must take our one-hour lunch break at exactly twelve o'clock noon and be back at exactly one o'clock sharp! We cannot leave work until the clock strikes five o'clock!

If we work too late, we might miss our kid's school event or game or be late for dinner. If we are late for work, we might get in trouble, maybe we will be fired, maybe we will be made an example of. We could lose a client or upset a friend because of our tardiness. Time is killing us at every turn!

Time exists for what seems an eternity, especially when we suffer or feel pain, yet when things are pleasant and enjoyable, time seems to fly by or simply not exist. When we are truly present in the moment, time stands still.

One of the immediate things that doctors do when we die is to mark the time of our departure. It is our death date, something that we mourn, solidifying the human measurement of time in our mind. It introduces us to our individuality and apparent mortality. We are lured into fear and the dread of an end of things all of which is created by the illusion of time.

All of this is because centuries ago, on a fateful day, one person made the keen observation that the earth rotated and revolved around the sun. This person was Nicolaus Copernicus. Yes, we can credit the ancient Babylonians, Egyptians, or even prehistoric time for the creation of time. But Nicolaus Copernicus's discovery led to the creation of time as we know it today. This measurement of time centuries later rules our lives, defining our existence and practically everything in our world!

Time scares the shit out of us—whether it is a fear of growing older, fear of dying, worry about not getting things done, stress about being late and so on!

So, Wayne found himself becoming anxious when the weekend or a vacation approached. Why? Because he felt he had to get things done on time before leaving for the weekend or, worse, a weeklong vacation. He worried that the work would not get done or something important would be overlooked until one day he stopped himself and his somewhat sadistic ritual of anxiety and restlessness to realize the world had yet to end nor did he get fired because something was not done. His realization was that it would be there when he got back. If something was important enough, he finally understood that a colleague would find a way to contact him or a teammate would step in and complete the work.

Fortunately, on this day, Wayne decided he was going to live forever by choosing to be here now. Thank you, Ram Dass! All we truly have is the present moment, now, which never begins or ends but rather just is.

Time was created by humankind in a relentless search for meaning. We are on a continual quest for purpose, finding the next best thing, seeking happiness and success. We continually find ways to extend time. At some point, we must ask ourselves why? We are living longer and longer, but does this bring happiness and a better life? Maybe it just extends our suffering unless and until we change our perspective.

Words to Live By

In the business world, time is everything, and the concept of being present seems impossible because apparently the early bird gets the worm. However, good things come to those who wait. Or is it nice guys finish last? Which one is true? How can we simultaneously be present in the business world and successful?

When you find yourself agitated or impatient, ask yourself, "Why am I agitated? Why am I angry? Why did I yell at my child, my spouse, my colleague?"

It is usually because of time. If you remove the pressure of time, life flows and anxiety is nonexistent.

Taking it one step further, once you are aware of how your thoughts and perspective of events, people, and things dictate your behavior, you will be able to mitigate angst, stress, and impatience.

New Hire

We get paid for bringing value to the marketplace. It takes
time ... but we get paid for the value, not the time.

—*Jim Rohn*

It was a beautiful July day in 2012 just a few months after Doe
Financial called it quits. They closed their doors, leaving hundreds of
employees on the street without a job. Wayne had been interviewing
feverishly for a new place to land. He had fortunately narrowed his
options down to two different companies, both of which were in the
same industry but very different in their core business and structure.

Recently, after finishing another round of interviews, Wayne
walked into the kitchen of his home to be greeted by his wife, Sue.
"How did your interview go?" she asked.

"Great! I nailed it. Now I have an offer from both Pigeon
Financial and M-80 Financial!"

"Wow! That's amazing!" Sue enthusiastically replied. "When do
you need to make a decision?"

"I told them that I needed to speak it over with you and would
get back to them in the next twenty-four to forty-eight hours."

"So, what do you think you're going to do?"

"I'm leaning toward the smaller company."

"Which one is that?" she asked.

"M-80 Financial, the IMO," Wayne replied, feeling better about
working with the independent marketing organization (IMO).

"Okay. Why?"

"Really?" He replied in a tone of frustration, despite knowing
she would ask such a question. *Is she doubting my decision?* he thought
to himself. She did a good job of bringing things to the surface for

Wayne; otherwise, he would obsess about it, letting it fester and build up in his mind.

"Yes, really!"

"Okay. Because I am tired of the corporate bullshit. Everything on the surface appears great. They say they embrace integrity, honesty, and transparency, which I believe is well intended. The problem is that management and many executives spit in the face of integrity and doing what's right. They treat their employees like crap and get away with it despite preaching these wonderful guiding principles. I feel like I am back in high school dealing with the same assholes who walked around doing whatever they wanted, pushing other kids around. The only difference is we're all now mature adults, apparently."

"That's funny! But I hate to say it's true." Sue laughed.

"There's this guy, Zig Ziglar, who wrote a book called *See You at the Top*, which is about business and sales success. Out of all his books and recordings, I have yet to read one that embraced a core message of lying, cheating, and treating people like crap. It could be possible I read the wrong book or that Zig Ziglar was full of shit, but I highly doubt it." Wayne smirked. "His books and teachings stressed the importance of honesty, loyalty, faith, integrity, and strong personal character. *See You at the Top* emphasizes the value of a healthy self-image and how to build it. I'm tired of getting lost in the mix at these big companies that fill management positions, not leadership positions. That's why I want to go with the smaller company."

"Okay. It sounds like you've made up your mind. But just make sure you aren't making your decision based on emotion alone. Is this the right job for you?"

"I don't know," Wayne mumbled.

"You have to know."

"Well, they're a family-owned company. The upside from an income standpoint is unlimited."

"Okay, that's good to know, but ..." She pressed him to talk it out with her.

Wayne sighed and continued, "But there's no guarantee with anything at this company, and that's the one part that makes me hesitate. And I did ask them for an offer letter though."

"Okay, what did they say?"

"They would have something to me in the coming days."

"Okay, good to know. What else attracts you to this company?" she persisted.

"The simple fact that I don't want to deal with the bullshit at these big companies any longer."

"You already told me that. Either way, I support your decision and know you will excel."

"Thanks for talking through it with me." Wayne's mobile phone started ringing. "Let me grab this. It's Gary calling."

"Okay. Love you!"

"Love you, too." Wayne answered the call from his good friend from college, Gary DeAngelo, to share the good news with him.

Wayne ended up accepting the offer with the smaller company, M-80 Financial, and declining the offer from Pigeon Financial. A couple of weeks later, Wayne traveled to Hartford, Connecticut, to meet the team at M-80 Financial to spend a few days in planning and strategy meetings.

Wayne took the Amtrak Regional Rail from Philadelphia Thirtieth Street Station to the Amtrak Metro North Station in Hartford, Connecticut, where his new business partner, John, picked him up. Wayne checked in at the local bed-and-breakfast, dropped off his bags, and then headed over to the office with John for their first day of meetings.

Meeting the owner, Peter, and the team was an eye-opener for Wayne, considering he recently came from Three Friends Financial, which was one of the best sales and marketing organizations on the wholesaling, marketing, and distribution side of the financial services business. Three Friends Financial was a family grown operation and responsible for Doe Financial's success as an annuity and mutual fund distributor. It was Three Friends Financial's approach to the business and their leadership that put Doe Financial on the map.

In hindsight, Wayne realized what a privilege it was to have worked at Three Friends Financial. Unfortunately, once Doe Financial purchased Three Friends Financial and took over the organization, the writing was on the wall that an end of an era would soon arise. Three Friends Financial was one of the first tremendously successful independent marketing organizations (IMOs), or broker general agents (BGAs). There was no other organization that rivaled them. The culture, professional development, and sales techniques taught by Three Friends Financial would never be replicated despite the dozens who tried.

M-80 Financial was like Three Friends Financial in that it was an IMO or BGA. It was also family owned with an entrepreneurial mind-set and no corporate bullshit, which attracted Wayne to the opportunity. He looked forward to working hard with a tight-knit group of people who built their success from the ground up.

On his first day at his new job, he immediately realized how fortunate he was to have worked at Three Friends Financial. M-80 Financial was an unorganized, poorly structured, immature team, which was quite the opposite of Three Friends Financial.

As his day progressed, regret crept into Wayne's mind about his decision to join M-80 Financial. He was concerned about the legitimacy of their business because they did not have a robust sales force as he had initially been led to believe. Their sales desk was not what he had expected. It was a far cry from what he was used to at Three Friends Financial. It remained unclear what their business structure was, and they were not very clear with regard to what accounts they were currently working with and which accounts they were seeking to bring on board.

The kid running the sales team was the owner's son, Jimmy, who displayed an extreme lack of maturity and professionalism. The financial services industry has an air of arrogance and materialism about it, and people brag about how much money they have and boast about the cars they drive and other materialistic bullshit, which was not Wayne's style. He enjoyed the business because of the earnings potential and the opportunity to impact and improve his accounts with the products he represented. He enjoyed the challenge as well, because this was an industry in which you could not afford to become complacent. You must always hustle and remain one step ahead of the competition.

Wayne's first impression of the owner's son was one of entitlement, as though he had been handed the job instead of earning it. His immature and unprofessional demeanor was less than appealing. His industry knowledge was lacking. He did not have a deep list of contacts or accounts. It was clear he based his self-worth on all the possessions he was able to afford because of his father's success. He bragged about his newest Rolex watch, which cost eight thousand dollars. He boasted about his thousand-dollar Berluti dress shoes. Jimmy continued his boasting while driving Wayne to lunch in his BMW 5 Series.

It was clear to Wayne from the moment he walked in the door that this kid was going to present a challenge and just might prevent Wayne from succeeding in his new role. This did not sit well with him, but he did his best to reassure himself that he made the right decision, despite the tsunami of doubt that overwhelmed him.

After lunch, they headed back to the office for their afternoon business sessions. During the planning and strategy meetings, Wayne noticed that his phone was extraordinarily active. Considering it was his first day at his new job, he disregarded the calls, deciding he would attend to them later.

At the end of the day, Wayne hopped a ride with John back to the bed-and-breakfast for a quick break before reconvening for dinner later that evening. On the ride back, they spoke about their meetings and plans for the following day. John was a good guy. He was the front man for Peter and responsible for hiring Wayne. If there was a silver lining in Wayne's decision to work at M-80 Financial, it was John. He displayed a professional demeanor and represented the company well.

"Pick you up around six fifteen for dinner. Sound good?" John said.

"Yes, sounds great. Thanks, John! See you in a bit." Wayne hopped out of the car and headed to his room at the bed-and-breakfast. Finally, with a reprieve from the business meetings, Wayne decided to check his messages. The first few messages were from his wife, dad, mother, and friend Gary, all who wished him well on his first day. The last message made Wayne hesitate as he listened, "Wayne, uh, this is Corey Reven at Pigeon Financial. I hope you're doing well." Wayne's heart started pounding, and he felt butterflies in his stomach. "Can you give me a call when you have a moment. I would like to speak with you about the job offer. We would like you to reconsider."

Wayne's jaw dropped. "Holy shit!" he muttered to himself. "What the hell does that mean? Reconsider?" His stomach churned. His heart was beating even faster, and his body trembled.

"Okay, reply to the message," he muttered to himself. Listening to the message again, Wayne shouted, "Holy shit! Oh my god! Maybe this is a sign. Get control of yourself before you call back. You need to be cool and collected." After he calmed his nerves, he returned Corey's call.

"Hello, this is Corey," the voice on the other end of the phone said.

"Corey, this is Wayne Renroc returning your call. Sorry, I missed you. I was stuck in meetings all day. Do you have a few minutes?" His heart pounded even harder than before, like it was about to jump out of his chest.

"No problem. Yes, I do," Corey replied.

"Great. What was it that you wanted to discuss?"

Without hesitation, Corey replied, "We would like you to reconsider joining our organization."

"Okay," Wayne calmly responded.

"Uh, we really like your background and what you'll bring to Pigeon Financial. We are willing to extend you a twenty-thousand-dollar signing bonus if you come onboard with us. Plus, another ten thousand after the first six months."

What the fuck? Thirty-thousand-dollars! Wayne thought to himself, almost dropping the phone. *Wayne, say something!* Thoughts jumped around the mosh-pit of his mind. *What do I say? I am here training for my new job. Shit!*

"Corey, thank you for your consideration, but I'd like some time to think this over considering I just accepted an offer with another company."

"I understand. How much time do you need?"

"Let me make a few calls. I'll get back to you either tonight or tomorrow at the latest."

"That works fine. Uh, if you have any questions, don't hesitate to call me. You have my number."

"Okay. Thank you, Corey. I'll get back to you shortly," Wayne said, trying to remain calm.

"Talk with you soon," came Corey's reply.

"Bye." Wayne ended the call. His heart raced, and his body shuddered as he paced around the tiny room of the bed-and-breakfast. His black wingtips pounded on the wooden floor, creaking with each step. He removed his shoes and continued talking out loud, "What the fuck! What the fuck! Oh my god! This is crazy. This must be a sign, especially after the debacle today. Okay, call Sue and let her know. It'll be good to talk this through with her."

Wayne tapped the screen on his phone, searched his *favorites* for his wife's number, and called her. The phone started ringing. "Come on, answer. Answer!" Wayne mumbled.

"Hey, baby! How was your first day?" His wife answered the phone.

"The day was okay, but I really didn't care for it much though."

"Why? What happened?" She interrupted.

"It's a small company, maybe too small, and I still am unclear as to what their structure is, who is on the external and internal sales team. I am not sure who their current accounts are. There are so many things that are missing. It's a little strange, and I have a bad feeling about this."

"Oh," his wife's voice faded.

"Yeah, I am not so sure about this," Wayne said hesitantly.

"Oh no. Really?" She responded with more concern in her voice.

"I can't explain it, honey."

"Oh boy," she said, in an anxious tone. "So, what are you going to do?"

"Well, you'll never believe it!"

"Believe what?" she asked with a worried excitement in her voice.

"I received a call today from the other company, Pigeon Financial."

"About what?"

"They want me to reconsider their offer. I just got off the phone with them, and they are offering me a twenty-thousand-dollar signing bonus and another ten thousand after six months."

"Holy crap!" his wife roared in excitement. "Are you serious?"

"Yes. What do I do?"

"Take it!" came her reply without hesitation. "Take it!"

"But I accepted this job, and I am here in training."

"Did they give you the offer letter? Did you sign a contract?"

"No."

"Well, then you have no commitment to them."

"Are you serious? So, you're saying I leave?"

"Yes. Why not? If your gut is telling you this is not a good thing, if in your heart you feel this is not where you should be, then go to Pigeon Financial."

"Okay?" He responded, still in shock at the turn of events.

"Why don't you call your brother. He will be a good person to bounce this off of."

"Okay. Let me do that now. I have to make a decision quick because I'm supposed to meet them for dinner in an hour."

"Okay. I love you. Whatever decision you make, I support it."

"Love you. Thanks!" Wayne ended the call and immediately called his brother Alex. Still pacing around the room, Wayne muttered to himself, "Come on, pick up. Pick up, Alex. Where are you?"

The phone stopped ringing when Alex's voice-mail message chirped in Wayne's ear. At the beep, Wayne excitedly spoke. "Alex. It's your brother Wayne. Can you call me back tonight? I need to talk to you. I am here in Connecticut training for my new job, and I just received a counteroffer from the other company. Call me!"

He continued pacing around the room, playing out the scenario. "Okay. I don't have a written offer letter for this job. I don't have a contract. I'm not all that impressed with what I saw today. Ah, I should call Gary." Wayne picked up the phone and called his friend Gary.

Gary answered. Wayne proceeded to explain his dilemma. "Hey, Gary! I am here in Hartford. My training went okay, but I am not too impressed with everything so far."

"Oh boy! That's not good," he replied.

"Nope. But it gets even better."

"Don't you mean worse?"

"No, I mean better. So, listen to this, I got a call from the other company today."

"What? Which company was that? The one in Seattle?"

"Yes! Pigeon Financial," Wayne replied.

"Oh. Okay. So, why'd they call you?"

"They extended a counteroffer."

"They what?" Gary replied in astonishment.

"They called me with a counteroffer and a signing bonus, plus another bonus after six months!"

"Holy cow! Really?" Gary exclaimed.

"No shit, right? What do I do?"

"Well, are you going to accept it?" Gary asked. "You would be going back to the corporate bullshit that you wanted to get away from."

"Yeah, I know. But, after today's experience I would take it. Although, I am not sure how to do it and if I even can. It just doesn't feel like good business."

"Listen, Wayne. I hate to say it, but this is business. These things happen all the time. They just never happen to me. Do you want to accept it?"

"I think so. I just feel awful. I am here in Hartford at the home office for training and am about to meet them for dinner in less than an hour."

"Ouch. Yeah, that's a tough one. Regardless, do what's in your heart, and go with it."

"Okay. Thanks, Gary. You are the best! I gotta go. My brother is calling me back."

"Keep me posted."

"Will do. Thanks again, Gary!"

"Anytime."

"Hey, Alex," Wayne answered the phone and proceeded to update Alex on the situation.

"Wayne, I got your message. That's great news!" his brother Alex said.

"Yeah, but what do I do? I just started this new job today, and I am in Connecticut for training. Can I really leave?"

"Yeah, you can. You owe them nothing. Did you sign an offer letter?" his brother asked.

"No. Everything has been verbal up to this point."

"Well, that's bad business and their mistake," his brother commented. "They should have secured you by extending an offer letter."

"You know, I asked them for one when they first offered me the job. I asked again before coming to training and again today. They still haven't given me the letter." Wayne was beginning to feel better about accepting the offer from Pigeon Financial.

"Well, then there's no question. You're a free agent."

"Okay. But I am still here in Hartford and am going to dinner in twenty-five minutes with the owner."

"Well, you need to pick up the phone and be honest with him. Let him know you have been approached by another company, and

46

they're offering something you can't refuse. Maybe he will come back with his own counteroffer, or he won't," his brother advised.

"Oh man. I know this is good, but this sucks at the same time! I feel awful."

"Wayne, this is business. You hold the cards and should not feel awful at all."

"Okay. I want to accept the other offer. I'll make the call."

"Okay. Let me know what happens."

"Thanks, Alex. You're the best!"

"Anytime. Love you, man!"

Wayne ended the call with his brother and took a few minutes to gather his thoughts. He rehearsed the call to his soon-to-be ex-boss: "'Peter, this is Wayne Renroc. I am sorry, but I am resigning.' No, that sounds stupid. 'Peter, this is Wayne. Do you have a minute?' No, it will take longer than a minute. 'Hey, Peter, this is Wayne. Do you have a few minutes? I don't know how to say this, but I just received a counteroffer from another company, and I am accepting their offer.'"

Wayne was quickly figuring out what to say. Time was of the essence, and he had to make the call soon. "Okay, no more practicing. Plus, John will be here soon to pick me up for dinner," he said out loud. He picked up his phone and searched for Peter's number. He tapped on Peter's phone number, and the phone began ringing.

"Hello, this is Peter."

"Peter, this is Wayne Renroc. Do you have a few minutes?" Wayne said firmly and confidently despite shaking like a leaf.

"Hey, Wayne. I sure do," he said enthusiastically. "We had a good day of meetings. I look forward to seeing you at dinner."

"Peter, about dinner. This is difficult for me to say, but I've been contacted by another company in the past hour." Silence on the other end of the phone. Wayne continued, "They extended a counteroffer that I cannot refuse. I understand if you're upset, but this is something I can't walk away from. I've accepted their offer."

There was silence on the line, which felt like an eternity. Wayne began to sweat, and then Peter responded, "Are you fucking kidding me! You son of a bitch! You can't do this! Who the fuck do you think you are?"

"Peter, like I said, I apologize. But I have to think about my family and my career. There's no easy way to do this, but I can't pass up this offer."

"You can't do this to me! If I ever see you again—" Peter continued his rage-filled rant on the other end of the phone, clearly not handling it well.

Peter's response made it much easier for Wayne to make the decision to accept the counteroffer. He had to find a way to end the call. "Peter, thank you for helping me with my decision. I wish you all the best."

"You motherfucker. I am going to kill you!" The phone went silent.

Wayne's body trembled. "What a fucking asshole! I can't believe that just happened. Holy shit, he's a fucking loose cannon. Okay, I need to call John," Wayne mumbled to himself. He dialed John's number, and he immediately answered.

"Hey, Wayne. I am almost there to pick you up for dinner."

"John, there won't be any need."

"What?"

"I'm so sorry, but I just accepted another offer. I was contacted by another company in the past hour. They extended a job offer that I can't afford to turn down. This is a difficult decision for me but an important one. You've been very accommodating throughout and nothing short of professional. I don't want this to damage any relationship we've established, but I understand if you're upset."

"Look, Wayne. I get it. These things happen. I appreciate your honesty and taking the time to let me know," John commented. "Did you call Peter?"

"Yes, I just got off the phone with him."

"How'd that go?"

"Bad. He was pissed off. I thought I was going to have to hang up on him, but he did instead."

"Yeah, that's Peter. He has a temper. He'll get over it though," John commented.

"Thank you, John. You're a good man."

"Well, I'm sorry I won't get to work with you. I wish you all the best."

"Thanks, John. You as well. Take care." Wayne immediately called his wife to tell her he was accepting the job at Pigeon Financial. Next was a return call to Corey Reven to accept the offer. He would start on Monday, August 6.

Words to Lead By

How do you handle adversity in business and life? Do you fly off the handle, like Peter, or do you handle things in stride? The anger, rage-filled taunts, and responses by people in positions of leadership are learned behaviors. Although it may seem to work in the short term, it creates more resentment and regret over the long term. True leaders find a way to take things in stride, manage their emotions, and lead with love.

What value do you bring to the marketplace, and how do you convey your value?

> "We get paid for bringing value to the marketplace. It takes time … but we get paid for the value, not the time."
> —Jim Rohn

☺ Welcome to the Nightmare

People don't leave companies—they leave management.

—*Young Entrepreneur Council (forbes.com)*

Wayne ended his new job with M-80 Financial to accept a better one with Pigeon Financial. A couple of weeks later, he found himself on the other side of the country in Bellevue, Washington, on August 6 for a team dinner with his new employer.

Laughter and light conversation echoed throughout the establishment as the hostess escorted him through the dimly lit restaurant. Upon reaching the executive dining room, all eyes were on him.

This grand occasion and welcome from Pigeon Financial made him a little uncomfortable. He greeted his new colleagues with a smile and a handshake. He felt as though he belonged. It was refreshing. This experience would prove to be very rewarding but also quite revealing and life altering.

That evening, Wayne was introduced to his business partner, Patrice, who was kind enough to spend her birthday evening at the business dinner with Pigeon Financial rather than among friends. It was the beginning of an amazing working relationship between the two. Both were passionate about their work. Both cared about the team and their clients. For both, it was more than just a job; it was an opportunity to make an impact and a positive difference for the company, their clients, and quite possibly the industry.

In less than two years' time, sales quickly doubled and then tripled and quadrupled. What Wayne, Patrice, and their fellow relationship managers accomplished was remarkable. It was astonishing and unexpected to see Pigeon Financial experience such monumental growth.

The bonus promised to Wayne was promptly paid after six months. A year later, Wayne was given the Relationship Manager of the Year award by the executive vice president of the division, Chad Wanderlust. The award was newly created to acknowledge and honor Wayne's strong work ethic, teamwork, passion, and ability to foster relationships and open doors, all of which blew the roof off from a sales perspective.

Unfortunately, this was the beginning of the end. Slowly, things at Pigeon Financial began turning into a nightmare of sorts. Their newest sales division supporting the company's fee-based annuity product, Reality Variable Annuity, was shutting down after launching less than two years prior. Nelson, the head of the Reality Variable Annuity fee-based annuity product relationship management team was brought in to take over the relationship management team for the retirement division that Wayne worked for. Wayne quickly found Nelson to be an outstanding businessman, an excellent leader, and an even better person to boot.

Ironically, Wayne learned that Nelson had been next in line as the head of the strategic relationship management team at Doe Financial a couple years prior, meaning Nelson would have been Wayne's boss, but it was not in the cards at that point in time. The timing was bad, transpiring just before Doe Financial made the announcement that they were exiting the annuity and insurance business.

Although it was in the cards for the two of them to work together, because of Doe Financial's failure during the "Too Big to Fail" era, it just was not meant to happen at that point. Therefore, Wayne and Nelson's acquaintance was momentarily averted until nearly a couple of years later when they both found themselves working at Pigeon Financial.

After several months with Nelson at the helm, the team was feeling confident and working very well together, continuing to rack up record sales for the retirement division.

Wayne's nightmare began on a Wednesday morning in September 2013. He was in San Antonio, Texas, spending a couple of days traveling with the local wholesaler. While he was getting a cup of coffee in the hotel lobby, Wayne's phone rang. "Hey, Nelson! What part of the world are you in today?" he answered enthusiastically.

"Good morning, Wayne. I am at my home base today. How about you?"

"I'm in San Antonio traveling with Nate. What's up?"

"Well, I wanted you to be the first one on the team to know. I tendered my resignation yesterday." Nelson's comments were followed by a moment of silence on the other end of the line. "Are you there? Can you hear me?"

"Uh, yeah. Did I hear you say what I thought you said?"

"Yes, Wayne. I have resigned."

"Oh no! Why? Is there anything I can do to help? What happened?" Wayne's heart sank.

"Well, the travel is too much for me. The constant coast-to-coast flying is taking its toll," Nelson explained. "Plus, I've had back pain for a number of years now, and it's getting worse because of the excessive travel."

"Wow! I didn't see this coming." Wayne sighed. "This was the last thing I expected to hear this morning." He was disappointed by the news, but deep down, he did not believe Nelson was being on the level with him. "I'm so sorry to hear the news. Does the team know?"

"I spoke with Chad, Ned, and Corey yesterday afternoon. The team doesn't know yet; they are next on my list to call."

"Is there anything I can do to help?"

"Nothing right now. I need to make a number of calls and wrap up some loose ends on my end. I will call you later."

"Okay. Thank you for letting me know. I'm sorry to hear the news. We were just beginning to gel. I wish you the best and will do anything I can to help you land somewhere else." Wayne ended the call. "Fuck!" He took a sip of his coffee and mumbled under his breath, "What the fuck was that?"

Less than a year into the job and Nelson resigned, without another job lined up! He just up and left. Who does that? People are not supposed to do that! Wayne always heard that a cardinal rule of business was to never leave a job without another one lined up. Looking back on it, Wayne should have seen it as a sign of the beginning of the nightmare.

Things at Pigeon Financial must have been pretty messed up for someone to resign the way Nelson did. The excessive coast-to-coast travel along with his back pain were legitimate reasons for resigning, but Wayne knew it was not the sole reason. Nelson was not telling Wayne the entire story. There was another underlying reason for his resignation, which he was not revealing, and to this day, Nelson has remained silent regarding his resignation.

Deep down, Wayne knew Nelson quit because he could no longer put up with, or fix, the glaringly obvious dysfunction among the leadership team at Pigeon Financial. The executive management team handled themselves like a bunch of middle school children. Wayne believed that Nelson had grown tired of the deceit, immaturity, and absence of leadership and professionalism among Chad, Ned, Corey, and Carl.

Could it be mediocre management pushed an outstanding manager and leader to quit? After less than a year and a half at the company nonetheless! Could it be that Pigeon Financial had a knack for pushing true leaders out? Could it be they were afraid that they would be found out for being imposters and their lies and deplorable way of management would be revealed? "People don't leave companies—they leave management," Wayne grumbled to himself.

Despite the tremendous success Wayne experienced, he was beginning to notice the dysfunction among the executives at the top which slowly ate away at his confidence and pride for his job. Despite doing their best to address it with executive management, much to their disappointment and frustration, there was little Wayne and his teammates could do to fix it. There was not much Nelson could do about it either, so he left. It took nearly five years for Nelson to recover and land on his feet again.

It was like watching a horror movie. The signs are everywhere about impending doom, devastation, and death. On the edge of their seats, the audience screams, "Watch out! He's going to get you! He's right there, you idiot. Run!" Yet the characters ignore the signs, hoping for the best until it is too late, and they are slaughtered. The audience groans, "You should have seen it coming. He was right there. Couldn't you see it?" This was the beginning of Wayne's nightmare.

Words to Lead By

Q: As a leader, are you strong enough to love your people rather than lose them because you cannot see past yourself, your ego? As a player, are you strong enough to leave loser leadership for real leaders who love and appreciate the value you bring to the marketplace?

"People don't leave companies—they leave management." This lesson goes for both employees and customers. A manager will lose staff if the employees think they're not being listened to or valued. Customers will stop using your products or services if they are dissatisfied with them. The quality and reliability of your products and services is a reflection of management.[1]

"A bad manager can take a good staff and destroy it, causing the best employees to flee and the remainder to lose all motivation."[2]

---

[1] "20 Business Lessons You Don't Want to Learn the Hard Way," January 2014, forbes.com.

[2] Brigette Hyacinth, "Employees Don't Leave Jobs. They Leave Managers," LinkedIn, June 2018.

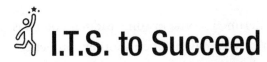

I.T.S. to Succeed

Steve Jobs succeeded because he put himself in the shoes of the consumer. He and Ive believed that unpacking was a ritual like theater and heralded the glory of the product.

—*Harvard Business Review (April 2012)*

Less than three years after he started working at Pigeon Financial, the dysfunction within the organization reared its ugly head and was wearing Wayne down. The longer he worked there, the more he understood why Nelson resigned without notice or another job lined up. They remained in touch and spoke often. Wayne tried to get Nelson to reveal the truth, the real reason why he resigned, but Nelson never strayed from his story.

Wrapping up the end of a grueling week of travel and business meetings, Wayne was at his home office on a phone call with his colleague Charlize. "I remember the day I realized that most companies, their employees, and management are constantly looking over the fence at the competition out of fear, rather than focusing on becoming better," Wayne observed. "Our accounts provide an overabundance of information about their business, the keys to the kingdom per se, and despite having this intelligence, most companies don't use it to their advantage. They often focus on embellishing their great products and features, sometimes to a fault. The industry is so competitive, copying one another's product designs, eventually the products end up looking the same. Bragging about how your product is the greatest and has the highest-paying features at the lowest cost is short-lived and shortsighted because someone else is going to come out with a product that's slightly better."

"Yep," Charlize agreed. "I'm tired of wholesalers comparing their 5 percent lifetime income to the competition, because someone will come out with 5.1 percent lifetime income or some hidden gotcha is revealed and the product isn't as advertised. Then another competitor comes out with a 5.2 percent lifetime income, touting how great they are, and the rider wars begin."

"If we're smart about it and take the information provided by our accounts to actually use it to our advantage, we will be far more successful. Learning about their business, how they get paid, what motivates them, their initiatives, pain points, technology, and resources puts us in a position to identify where our products fit. Knowing our accounts better than they know themselves positions us to beat the competition and succeed, even if our product is slightly inferior. And having a great product will make us unstoppable," Wayne continued. "When our accounts provide the same firm intelligence to twenty or thirty investment product companies and management tells their sales force to go after it, you will have twenty or thirty babbling idiots saying the same mindless crap to the same audience over and over again. After seeing this mindlessness repeated ad nauseam by sales teams throughout my career, I knew it was time for a different approach. I'm not here to sell a product. I'm here to put a dent in the universe. This is when I came up with my business model *I.T.S. to Succeed.*"

"Huh?" Charlize replied.

"In Their Shoes to Succeed," Wayne said.

"In Their Shoes to Succeed?" Charlize repeated.

"Yes! Back in 2011 when I was at Three Friends Financial, I was traveling to New York for a meeting with Fred and Barney Corp., which is now Flint Rock Group or Flint Rock Corp. I lost track after all of the name changes and M&A activity."

"Oh yeah, Flint Rock Group. They're still trying to figure out what the hell they're doing over a decade later." Charlize chuckled.

"I was on the Regional Rail train heading to New York to meet our national sales manager and a couple other colleagues. During my commute, I had to hop on a weekly project sync call for an upcoming product launch to ensure everything was on schedule."

"Were your calls as discombobulated as ours?" Charlize asked.

"Hell no! In fact, they were very well coordinated and productive. Despite being nearly three years since the devastation caused by the 2009 financial crisis, we still felt the effects. At that point, I could hear the frustration over the phone. Because of the extensive layoffs, we were doing the same amount of work with fewer people. It was fortunate to still be employed, but doing the job of three people for the pay of one was insane."

"That's what it feels like working here. Never have I worked so hard for so little, and making things even worse, I've never worked for a company that didn't get along. Sadly, it took me three years to realize it, but the management team here is inexperienced and very self-centered. As for Carl, I have absolutely no respect for him and find it very difficult to look at him knowing all of the awful things he has done. It still blows my mind to see him in charge of the broker/dealer, sales operations, and the sales desk," Charlize continued. "He doesn't know what the hell he's doing, and the entire sales force even sees right through his bullshit."

"Well, working for Three Friends Financial was the best career experience I ever had. They provided me with the opportunity to grow and succeed on so many levels. They equipped me with industry knowledge, sales skills, presentation skills, relationship skills, and business acumen unmatched by any other sales organization or training program. Pigeon Financial is a goddamn joke compared to Three Friends Financial."

"You certainly did work for one of the best in the business, and the money some of their wholesalers earned was obnoxious."

"Tell me about it! The wholesaler I worked with back in 2005 showed me one of his commission checks for fifty-five thousand dollars. Fifty-five thousand dollars in one month!"

"Don't remind me. I have been making less money every year since working here. You know they don't pay us enough! I keep telling Chad we are the lowest paid relationship management team in the industry."

"What does he say to that?"

"Nothing. Corey even tells me we're paid the industry average."

"Really?"

"Yep."

"Well, I am happy to be working. At least I was for the first couple of years. I've come to see Carl, Ned, and Corey's true colors and am beginning to resent working here. They're so smart, yet they seem so stupid at times. Corey and Carl keep climbing the corporate ladder, and I don't get it. This corporate bullshit was one of the reasons I declined the initial offer to work here. And here I am dealing with the games and bullshit again."

"You're right, but what can we do about it?"

"I don't know, but something's got to give. You know I experienced the same incompetence at Doe Financial when they bought Three Friends Financial. The executive management team at Doe Financial were very intelligent but didn't have a sales bone in their body, and common sense was fleeting. They were atrocious at leading and nurturing their employees. What really disappointed me was when Skip Armah whispered into Ned's ear that we made too much money after we crushed it in 2013."

"Did he really say that?" Charlize gasped.

"Yes, he did! He said it to Ned during our midyear planning meeting in 2014. Skip walked into the meeting room, and Ned jumped out of his chair to greet him. Ned was always a hot mess when Skip was around. Skip put his hand on Ned's shoulder and said to him, 'You know, you guys made too much money last year.' Remember how much we made that year? Everyone made a shitload in incentive comp. I will never understand why it's considered a bad thing to make too much money. I mean, when you kick-ass and blow the established sales goals out of the water, then you should get paid for it."

"True, but not when you're a publicly traded company," Charlize immediately replied.

"Yeah, I get it. But seriously? Everyone earned it. We busted our asses, saw the opportunity, and embraced it. We shouldn't be punished for making the company money!"

Publicly traded companies must meet Wall Street's quarterly earnings expectations. Their focus is on making shareholders wealthy rather than the employees. So, instead of paying the employees, the shareholders are paid.

Wayne continued, "This is conjecture, but Doe Financial failed for a few reasons; for starters, it was due to shitty leadership, and their international business was a mess. Having a hedge fund manager as one of their biggest shareholders didn't help either. In short, the hedge fund manager forced Doe Financial to fold after giving them an ultimatum to increase shareholder value. The hedge fund manager held the cards as a majority shareholder; his actions and words could have either helped or hurt Doe Financial's stock price. At the end of the day, they sold their annuity and insurance business and closed their doors. The financial crisis in 2009 was the final straw that broke the camel's back, and a lot of camels' backs were broken back then.

"Do you remember what Ben Bernanke said after his term as the Federal Reserve chairman was over?" Wayne asked Charlize.

"I believe he said that it was the worst financial crisis in the history of the markets, even worse than the Great Depression," Charlize replied.

"Yep, he also mentioned that twelve of the thirteen most important financial institutions in the United States were at risk of failure within a period of a week or two. That's insane! After surviving the crisis, I came away with a greater appreciation for what a gift it was to be employed by Three Friends Financial. Although I certainly didn't come out unscathed because I eventually lost my sales territory. Thankfully, they gave me another opportunity when they offered me a relationship management job in national accounts. Not only did Three Friends Financial make a lot of people wealthy, but they also looked out for their people as well. At the time, I was thrown around like a pinball from wholesaling to relationship management for mutual funds in the wire house channel and then moved back to covering annuities in the banks. I was certainly out of my comfort zone, but nonetheless they gave me an opportunity and I made it work.

"Adding to the fear of another round of layoffs was the frustration of the extreme workload. The days of fat commission checks would soon be a thing of the past. It became more difficult to generate sales, and wholesalers had to work exceedingly hard to regain the trust of financial advisors. Even when they did, they still had to earn their business. The wholesalers' roles shifted from proactive sales to reactive, defensive sales."

"National Accounts had the same challenges dealing with their accounts as the wholesalers did with their advisors," Charlize stated.

"True. Everyone spent their time explaining the company's financial strength ratings and stability instead of explaining how the investment they represented helped clients achieve their investment goals. Even when we found a way around the objections regarding the viability of the company, we still had to convince our accounts and advisors that they should offer the product to their clients."

Wayne and Charlize continued their conversation about the industry, their careers, and the travesty that was occurring across the industry.

———◆◆———

Relationship management teams at most of the insurance companies had to convince their accounts that the company would still be in business to honor their financial obligations during the crisis. Doe Financial was one of the biggest insurance companies with the industry's largest sales force, and when they called it quits, it was a complete shock to the industry.

This was second in line to the failure of UIC Financial, which was apparently too big to fail, yet they failed. Of course, they were rescued because the country and the world economy could not allow them to fail. If they failed, it would have sparked a global crisis. The entire financial system might have collapsed, and who knows what that would have meant for the country?

The conversations Wayne and his peers had with accounts shifted from product development and retirement solutions to company ratings and the risk-based capital (RBC) ratio. Before the crisis, no one really knew what an RBC ratio was.

The irony in all of this was that company ratings are all subjective and basically the opinion of independent rating agencies that comment on the financial strength of an insurance company and its ability to pay claims. It is just an opinion and not a fact or a guarantee.

Ratings do not have much to do with how well an insurance company's securities are performing. Wayne believed this was Doe Financial's Achilles' heel in the way they managed the underlying investments in their book of business.

Doe Financial expanded into Canada, the United Kingdom, Japan, and Germany. Apparently, the leadership team in charge of product development at Doe Financial did not properly hedge and manage the underlying portfolio, which contributed to their failure.

Their US book of business and assets were fine, but their international books of business were what did them in. After successfully launching an annuity product in Japan, they had to reverse course. In a meeting with the executives from Japan, Wayne learned something that you do not see every day. Their wholesalers were no longer selling Doe Financial's annuity product, but rather their marching orders were to pressure advisors to have their clients liquidate their accounts and close their contracts.

This is conjecture, but the only way to protect the company was to deploy an anti-sales force who were focused on liquidating as many annuity contracts as possible because they did not properly hedge the income and death benefit guarantees.

In effect, the wholesalers' job was to get clients to cancel their annuity contracts despite being good retirement investments for them. The insurance company could no longer honor the guaranteed death benefit and guaranteed lifetime income riders, which were the reason clients invested their money in the products in the first place.

Another irony was that the insurance company's ratings remained strong leading up to the crisis. There was no hint of Doe Financial's or UIC's issues. Financial advisors were telling their clients the insurance companies were stable and safe; therefore, the clients' investments were safe. Of course, the rest of the story is history; both Doe Financial and UIC Financial failed.

The question that needed to be asked and addressed was how could these companies fail if their ratings were so strong? And how valuable are these ratings agencies if they are unable to even reveal what a company's financial strength truly is?

The problem as Wayne saw it was that insurance company ratings are based on the financial strength of the insurance company's underlying investments that back their annuity and insurance guarantees. So, how do you know whether the underlying investments that, in effect, contribute to the insurance company's financial strength are any good? Do shareholders know who manages those assets, and is there any way of knowing if they are taking on too much risk or gambling with their money?

So, when all of this happened, most insurance companies and financial firms saw their portfolios plummet. They experienced tremendous losses in collateralized debt obligations, mortgage-backed securities, and credit default swaps.

Never really understanding the intricacies of that type of investing, Wayne regretted ever learning about it, too much information. In short, it was a legalized form of gambling. Credit default swaps are basically bets on whether the collateralized debt obligations (CDOs) and mortgage-backed securities will default. Although the underlying investments appear to be strong, there is no guarantee they will perform well in a market crisis. Adding to the confusion, insurance company ratings are not really what they appear to be on the surface. They can have several underlying insurance companies, called cohorts, which fall under the main company, which is referred to as the umbrella parent. This makes it even more difficult to gauge their ratings. It is sort of a shell game.

Despite being too big to fail, UIC Financial did in fact fail. As a result, in Wayne's industry, everyone became experts at explaining RBC ratios, which was something no one really understood prior to the crisis and most still do not understand.

What seemed to be a single entity as an insurance company was actually composed of several smaller insurance companies or entities. Each of the entities, or cohorts, had their own individual credit rating. Despite UIC Financial being a diversified company with over a hundred separate insurance entities back in 2008, they still failed because of their wrong bets on CDOs. They basically gambled on CDOs, which led to their failure.

Next came TARP funding, and some of the largest insurance companies applied for government bailout funding; Doe Financial applied and still failed. The Troubled Asset Relief Program, or TARP, was a US economic program designed to ward off the nation's mortgage and financial crisis, known as the Great Recession.

The irony was that the financial ratings of many of these insurance companies were the strongest among their peers, and somehow, they still failed. The good news though was that the insurance industry is set up so the investor does not lose money in the event of failure. Meaning these behemoth insurance companies that exited the business still honored their insurance contracts and guarantees.

An inordinate amount of pressure was placed on clients to liquidate their accounts with buyout letters, which freed the insurance company of their financial obligation to honor the lifetime income and death benefit guarantees. After surviving the drama of the Financial Crisis and the massive layoffs, the overworked and underpaid era ensued.

The fallout from the Great Recession would be felt for years. The mounting stress, growing uncertainty, and unrelenting excessive workload took its toll on people.

While reviewing the current projects, product launches, and product updates with the various departments, Wayne could hear the fatigue and impatience in his teammates' voices. He even found himself losing patience and becoming frustrated with the heavy workload and apparent lack of response from his accounts.

It was in that moment when he realized his accounts were suffering as much as he and his teammates were, if not more. No matter the amount of work they had in front of them, when it was cleared it off their plate, relief was nowhere to be found. Once a task or phase of a project was finished and delegated to another department or client, Wayne was at their mercy, having to await their response.

Deadlines and respond-by dates were ignored. Messages were not returned. Phone calls were not answered. He had to chase people down. Even when he got them on the phone, it was a challenge to get them to provide the status of the work item or project.

It was an awful business experience, one that he would not wish on his worst enemy. He was running full sprint on a hamster wheel to hell with no end in sight. All that he accomplished was exhaustion and frustration. Even when tasks or projects were completed and returned, much of it was done half-assed because people did not have enough time to complete the work as thoroughly as they once did.

Rumors began making their way around the office about Doe Financial being the next one to fail or show up in the mergers and acquisitions headlines. This additional noise did not help matters. Of all the stories, rumors, and fake news, none of them were right except for the failure part.

The teams went around the horn from department to department discussing account after account and the status of the product updates. Then things came to a head when a team member expressed her frustration regarding a client not responding in a timely fashion to her requests.

It was very difficult to provide an update on an account when the account had gone silent—that is, ghosted—leaving the team member with egg on her face. They all lost sight of the purpose of their work; the quality of work suffered while employees simply pushed work off their plates onto someone else's simply to get a moment to breathe.

Colleagues threw tasks over the proverbial wall to fellow colleagues and accounts just to remove them from their workload. The problem with that approach was that the tasks piled up on the other side of the wall, on the desks of colleagues and accounts who happened to be as overworked and frustrated as they were.

It got to a point at which the appreciation of being employed faded, and they hoped to be the next one laid off! They all had their heads down, throwing their work around to others in an insane cycle of incomplete work. No one even considered for a moment what was happening on the other side of the wall.

If the teams took just a moment to see that their colleagues and accounts were as overworked and stressed as they were, Wayne believed things would have been different. In sensing his own frustration and seeing it in others, Wayne decided to look over the wall.

When he did, he saw the same big stinking pile of frustration on top of a heap of tasks and projects. People were doing their best in a very challenging and uncertain time, but most of the tasks and projects were meeting their demise in a task and project graveyard. With deadlines looming, he could feel the angst and stress over the phone line, so he abruptly interrupted the call.

He asked everyone to consider why it was happening. He asked them to do their best to understand that their accounts were going through the same thing they were, and they, too, were overworked. Lobbing work over the wall to their accounts only increased their workload and exacerbated the dysfunction and incomplete work.

Wayne decided to change his perspective by putting himself in his accounts' shoes. He asked the team to do the same thing with their accounts and even colleagues.

For every work item they threw at their accounts, there were another twenty to thirty companies doing the same thing, throwing the same work items over the wall at them. Imagine how they felt! They were bombarded with request after request from twenty or thirty different companies and did not have the people to handle the work. Everyone was experiencing the same frustration and burnout.

Understanding that their accounts were as overworked and stressed as they were provided Wayne with an entirely different perspective. He asked the team to be more conscientious in their communication with accounts as well as with one another. Being more understanding, patient, and empathetic would make everyone feel better about their work, and it was Wayne's belief that their accounts would be more willing to get things done. Being empathetic to their accounts' plight, which was also Wayne's and his colleagues' plight, would contribute to a reduction in the stress and anxiety everyone was experiencing.

That was the moment when Wayne came up with his business approach of *I.T.S. to Succeed, or **In Their Shoes** to Succeed.*

The premise is for a business or partnership to succeed, by putting oneself in the other person's shoes, the shoes of work colleagues, employees, clients, and customers. When someone sees it through their client's eyes, or from their perspective, things become easier.

I.T.S. to Succeed enabled Wayne to view business through a different lens, a lens which most never considered. This approach enabled him to exceed expectations when everyone else thought it to be impossible. His approach was fueled by Steve Jobs and his approach to Apple products through the experience of the customer.

I.T.S. to Succeed was accompanied by "Know your partners better than they know themselves." Understanding his accounts and clients' way of doing business, knowing their initiatives, their tools, their resources, and even their pain points allowed Wayne to identify and create new sales opportunities. Wayne's approach identified a scratch they didn't know they needed to itch.

Instead of leading with product, he ended with product. He made it about knowing his accounts and clients—what made them tick, what made them money, how they got paid, what their initiatives and goals were. The days of leading with product were a thing of the past, and it was something Wayne did not embrace even when he was a wholesaler.

Knowing the advisor's firm better than the advisor does gives the wholesaler leverage. Although this dedication and understanding of an advisor's business may not result in immediate sales, eventually it leads to greater and more frequent opportunities while fostering a longer-lasting relationship.

Words to Lead By

Q: Do you apply an approach to your business similar to I.T.S. to Succeed? We all have a product to sell. The best way to generate interest is to put yourself in the shoes of the consumer who needs your product or service. Knowing your clients better than they know themselves and seeing things from their perspective better positions you for success.

If you know the enemy and know yourself, you need not fear the result of a hundred battles. If you know yourself but not the enemy, for every victory gained you will also suffer a defeat. If you know neither the enemy nor yourself, you will succumb in every battle.
—Sun Tzu, *The Art of War*

Howard Schultz put himself in the shoes of his father, in the shoes of the village in Italy that sparked his passion. His tagline was "A place for conversation and a sense of community. A third place between work and home." The Virgin Group succeeded because Sir Richard Branson loves his people.

Steve Jobs succeeded because he put himself in the shoes of the consumer. He believed that unpacking was a ritual, like theater, and heralded the glory of the product.

When you open the box of an iPhone or iPad, we want that tactile experience to set the tone for how you perceive the product.
—Steve Jobs

The Teacher Left the Classroom

You never walk alone. Even the devil is the lord of flies.

—*Gilles Deleuze*

Imagine this scenario. You are in middle school or high school, and halfway through the school year, the teacher doesn't show up for class. No big deal, right? This sort of thing happens all the time, and a substitute teacher usually comes in to teach the class.

But this time, it's different. No substitute teacher arrives. Actually no one arrives! Yet the students sit in class at their desks, maintaining good behavior because they expect a teacher or an authority figure to show up at any moment.

They sit in class until the final bell rings and then head home for the day. Yet, the next day of school goes by and still no teacher! The students arrive in class and still behave accordingly in anticipation of a teacher arriving. Yet, no one arrives! Eventually, after no authority figure shows up, a student daringly shoots a spitball across the room. He sits at his desk in silence, remaining as inconspicuous as possible, waiting to see what transpires from his inappropriate act just in case someone is watching.

When nothing happens, he does it again. *Pfft*, a saliva-soaked ball of mush flies out of the straw and soars across the classroom. Flying above the students' heads, it speeds toward the front of the classroom until *thwack*, the spitball smashes into the whiteboard and adheres itself to the board.

Seeing what is going on, the students begin to act up. Another student throws a paper airplane across the room. Gliding through the air, it slices through the silence, opening to a roar of laughter from

71

the class. As a precaution, they quickly go silent in case someone suddenly appears. Yet again, nobody is there. They get away with their antics!

Still, without a teacher or anyone there to keep any semblance of peace, the students gradually become more daring. Ultimately, they end up not doing their work. Instead, they decide to do whatever they want because the teacher left the classroom. There are a few students, though, who try to maintain the peace and adhere to the rules, but they quickly become the minority. Balls of paper fly through the air. Students are scribbling on the whiteboard. Some are standing on their desks, throwing pencils into the soft ceiling tiles above, peppering the ceiling and giving it the appearance of classroom stalactites. Some of the students even leave class and never come back! Well, the teacher left the classroom at Pigeon Financial and was never coming back.

This *Lord of the Flies* scenario was quite frightening. Wayne and his teammates were astute enough to keep the ship afloat as best they could. They forged forward without a leader, doing their best to keep things orderly and professional. Management had their heads in their asses, serving their egos with their eyes glued to the numbers while neglecting the names, their people.

At this point, Wayne was desperate for change. He begged and pleaded, even roared, for leadership at Pigeon Financial to change the way things were for the better. He even asked upper management to relieve him of his work duties, asking them to let him go on multiple occasions because he could no longer tolerate working for such abhorrent leadership.

He witnessed the disintegration of employee morale ignited by upper management's increasing ignorance and neglect. The lack of productivity, extreme negativity, and deteriorating morale contributed to thousands of dollars being thrown out the window simply because people were not doing their work. Money and time were wasted on unnecessary calls and meetings that seemed to be more of a cover for the sake of looking productive—that is, fake work.

The more he expressed his concerns regarding the low morale and negative work culture, the more management seemed to ignore his pleas, taking no action. The longer this went on, the more it fed his desire to move on, but he was continually lured back in with the enticement of a promotion. This kept him engaged because he wanted to help, and he truly believed he could make a positive difference.

Since joining the company in 2012, he had done an outstanding job of meeting and exceeding expectations, opening doors, and deepening relationships. His insight, knowledge, and determination were a big contributor to the company's unprecedented success. As he incorporated his business approach of *I.T.S. to Succeed* to his role in relationship management, the company catapulted up the ranks among industry peers and ahead of the behemoths.

After being honored with the Relationship Manager of the Year award, Wayne was then elected as a member of the field advisory board, which was a select few sales leaders who collaborated on product development, marketing strategies, and the overall direction of the division. This was complemented by an award of shares of company stock and participation in the employee stock ownership plan.

Wayne's work ethic was unmatched. He brought a deep understanding of, and passion for, the business. More important, he knew how to motivate and move people into action. His approach to the business and the marketplace of knowing his clients better than they knew themselves could not be ignored, which created an energy and excitement that was contagious.

He had earned the respect of the sales force because he, too, had previously been a wholesaler. He earned the respect of his teammates because of his positive energy and passion for the role. Plus, he was willing to share his knowledge and approach with his teammates to help them become better professionally. He opened more doors, established new relationships, and improved existing relationships as never experienced before by Pigeon Financial.

Countless discussions with Corey and Ned took place regarding an opportunity for Wayne to lead the team. He also spoke with Chad on occasion about a potential promotion.

Unfortunately, it was a very slow process with very little follow-through. The discussions about a potential promotion seemed to be just idle words paired with the empty promises from Corey and Ned about taking steps to improve the dysfunction in the workplace. It slowly ate away at Wayne's passion and desire for his job. Unfortunately, the more they spoke about a promotion, the less he believed it was going to manifest.

There was a time when Wayne embraced a deep sense of pride and excitement for his work. Now he found it increasingly difficult to ignite that spark. It was even a challenge to summon the energy to get out of bed each day to go do the work he once loved and was energized about. His frustration mounted with the growing disruption and toxicity among employees and leadership alike.

Wayne and his teammates seriously wondered whether management was fabricating work and activities to subtly validate their high-paying management positions, thus making them irreplaceable. Their schedules were full of tasks, calls, projects, and meetings, which looked great in black and white. Although, being a participant in these meetings and calls, Wayne and the team began to see how inefficient and ineffective things were.

Wayne remembered as a child helping his parents with the yard work in the fall. He believed that if he raked the leaves as fast and as hard as he could, it meant that he was successful and productive. But all he did was move the leaves from one side of the yard to the other, and no real work was actually done. But, in his childish mind, he felt as though he was successful because he was breathing heavily and sweating.

Despite his hard work, his parents were frustrated by the inefficiency. It was more of a burden on them because they had to complete his unfinished work in addition to the work they were doing. It was a matter of whether his parents allowed him to continue doing inefficient and ineffective work only to clean up the mess he left behind, which always led to their continued frustration, or the next time his parents had yard work to do, they did the work themselves. An even better scenario would be to take the time to teach him how to properly complete the work in a more efficient and effective manner. His parents chose to teach him how to do the work properly, which ultimately reduced their workload, allowing them to complete more work in less time.

This busywork created by upper management was like moving the work from one side of the desk to the other or scheduling a conference call to discuss the moving of the pile of work. In mindless call after mindless call, they would discuss the moving of the same pile of work, to go to work once again, moving it to another spot on the desk or the project plan. Then another call was scheduled to strategize about the same pile of work again. This busywork, or fake work, occurred over and over again. It led Wayne and his teammates to believe upper management did not know what they were doing and possibly were creating this busy work to appear productive, thus validating their positions, or, worse, they were purposely preventing things from improving for fear that they would be exposed for the frauds they were and replaced by true leaders who knew what they were doing. Maybe that was why Nelson resigned, because they felt threatened by him and pushed him out because of their ignorance.

Just because someone works hard at something does not necessarily make them a success. Very inefficient work processes are complete time wasters, sucking energy and resources while deflating employee morale. Wayne and his teammates noticed that the employees who had strong work ethics, pride, and integrity ended up cleaning up the mess from the inefficient, untrained, and unmotivated employees. But this also made them less productive and more stressed, leading to burnout. Wayne and his teammates were working for an upper management team who, despite their intelligence and impressive ability to analyze numbers and data, were grossly incompetent and ignorant of the welfare of the team.

When other teams began dropping the ball, the issues became chronic and embarrassing. The lack of appropriate training and guidance from upper management contributed to an overabundance of incomplete and error-laden work. With no one present to guide them and hold them accountable, things worsened. The blind were leading the blind, and the workplace gradually became more disruptive and toxic.

It was as though they fabricated this fake work phenomenon so that when issues arose, upper management could then rush in to address and resolve the very issue they created. This made it appear as though they were improving the workplace when in reality, they were fixing the very issues they created.

This was a serious issue that was negatively affecting the team, slowly eating away at their morale as well as the morale of the sales force and other departments. Time after time, the promises for a promotion kept coming, but a promotion was nowhere in sight. The more Wayne witnessed the chronic dysfunction, the more he wrestled with the idea of even wanting a promotion. Deep down, he desired the opportunity to improve the workplace, but he dreaded working among the self-serving leadership team at Pigeon Financial.

Nelson's replacement, Amy, came in to run things as the third head of relationship management. Less than a year after she took on the role, she was gone. They fired her, after more than ten years at the company. Corey would soon be back at the helm. During one of their many trips to the home office in Bellevue, Wayne and Charlize walked back to the hotel after a day of meetings, figuring out what the next steps were.

"You were right. The writing was on the wall all along regarding the dysfunction here," Wayne commented.

"From my first day setting foot in this place, it was pretty clear that upper management embraced a strange view of relationship management, a sort of love-hate relationship," Charlize said and continued, "They've always maintained this belief that the team isn't necessary, and if they could do it themselves, they would, but they can't. But they need a relationship management team just as much as they need a sales force."

"Well, their obsession with automation clearly spits in the face of having a sales force. If they could replace the wholesalers, they would do that as well, but they can't," Wayne added.

"If they could find a reason to eliminate the entire team and the relationship management role, I believe they would in a heartbeat."

"I find it laughable that we are going on four managers in almost four years," Wayne scoffed.

"It's an embarrassment. That's what it is! The abhorrent dysfunction in this company, which starts at the top, is trickling down to the employees and continues to divide the teams. Did I tell you what Corey said to me last week?"

"No, I don't think so."

"Get this. He asked me to stop talking on the team calls and to give the rest of the team an opportunity to speak."

"Bullshit!"

"I bullshit you not. So, on yesterday's call, I was silent. I didn't say much other than a few brief comments."

"Come to think of it, you were pretty quiet."

"Then he calls me to ask why I didn't say anything on the call. In one moment, he confronts me, telling me I am speaking too much, and in the next, he wants to know why I am so quiet. I really don't think they know what they are doing," Charlize stated in exasperation.

"Leaders who don't listen will eventually be surrounded by people who have nothing to say. Corey and Carl shouldn't be in positions of leadership. It astonishes me to see them turning a good company into a place people despise. They are surrounded by employees who no longer have anything to say, and they don't even see it or just don't give a shit about it."

They stood at the corner, waiting for the light to change.

"So, do you think they'll hire someone to run the team again?" Wayne asked.

"I really don't know. Maybe Corey will remain and end up running things again."

"What about you?"

"What do you mean, what about me?" she responded with a tinge of annoyance.

"Look, Charlize, you are good at what you do and understand what makes relationship management successful. Have you ever considered running the team?"

"No," she replied without hesitation. "Look, I would consider it if things were different. I spoke with Amy about it a week ago, and she said I was crazy to even consider it. And, even if I did, two years is all I would put in."

"Why?" Wayne asked as they crossed the street.

"They would either find a way to get rid of me, or I would end up leaving because of the stress. There is no way I would pursue a management role with this company as long as Corey, Carl, Ned, and Chad are running things."

Each time Wayne and Charlize had this conversation, her stance remained the same; she was unequivocally against it. Not because she couldn't do it, but because she knew how fucked up Pigeon Financial was.

Knowing this should have stopped Wayne from even thinking about pursuing a management role. Especially considering how things continued to get worse, he should have taken notice and walked away to let another candidate, or victim, give it his or her best shot. But the power of pride and ego has a strange way of clouding one's judgment, leading us to do things we oftentimes regret. This was one of those times Wayne regretted.

"Well, Corey keeps sucking me into his little hell," Wayne replied.

"What do you mean? Did he offer you a job?"

"No, not yet at least. Although he and Ned have been dangling the idea of a promotion in front of me for over a year now, but nothing ever happens. He keeps talking about more responsibility, whatever that means, and then Corey asked me to create a roles and responsibilities proposal for relationship management, outlining the roles and responsibilities for the internal relationship managers and the sales operations managers."

"You know he asked me to do the same thing."

"No, I didn't. What did you say?"

"I told him I'd look into it, but I never followed through. If he really wanted something, he would have pushed me to do it. Plus, I'm confident it will be a work in futility."

"Well, he continues to suck me in. Regrettably, I jumped at the opportunity."

Wayne and Charlize walked through the revolving door to their hotel, continuing their conversation in the lobby.

"You did?"

"Yep."

"When are you supposed to start?"

"As soon as possible. He wants something in the next month or two. Before I do any work, I want to get together with the team to get their input."

"Wayne, you know I will help you in any way I can. You should set up a call with the team as soon as possible to discuss this."

"Good idea. I will coordinate a call for this coming Friday."

"Thank you for standing up for the team. I hope this works out for you."

"Yep. Me too. See you at dinner." Wayne said as he headed to his hotel room for a break before convening for dinner later that evening with the team.

Words to Lead By

Q: As a manager, or leader, are you there for your people while providing them with the freedom to grow and thrive? Are you able to identify and build upon their strengths? Are you, also, able to identify their weaknesses and turn them into strengths instead of degrading the people?

Lord of the Flies explores the dark side of humanity, the savagery that underlies even the most civilized human beings. William Golding intended this novel as a tragic parody of children's adventure tales, illustrating humankind's intrinsic evil nature. He presents the reader with a chronology of events, leading a group of young boys from hope to disaster as they attempt to survive their uncivilized, unsupervised, isolated environment until rescued.[3]

Lord of the Flies is a 1954 novel by Nobel Prize–winning British author William Golding. The book focuses on a group of British boys stranded on an uninhabited island and their disastrous attempt to govern themselves.[4]

---

[3] https://www.cliffsnotes.com/literature/l/lord-of-the-flies/book-summary.
[4] https://en.wikipedia.org/wiki/Lord_of_the_Flies.

Asshole's Fable—The Manager Who Cried Wolf

A liar will not be believed, even when telling the truth.

—*Aesop's Fable*

After their visit to the home office in Bellevue, Wayne began gathering the information for the proposals, much of which had already been created by his colleague Patrice a few years prior. Using her research as the foundation, he spent countless hours working with the team, soliciting their advice and insight, as well as that of their accounts and competitors.

Gleaning the perspective from different vantage points provided the backdrop to create the best representation of relationship management possible. If the mess that had been created within the walls of Pigeon Financial was going to be fixed, this was the only chance aside from replacing the upper management team.

Clearly identifying the roles and responsibilities was the easy part, since they had already been established through Patrice's work and the team understood what needed to be done. The uphill challenge was the constant turnover of managers, the continual reshuffling of the deck regarding the organizational structure, along with continued inconsistency and ignorance of the mounting issues and disconnect.

The relationship management team was the face of the organization for their accounts; broker/dealers, banks, and wirehouse firms nationwide. They were the hub of a wheel connecting the spokes; all the different departments, executive leadership, product, sale operations, marketing, and national sales with the executive leadership, product, operations, marketing, and sales teams of their accounts. The driving force behind the proposal was repairing the damaged and disconnected relationship between the relationship management and sales operations teams at Pigeon Financial.

The challenge lay with the sales operations team, who no longer held up their end of the bargain. The sales operations team continued a downward spiral of subpar, error-laden, and often incomplete work, which was the result of an absence of coaching and leadership. Wayne and the relationship management team routinely stepped in to correct those errors and cover up the poor results.

Although separate departments with differing job responsibilities, they operated under the same division and supported the same product line and the same accounts. Their success was interdependent. For an annuity product to be available for sale at an account, the relationship management team engaged with senior management at their assigned accounts. Their focus was on opening the door to initiate discussions between key stakeholders. Once a product received approval, the door was opened for the sales operations team to ensure that everything worked: systems, paperwork, electronic order entry, and more. The same applied with the marketing team, their job was to create and then secure the approval of the marketing materials from their assigned accounts. Collaboration and a clear understanding of each team's roles and responsibilities were critical to the overall success of the division and ultimately the company.

Once Pigeon Financial's relationship management team received approval for their annuity products, then next step was to create the project launch document providing the sales force with the product and firm intelligence necessary to engage the financial advisors at their dedicated accounts.

The relationship management team quarterbacked all of it and took exceptional pride in how they represented themselves and the company despite the unprofessionalism and incompetence of Ned, Carl, and Corey. Unfortunately, the constant unpreparedness, inaccuracies, unreliability, and often foolishness within the division grew tiresome.

The relationship management team did their best to get the job done despite the continued inaccuracies, and when something went wrong, all eyes would be on the relationship management team. They were the fall guys if things did not work out, which was just the nature of the role. The lack of guidance and leadership also bled over into the marketing department, which did not make things any easier for the team. The marketing department's continual ignorance of their accounts' marketing processes and approval requirements contributed to the chronic issues, delays, and rework. This occurred and reoccurred each time a new product or marketing brochure was created.

In structuring the proposal, Wayne and the team acknowledged how critically important it was for the document to contain the right information and statistics to align with Corey's personality style and business mind-set. No fluff, no rah-rah, no teamwork, no camaraderie, just the facts.

Just over a month later, the proposal was ready. This was around the same time as Wayne's annual review meeting in Charlotte, North Carolina, with Chariot Horse Advisors. This was an opportune time for Wayne to sit down with Corey and review the proposal considering the Pigeon Financial executive management team would be in town for the meeting.

Having flown in the evening before, Wayne scheduled breakfast with Corey the following morning, Tuesday, December 6. The plan was to meet at Panera Bread on College Street to review the agenda of meetings for the day and find time to discuss the proposal later that afternoon. During breakfast, Wayne handed Corey a copy of the proposal with the intention of providing him enough time to review it in advance of their meeting later that day.

When their day of meetings concluded, Wayne and Corey convened at the food court of Tower Three in the business complex on South Tryon Street. Wayne was eager and a little nervous. He pulled an aluminum chair away from the table and sat down across from Corey. Leaning over in his chair, he grabbed the proposals from his bag. Avoiding the crumbs left over from the lunch crowd that had recently departed, Wayne slid a copy of the proposal across the table toward Corey.

After an initial exchange of small talk, they jumped into their discussion.

"Tell me about the proposal and what you hope to accomplish," Corey started.

Considering the dozens of conversations that had taken place leading up to this meeting over the past several months, Corey had a very clear understanding regarding what Wayne wanted to accomplish with the proposal. Wayne's frustrations were coming to a head after repeatedly answering the same questions from Corey months leading up to their meeting.

When emotions are introduced into any situation or relationship, things can easily become clouded. Tension escalates, and even the best-laid plans can easily go astray. This was Wayne's Achilles' heel.

For Wayne, this was another indication that Corey was either too overwhelmed to take the time to prepare for their meeting, simply did not give a shit, or maybe simply did not know what the hell he was doing.

Wayne's expectations of his boss were not at all unrealistic or absurd, but Corey's continued ignorance of the issues was a core reason for the corrosion of conformity, which contributed to the growing masses of actively disengaged employees.

Doing his best to hide his mounting anger and frustration with Corey, Wayne continued reading the document verbatim. Taking a deep breath, Wayne spoke. "Corey, the proposal is intended to do three things: first, to define the role of relationship management and sales operations within the division; second, to align and identify the responsibilities for the involved parties, relationship management and sales operations," Wayne droned on. Any enthusiasm or passion that once existed had been extinguished. "Lastly, this will ensure the continued success of relationship management by providing a more efficient process, ultimately leading to a more effective, productive, and satisfied team, resulting in sales and revenue targets being met, if not exceeded."

Corey continued to pose questions that were clearly addressed and answered in the proposal. The issues addressed in the proposal had been voiced over the past few years by the team without any response from Corey until now. But Corey continued to pose the same mundane questions with no follow-through.

His frustration with, and growing distrust of, Corey sank its claws in deep, and any respect that Wayne once had for him had long departed. In his usual monotone style, Corey posed yet another mindless question, "How do you define relationship management?"

Wayne's heart sank as he read the definition of relationship management directly from the proposal. "Corey, relationship management, as stated on the bottom of page two, is defined as a systematic approach to grow and maintain a named set of the division's most important accounts to understand their organization and uncover opportunities that will maximize mutual value and achieve mutually beneficial goals. It's difficult to accurately define relationship management, considering the various aspects of the role and the departments with which the team must collaborate to successfully launch products and deepen client relationships."

"Cool. Uh, how do you see the team being structured?" came Corey's rote reply.

Refraining from saying anything he would later regret, he continued to review the proposal. "The intent is to establish a clear delineation between the role of relationship management and sales operations as depicted on page three. In identifying the responsibilities, it's just as important that the internal relationship managers are aligned with an appropriate sales operations manager, allowing them to remain in sync with accounts, product updates, product launches, campaigns, and more," he continued. "To ensure this was the best approach for the division, we consulted with team members, our accounts, and even our competitors. We used the existing work that had been created over the past several years as the foundation while incorporating research reports and findings from a third-party research company.

"But my main concern, Corey, is whether my understanding and definition of relationship management is aligned with yours. For example, if I believe relationship management is supposed to be 'X,' and I propose how it should be implemented based on the foundation of 'X,' yet you believe it to be 'A,' it probably doesn't matter how great a job I do explaining 'X' if your mind is already sold on 'A.' I need to know how you define and see relationship management and our collaboration with other departments. I need you to explain your views because I don't care to continue pushing my view of relationship management if you have an entirely different concept in mind."

Wayne was quickly losing his interest and desire to improve things, because Corey seemed to have an entirely different understanding of relationship management and was not forthcoming about it. Wayne trudged forward anyway. "Turn to page three. You will see our proposed structure, which is based on the foundation currently in place. There needs to be a clear delineation between our roles and responsibilities and the roles and responsibilities of sales operations. As mentioned previously, the sales operations managers are pushing most of their work onto the internal relationship managers. The internal relationship managers are overworked doing the work of the sales operations team as well as trying to complete their own work. It has gotten out of hand and has negatively impacted the quality of the team's work. It doesn't help matters either to see work slipping through the cracks with the marketing team as well."

"Uh, I'm not sure we can do that," Corey said after looking at the team structure outlined in the proposal. "Are you proposing we hire a manager for internal relationship management?"

"Yes. The intent is that Patrice or Hank would fill that role, or another identified individual. Elaine cannot continue running both sales operations and the internal relationship management team. She has very little knowledge about relationship management and has been incapable of even addressing the issues within her own team. We also suggest that you hire someone to oversee the entire relationship management team—external and internal. You have too much on your plate, Corey. How can you effectively manage the relationship management team along with sales operations, national sales, and marketing? For this to work, we must have some structure with clearly defined roles and responsibilities. In addition, it is critical that we have the support of both you and Carl for this to be successful."

"Uh, we just hired Elaine, and she doesn't have enough people reporting to her. That is why we moved the internal relationship managers under her. She does not have enough people on the team to validate her director title, with only the sales operator managers. So, we decided to the internal relationship managers needed to report to her. I am not sure I can justify hiring a manager for the internal relationship managers or a manager for the relationship management team. It's not in the budget."

It had become apparent to Wayne and the team that the decision to hire Elaine was not well thought out. Elaine knew next to nothing about relationship management. This was yet another "set up for failure" story for the books at Pigeon Financial. Carl historically hired people who would do as they were told rather than lead and improve the team. He did not want someone who would see through and challenge his bullshit and habitual lies. Elaine was the perfect fit.

The last thing someone who has been recently promoted wants to do is push back. The saying goes, "Don't bite the hand that feeds you." Well, the hand in this scenario needed to be cut off at the elbow, but no one would do it.

The good news was that she eventually broke free of his deceit, about a year later, when there was yet another reorganization. No longer reporting to Carl, her eyes had finally been opened to the dysfunction and his bullshit. She no longer served a purpose and no longer could help move Carl's agenda forward. In his usual style, he turned his back on her as he had done with Ned and countless others while he climbed his way to the top.

"Let's plan on scheduling a follow-up meeting. In the meantime, I want you to put together a proposal highlighting your plan for implementation, clearly defining the specific job responsibilities of relationship management and sales operations," Corey concluded.

"Okay. Thanks, Corey. When do you want this completed?" Wayne reluctantly complied.

"Uh, let's get together in another month. Reach out to Deanna and schedule our next meeting."

"Okay. Sounds good," Wayne said with a bullshit smile as the meeting concluded. He stood up from his chair, shook hands with Corey, and headed back to his hotel.

Wayne immediately called Charlize to fill her in on the meeting.

"Hey, Wayne," Charlize answered the phone. "How'd your meeting go?"

"It was bullshit! The first question he asked was, 'Tell me about the proposal and what you want to accomplish.'"

"Okay. But didn't we put that in the proposal?"

"Yes. He knows exactly what we want to accomplish. We have been talking about this for three goddamn years."

"I agree. But you have to keep your cool and play along with this. We really need some positive change, and this is our only opportunity."

"Yep." He sighed. "I am just tired of his bullshit. He asked me to define relationship management, which you know we have discussed ad nauseam. It's the same shit over and over again."

"What did you say?"

"I pointed to page two and proceeded to read the definition," Wayne said in frustration. "All of his questions were answered in the proposal exactly the way we planned, but he still asked them."

"Did he say anything about the structure of the team? The IRM manager and team lead for the RMs?"

"When I suggested he hire Patrice or Hank to run the IRMs, he pushed back, saying he doesn't have it in the budget. Oh yeah, plus he can't take the IRMs away from Elaine because of her director title."

"I told you! They gave her that promotion because Carl wanted another minion to do his dirty work. But they screwed up not knowing that a director must have at least five direct reports, and she only has four sales ops managers on her team. That's why they moved the IRMs under her. It's such a cluster fuck!"

"Well, I also suggested he hire someone to run the RM team, and he said he couldn't."

"Let me guess, no budget."

"Yep! Every time we zig, he zags. He doesn't see things the way we do. I wish he would tell us so we can move on."

"Remember, Wayne, he doesn't understand how to run relationship management. It's as though he doesn't want someone to come in who knows what the hell they're doing. Look at Nelson. He was the perfect person for the job, and they drove him out. Ned, Corey, and Carl were fighting him tooth and nail on practically everything. They saw him as a threat. He realized he couldn't make any positive changes and grew tired of constantly fighting them, so he left."

"I have lost all respect for Corey. He continues to make comments about how much of a pain in the ass you are, which doesn't help. He clearly doesn't see how much you bring to the team, how much you contribute, and how well you know your accounts."

"Thank you, Wayne. So, what happened? How did you end the meeting?"

"He asked me to create another proposal."

"Another one?"

"Yep. He wants me to create another proposal outlining how I intend to implement the first proposal and clearly define the specific job responsibilities of relationship management and sales operations."

"Isn't that what Patrice's document already does?"

"Yes, of course," Wayne laughed.

"And he wants you to create a proposal about something that's already been created and he hasn't acted upon? Well, I guess it's good that he didn't reject it altogether and you have another shot at fixing things," Charlize commented.

"Yeah, I guess you're right," Wayne said with a sigh. "I've never worked for a company that prided itself in creating work for the sake of looking busy. The truth of the matter is that we could have made an immediate impact if we were given the authority to implement some of these changes. It's a bunch of bureaucratic bullshit. I don't need a title or a promotion. Just the ability and authority to make the necessary changes. Corey and Carl can continue managing in their fucked-up, self-serving, mindless style while we actually get shit done."

"Wayne, that's what we're already doing!"

"You're right, but I'd like to do it without fighting them tooth and nail on practically everything."

"Good point. All we need is the ability to implement some of these changes without going to committee, without going to Corey and Carl for approval. But you and I know that'll never happen. For a guy who told me he wasn't a micromanager, I'm not so sure he even knows what that means. They're losing control. They can't keep running things this way. Fortunately, we've been able to keep things sane, but we're paying the price and are now labeled as instigators of the chaos that they ignited around here. Elaine and Fiona are under Carl's influence and don't see through his bullshit, yet. I've got to believe eventually it's going to come to a head."

"I'm tired," Wayne said with a deep sigh. "I need a break from this."

"I agree. It's giving me a headache." Charlize sighed.

"Catch you later?"

"Yep." Charlize hung up.

After that meeting, Wayne immediately began working on the second proposal but with less enthusiasm than before. In any other scenario, someone would have been thrilled to be given an opportunity to create a second proposal outlining the roles and responsibilities of the team.

It seemed Pigeon Financial was being run by an upper management team who did not have everyone's best interests at heart but instead their own. The desire for a promotion was fading, and Wayne was growing tired of management creating work, all of which disappeared into a black hole of inaction, no follow-through, and no ownership. All the while, it was the employees who did the work that created success for the organization and executive management.

One doesn't need to go to business school to see the atrocities and inefficiencies at play. This too-busy-to-give-a-shit phenomenon allows upper management to float around, riding on their egos, pointing fingers, pounding their chests, and delegating work. They move on to the next executive meeting to sweep in once again, create mindless work, and then float off into the ethers never to return.

Regardless, Wayne moved forward with the plan and began working on the second proposal with the team. It didn't require too much work, considering Patrice had already created the roles and responsibilities document highlighting the specific tasks and responsibilities for the team a number of years prior, so it was resuscitated from the project wasteland.

Less than two months later, toward the end of January 2017, the second proposal was ready. This time around, they would review it on a conference call with the entire external and internal relationship management team. It was good to have the support of the team on the call to give a stronger voice to the proposal and what Wayne hoped to accomplish.

The challenge remained the same, which was aptly reflected by Charlize's comments at the outset of the call: "The core issues have never changed. Personalities have changed, but the core issues have remained the same." Charlize knew how to strike a chord and get to the point. She concluded her comments with the following words:

"This is a very senior group of people you have to leverage. Sharing that and giving it a voice will only make this place better."

This was not the first time these words were spoken. The right words were said at the right time. Unfortunately, Charlize's words fell on deaf ears, again. Corey and Carl were so busy spreadsheet coaching, knee deep in automation and data analysis, that they missed the core issues that had always prevailed. Because of his strong will and determination, Wayne remained engaged, hoping to forge the positive change he and the team desired. The proposals were the only remaining hope the team had left for any positive change to manifest.

Wayne looked for the best in people, trusting them at their word, which was a mistake. The absence of follow-through and implementation by Corey and Carl grew tiresome. If only he had sought clear direction from Corey at the outset regarding this apparent promotion by asking Corey what his intent was, maybe Wayne could have anticipated what was to come next. This was another lesson Wayne would learn the hard way.

They needed someone to take ownership of the work and make the critical decisions to implement change. Each time Corey made a comment about giving Wayne more responsibility to lead the team, which meant the possibility of a promotion, nothing resulted other than more work, more proposals, and more calls. The longer they dragged this out, the further away Wayne retreated until he eventually stopped showing up. He mentally checked out.

Like the fable of "The Boy Who Cried Wolf," a new fable was born: "Asshole's Fable—The Manager Who Cried Wolf." In Aesop's Fable, "The Boy Who Cried Wolf," the story culminated in a sad and tragic ending when the sheep were slaughtered by the wolf and the wolf eventually killed the boy. The continual lies and fake work from Corey and Carl were reminiscent of the boy in the fable with his continual lies. When the boy cried wolf the first time, the townspeople (employees) rushed in to help him. When he cried wolf once again, the townspeople, because of their integrity and commitment to their work, came running. Of course, there was no wolf (no ownership, no promotion, and no action) to be found. Eventually, after numerous cries, the townspeople grew tired of the boy's lies. When the wolf did in fact arrive, the boy cried, "Wolf!" but no one arrived. Not a single townsperson came running. After hearing the boy's continual lies and bogus cries for help, the townspeople no longer showed up.

For those who are in positions of leadership and management, please don't allow your ignorance and false cries to lead to the slaughter of your sheep (employees).

Wayne often wondered how Corey, Ned, and Carl would react if their own kids were treated in a similar manner. When they found out that their kids, their loved ones, were being lied to, sexually harassed, and treated like shit in the same way they lied to and treated their very own employees, one has to wonder if they would idly stand by and allow this abhorrent treatment of their loved ones to continue.

Eventually, Wayne stopped showing up. He stopped responding to the redundant and mindless requests that upper management continually created. There was no method to their approach, no method to capture the recurring tasks and requests that would improve efficiency and effectiveness. Upper management never implemented a process to capture and mitigate this rework. Therefore, employees continued wasting valuable time and resources.

The irony here was that this would have been a good use of automation. But they were so busy with their heads up their asses they missed the opportunity entirely to make improvements using something they so adored, automation.

Corey requested that Wayne create yet another proposal outlining the first two proposals and a rough outline of the account alignments.

By the time the third proposal was ready in July, Wayne was at his wits' end. He felt tired and defeated. Any semblance of the pride and confidence he had once embraced had been destroyed. It was surprising he hung on for that long. Then a miracle of sorts occurred. To everyone's surprise, a call was scheduled by Corey and Carl to walk through the roles and responsibilities with both teams, relationship management and sales operations.

Unfortunately, that was as climactic as it would get. Corey and Carl kicked off the call with their version of the roles and responsibilities and then handed the call over to Elaine to walk through in her robotic recitation of the slide notes.

Although Wayne and his teammates were dialed in for the call, they were tuned out mentally. It was the same surface talk and bullshit from Corey and Carl. Other than filler questions and comments, Wayne and the team remained silent on the call, except for Charlize. She called attention to the continual rework and lack of implementation, but Corey brushed her comments aside with his usual tone of annoyance.

The hour-long call had ended and so had the roles and responsibilities project, once again. Carl and Corey took the team's work, repurposed it, presented it, and did absolutely nothing to enact the changes. There was no ownership of the project, meaning the roles and responsibilities proposals died another miserable death. The team calls with Carl and Corey were a graveyard, where all ideas and hope went to die, along with the morale of the team.

The root of the problem with relationship management was the relationship part. Relationships represent a human connection and cannot be measured or replicated with analytics. This was Corey's handicap because he lacked any signs of emotional intelligence. Corey was 99 percent left-brained and more concerned about artificial intelligence than emotional intelligence.

It felt as though he was living a modern-day version of Aesop's Fable "The Boy Who Cried Wolf," but this fable was more like "Asshole's Fable—The Manager Who Cried Wolf." Like Aesop's Fable, this too would soon meet with a tragic ending.

Words to Lead By

Q: As a manager or leader, are you able to put yourself in the shoes of your people? (I.T.S. to Succeed!) Are you smart with your words? Do you make empty promises or comments to your people that you do not follow through on? Pay attention because your people are paying attention.

Aesop's Fable "The Boy Who Cried Wolf"

The tale concerns a shepherd boy who repeatedly tricks nearby villagers into thinking wolves are attacking his flock. When a wolf does appear and the boy again calls for help, the villagers believe that it is another false alarm, and the sheep are eaten by the wolf. In later English–language poetic versions of the fable, the wolf also eats the boy.

The moral stated at the end of the Greek version is "this shows how liars are rewarded: even if they tell the truth, no one believes them."[5]

A bored boy tending sheep cried, "Wolf!" to get attention. He did it again, and people came. A third time and the boy was ignored. Goodbye, flock. A liar will not be believed, even when telling the truth.[6]

---

[5] "The Boy Who Cried Wolf," Wikipedia, https://en.wikipedia.org/wiki/The_Boy_Who_Cried_Wolf.

[6] "The Boy Who Cried Wolf," Fables of Aesop, https://fablesofaesop.com/the-boy-who-cried-wolf.html.

On the Shoulders of Giants

My life was built on a foundation of parents, coaches,
and teachers; of kind souls who lent couches or gym
back rooms where I could sleep; of mentors who shared
wisdom and advice; of idols who motivated me ...

—*Arnold Schwarzenegger (Tools of Titans, Ferriss 2016)*

It was early spring 2017, Wayne was on a morning flight to Charlotte, North Carolina, for a meeting with Barry Antiverse, the senior vice president of annuity products at Chariot Horse Advisors, to discuss Pigeon Financial's new product.

Wayne lost himself reminiscing about one of the greatest business lessons of his storied career from nearly twenty years prior. The year was 1998; Wayne worked for Roguehouse Financial in Phoenix, Arizona. He had not yet learned how to effectively be assertive and close sales without pissing off the prospect, or without losing the sale entirely. "Always be closing" has been the motto for decades in sales, but for someone who has not yet learned the elegance of closing, it can be awkward and difficult and lead to failure more often than not. Ultimately over time through persistence and perseverance you learn to get up over and over again, which paves the way to success.

Wayne was gathered with colleagues in the Roguehouse Financial conference room for a morning huddle with Bryce Roguehouse, the owner and their boss. "So far, Wayne, Dennis, Kris, Tony, Kyle, and Adam are on target and have brought in at least two plans this week with checks in hand. Great job! And some of you are on target to exceed your goals. Keep up the good work." Bryce smiled to the team. "Although, there are those of you who have not collected a check or sold a new plan this week." His tone and demeanor of love and support changed to a fiery intensity of frustration. "If any of you come back to the office tomorrow morning without a check, you will not—I repeat, will *not*—get paid!" he roared.

This was one of those rare moments when Bryce showed his frightening and intimidating Hitler-esque side. He was a towering presence of intimidation, as his nostrils flared and the tiny dark pupils of his eyes grew like the opening of a tunnel growing larger and larger into an empty circle of darkness. His healthy pale complexion had morphed into a blood-red hue.

"Oh shit! What is he going to do?" Wayne mumbled under his breath. He glanced around the room at his peers to gauge their reaction but ever so briefly because he did not want to break eye contact with his boss for too long in case he attacked. All of those present in the conference room sat motionless staring straight ahead at Bryce like deer frozen in the hypnotic glare of headlights. Unflinching, they stared with bated breath, fearing for their jobs, even their lives. Tension filled the room. Bryce's words broke the silence. And for some, his words broke their pride.

Bryce picked up an envelope that had sat on the table in front of Wayne's colleague Lance. He pulled Lance's commission check from the envelope, and the envelope floated toward the floor. All eyes were on Bryce holding the commission check in front of the group like a sacrificial lamb in an offering to the gods. Then he spoke. "If you can't close any plans today and come back without a check, you will not get paid!" Bryce Roguehouse repeated his words. Grasping the check between his fingertips with both hands, he pulled his right hand toward his chest and his left hand forward away from his torso. Scrrippp! The commission check was no more! He tore Lance's paycheck into pieces! The sound of the commission check being ripped to pieces tore through their hearts and egos. It screeched through the air, screaming into their ears with a message, a threat!

Despite Wayne's success at Roguehouse Financial and the praise Bryce Roguehouse gave him moments prior, he didn't understand why Bryce would make such a threat. This rattled Wayne. He feared what would happen if he did not collect a check at his appointment later that evening.

"Do you understand!" Bryce roared.

The room fell silent. *What the fuck just happened?* Wayne thought to himself. *Did he just do what I think he did? Is this guy insane?*

Tony let out a quiet chuckle and muttered, "Heh! He just tore up your commission check, Lance. That's funny!"

Bryce looked over at Tony. "Just because you are one of our top reps doesn't mean you get a free ride. This applies to you as well, Tony!"

Tony sat back in his chair and mumbled under his breath, "Whatever, you psycho."

"Would you shut up?" Kris whispered to him.

For the rest of them, Bryce's message was received: "Get the check." The meeting concluded, and they all walked out of the conference room on their way back to their desks.

"Can you believe he did that?" George said.

"Lance, dude! Was that really your check?" Dennis asked.

"Yes!" Lance replied. "What the hell was he thinking?"

"How much did that set you back?" Tony asked.

"That was a seven-thousand-dollar commission check! I can't believe Bryce did that! He's an asshole," Lance griped.

"You can get another check issued, right?" George asked.

"I don't know. I sure hope so because that would really suck if I can't get a new one," Lance moaned.

"Yeah, they'll reissue a check," Dennis confirmed.

"Man, I hope so!" Lance exclaimed.

Ding. Ding. Ding. The gentle sound from the front of the plane awoke Wayne from his daydream. The flight attendant began speaking over the intercom.

"Ladies and gentlemen, we have begun our descent into Charlotte. Please turn off all portable electronic devices and stow them until we have arrived at the gate ..."

Wayne's flight safely arrived in Charlotte. He grabbed his bag from the overhead compartment and exited the plane. Walking though the terminal, Wayne casually meandered through a crowd of anxious travelers on his way to baggage claim to meet his Uber ride.

Chariot Horse Advisors had become such an important client and Pigeon Financial's number one indexed annuity account because of Wayne's efforts. He opened the doors, which created opportunities for the sales division to be successful, so much so that Pigeon Financial built their new products based on Chariot Horse Advisors' product guidelines, parameters, and approval specs. All new product initiatives and launches that were brought to the table for approval with all other accounts lived and died based on Chariot Horse Advisors.

Prior to the meeting, Wayne's boss, Chad, made it very clear that Wayne must secure the product approval from Barry. His approval would allow the product team, national accounts team, marketing team, and operations team to move forward with the project. If Barry declined, the entire project would be stalled not only with Chariot Horse Advisors but all other accounts as well.

Wayne's experience at Roguehouse Financial twenty years prior had proven to be one of his biggest and most influential career lessons. Wayne's upcoming meeting with Barry seemed quite similar and could have easily gone off the rails just like his experience in 1998.

Wayne's Uber ride arrived, and he hopped into the back seat. Listening to music on his Air Pods, he lost himself, once again, recollecting his experience at Roguehouse Financial back in 1998 ...

The sun was setting, and Wayne was on his drive to North Phoenix for the initial interview with a young couple. The initial interview was the first face-to-face meeting with prospective clients after closing them over the phone and getting them to commit to the initial interview. As with the cold calls, this meeting was even scripted. Wayne rehearsed the script on his drive to the appointment.

Arriving at their home, Wayne parked his car and turned off the ignition. The interior lights flashed on, and he gathered his materials for the meeting. Taking a huge breath, he closed his eyes and exhaled. "Here we go," he said to himself. "Don't fuck it up!" He yearned for a beer, or six, to help calm his nerves.

Upon exiting his car, he locked the door and began his walk up the pathway toward the front door of the home. After straightening his tie and his jacket, followed by a quick zipper check, he knocked on the front door. An attractive young woman opened the door. Wayne greeted her with a smile and a handshake. She introduced herself and walked him into their kitchen. Her husband joined them as they exchanged greetings. They were very cordial welcoming him into their home. At that moment, he felt confident he would secure them as clients, unless of course he somehow managed to fuck it up.

Opening his portfolio, Wayne handed the planning documents to the husband and wife and began reciting his script. The meeting went very well. Wayne gathered all their financial information, statements, and records. He had everything he needed and a commitment from them to work with Wayne, except for a check! Then he heard his boss's threat from earlier that morning shoot through his mind like a rifle shot: "You better come back with a check! Or you will *not* get paid!"

Collecting himself, Wayne straightened his tie, buttoned his suit jacket, and promptly walked out the front door, down the walkway toward his midnight-blue Toyota Maxima. His phone rang.

"Hello," Wayne answered.

"Wayne, hey, man, it's George."

"Hey, George. What's up?"

"I wanted to see how your appointment went. Did you get a check?" he asked.

"No." Wayne sighed.

"Really?"

"Yep." Wayne sighed.

"What about Bryce? Do you think he is going to be pissed off?"

"I don't know, and I really don't give a shit," Wayne said in frustration.

"Really?"

"Yeah really!" Wayne exclaimed. "Dude, I lost my client *because* I asked for a fucking check."

"What do you mean?"

"The meeting was a success. I got everything I needed from them; they completed the fact finder, gave me all their statements. Everything! Except …"

"A check," George finished his sentence.

"Yep!" Wayne yelled. "Dude, I had them. They were my client. I knew it but felt that it wasn't the right time to ask them for a check. They weren't ready. But all I heard was Bryce yelling this morning and tearing Lance's commission check to shreds. So, I pressured them and told them they needed to pay me two-hundred and fifty dollars to work with me."

"Really?"

"Yep."

"So, what did they say?"

"The guy practically threw me out of their home. He told me to leave and to never come back! This is bullshit!" Wayne yelled.

"Oh, man. I'm sorry."

"Yeah, me too. I don't want to ask for a check when I know the client isn't ready and especially when I'm not ready to ask. Why did Bryce do that? Now I'm fucked! I lost the damn sale, the client, and any opportunity for future business or referrals. Shit! That is like the trifecta of fuckups! Why didn't they coach us on the right and wrong way to close the sale, especially in the pressure of the moment?"

"Dude, you'll be fine. At least you tried. I am sure he'll be happy that you asked for the business. Now it's a matter of learning how to ask for the business without pissing off the client." George chuckled at Wayne's expense.

"Ha, ha! Funny!" Wayne replied. "I need a beer, maybe several."

"Catch you tomorrow, Wayne."

"Thanks for calling. Have a good night."

"Yep, you too, bud."

———

The Uber driver pulled up to the Marriott City Center Charlotte. "Sir, we are here."

Wayne awoke from his daydream, exited the car, and was greeted by the bellman. Wayne was still lost in his business experience from long ago and would use that experience to his advantage. This time around, Wayne had to "get the check" from Chariot Horse Advisors, in the form of getting the product approved. He approached the entire situation and his relationship with Chariot Horse Advisors from a short-term and long-term perspective. What points could he afford to lose today, giving his "opponent" a false sense of security, in order to win the match?

Wayne knew his client Barry well and heeded his words over the years about other account management teams who rubbed him the wrong way with ignorant demands and comments. Barry rarely forgot or forgave them for the error of their ways and was not shy about sharing his frustrations. Over the years, Wayne had listened intently to Barry, who often expressed his frustration with account managers at the other annuity companies who demanded that he approve their product. They would even impose upon Barry that Chariot Horse Advisors meet their demands simply because they invested money to establish the relationship. They expected things to be done their way with immediate results.

Wayne understood what rubbed Barry the wrong way, as well as what appeased him.

———

Many of the scenes in the boardroom of our adult years do not stray too far from the experiences in school and on the playground of our youth. Kids act irrationally, or like assholes, continually badgering other kids and even adults to get what they want. They whine, complain, and throw temper tantrums in the boardroom just like they once did on the playground and classroom of their youth.

The incessant badgering from a child is relentless with absolutely no regard for the other person's vantage point or situation. The child continues with their badgering until they either piss off the other person who eventually tells the kid to take a hike or caves under the pressure, giving in to the child's demands.

Either way, a resentment for the way the child approached the entire situation remains. The child is solely focused on their own selfish needs without any regard for the needs of the other person or people. Focused on their own interests, they leave a trail of resentment and damaged relationships in their wake. Most adults and parents exercise patience and forgiveness, allowing the child to learn and mature. Not so much in the boardroom of life during our adult years. This was Barry's world. He was continually badgered by account managers who asked for what they wanted or, even worse, demanded what they were told they should demand without thinking, without asking the right questions, and without understanding why they were doing what they were doing in the first place. These professionals rarely took the time to understand Barry or what he and his product team needed in order to succeed.

Not much had really changed from the days on the playground other than Wayne was now dealing with grown adults who were responsible for investment products that generated millions of dollars in sales and revenue and the billions of dollars received from investors who trusted these apparent leaders with their money, believing that they would do the right thing and not lead them astray. Barry had a responsibility for these investors and looked out for their best interests by approving the best investment products. In doing so, he would not approve just any product or give in to the temper tantrums of account managers.

Wayne saw account managers destroy their relationship with Barry repeatedly because of their shortsightedness. Wayne was not going to be that guy. He knew that Pigeon Financial's sales were as important to Chariot Horse Advisors as they were to Pigeon Financial. Wayne recognized the trends in the industry and the marketplace. The trends clearly indicated that Chariot Horse Advisors would eventually have to come around and approve the product.

If Barry ignored the trends, the result would be even more tragic than it was after the 2008 Financial Crisis because sales at Chariot Horse Advisors would continue to dwindle, which would translate into dwindling revenue. The likelihood of approval was practically a given considering Pigeon Financial's tremendous success at Chariot Horse Advisors as the number one indexed annuity carrier in their firm. Wayne knew that and understood it was just a matter of time.

Yes, Chariot Horse Advisors needed Pigeon Financial as much as Pigeon Financial needed Chariot Horse Advisors. But, unlike upper management and other account management teams, Wayne wasn't an asshole about it. He did not spit in Barry's face by throwing a tantrum and telling him they owed him because Pigeon Financial was their number-one carrier. He didn't bitch and moan about how much time and resources they dedicated to Chariot Horse Advisors. That was the nature of the business; you invest time and money into onboarding an account. Just because an annuity company lands an account does not mean the sale and success will magically appear. It is a matter of nurturing the relationship.

Ned Desilent, the executive vice president of Pigeon Financial's retirement division, was a bull in a China shop. He looked at the bottom line. If sales and revenue did not instantly appear, heads were going to roll. There was very little rapport and zero nurturing of the relationship to plant the seeds for success. Bryce Roguehouse's approach to the marketplace back in 1998 was similar to Ned's and many of the so-called leaders Wayne had worked for over the years. This was how loser leadership approached the marketplace.

In the business world, rooms are filled with big egos. When you have a room full of executives with big egos, it become a childish contest of who is the smartest, who has the most money, and a bunch of other bullshit. They often get lost in who has the biggest dick while losing sight of why they have dicks in the first place.

Wayne cringed upon realizing that not much had changed from the days on the playground as a child to the days in the boardroom as an adult. It took some time, but after many years of working with C-level executives and the big egos in the financial services industry, Wayne learned how to read people and how to get things done without being an asshole or a bull in a china shop.

He believed there was another way to conduct business. By becoming a student of the business and of emotional intelligence, Wayne knew how to effectively manage the emotions of his clients while steering them in the direction the industry was headed. Instead of creating headwinds and confrontation with his accounts, he learned as much about them as he could, which put him in a winning position.

Before scheduling his trip, Wayne realized it was too soon to pressure Barry for his approval of the new product. Instead, Wayne would plant the seed and nurture it until it sprouted. Knowing that Barry's team supplied him with the research and product intelligence, Wayne was going to put on a full court press from an intelligence vantage point—emotional intelligence, industry intelligence, and Chariot Horse Advisors' very own firm intelligence.

The challenge Wayne faced was whether he should let the executive management team at Pigeon Financial know about his approach. He feared they would not understand, and in their shortsightedness, they would focus only on getting the product approved by funding their chests and demanding that Barry approve the product.

Wayne kept his plans to himself. The product was a little cutting edge with investments that were new to the industry. Not having a track record of performance didn't help matters, and the investment concept was something firms were still trying to grasp. Based on prior dialogue with Barry and his team, it was clear to Wayne that Barry wasn't ready for a product like this, yet. So, why push it in the short term, risking long-term damage to the relationship?

———◆————

Wayne arrived at the Chariot Horse Advisors office building, Tower Three, and checked in with Veronica, who was head of security. She was an interesting woman and very temperamental. In one moment, she was an angel, all smiles and full of bubbly conversation. In the next, she could be mean and a downright grump. Wayne was never sure which version of Veronica he would get when checking in at the security desk. Thankfully on this visit, she was her angelic self when Wayne greeted her.

Wayne meandered over to the bank of elevators and pressed the button between the elevator cars, and the elevator doors glided open. He entered the elevator and pressed the button for floor eighteen, and the doors gently closed. It was the same routine for the past ten years. Upon arriving on the eighteenth floor, Wayne was promptly greeted by Jocelyn and her peers with smiles and hugs.

Wayne walked toward Barry's office, ready for a war of wills. For the good of the future and the relationship Wayne would not raise arms against Barry. He was prepared to surrender in that moment, knowing he would eventually be triumphant.

With a big smile and an enthusiastic hello, Wayne greeted Barry, "Barry, how are you doing? Great to see you!"

"I'm great, Wayne. How are things at Pigeon Financial?"

"Great, we are still selling the heck out of our indexed product with you guys. The retirement team has been fantastic supporting our sales team."

"Great to hear, Wayne. Thank you for all of your efforts."

"My pleasure, Barry. Is this time still good?" Wayne cordially asked.

"Of course. Have a seat."

"Thank you, Barry." Wayne sat down at the table in Barry's office and placed his navy-blue Tumi backpack on the floor next to his chair. "How much time do you have?"

"I have a call I need to jump on at two o'clock," Barry said as he sat down in his chair.

"Okay. Let's get started then," Wayne replied.

"So, what do you have for me, Wayne?" Barry got right to the point.

Wayne was prepared for the meeting with his finger on the trigger, somewhat anxious about getting down to business. Leaning over in his chair, he reached down into his bag to grab the spiral-bound product pitch deck. Opening the pitch deck to the product overview page, Wayne gently slid it across the table toward Barry. "Prior to our meeting today, I mentioned the product that we're looking to develop and launch with Chariot Horse Advisors is a hybrid indexed annuity product, which you see on page five of the deck."

"Let me stop you right there, Wayne." Barry looked up and peered across the table at Wayne. "If you are here to ask me to approve one of these volatility-controlled indices, you have another think coming."

Unfazed by Barry's comments, expecting this sort of response, Wayne asked, "What do you mean?"

"If this product has a volatility-controlled index, let me tell you they're shit. I have yet to see one perform any better than the S&P 500, which everyone knows and is comfortable with. Advisors are not going to explain a volatility-controlled index to a client. They barely understand the S&P 500 index."

Wayne listened intently to Barry's comments. Not yet convinced of the viability of the investment strategy himself, he certainly was not going to pressure Barry into agreeing to it, at least in that moment.

"If that's what you're going to show me, I'm sorry, but I'm not going to budge," Barry continued. "In addition, if you have a buffer or margin on the index, we are not even considering them at this point. You have a challenge ahead of you, Wayne. Even if we were to consider a volatility-controlled index, it is still dead in the water with a margin or buffer. The products must have an index cap."

"Barry, that sounds fair, and I understand your stance," Wayne replied. Never turning past page five, he closed the pitch deck. It lay stranded as though a lost ship in the middle of an open sea of nothingness.

Wayne continued, "If you have conducted your research regarding these products, especially risk control indices and have not found a reason to consider them, I'm not going to press you on this, Barry. At this point, I don't have any stellar performance figures that are going to change your mind." He casually sat back in his chair.

Barry turned his gaze away from the pitch deck, lifting his eyes toward Wayne's with a baffled expression. "Don't you have to report back to Chad about this?"

"Yes, I do, Barry," Wayne firmly replied.

"Aren't you concerned about going back to him without a product approval?"

"No, I'm not. Listen, it's clear these indices are relativity new to the marketplace. You have conducted your research and made it clear they don't appear to be any better than the S&P 500, which all investors know and are familiar with. I will handle things at the home office with management, but all I ask is that you keep the door open. I need to conduct more research. When I do, I will come back and share my findings with you. Quite frankly, we need to provide you with more concrete data and evidence upholding our stance that this product will be a benefit to you and your business. Again, all I ask is that you keep the door open so we can continue the dialogue because I will be back."

"Sounds fair, Wayne," Barry responded with a slight chuckle of disbelief and a look of astonishment.

Wayne stood up to shake Barry's hand. "Thank you for your time, Barry. I value our relationship and am not going to jeopardize it by pressing you on something that you are clearly not ready for. Please keep the door open. It's important that we work together to understand these new indices."

"Thank you, Wayne," Barry replied with a grin.

At that moment, Wayne knew he had won Barry's trust and respect. Seeing what was transpiring in the industry and product trends, Wayne deeply believed Chariot Horse Advisors would be forced into a position in which they would have to reconsider. The rapid upswing in indexed annuity sales and the declining sales trend in variable annuities made it clear where the industry was headed. It was just a matter of time.

Wayne did not need to close Barry with a hard sales pitch or tactic. The meeting concluded, and although Wayne surrendered in that moment, he was victorious a few months later when Chariot Horse Advisors approved the product.

Words to Lead By

Q: How did you (will you) become successful? Do you (will you) ride on the shoulders of giants, or do you (will you) step on and over the bodies of others pushing them down to get ahead?

What Is Emotional Intelligence Leadership?

Emotional intelligence is also useful in leadership positions. On the job, leaders oversee and manage people, and this trait contributes to them being approachable, influential, and decisive.

Emotional intelligence in leadership often means an ability to tackle stressful situations and address problems without yelling or blaming others. The goal is to foster an environment that encourages others to succeed.

Emotionally intelligent leaders know how to deal with conflict in a manner that motivates their team, rather than disheartens it. They're also aware of why their team players respond in a particular manner.

Performance is sometimes tied to emotion, and emotionally intelligent leaders have the ability to discern what makes their team happy. Encouraging a happy environment can improve productivity.

Five elements define emotional intelligence.
These components include the following:[7]

Self-awareness	Self-awareness is being conscious of your own feelings and motives. Emotionally intelligent people often demonstrate a high level of self-awareness. You know how your emotions affect you and others, and you don't allow your emotions to control you.
Self-regulation	People with the ability to self-regulate don't make impulsive decisions. You pause and think about the consequences of an action before proceeding.
Motivation	People with emotional intelligence are productive and driven. You think about the big picture and assess how your actions will contribute to long-term success.
Empathy	Emotionally intelligent people are less likely to be self-centered. Instead, you empathize with others and your situations. You tend to be a good listener, slow to judge, and understanding of the needs and wants of others. For this reason, an emotionally intelligent person is often seen as a loyal, compassionate friend.
Social skills	It's easier for you to collaborate and work in teams. You tend to be an excellent leader because of your strong communication skills and ability to manage relationships.

---

[7] OPM.gov, *Policy, Data, Oversight Assessment & Selection, Emotional Intelligence Tests.*

Here are a few signs that could indicate emotional intelligence.[8] You are..

- viewed as an empathetic person by others
- an excellent problem solver
- not afraid to be vulnerable and share your feelings
- able to set boundaries and not afraid to say "no"
- able to get along with people in different situations
- able to shrug off a bad moment and move on
- known to ask open-ended questions
- able to accept constructive criticism without making excuses or blaming others
- an outstanding listener
- not afraid to admit your mistakes and apologize
- self-motivated
- capable of understanding your actions and behaviors

---

[8] "What You Need to Know about Emotional Intelligence," November 2018, healthline.com.

Addict—Mindlessness Man

All men's miseries derive from not being
able to sit in a quiet room alone.

—*Blaise Pascal*

Our greatest fear is sitting in silence
with our own thoughts.

—*Eckhart Tolle*

It was a Thursday afternoon in June 2017. Wayne and his childhood friend Tyler enjoyed lunch at their favorite sushi restaurant, Yuki Sushi. When not on the road traveling, Wayne took the time to reconnect with friends over coffee or lunch. Engaging in conversation, they enjoyed several sushi rolls. Their nostrils flared and eyes watered from an overabundance of wasabi.

"Inconspicuously taking control of my life, influencing my decisions and behavior, it overwhelmed my ability to focus and be present in the moment," Wayne explained. "Tugging at my soul, this psychotic mental dance became very tiresome, sucking the life out of me! Every moment of every day, I yearned for it while pushing my loved ones aside so I could get more."

"What are you taking about?" Tyler asked in a slight tone of annoyance.

"There was no debating it; I was addicted. It defined me and validated my existence."

"Dude, what the hell are you talking about?" Tyler asked.

"Dozens of times each hour and hundreds of times throughout each day, I was in desperate need of more. I was searching for some sort of salvation in each hit. I lost sight of everything. I didn't know who I was any longer."

"Are you trying to tell me you have an opioid addiction or something?"

"No!" Wayne gasped. "Let me clarify. I know that I'm an addict and even wager that you're an addict."

"Come on, Wayne. You know I had problems in the past, but I've moved on."

"All I am saying is that we are all addicts of a different sort these days, and I am not talking about drugs or alcohol. This is entirely different and quite possibly worse because it is so unassuming."

"Okay. Then what the hell are you talking about?"

"Sorry. I didn't mean to upset you. Let me continue. I felt like my life he'd been taken hostage by an unlikely culprit that coaxed me in with promises of immediate gratification and power while maliciously taking over my life." Wayne continued to share his concerns.

He allowed it into his work and even into his home and personal life. It got to a point at where he was not sure if there was a way out or if he would ever get over his addiction. It had become so bad that he began to worry about his kids becoming hooked. He feared that they would fall victim to its devious lure. Once he became aware of it, he saw that it was more prevalent among his friends and family than he thought. Wayne was just another victim on a long list of victims.

"Everyone I know is addicted. Even when walking through town, sitting in a business meeting, enjoying lunch or a cup of coffee, I am surrounded by people bowing their heads in quiet desperation and mindlessness. It looks like they are in prayer or some sort of trance." Tyler listened intently when Wayne asked, "Are you okay?"

"Yeah!" Tyler laughed. His eyes were wide open and full of tears from the mouthful of wasabi he had just inhaled.

"Don't rub your eyes! You don't want to get wasabi in your eyes. That will make it worse," Wayne gasped, handed Tyler a napkin to wipe his eyes.

"Okay. I'm good. Go ahead. I'm listening."

Wayne found himself bowing his head to this deity while walking through the airport the prior week. With his bag in tow, he navigated through a sea of people who also paid homage to what seemed to be some sort of supreme being. Every few minutes, he lifted his head to make sure he was walking toward the correct terminal to quickly lower his head once again to get more.

"It sucked me in under its spell, I needed more of it every day. It pulled me closer and closer into mindlessness. My smartphone had gradually taken over my life, validating my existence and defining who I was."

"What is wrong with you? I thought you were in serious trouble!" Tyler responded in frustration. "You're talking about your damn iPhone?" He scoffed. "You had me worried."

"Well, in a way it is serious." Wayne smiled. "Practically every minute I found myself eagerly looking at my iPhone like an addict needing another hit. It was about time I looked up and woke myself up from this nightmare!"

"Now that I understand what you're talking about, I know I'm an addict!" He laughed. "Practically everyone I know is mesmerized and paralyzed by their damn smartphone."

"That's my point! I don't think people realize they're addicted to their smartphones."

"I agree. I'm just glad you're not an opioid junkie." Tyler laughed.

———◆◆———

Wayne explained to Tyler how his smartphone made him feel completely mindless and lost. Like some sort of evil power overwhelming his life. A Marvel Comic action antihero of sorts called *Mindlessness Man*. Mindlessness Man is an antihero who can no longer think for himself. His strength, salvation, and identity can only be found in his smartphone through the thousands of messages, texts, posts, replies, invitations, shares, and likes he receives day in and day out.

Even when taking his dog for a walk, this antihero *Mindlessness Man* would appear. While at home eating dinner with his wife and kids, *Mindlessness Man* sucked him in with its powers. Unable to resist the urge to check in, Wayne was continually swept away from the joy of the moment.

Wayne missed out on so much of his life because he was searching for meaning outside of himself, losing sight of what was most important. Instead of listening to his daughters tell him about their day, all he heard was the *ding* of his phone alerting him of the urgency in the latest message from work or a social media post. If *Mindlessness Man* were an actual Marvel Comic action antihero, his theme music would be the *ding* of Wayne's iPhone calling him into action, mindlessly sucking him away and destroying his life.

"*Mindlessness Man!*" Tyler chuckled. "That's interesting and at the same time a little sad. You're right, though. I do the same thing and have no fucking clue I'm doing it. You are right though; it is an addiction."

"Gradually and then suddenly it screws up your life," Wayne said.

"Yes, and on an entirely different level than drugs or alcohol."

"Yep. This is far more subtle than caffeine, alcohol, cocaine, pot, oxycodone, or other drugs. We don't readily display the signs or side effects from our smartphones and social media, but it fucks with our lives and minds," Wayne continued. "My daughter recently had her sixth-grade band concert at school. We arrived early to get seats in the front. I sat in the front center ready for her performance when *Mindlessness Man's* superpowers lured me away. If you were there, you would have seen my head tilted toward the ground as though I was under a trance. Lured in by Mindlessness Man's hypnotic ways, I was incapable of breaking my gaze away from my smartphone. For what I thought would be just a moment turned into minutes of mindlessness until I finally found the courage to break my gaze away from my phone. When I looked up, I realized that I had missed my daughter's recital!"

"Seriously? That was a real loser move!" Tyler chuckled.

"Thanks. That makes me feel so much better." Wayne couldn't help but laugh at the situation. "I was so pissed off for believing in the fucked-up delusion that my identity was my work. I had to ask myself a very revealing and frightening question: 'Who am I without work?'"

"Well, did you answer yourself?" Tyler smiled.

"I was faced with a sad reality that my existence was based on my career," Wayne responded. "For some sadistic reason, I find my worth in my iPhone. In all the emails, text messages, and phone calls. It's with me everywhere I go. Did you notice that I have two damn phones! If that's not a sign, I don't know what is."

"That is sad!" Tyler remarked sarcastically. "But isn't that normal? Don't we all use email, text messages, webinars, and phone calls as tools to make us more productive?"

"Yeah, but it's everywhere, and I can't escape it. I receive more than a hundred emails every single day. And that's only from work. I easily get more than that in my personal email. It's become more of a hindrance than a helpful tool. I believe at one point it made us more productive but quickly lost its usefulness. Now it's used for practically everything. Instead of picking up the phone to call, people send an email or a text message. The amount of time it takes to create and send an email is so much more than the time it takes to pick-up the phone and call someone. I believe it makes us more inefficient."

"Well, have you noticed we don't even speak to one another anymore?" Tyler interjected. "We can't even find the time to leave a voice mail. All people do is call and hang up without leaving a message. Is there an unwritten rule somewhere that I missed that says you're supposed to call someone back after they call you without even leaving a message? Are we that fucking lazy?"

"Oh gosh! I have a colleague who does this all the time!" Wayne sighed. "Email chains are just as bad. There seems to be this unwritten protocol that everyone must reply to group emails. It's this domino effect of people replying with mindless bullshit responses like 'Thanks, that makes sense, ditto, agree, good idea,' and so on.

These mindless email replies are a complete waste of time and make us less productive."

Tyler chuckled with a smirk. "Heh, heh. I get it. We don't even spell words anymore in our messages. Instead, we use cryptic anagrams, acronyms, and emojis."

"After a while, this mindless ritual became tiresome with no end in sight. My smartphone was gradually making me insane! The insatiable desire of looking at my iPhone lures me in like the moth that found its way into the living room that same night. I was mesmerized by this stupid creature darting around, flying in circles, and zigzagging all over the place. Then it found its way inside the lampshade charging at the bright lightbulb like a Kamikaze pilot on an apparent suicide mission. The moth bounced off the hot light bulb and circled back again in another attempt to complete its mission."

"That is so true! Why are they so stupid?" Tyler smiled, shoving another wasabi-coated spicy tuna roll into his mouth.

Wayne shared his experience of the moth with Tyler. Continuing its relentless pursuit of the lightbulb, the moth frenetically smashed head-on into the lampshade. Furiously flapping its wings, it looked like it was attempting to topple it over.

The moth darted all over the place, leaving a dusty print from its wings and torso on the lampshade. Eventually it grew tired and took a moment of reprieve, resting on the inside of the lampshade. After regaining its composure and bearings, this stupid moth resumed its insane suicide mission. Then a question popped into Wayne's head, *For what? Why does this moth unremittingly dive at the light bulb? What the hell is it trying to do?*

His daughter shrieked in fear when she noticed the moth, thinking it was a bee. She ran out of the room screaming that she saw a bee. Wayne tried to calm her fears, letting her know it was just a moth.

When she came back into the living room, Wayne showed her the moth. They watched it fly around like crazy, bouncing off the lightbulb when he suggested that she ask Siri why moths behave like that.

She jumped up, grabbed her phone, and asked Siri, "Why are moths attracted to bright light?"

"Okay, I found this on the web for 'why are moths attracted to bright light?'" Siri replied.

They found an article on the internet entitled, "Why Are Moths Drawn to Artificial Lights?"

The article described it as someone with an unswerving yet self-destructive attraction like greed, lust, or just the thrill of the chase. It continued to explain that there have been a handful of theories as to why moths make suicidal nosedives toward burning candles and artificial lights. Long story short, there was no good explanation why moths are attracted to bright lights.

Wayne was dumbfounded. "Moths kill themselves for no reason," he commented to Tyler. "That's just stupid! But you know what is even more disturbing?" Wayne asked without allowing Tyler to answer. "I feel like that goddamn moth!"

"What do you mean?"

"Well, not to be morbid but the next day the moth was dead. It lay there on its back motionless in defeat at the base of the lamp. That stupid moth killed itself in a neurotic and maniacal pursuit of the light for no apparent reason!

"I often wonder whether we're like a moth," Wayne continued. "But rather than a bright light, we are maniacally drawn to success, titles, money, and material things. Do we end up just like the moth? Mindlessly and neurotically, I check my iPhone all the time. And I am doing it right now as we speak. I feel like a fucking moth mindlessly chasing something for no reason and with no result in sight, other than my demise as a human."

"I've heard that smartphones trigger a release of dopamine," Tyler added. "Which explains our attraction or addiction to them. I get what you are saying, but why are you so upset about it?"

"Because I feel like I am losing my mind chasing after success, chasing email after email, call after call, text after text. I tap the screen to check the time or to see if there are any new messages practically every damn minute if not more often than that. It's insane.

Then I check my phone again because I never really paid attention to what I was looking at in the first place. Like that stupid moth I am constantly drawn to my iPhone and my work, making sure I don't miss anything. Yet, I end up missing everything. God forbid I miss another mindless conference call or meeting! If I keep this up, I'll be the one lying on my back dead from the mania."

"Yep! Smartphones are the reason why you feel like you're turning into a dope." Tyler chuckled. "Technology is an enabler. It enables us to do so many things that were not previously possible. All without leaving the comfort of our home, we can shop for groceries, shop for a car, invest, read a book, listen to music, make phone calls, send messages, get directions, play games, study, research, and even take an eye exam!"

"I guess the good that can be gleaned from this is that it enables many of us, including me, to make a living," Wayne conjectured.

"Yes, it's a tremendous tool for business, work, and life. But the question always lingers about whether we are any more productive. I do my best to use it as a productivity tool for work and leave it in my bag at the end of the day. Although I have read research that indicates our smartphones really have *not* had an impressionable improvement on productivity."

"I believe that," Wayne commented. "We need to look up from our phones and pay attention to what is going on around us instead of seeking validation in someone else's comment, post, text, or email."

"Or the simple fact that we lose sight of life because we get sucked into work twenty-four/seven. It's good to pause and provide ourselves an opportunity to let go occasionally."

"Yeah. I really need to pause and look around. I have failed miserably at simply enjoying life," Wayne confessed. "Being present in the moment is really hard to do."

"I agree. You know I tried that the other day when I drove my six-year-old daughter to school. She usually has about ten to fifteen minutes to play with her classmates on the playground before the school bell rings. On the day, I purposely left my iPhone in the car."

"That's a good idea. I should try that."

"Yeah, it was pretty awesome. A huge sense of relief came over me. Well, of course, this was after the initial panic I felt because I didn't have my phone by my side." He chuckled. "So, I just hung out, watching my daughter play with her classmates, and I was fully present in the moment. I noticed other parents with their heads down, gazing into their phones. *Mindlessness Man* took away that moment of joy with their child. Last week, I sat on a bench at the school playground when one of my daughter's classmates came over and sat down next to me. We talked about our favorite colors. Then we looked at the clouds floating by and shouted out what shapes and animals we saw."

"Really?" Wayne asked.

"Yep! It was so amazing. Then the bell rang. I haven't felt that good in a long time."

Wayne read that that there were well over thirty-one million Facebook posts per minute and 325,000 tweets per minute into the black hole of social media. Every minute! Of the nearly one-and-a-half-billion Facebook users, each one posts thirty-one times every single day! And most of it is stupid, mindless shit. There are over seven billion people in the world. Almost a quarter of the world's population uses Facebook!

Wayne decided to power down his iPhone and walk away, and it felt great! Many of his anxieties magically vanished when he powered down and walked away from his iPhone. We need to pause and provide ourselves with an opportunity to let go. More people should power down and walk away.

He felt frustrated by how he had lost control of his life. Dr. Wayne Dyer used to speak of a feeling of being "nowhere," but when we make the slightest change to the letters and add a space, nowhere becomes "now here."

His iPhone was to blame for exacerbating the power *Mindlessness Man,* this newly found action antihero, had over him. He became an expert at missing out on life. Unbeknownst to him, he was engaged in an in-deliberate practice of not being there.

Wayne read about the concept of deliberate practice when he read Malcolm Gladwell's book *Outliers* (2008). The 10,000-hour rule, deliberate practice concept stuck with him. His realization was that he had been spending more than 10,000 hours on what he called an "in-deliberate practice." An in-deliberate practice is the opposite of deliberate practice, in a detrimental fashion. For example, constantly focusing on and worrying about what he did or said the day or week before created stress about what he would do the following day or week. This in-deliberate practice easily allowed him to miss nearly every moment until now.

Considering humans are creatures of habit, most of us spend our lives focused on *in-deliberate practices*, which are often difficult to identify. Even when they are identified, it is even more challenging and often troublesome to change them. This is where the *10,000-hour rule* shines because it takes focus and dedication when making a positive change. It requires putting forth a concentrated effort to do something new or to become an expert at whatever it is you are changing, improving, or perfecting. Wayne thought about all the moments in his life when he was nowhere, not present, missing the joy of being with friends and loved ones. He felt as though his entire life had passed him by right before his eyes and he had done nothing about it, until now. This was a tipping point for him—another Malcom Gladwell book, *Tipping Point*, which he loved.

Wayne was growing tired of feeling like a moth, restlessly and relentlessly pursuing a bright light until meeting its demise. His ego's mindless pursuit of success and desire to have all the meaningless possessions people accumulate until we die no longer made sense to him. Not truly knowing who we are is the tragedy. His realization was that most people do not truly enjoy all of the possessions they accumulate. Rather they spend most of their time boasting to others about what they have, comparing themselves and their possessions to other people in a mindless cycle of insanity. Making it worse, most of these people spend a great amount of energy and time trying to protect and keep what they have so they can brag about it to people. Without their possessions, they have no identity; they are no one and nowhere.

Words to Lead By

Q: Where do you find meaning? Hint: Look within, not without.

Our greatest fear is sitting in silence with our own thoughts.
—Eckhart Tolle

We are not our bodies, our possessions, or our career.
Who we are is Divine Love and that is Infinite.
—Dr. Wayne Dyer

Encounter with a Buddhist Monk

> Be here now.
>
> —*Ram Dass*

It was the second week of August 2017 and another week of business trips to Southern California for Wayne. After spending the first day and a half in San Diego and Los Angeles, he was heading to Pigeon Financial's home office in Bellevue on the second leg of his trip for quarterly business meetings with senior management.

American Airlines Flight 605 sat on the runway at the Los Angeles International Airport awaiting takeoff for Seattle, Washington.

It was astonishing to see how his mood had shifted from blissed to pissed in one hot minute upon entering the airport. Although he had enjoyed meeting with his accounts over the last day and a half, he dreaded heading to the home office for another day of mindless meetings with executive management. A year ago, he would have welcomed the opportunity and looked forward to these meetings, but they were becoming something he abhorred. Glimmers of the passion and enthusiasm he once had for his job would reappear occasionally, shining for the briefest moment but quickly fading like a shooting star.

That weekend, during a session with his life coach, Marianne, he mentioned his back pain. Expressing his concerns about work, she addressed his worries and channeled his energy. Suddenly and somewhat mysteriously, his back pain vanished. But it returned just as quickly as it vanished. His back ached, and his neck hurt. It felt as though a knife had been thrust into his spine.

He headed to the security checkpoint at a hurried pace among the herd of crazed travelers with their luggage in tow. Looking off in the distance, he spied the maze of security ropes. The ropes, intended to maintain order and keep people in line, zig-zagged back and forth, seemingly going nowhere. He paused for a moment, pondering how analogous it was to his career: frustrating, slow moving, winding with twists and turns seemingly going nowhere.

Maintaining his hurried pace, he scanned the area up ahead for long lines of travelers who might impede his path, but to his surprise, there was a vast openness awaiting him. Drowning out the chaos of the noise in the airport, he listened to Volbeat's "The Nameless One" pounding in his ears through his Bose earbuds. To his surprise and delight, there was no one in between him and the maze of ropes at the security checkpoint. This was peculiar, especially at a very busy airport like LAX. "Wow! This is amazing," he muttered to himself. "There's no one here!"

He forged forward in a frenetic pace to catch his flight. Then in his direct line of sight, up ahead, he noticed a petite woman clothed in an earthy-colored robe, floating gracefully along. He slowed his pace to observe this angelic woman. Her head was nearly as bare as his. *She must be a Buddhist monk*, he thought to himself. *I wonder if she's going the same way I am.*

Just before reaching the entrance to the security line, she paused. Glancing down to study her boarding pass, she then looked up ahead toward the line trying to figure out the next step on her journey. Everything around Wayne slowed down. He sensed her every move, which was orchestrated with a deliberate calmness. She was clearly in the moment and nowhere else. Even amidst the chaos of hundreds of frenetic travelers, hurry did not exist for her even though she too needed to reach her destination.

Wayne forged forward at full speed because, sadly, hurry still existed for him. It was all he seemed to know. Without hesitation, he zipped past her so he could be the first in line.

Proceeding through the winding maze of ropes, he converged with another line of travelers. After all the haste to be the first in line, he was now last in line! Out of the corner of his eye, he once again spied the angelic woman, who was slowly gliding in his direction, eventually easing up next to him.

He was overwhelmed with a feeling of shame about his need to be first in line. His thoughts jumped around the mosh-pit of his mind: *What is wrong with me? I could have stopped and offered to assist this wonderful woman, this beautiful spirit. In my ignorance and self-centeredness, I rushed past her to be the first in line, to go somewhere I no longer care to go!*

Wayne felt the presence of her energy. Like the sun lighting up the world, a warmth of love and peace emanated from her. She did not need to say anything. He could feel it!

Immediately *Be here now* popped into his mind. He could hear the words of spiritual teacher Ram Dass: *"Ahh, here you are. Be in the moment. Be here now."* The words landed upon his ears, but he did not heed them. Instead, he continued on his frenetic journey.

Feeling as far as possible from being in the moment, he wondered which moment he was really in. Aside from being the first in line, the first through security, the first to get his stuff, and the first to the gate, he was lost.

Still waiting to pass through the security checkpoint, he was far removed from the moment. In his mind, he had already made it through the line. Anxious about his next step, he already saw himself picking up his luggage, grabbing his stuff from the drab gray bin, and putting his shoes back on his feet and his belt back around his waist. All that mattered to Wayne in that moment, and his life at that point, was making it through the winding ropes of the security line and most importantly figuring out where to get a cup of coffee once he had made it through.

Wow! Is this really where my head is at? he thought to himself. *Clearly, I am not in the moment and far from "being here now."* This both saddened and frustrated him.

Despite being absent from participating in the present moment, the experience tugged at his mind. Her presence deeply moved him. He felt her energy all around him. Deep down, he yearned to glance at her out of admiration and respect, but he could not bring himself to do it. He did not want to make her uncomfortable by staring at her like some crazed stalker. Instead, he glanced at her out of the corner of his eye, daydreaming about approaching her with a simple "Hello." Even better, a hug would have been preferable, so he could absorb her peacefulness through some form of human osmosis. He did no such thing and continued his maniacal way through the line.

He slowly moved along the procession of passengers until both lines merged. Mustering up a tinge of courage, he gestured for this kind woman to move ahead of him. This was his lame attempt at releasing some of the guilt he held on to after zipping past her so he could be the first in line. With enlightened eyes, she looked at him and gracefully gestured with her hand for him to move ahead. She seemed to sense his frenetic pace and most likely wanted to distance herself from his misaligned energy. He conceded and continued moving along.

In that moment, it hit him that her slow and deliberate gesture resembled a mudra, of sorts, like the Varada Mudra, denoting the act of charity and benevolence. He wondered what she was feeling and thinking while surrounded by hundreds of frenzied travelers. *Does she even notice any of it? She must sense my frustration and impatience. You don't need to be an enlightened being to feel my misaligned energy.*

They slowly trudged along next to the long stainless-steel table, placing their luggage on top of the table and their items in the gray drab plastic bins. Glistening in the bright lights shining down from the ceiling above, he found himself lost again. Staring at the scrapes and scratches ingrained in the table from the thousands of travelers who had gone before, Wayne pondered all the scrapes and scratches he had endured throughout his career.

Snapping out of his daydream, he heard the commands from the TSA agent: "Shoes off! Remove everything from your pockets! Remove your laptops from your bags! There should be nothing in your pockets! Keep moving!" Awakened by the barking commands of the security agent, he noticed this angelic woman placing her items in the drab gray plastic bin. Her suitcase remained alone, standing upright next to her as she organized her items.

This is my opportunity to redeem myself and, in some way hopefully connect with this amazing and peaceful being. In that moment, Wayne decided to gently pick up her suitcase and place it on the table.

Looking into his eyes, in the softest voice, she whispered her words of gratitude. Deep down, he still desired to make some sort of connection with her. Maybe he could speak with her, hug her, shake her hand, or something. His reluctance and fear of embarrassment prevented him from doing anything at all.

After placing his shoes, belt, laptop computer, iPhone, and other items in the bin, it was his turn to slowly trudge along the stainless-steel table toward the dark black conveyer belt. He helped to pull her bag along the table onto the rollers until it disappeared into the black hole of the scanner. Although the human eye could not detect what was inside the luggage, the scanner revealed everything hidden behind the protective outer shell of the suitcases.

Underneath Wayne's outer shell was his truth—the person he yearned to be but was afraid to reveal for the world to see—afraid of being judged, afraid he would not be accepted, that he would not fit into this corporate world of greed, ego, and the need to be number one. The mosh-pit of his mind became increasingly rambunctious when he asked himself, *Can I love those who I work with and still succeed?*

Nearing the end of this encounter, he desired to remain with this angelic woman for a while longer to somehow find a way to soak up her divine light and leave the world behind. Upon making it through the security screening, they collected their things from the table situated at the other end of the conveyer belt. Still by his side, she looked toward him with loving eyes and expressed a gentle, "Thank you."

Wayne smiled. He grabbed his bags when a sudden and crisp sting of life smacked him in the face, awakening him from his daydream, and he continued his journey. The mosh-pit of his mind kicked into high gear when *Mindlessness Man* reappeared. *Wake up! Get going. Get your coffee! Check your email! Check your voice-mail messages. Are you supposed to be on a conference call? Where's your gate? Get to the gate as soon as possible and get in line so you can be the first on the plane. Make sure you get on early so you can find an overhead storage bin for your suitcase. Make sure you have something to read. Make sure your laptop is nearby so you can do some work. Did you go to the bathroom? You don't want to be stuck in a window seat unable to get up for a bathroom break during the flight.*

His shoulders and back surged with pain from carrying the burden he placed upon himself. He tightly clenched his jaw, grinding his teeth in anticipation of the business meetings that afternoon and in the coming day.

He pondered this brief encounter with this enlightened woman. *Really? Is this the life I envisioned? Is it possible that this is all my doing? I don't have to feel this back pain. I don't have to clench my jaw. I don't have to grind my teeth. It is all up to me. Could it be that the peacefulness this woman embodied is also within me, and all I need to do is allow it to manifest?*

Before he knew it, the airplane took flight toward the heavens, carrying him to his next destination. He traveled in the heavens at over 375 miles per hour, disconnected from the rest of the world forty-thousand feet below him. At his destination, the plane touched down. A gray cloud of doom spewed from the friction of the wheels screeching on the concrete runway, signaling touchdown as the 144,000-pound behemoth returned to earth once again.

Bracing for impact, he dug his feet into the thin carpet of the airplane cabin, causing his toes to scrunch together in his glossy black wingtips. At touchdown, he bounced out of his seat. He clenched the hand rests to hold himself safely in place while the seatbelt tightened around his torso as he slid forward in his seat.

It took but a moment until the Boeing 737 was floating on the tarmac, heading toward the gate. As he landed in yet another city, the rumble of the touchdown was his signal to reconnect to the chaotic world.

Being disconnected from the rest of the world while in the air provided a little respite from the chaos of work and the lure of his smartphone. Of course, this was made easier considering the absence of inflight internet service, which allowed him to remain disconnected during the brief time he was in the air.

Once he was on the ground, *Mindlessness Man's* addiction and allure tapped him on the shoulder, reminding him that the chaos of work awaited him. His right thumb instinctually tapped the home button on his smartphone. When the screen lit up, his forefinger gently caressed the screen like a magician's wand swiping in an upward direction as though he were flicking a bug off the screen. The phone's menu floated into view. He immediately tapped the airplane icon with his forefinger, disabling airplane mode.

The icons on his home screen lit up like the Fourth of July with the latest email, voice mail, and text message notifications. In a matter of moments, he would be reunited with his salvation, a mailbox full of dozens of new messages awaiting his reply.

The flight attendant's voice roared over the airplane speakers. "Ladies and gentlemen, welcome to Seattle-Tacoma International Airport. Local time is 2:35 p.m. The temperature is sixty-five degrees. For your safety and comfort, please remain seated with your seat belt fastened until the captain turns off the fasten seat belt sign. This will indicate that we have parked at the gate and that it is safe for you to move about. At this time, you may use your cellular phones if you wish."

He had heard this message hundreds of times and never really listened. The flight attendant's words filled the cabin. The airplane rumbled and creaked as it taxied to the gate. Psyching himself up to get ready to jump into work again, he imagined Michael Buffer roaring over the airplane speakers, "On behalf of American Airlines and the entire crew … let's get ready to *rumble!*"

With a laser-like focus, he stared intensely at his iPhone. The email icon lit up. The tiny red circle exploded like a red sun rising. Inside the little red circle, the digits rapidly ascended, tallying the new messages flowing into his inbox from cyberspace. Quickly the red circle turned into an oval as the number rapidly reached double digits; *five, ten, fifteen, twenty, twenty-five, twenty-six, twenty-seven …*

With each new message filling the email icon, he was filling with angst and dread. It was time to rumble!

His phone was replenished with the latest drama, issues, fake work, and other bullshit. He was ready to jump into action, take control of the situation at hand, and save the day. "Shit! I hate this!" he mumbled to himself.

"You are reconnected, huh?" the passenger sitting next to him commented.

"I'm sorry, what?" Wayne replied, looking over at the guy.

"Did your phone blow up with messages while we were in flight?"

"Oh yeah." Wayne chuckled. "It certainly did."

"I know how you feel. I waste so much of my time reading senseless emails. Even worse spending time on conference calls that don't accomplish anything. Speaking of which, I have to dial in for a conference call in a few minutes."

"Yes, same here." Wayne chuckled some more. "I feel like I'm brainwashed by work, the calls, messages, meetings, most of which are not very productive."

The stranger nodded his head in agreement with a slight grin.

"May I ask you a question?" Wayne asked.

"Sure," the stranger replied.

"How do you deal with it?"

"With what?"

"All of the bullshit," Wayne responded.

"I don't really. I just focus on doing my best and have learned to let go of the bullshit and not get involved in the drama. Plus, I know that if I get sucked into the negativity, I will end up stressed out and act more like an asshole. So, I learned to focus on the good and surround myself with the right people."

"I want to let go and focus on doing my best, but my fear is that if I let go, the wheels will really fall off, and the blame will come back on me and my teammates," Wayne passionately replied. "The management at my company is a self-serving group of people who completely disregard their employees. There is too much busy work, or what I refer to as fake work, which is like the fake news we keep hearing about in the media. Executive management wastes so much of our time and resources with this fake work, which translates into thousands of dollars being wasted because of inefficient and incompetent management."

The man didn't respond.

Wayne continued, "Sorry, I didn't mean to lay all of that on you."

"No, it's totally fine. I get it. I've been there. I was just processing it because it sounds so familiar to my career and many of the executives I've worked with."

"Oh, so what did you do about it?" Wayne asked.

"I changed my perspective and my job. Maybe it's time for you to do the same, but your perspective needs to change first before you change jobs. What you are really changing is your boss or management, not the job. But it won't be any different for you until you change your mind-set."

"Yeah, I guess you're right," Wayne sighed.

"It sounds like you need to disconnect for a little while longer to reflect and refresh. Life's too short, as they say. You sure as heck don't want to wake up one day realizing you missed your life because of a shitty career and awful management. You can't get it back." Wayne hung onto the stranger's every word. "Do you have kids?" the man asked.

"Yes, three daughters."

"Great! How old are they?"

"Eleven, nine, and five."

"Well, my kids are a little older, but I missed them growing up because my priorities were out of whack. I had to walk away, reflect, and refresh. My perspective changed, and I have a greater appreciation for life and career. I learned about Rule Number Six from this guy Benjamin Zander, who is the conductor and musical director of the Boston Philharmonic Orchestra."

"Oh yeah! I know who he is!" Wayne enthusiastically interrupted.

"Good. So, you know about Rule Number Six."

"I do! I met him at a conference in Boston several years ago. I had an opportunity to shake his hand and get my picture taken with him."

"Well, when you get a chance, revisit Rule Number Six because it sounds like you have forgotten about it," he advised.

"Yep. Thank you," Wayne replied in appreciation. *Ding.* The airplane speakers rang, alerting the passengers that it was safe to remove their seat belts. The sound of seat belts unbuckling echoed throughout the cabin *click, click, click, click, click,* followed by passengers springing up out of their seats like jumping beans.

"It was nice speaking with you," the stranger commented as he grabbed his bag from the overhead compartment.

"Huh?" Wayne mumbled, lost in the words he had just heard. "Yeah, you too. Thank you. Safe travels."

"Remember Rule Number Six: 'Don't take yourself so damned seriously.'" The stranger smiled and went on his way.

Wayne was humbled by this divine light that manifested in his life. Although the moment was ephemeral, the experience of this wonderful woman and businessman entering his life will remain for an eternity.

Words to Lead By

Q: Do you take yourself too damned seriously?

Rule Number 6: The Transformative Power of Lightening Up and Practicing the Art of Possibility:[9]

> Two prime ministers are sitting in a room discussing affairs of state. Suddenly a man bursts in, apoplectic with fury, shouting and stamping and banging his fist on the desk. The resident prime minister admonishes him: "Peter," he says, "kindly remember Rule Number 6," whereupon Peter is instantly restored to complete calm, apologizes, and withdraws. The

---

[9] Zander and Zander, *The Art of Possibility* (2000).

politicians return to their conversation, only to be interrupted yet again twenty minutes later by an hysterical woman gesticulating wildly, her hair flying. Again the intruder is greeted with the words: "Marie, please remember Rule Number 6." Complete calm descends once more, and she too withdraws with a bow and an apology. When the scene is repeated for a third time, the visiting prime minister addresses his colleague: "My dear friend, I've seen many things in my life, but never anything as remarkable as this. Would you be willing to share with me the secret of Rule Number 6?" "Very simple," replies the resident prime minister. "Rule Number 6 is 'Don't take yourself so goddamn seriously." "Ah," says his visitor, "that is a fine rule." After a moment of pondering, he inquires, "And what, may I ask, are the other rules?"

The host replied, "There aren't any."

When we can be in the moment, we no longer feel compelled to watch the clock. Whatever your work might be, bring all of yourself to it. When you are fully present, you may find that your labor is no longer a burden. Wood is chopped. Water is carried. Life happens.
—Life Hacker, Patrick Allan

Names before Numbers— The Moment I Realized I Was Working for an Idiot

The twin brother or sister of efficiency is elegance ...
Because in elegance you also have the art.

—*Tim Ferriss*

That afternoon, Wayne checked into his hotel and immediately went to the home office for his one-on-one meeting with Corey. This meeting was a semi-annual review of sorts in which Corey spent time individually with each team member to discuss what was working, what was not working, what needed improvement, and so on.

It was a beautiful afternoon in Bellevue, Washington, with clear blue skies above. Wayne walked from his hotel to Pigeon Financial's Home Office. Listening to Volbeat's "Battleship Chains" on his iPhone, he walked up Northeast Eighth Street. The music pounded through his earbuds into his ears, drowning out the world around him.

Walking up the steps, past the fountain, he approached the revolving doors to the office building. The water from the fountain shot into the air, returning to the pool of water below. The sound of the water splashing into the base of the fountain was drowned out by the lyrics pumping into his ears, "You got me tied down with battleship chains. Fifty foot long and a two-ton anchor."

Immediately upon entering the building through the revolving doors, Wayne eyed the umbrella station. With a childlike curiosity, it always amused Wayne to see the umbrella stations scattered throughout the city in office buildings and hotels. Because Seattle, and neighboring Bellevue, were the rainy cities, umbrellas were available for people to borrow at their convenience. It was a sort of umbrella honor code in which people would take an umbrella and replace it. This turned out to be a lifesaver for Wayne on a few occasions when he got caught in the Seattle rain.

He swiped his badge on the console at the elevator doors and tapped floor number 9 on the screen. The display flashed "B," directing him to elevator car B, which would take him to the ninth floor. Once inside the elevator, there was no turning back, since number keypads were nonexistent inside the elevator cars. Your destination was set, and there was no way of changing it once you entered.

The elevator car quickly reached the ninth floor, and the doors slid open. Wayne exited the elevator car and took a right turn toward the doors to the office. After he swiped his badge on the black card reader, the red light turned to green, followed by a beep, signaling the door unlocking. Wayne removed his Bose earbuds from his ears to welcome the sounds of the world around him.

He immediately headed to the conference room for his meeting with Corey. Corey was already there finishing up a conference call when Wayne entered. He stood up to greet Wayne with a handshake and sat down again. Wayne turned on his laptop and checked his email while sitting in silence as he waited for Corey to wrap up his call.

A couple of minutes later, Corey's call ended. "Hey, Wayne. How was your flight?"

"Good. It's always a quick flight from LA," Wayne replied.

"Sure, beats the coast-to-coast flights. Right?"

"Yep. So, where do you want to start?" Wayne jumped right into their meeting. The sooner he got started, the sooner it would be over with.

"Well, uh, let's talk about the questions I sent you in advance of this meeting."

"Okay, sounds good," Wayne replied. "I believe you were looking for feedback with regard to improvement in the division, things that are working, not working, and so on."

"Yep."

"Names before numbers sums it up, Corey."

"What does that mean?"

"We have experienced tremendous success with our firms. But as things continue to grow, I see a trend that appears to be a little heavily weighted on the numbers, metrics, and analytics."

"Okay, that's good though. Right?"

"Yes, of course it is. But, Corey, I believe we are losing sight of the names in favor of the numbers."

"What does that mean?"

"Our sales and activity numbers cannot and will not happen without our people," Wayne continued. "To put it another way, will we achieve our sales, revenues, and profits without our people?"

"Uh, probably not."

"I am sure you agree that the numbers do not and will not happen if you don't have the right people to do the work. Do you follow me?"

"Okay, what are you getting at?" Corey asked in a tone of annoyance.

"The success with my accounts is certainly not because of my intense focus on the numbers. Rather, I have learned to embrace the names, the team, and our accounts. Ultimately, the result is our success which is captured and reflected in our extraordinary sales numbers. Do you remember the book *The Energy Bus* you recommended the team read?"

"Yes."

"Thank you for the suggestion by the way. The book was very insightful on many levels. Do you happen to remember Rule Number Eight from the book?"

"Uh, no."

"Rule Number Eight is 'Love your passengers,'" Wayne firmly stated.

"Okay?"

"As I just mentioned, and you confirmed, our numbers are meaningless and will not even happen if you don't have people to do the work. If that's the case, which it is with any business, wouldn't it make sense to embrace the people who put up the numbers?" Wayne continued without giving Corey an opportunity to respond. "Corey, my point is that we need a Rule Number Eight. You have to love your people!"

"Okay. Makes sense," came Corey's reply. This was one of his usual replies, in addition to "Cool," and an all-time favorite, "Put together a report showing how this results in sales."

Wayne continued, "The team is lost, and we need someone to lead us. You have way too much on your plate to effectively run the division. How long do you think you can run national sales, operations, and relationship management effectively before you really lose control?"

"What do you mean?" Corey asked in surprise.

"Corey, I continually drop you hints about the low morale of the team. I've told you on multiple occasions how much the team is overworked trying to keep things afloat. It's becoming increasingly frustrating to continually see the team correcting the chronic errors caused by the sales ops team. We're doing the work of the sales ops team because their work is shoddy at best, and some of them are not even showing up to do their job."

"What are you talking about?"

Wayne was becoming visibly upset and annoyed by Corey's continued ignorance of the situation. "Corey, technically you are my fourth boss in as many years. When you brought in Amy to run the team after Nelson unexpectedly resigned, she was set up to fail from the get-go. And I think you knew it! We keep cleaning up these messes because no one is managing our team, and no one is managing the sales ops team."

"Wayne, things seem to be pretty good to me. We have weekly calls with the team, and everything is on target. I haven't heard of any of these issues from anyone else."

"Corey, you don't see it because no one tells you about it." Wayne continued, "I'm dumbfounded watching this company, which prides itself in efficiency and metrics, throwing thousands of dollars out the window each day because of lost productivity from all of your disengaged employees."

"Give me an example," Corey said in an emotionless tone while looking at his computer screen.

"We are picking up the slack from the sales ops team. They aren't doing their job. Quite frankly, they don't know what they are doing. Some of them aren't even showing up for work, while others are taking it upon themselves to work from home. Corey, they are not remote employees! Patrice is the only remote employee. Fiona has been working from home two to three days a week. Mandy has more doctor's appointments than anyone I've ever worked with. On top of that, she's taken it upon herself to work from home once or twice a week. Whether you want to acknowledge it or not, they resent Patrice for working remotely, and that's bullshit! She has a legitimate health concern that prevents her from coming into the office. No one is there to manage the team. They haven't had a manager to oversee them for months and are doing whatever they want. We're cleaning up the mess for their incomplete and incompetent work. We can't afford to let things slip, so we step in. We are overworked, burnt out, and tired of doing everyone else's work on top of our own work."

"Come on, Wayne, you need to be more objective," Corey reacted. "If you looked at this from our perspective, you might understand what's going on."

"Okay, Corey. Please tell me what your perspective is. Help me understand what's going on. I'm all ears."

"I don't see that at all. I haven't heard anything from sales operations regarding the issues you raised. We just launched our latest product, which was a success, and our sales numbers look great," Corey commented.

In that moment, it became clear to Wayne that Corey most likely would never understand. Wayne was dumbfounded by Corey's ignorance of the dysfunction. He was blinded by the numbers. All he saw was the black and white of the numbers on his spreadsheet. "Corey, no one is going to tell you what's wrong. They would rather remain silent out of fear of getting in trouble or, even worse, fired. Elaine is now running sales ops, as well as the internal relationship management team despite her complete lack of experience and knowledge of relationship management. She doesn't know what she's doing, and no one seems to be there to guide her. The team keeps trying to help by letting her know what is going on and correcting all the mistakes, but for whatever reason, she's not listening. You guys are setting her up to fail just like Amy and Nelson. The launch document for the upcoming product changes, which sales ops owns and is responsible for, was not completed. Despite it being their project, somehow, they were convinced that they were not responsible for completing the launch document. So, when it wasn't completed, the relationship management team completed it and cleaned up their shit, again! But, for some reason, whenever we step in to help out, we get our wrists slapped and reprimanded by Elaine for cleaning up her team's mistakes. What the hell is going on, Corey? Someone needs to get their shit together."

"Okay, Wayne. I think you need to step back and think about what you are saying," Corey barked. "Like I said, none of these issues have been brought to my attention, and I have not heard any of this from Carl or Elaine."

Realizing this conversation was not going anywhere other than a heated argument, Wayne conceded. "Corey, I apologize for my outburst. I still believe you have too much on your plate, and I sincerely would like to help. I love the work I do, and although we have done a great job building positive momentum, we are overly focused on the numbers and need to place an emphasis back on the names, on the team. All I ask is that you remember *Rule Number Eight* and love your people! You should be leveraging the team's talents and experience to make you and the company even more successful. But you have to be present. You have to include us. We cannot do this when we don't have anyone supporting us. More importantly, we need someone on the team who can institute change."

"I have to jump on another call. Why don't you put a report together highlighting what you mentioned? We'll see if there is something we can do."

"Okay. Corey, all I intend is the improvement of the team's morale and to continue our success." Wayne sincerely wanted to make this work in an open and honest collaboration. Yet, he could not help but be annoyed by Corey's infatuation with the numbers and ignorance of the issues.

"We'll see you at dinner tonight at Joey's, right?"

"Yep. Six o'clock. See you then. Thanks." Wayne walked out of the conference room. "Another fucking report? Come on!" He mumbled to himself. "A report isn't going to fix the dysfunction and shitty morale. He is so fucking blind to what's going on."

He strolled through the office around the maze of cubicles and sneaked into another conference room to call Charlize. She was a great sounding board. Plus, she shared the same frustrations as Wayne did. She did not care for the bullshit that was taking place at Pigeon Financial and was certainly not shy about voicing her concerns and frustrations with Corey—although he tended to ignore her comments.

Wayne unlocked his iPhone and tapped the phone icon with his finger. His contacts popped onto the screen. As he tapped on the star at the bottom of his phone, his list of favorites appeared with Charlize's name at the top.

He tapped her name, and the phone started ringing. Charlize quickly answered, "Hey, Wayne! How are you doing?"

"Hey, Charlize! I'm good. Do you have a few minutes?"

"Yeah. I'm just dealing with the usual fire drills, the product updates and battling with sales ops to get their shit done. Do you know they screwed up another communication to my client? As usual, Adam and I have to go back and clean it up! It's the same bullshit. Nothing ever changes here."

"Yeah, I'm not really surprised. Something has to change, though. By the way, I wanted to let you know I had my meeting with Corey today."

"That's right. You're in Bellevue this week."

"Yep. I just got here today for my meeting with him. We have a team dinner tonight and meetings all day tomorrow."

"So, how'd it go?"

"It's the same shit with him," Wayne replied with a sigh. "I keep urging him to pay attention and love his people. Do you remember *The Energy Bus?*"

"Yeah, but I really didn't read it," Charlize said.

"I didn't read it at first either but am glad I finally did. It's a very insightful book and discusses the ten secrets, or tips, to approaching life and work. I urged him to follow Rule Number Eight from the book. Of course, he had no idea what the rule was."

"Neither do I. What is it?"

"It's 'Love your passengers.' He asked me what he needed to improve, and I said he has to put the names before numbers."

"What does that mean?" Charlize interjected.

Wayne elaborated on his meaning of names before numbers for Charlize. In addition, he explained how he could not quite understand why management would mandate the team read a book, when they themselves did not embrace the words and lessons in the book. Often, management was ill prepared to have an open and constructive dialogue about the very book they required the team read.

Wayne read the book and embraced it. There it was in black and white on the pages of *The Energy Bus*; the words read, "Love your passengers." It made perfect sense that Corey should embrace Rule Number Eight, yet it eluded him, which frustrated Wayne. He was baffled by Corey's ignorance of the book's lessons and suggestions.

It was clear they were attempting to metric and automate everything. This is something that can be done successfully and effectively, but leadership must also learn to love their people to be successful. As with automation and relationship management, there are too many aspects to the job that make it nearly impossible to automate, such as people skills and relationship building. Knowing accounts better than the accounts know themselves cannot be captured on a spreadsheet. Nor can knowing how to speak to people, knowing how to negotiate, or knowing how to establish trust and respect. Spreadsheets and analytics do not and cannot capture this.

Wayne continued his phone conversation with Charlize. "I just read a recent Gallup employee engagement research article the other day that said that more than 50 percent of employees are not engaged at work."

"I'm not surprised to hear that," Charlize replied.

"People are generally satisfied at work but are not connected to their work or the workplace. They usually show up, do the minimum required but, in a heartbeat, will leave for a slightly better job," Wayne continued. "Then you have the other 10 percent or so who are actively disengaged, meaning those employees who have miserable work experiences. Between those two groups, that is about two-thirds of all employees who basically hate what they do."

"That sounds like Pigeon Financial. In the six years I have been here, not much has improved. It's gotten worse. Corey, Carl, and Ned are driving this place into the ground. They get away with it because we keep cleaning up their mess, and they are fortunate that the wholesalers do a great job of selling our product. It's the wholesalers who are making these clowns successful. Plus, Amy is the one responsible for creating our indexed annuity at the perfect time when the industry began selling these products, which made these knuckleheads look like they were great leaders when they are subpar at best."

"I do have to give credit where credit is due," Wayne added. "Despite his volatile personality, Ned has done a pretty good job positioning the product for success. But overall, they cannot seem to get past the numbers, even themselves, to see their people, or to love their people. So, I got the same bullshit response from Corey when I urged him to love his people."

"Let me guess, he said, 'Uh, makes sense. Why don't you create a report?'" Charlize mocked Corey in an emotionless tone.

"Pretty much. He said that no one brought any of these issues to his attention."

"Of course, they haven't. They don't know what they're doing because no one has shown them how to do their job. Don't think for a second that they're going to jeopardize their positions by telling Corey or Carl how screwed up things are. Plus, they probably don't even know how messed up it is because they haven't worked anywhere else. Dysfunction and deceit are all they know."

"Since I wasn't getting anywhere with Corey, I stepped back and apologized for my words. I just let him know that I wanted to help, that the team wants to help. He has so much talent on this team, and it's going to waste."

"As I've said before, I really don't believe they're going to change. I am getting too old for this shit! I just spoke with a friend who was recently laid off after years of working for the world's largest telecommunications, media, and technology companies. They even laid him off after he received an outstanding performance review and saved the company over ten million dollars the year before. His employer certainly didn't put their names before their numbers. I see the same thing happening here, and it scares the shit out of me."

"More and more of these large companies don't seem to give a shit about their employees. They appear more concerned about the health of their numbers rather than the health and morale of their people. Have you seen the movie *The Accountant*?" Wayne changed direction.

"Yeah, isn't that the one with Ben Affleck?"

"Yep. Do you remember the character he portrayed in the movie?"

"I don't know the guy's name, but I remember he was some sort of freak with numbers and killed a lot of people."

"The guy's name was Christian Wolff. He was this math savant who loved numbers more than people. He worked for some of the world's most dangerous criminal organizations, but his cover was as a small-town CPA."

"Now I remember the movie."

"Don't you see the likeness?"

"Likeness to what?"

"Not what, but whom."

"Huh?"

"Think about it."

"Oh! I get it!" Charlize interrupted. "Oh my gosh! Corey's behaviors are eerily like Christian Wolff's. I have to tell my husband. He's going to crack up."

"Yeah, but it's more disturbing than funny. Corey fits Ben Affleck's character, Christian Wolff, to a T, minus the killing…as far as we know." Wayne chuckled. "Although his extreme absence of emotion and total disregard of employees could easily be considered the same as killing someone's confidence and pride."

"Now that's funny!" Charlize laughed. "I'll have to watch that movie again."

"On another note, what did you think about Carl's bullshit comments on the conference call yesterday?"

"I think he makes up half the shit he says, and I don't know how he gets away with it!" Charlize exclaimed. "No, actually I do know. He's good at playing the favor of whoever will get him ahead. I've always said he's a player. When I was first hired, he was pandering to Ned but then turned on him and threw him under the bus when Chad was promoted. Ever since then, he's been playing Chad like a fiddle, and Chad has no clue!"

"I'm astonished how he has risen through the ranks at this company."

"He's very intelligent though and too smart for his own good."

"Well, it has been said that high intelligence is a trait of a sociopath," Wayne interjected. "They are charming, grandiose, and promiscuous."

"Wow! That sounds eerily like Carl."

"I am not saying everyone who is intelligent is a sociopath, but high intelligence is probably what makes them so believable to others. In addition, they lack empathy, don't feel guilt, have a limited and shallow emotional experience, and get bored easily. In addition, psychopaths usually focus on satisfying their immediate desires and rarely work on achieving any long-term goals. Sounds like Carl, right?" There was no response on the other end of the line. "Charlize? Are you there?" Wayne asked.

"Sorry. I'm here. I just didn't know what to say. That sounds exactly like him!"

"Oh wait, it gets better. Psychopaths are fast talkers, and what they say is mostly, if not entirely, false. They make big promises, tell big stories with no basis for them or no experience at whatever they're planning."

"Wow!" Charlize gasped. "Carl has Chad eating out of his hand. Something must change. Someone has to stop him. I hate to leave it like this, but I've got to go. I have a call in a couple minutes," she commented. "Let's continue talking about this."

"Talk to you later."

"Bye."

Wayne left the conference room and walked over to catch up with his teammates. He always enjoyed seeing them, but it pained him to know they felt like prisoners who couldn't say anything. They could not be honest and express their true feelings and frustrations except among one another.

Words to Lead By

Q: As a leader are you crunching numbers to lead your names (your people), or are you loving your names (your people), allowing them to create your numbers? You must embrace and understand both, not one over the other. It must be a healthy balance and harmony.

Q: When the shit hits the fan, do you crunch more numbers and push your names (your people) even harder to perform, or do you know how to truly motivate your names and trust that they, through proper guidance and leadership, will do the work necessary to succeed?

Q: Are you strong enough and know the marketplace and your employees well enough to let go of the numbers when necessary and embrace the names and vice versa?

Wayne loved crunching numbers and running spreadsheets, but he also understood they would never accurately reflect the human emotional investment in, and connection to, the workplace. He understood that for a company to succeed, leadership had to invest in their people first. The people are what make the profits possible. The numbers are what allow a business to keep track of their success. Where many businesses and leaders fail is when they lose sight of the names over the numbers.

People will work hard, but a heavy pace cannot endure without some sort of reprieve. People will become tired, and if there is no motivation other than money and a hard-charging manager, the people will eventually abandon them by leaving or being one of the many actively disengaged.

Based on years of working with sales professionals, Wayne knew that his top performers would rather die than fail at their job. Understanding this, when things became difficult, rather than crunching numbers and pressing his people to do more, he would look to them to find a way to maintain their relationships, their clients, because they understood what they needed to do to succeed.

This is contrary to most managers and leaders. When things become difficult, they crunch more numbers; they demand people work harder and do more work, which leads to stress and burnout. Sort of like the kid who helps his parents with yard work and feverishly rakes leaves but only moves them from one side of the yard to the other. He does it repeatedly, expecting different results, but he just becomes tired and quits.

Knowing the process and knowing the people, Wayne knew he could temporarily shift his focus onto nurturing their client relationships so they could better understand what they needed to thrive during uncertain times, when they were not selling. Stop it! Stop pressing the wholesalers to do more work by increasing their activity numbers. During difficult times, pressing your people by sinking your head in spreadsheets and numbers when clients aren't buying will not solve the problem. You must find an opportunity to rely less on the numbers, the analytics, and be brave enough to focus on the names (mother the sales force and your clients). If they nurture their relationships to find ways to thrive during difficult times, your salespeople will be rewarded by increased numbers, sales, when the turmoil subsides. Once this occurs, the shift can be turned back toward the numbers and activities, allowing you to maintain and grow your business.

You cannot afford to love your numbers over your names; nor can you afford to love your names over your numbers. You must find some semblance of balance and harmony between the two and know when to put an emphasis on one versus the other while always bringing both back to balance.

> You have a lot of facts but very little wisdom. Information is knowing that water is H_2O. Wisdom is knowing how to make it rain. Information is being able to make a diagnosis. Wisdom is being able to heal.
> —Robert Wright

Mediocre Management Massacre

So you've got to ask yourself, "Why aren't they doing as well as they should be?" Fully 90% of the time, the reason is management ... The system is so flawed that you can't get mediocre managers out.

—*Carl Icahn (Money: Master the Game Robbins 2014)*

Sales at Pigeon Financial were still doing extremely well. They were quickly becoming one of the top selling indexed annuity companies in the industry. The Catch-22 was that when sales were rockin' and rollin', it was much easier to brush aside the cluster fuck that was taking place behind the scenes.

When things are going extremely well, everyone is happy, especially when money is being made. This makes it easier to brush aside the dysfunction and toxicity that is taking place behind the scenes. But when people look behind the curtain to reveal the mess, they quickly pull it shut and walk away because they don't want to deal with the bullshit, or acknowledge it, and possibly jeopardize their job. Plus, when everything is working and money is being made, why fix it if it does not appear to be broken?

Wayne's good friend Gary from college had forged a successful career in pharmaceutical sales over the course of fifteen years. Gary was one of the kindest individuals anyone would ever meet. He was always striving to be the best and never rocked the boat, regardless of how often his territory was changed or how often he had to prove himself to a new manager.

He always excelled at whatever it was he put his mind and heart into. But he also put up with the bullshit and made excuses for the crap management put him through even after fifteen years of success working for the same company. Despite Gary's honest and excellent work ethic and continually exceeding his goals, he somehow ended up getting pushed to the bottom practically every year.

Wayne and Gary had frequent conversations about the business world and leadership. Wayne often found himself annoyed by Gary's excuses for ineffective and incompetent management, although they saw eye to eye regarding the need for a structure and hierarchy within organizations. Done properly, this ensures a healthy collaboration and communication among departments and leadership, which maintains a rewarding and successful workplace.

Wayne's frustration remained with those companies that placed people in positions of leadership and management who acted more like tyrants rather than leaders. Gary would often brush it aside because he viewed it as a natural part of running a business, and there was not much anyone could do about it. This infuriated Wayne. He was not going to sit on the sidelines to watch people in positions of power run rampant, making a mockery of leadership and a nightmare of the workplace.

During one of their regular Friday night conversations, Wayne and Gary were in another heated conversation. "But, when the good times come to an end, when things get tough, the competition is breathing down your neck and sales are more difficult to come by, the fall guy is typically the employee," Wayne stated passionately. "If layoffs are going to happen, no matter how great an employee is, they're usually the first to go. Even if a manager sucks at their job, they won't hesitate to cut an employee loose before they do it to themselves despite their incompetence and awful leadership. I'm tired of people being viewed as just a statistic who can easily be removed. I've seen managers conceal the toxic shit show that takes place behind the scenes because they know full well if the disaster is revealed, it will be their necks on the line. Despite management being responsible for the failure and leading the employees down that path to disaster, they will deny everything and point the finger directly at the employees. This toxic work environment festers. It's sort of like being diagnosed with advanced stage cancer. Despite all appearances on the outside of being healthy and perfectly fine, inside, that person is dying, and in this case, it's the employees whose pride and confidence are dying. No matter how hard the employees work to get rid of the toxicity, it continually recurs because it hasn't been identified or acknowledged by self-serving and negligent management. Cancer does not consider itself a killer, but everyone knows it as such. Shitty management does not consider itself a morale killer, but employees do. A shitty manager does what they believe they're supposed to do, which is manage and boss people around rather than teach and lead."

"Okay, Wayne. You're being a little extreme. By the way, I haven't been fired or laid off after all these years. So, I believe it's more than just being a number."

"True, you haven't been laid off, and I'm glad that hasn't happened. But you are in the goddamn pharmaceutical industry. The trillion-dollar pharmaceutical industry! Of course, you haven't been laid off. Everyone is making money hand over fist." Wayne paused to take a breath. "Hear me out. We are exceeding sales goals, and when you are blowing through your goals, it's easy for upper management to hang their hat on the astounding success by showing off the company's sales numbers. The CEO is happy. Even the shareholders are happy. Of course, the dysfunction and toxicity remain hidden from the CEO because sales are surging, and that's all that matters. All the while, the names, or employees, are miserable. They're actively disengaged from work, which is a slippery slope of devastation. I am not sure which is worse, the management team not telling the CEO about the toxic work environment or the CEO being aware but turning a blind eye because their priority is with the profits versus the people. Even the shareholders' interests take precedence over the employees' welfare, despite it being the employees' hard work that drives the sales and revenue, which in turn drives the company's value and success."

"Interesting. So, are you saying that the CEO doesn't see these actively disengaged employees because upper management has basically kept it hidden?"

"Yep, pretty much. Although there are other factors that play into this. Upper management cannot afford to reveal how messed–up things are because if they revealed the atrocities created by their ineffective management, they'd be looking for another career," Wayne continued. "So, instead, the employees drown in a pool of negativity, slowly losing interest in their work and becoming actively disengaged. In some cases, employees lose confidence in themselves and their ability to do their job. They just show up to work, do their job because they have to, and believe there's no other way or nothing else for them."

"Wow! I am speechless. Is this really happening?" Gary asked.

"You betcha! Instead of heeding the cries for help from employees regarding the declining morale and dysfunction, management decides instead to deploy online surveys to gauge employee satisfaction. Listen, we were recently asked to complete one of many online surveys. My colleague Jean started the survey and stopped after the first three questions because the questions didn't make any sense and didn't even pertain to our job. It was a generic template! Most of the questions had nothing to do with our specific job functions or even our industry. When Jean mentioned the survey, I opened it up to read the first few questions. And you know, she was right! I was blown away by how inaccurate it was."

"That tells me they didn't conduct the proper due diligence when selecting the survey or the survey provider."

"Yep. It appeared the intent of the survey was to gauge the roles and responsibilities of the team. Which is all good and well except for the fact that this had been addressed with the roles and responsibilities proposals we already created for Corey."

"Oh, yeah. I remember. Wasn't that when I asked you if you were a Six Sigma black belt?"

"Yep. That was the report."

"Dude, that was impressive. Even more so considering you never studied Six Sigma."

"Well, it didn't matter. They failed at implementing anything we advised. So, we decided to take things into our own hands with the survey."

"Oh no! What'd you do?" Gary gasped.

"We completed the survey together as a team," Wayne said matter-of-factly.

"What? How'd you do that?"

"On one of our private team conference calls, we walked through the survey together. We took turns reviewing the questions and then discussed the appropriate response as a team."

"No, you didn't!" Gary exclaimed.

"Oh, yes we did!" Wayne responded with a chuckle.

"So, what happened? Did anyone find out?"

"Nothing. Absolutely nothing happened. We never heard anything from Corey or Carl after that. The survey died a slow death in the project and task graveyard with the dozens of other projects and tasks that were a complete waste of employees' time and the company's money."

"We have surveys each quarter. I've always enjoyed completing them and never felt the need to be dishonest," Gary commented in his usual style, not wanting to rock the boat.

"I understand, but on the flip side, I don't condone the way Pigeon Financial and many other companies treat their employees when, instead of listening to them, they decide to have them take a survey, which is so impersonal. Plus, I don't buy into the apparent confidentiality of these surveys."

"Well, you certainly have always had the balls to challenge the status quo. I admire you for standing up to the bullshit and stepping out of line to challenge the way things are done for the benefit of your colleagues and the workplace."

"Oh yeah, the other part of these surveys is that no matter how awful the results, upper management finds a way to interpret the results in their favor. This makes surveys another flawed tool. All of this leads me to seek an answer to the question of why employees can't be honest in the workplace."

"Do you really think they can't be honest?"

"Oh yeah. Without a doubt. Let me put it to you this way. They can be honest, but most aren't for fear of being reprimanded or worse. While I was working at Doe Financial, my manager walked into the office and asked me if I had too much work?"

"What is wrong with asking that?" Gary replied.

"This was after the 2009 market crisis and half of the company was laid off. The same amount of work remained, but it was being done with more than half of the people no longer there. Actually we lost two-thirds of our team. We were on our heels defending our business, explaining our ratings, confirming the financial strength of the company, and persuading our clients to still do business with us. Understanding that was the backdrop, what kind of manager poses a question such as that? That's simply ignorance to what's taking place."

"Not attuned to what's going on."

"Of course, we had too much work! Everyone had too much work. We were worried that our next day at work would be our last. I wasn't about to embellish the truth. Plus, they should have known we were overworked. I don't believe they were ready to hear the truth. So, I misrepresented the situation."

"I think you could have been honest with your manager. You just need to phrase it in the right way that is not antagonistic or retaliatory."

"Point taken. Yes, I agree."

"Remember the movie *A Few Good Men*."

"Of course! Who doesn't?"

"The pivotal scene when Tom Cruise, Lt. Daniel Kaffee, is cross-examining Jack Nicolson, Col. Nathan Jessup." Gary begins quoting the movie, "'I want the truth!' 'You can't handle the truth!'"

Wayne laughed. "That is the business world except that lives are not at stake, or at least they don't appear to be. We are not at war or defending our nation, but sometimes it feels as though we are at war and defending our rights as employees. I love that movie and that scene. It's such a powerful one! Colonel Nathan Jessup committed crimes because he was in a position of power and lost sight of the real reason why he was doing what he was hired to do and was arrested. Of course, he probably was acquitted of all charges and went on his way."

"Sadly, the more you speak about this, the more I see the same thing happening where I work. That is why I just put my head down and do my job."

"Yep! That's what practically everyone says. They ignore this shit and allow it to continue unchecked. Then they make comments like 'It's like that everywhere.' 'I just do my job and go home.' 'The grass isn't always greener.' That's fucking bullshit! Why doesn't anyone do anything about it?"

"What can we do?"

"Say something. Do something about it. Get another job! I am proud to be a part of the success, but at what cost? It was pretty awesome becoming the best in our product category while the behemoths are left wondering how in the world this no-name company garnered so much business. Industry peers congratulate me on the success, and even competitors offer words of congratulations. When clients comment about our tight-knit family environment, it makes me want to throw up. They think we are some sort of Brady-Bunch or Leave-It-to-fucking-Beaver perfect family. They never see the bullshit and dysfunction behind the scenes that's eroding morale."

"Is it really that bad?"

"Yes. Remember the guy, Carl, I work with?"

"Yeah. The sociopath."

"Yes, that's the guy. Well, no one has called him on his bullshit because he's so good at it. He's so convincing. Plus, being in an executive position makes him practically untouchable. So, his lies have become bigger and more ludicrous. On top of that, he's having an affair with a girl he promoted to director of the internal sales desk, which was not deserved or earned. I've worked for women who ran sales desks, who were amazing at their jobs, and this girl is nowhere in the vicinity. Of course, people let it go because there really was nothing that could be done about it. He routinely shows up intoxicated during business functions, openly making derogatory remarks about his employees and making sexual advances with practically every female he encounters! What's really fucked up is that this behavior is so common that people turn a blind eye and just accept it."

"Yeah, I see some of that here." Gary sighed.

"Despite this guy's sociopathic tendencies and his ineffective and incompetent management style, no one, not a single person, has done or said anything about it. And you can't get rid of these managers. They're in positions of power, and when it's your word against theirs, you're fucked. And for employee well-being, ha! I call bullshit." Wayne laughed. "I was always under the impression that human resources was there to support and protect the employees when it came to workplace morale and mistreatment. On the contrary, at Pigeon Financial, the human resources department is there to cover up executive management's misdeeds and mistreatment of employees. In effect, the human resources department is condoning the behavior of these assholes, thus making them untouchable!"

"Are you serious? What the heck is going on there?"

Wayne continued sharing his experiences with Gary. All of it finally made sense the day Wayne and the team caught Carl in one of his lies. Once you catch the first one, all the others become obvious, and you can't help but wonder how in the world you missed it all along. The floodgates of lies opened, and they drowned in an ocean of misrepresentation.

During an executive meeting, Carl was reviewing the project calendar with the team. Carl had a new person, Fiona, running the project management team, since the previous guy, Sigmund, resigned. Sigmund, in his own words, said that he "could not trust Carl as far as he could throw him." There was a great amount of deceit and mistrust between the two. Sigmund finally saw through the lies and eventually left the company.

Carl commented that he recently spoke with Sigmund, making up some bullshit about their apparent conversation and how great Sigmund was doing at his new job. Next, Carl mentioned that Fiona really stepped things up, making project management sing since Sigmund's departure—when Sigmund laid the foundation for project management prior to his departure and Fiona walked into what he built.

In the middle of the meeting, Wayne's colleague Jean texted Sigmund to ask if it was true that Carl spoke with him. She knew how much he despised Carl and didn't believe for a second it was true.

Sigmund immediately replied, saying that Carl was full of shit. He hadn't spoken with that asshole since he resigned and really didn't care if he ever spoke with him again. Carl was the reason Sigmund left the company. At that moment, Wayne and the team knew Carl was making shit up right there on the spot. He blatantly lied about speaking with Sigmund. Moments later, he fabricated the status of an account they were trying to onboard. In his confidence, he stated that the client was ready to move forward, all the agreements were awaiting approval, and they would be live in a few weeks.

Everyone in the meeting noted his comments and moved on to the next agenda item, except for Melanie. This was her account, and the look on her face was priceless. It was clear by the expression on her face that she was stunned and not sure how to react. As professionally as possible, she interjected by commenting about a recent call with the client, who informed her that things were stalled and were nowhere even close to moving forward.

Wayne was having such a great time in his first few years working at Pigeon Financial. He even thought things were better than they were until the recurring signs of instability within the company revealed themselves. The writing was on the wall when Nelson unexpectedly resigned and then when they fired Amy. At that point, he should have run for the exits, but instead, he stayed. It was like witnessing a car crash. You know you should leave and look away from the horror, but you can't. You just stand and stare at the tragedy as it unfolds.

Words to Lead By

Q: Are you just a manager with a title, or are you a leader who is willing to love your people, allowing them to rise up and rise above?

"So, you've got to ask yourself, 'why aren't they doing as well as they should be?' Speaking of the overall success of American companies. 'Fully 90% of the time, the reason is management … The system is so flawed that you can't get mediocre managers out.'"

That quote from Carl Icahn pretty much sums up the pulse of the industry, of corporate America. "These managers might have a title, but that doesn't mean shit if you can't connect with people and motivate them, move them, and inspire them."[10]

"For twenty-five years, you paid for my hands when you could have had my brain as well—for nothing." This was a comment from one of GE's appliance workers.[11]

Definition of human resources from *entrepreneur.com* is as follows: "a human resources department is a critical component of employee well-being in any business. Any mix-up concerning these issues can cause major legal problems for your business, as well as major employee dissatisfaction."[12]

---

[10] Robbins, *Money, How to Master the Game* (2014).
[11] Welch, *Winning* (2005).
[12] www.entrepreneur.com.

Coaching is about Behaviors, Not Outcomes

We've found that what often happens is that managers focus on outcomes rather than behaviors in coaching conversations ... Some members like to call that "spreadsheet coaching." It's focused on business results, not behaviors, and it's delivered in a one-size-fits-all manner—everybody gets the exact same treatment. But done well, coaching is about behaviors, not outcomes.

—*The Challenger Sale*

Wayne sat at the kitchen table, enjoying his morning cup of coffee. Lost in his thoughts, he wondered if he had it all wrong. He found himself questioning whether he was brought up the right way.

Deep down, he believed his parents brought him up right, teaching him to be honest, to always give it his best, to work hard, and to treat others with kindness and respect. Following their guidance and embracing the positive virtues they taught did in fact bring him success, but what confounded him was the behavior displayed by executive management at the companies he had worked for over the years. The positive virtues that Wayne was taught seemed to elude many of the executives he worked for. This made him question what he was doing because they seemed to have met with more success than he had up to that point.

He worked his ass off to get where he was. He did what was asked of him and exceeded expectations. Through the years, he noticed a recurring trend with executives and upper management. They seemed to care very little about their people and were ignorant of the internal conflict, the lack of support and camaraderie among employees.

His frustration at Pigeon Financial was with the feeling that he, and his teammates, were continually pushed aside by management. The management team had become increasingly belligerent and unwilling to listen to their suggestions and feedback regarding the betterment of the team and the division. It did not start out that way, but gradually over time it seemed Wayne and his teammates no longer had a voice.

Wayne loved his parents and grandparents for their guidance, but he felt as though it was all a lie. Witnessing how poorly upper management and executives treated their employees fed his doubts.

The values my parents instilled in me seem to elude the leaders at Pigeon Financial. Maybe I should start lying, cheating, and treating people like shit so I can get ahead because that seems to be the mind-set of executive management. If you can't beat them, join them. Wayne continued processing his many thoughts. *There seems to be some sort of compromise when you are in management in which you have to set aside what you innately know is right for what instead is the best for the company and leadership, even if it neglects employees or hurts them.*

The more honest and hardworking he was, the harder it seemed for Wayne to move up. He knew there was more to being a true leader than a title and labeling employees as a number or statistic. He got up from the kitchen table and walked to his office where he grabbed the book *The Challenger Sale*, which Ned gave to the team as required reading a couple of years prior.

The book was an excellent guide for business and sales. Wayne read it. He listened to the audio version. He studied it. What he found in the pages of *The Challenger Sale*, clear as day, was Corey, Ned, and Carl's failing. It was referred to as "spreadsheet coaching." The book highlighted this as a poor way of leadership, and it was Pigeon Financial's failing. According to *The Challenger Sale*, spreadsheet coaching is as follows.

> We've found that what often happens is that managers focus on outcomes rather than behaviors in coaching conversations, saying things like, "Your conversion

rate is way down. What's the problem? Aren't you following the process?" That's not really what you should be after. Some members like to call that "spreadsheet coaching." It's focused on business results, not behaviors, and it's delivered in a one-size-fits-all manner—everybody gets the exact same treatment. But done well, coaching is about behaviors, not outcomes.[13]

Corey, Carl, and Ned were spreadsheet coaches! They were so far lost in the numbers that they neglected the names, the people, and Rule Number Eight: "Love your people." It got to a point at which they created spreadsheets to track everything, even spreadsheets to track existing spreadsheets. Conference calls were scheduled to talk about what was discussed on previous calls instead of taking action, owning the work, and actually accomplishing something.

Of the dozens, if not hundreds, of books published on success and leadership, Wayne had yet to find one that bragged about how a company's spreadsheets and metrics were the ultimate reason for their success. Spreadsheets, metrics, and automaton are important tools that contribute to the success of a company, but they are not the magic pill for success. Any good manager worth their salt understands that true success is attributable to a healthy balance and respect of both the names and the numbers.

In Wayne's experience, the more metrics and analytics management places on a sales team's head while neglecting their sales skills and entrepreneurial spirit, the more they were encroaching on dangerous ground.

What ensued was a manipulation of the numbers by the sales force. They provided management with what they wanted to see and hear rather than open and honest feedback. Yet, the sales team went about doing their business the way they knew would result in

---

[13] Excerpt From page 311 Matthew Dixon and Brent Adamson, *The Challenger Sale* (2011) (iBooks), https://itunes.apple.com/us/book/the-challenger-sale/id440415589?mt=11.

success while providing manipulated numbers to management. In short, the entire process was bastardized because management had their heads so deep into spreadsheets and metrics that they lost sight of their people and what ultimately made them successful.

The irony of Pigeon Financial's love of automation and spreadsheet coaching was their headquarters being located near Amazon, the poster child of automation and spreadsheet coaching, which was in neighboring Seattle.

Amazon was an excellent example of this automation obsession and frighteningly so. Pigeon Financial was pushing toward automation and gradually began treating their employees like a statistic rather than a person with a family and life outside of work.

> It will be no surprise if Amazon becomes the first business to fully automate. A company that resents even its workers basic right to a break will only find people a frustration to its aims. Amazonians who left their workstation to go to the bathroom would be promptly hounded by senior employees. Stories abound of workers afraid to stop, pissing into bottles at their desk. Your tracker, after all, is recording. As such, everything you need to do must be done on your breaks. But given the size of the warehouse—and the fact that to get in and out of it, you must go through airport-level security—it tends to take three to four minutes to just make it back to the canteen. If you get a full five minutes to sit down, you've done well.[14]

Wayne's frustration mounted. He believed companies should represent their employees, rather than resent them. The number one wholesaler for Pigeon Financial became the number one wholesaler because of his talents and his ability to build relationships with his advisors. He had a way of connecting with them, to help them

---

[14] Cameron Brady-Turner, March 2019, https://onezero.medium.com/relentless-com-life-as-a-cog-in-amazons-e-tail-machine-d46b3ef05eb8.

understand how Pigeon Financial's products benefitted the advisors' clients. His job was to sell and hit his sales goals and he did so year after year, even exceeding the established goals.

This guy was the number-one wholesaler because he built a business with long-lasting, trusting relationships with his advisors. He did such a good job that his internal counterpart did not have enough time in the day to make the automated scripted calls that Darlene, Carl, and Corey mandated the internal sales team complete.

Despite being the top sales territory, they fired his internal counterpart because he did not follow their unproductive and ineffective metrics. When a manager rules with an iron fist and idolizes metrics as the golden rule, then that manager will meet with failure over the long term.

Loving your people is not taught in schools or universities. Rather we are taught to lead from a place of facts, force, ego, and fear, idolizing the numbers and analytics. If you threaten your kids or students, yell at them for speaking their mind, or demand they do what you say because you are in a position of authority, eventually, they will come to despise their work, possibly even rebel and stop doing their work entirely or will no longer show up.

They will learn to say what you want to hear instead of sharing the truth. Being willing to listen to and act upon honest feedback will improve the business and company. It makes leadership better. It makes the parent better. It makes the teacher better. But the absence of this "transparency" will lead the employees, kids, and students to lose respect for their boss, parents, and teachers. Eventually, the employee, child, or student finds a way to manipulate the rules and ends up doing what he or she wants anyway.

The book *The Wisdom of Failure; Losing Balance between "What" and "How"* captures this dynamic as follows:

> We are also a very goal-oriented culture in which status and success are paramount. We're proud when we're at the top of our game and when others see we're there. But we probably don't spend enough

time considering how we got there. Jennifer Robin, coauthor of *The Great Workplace: How to Build It, How to Keep It, and Why It Matters* and research fellow with the Great Place to Work Institute, tells us that in great workplaces, rather than focusing exclusively on goals—the "what" of success—leaders also take time to focus on process—the "how." Like management and leadership, or tactics and strategy, both are necessary, and so is paying attention to both. Attending to how goals are achieved, rather than the goals themselves, builds strong relationships and solid business acumen—and knowing how we achieved what we achieved (or failed to do) can educate us about the real basis of our success.[15]

Steve Jobs was quoted as saying, "My passion has been to build an enduring company where people were motivated to make great products. Everything else was secondary. Sure, it was great to make a profit, because that was what allowed you to make great products. But the products, not the profits, were the motivation. Sculley flipped these priorities to where the goal was to make money. It's a subtle difference, but it ends up meaning everything—the people you hire, who gets promoted, what you discuss in meetings."[16]

So, when it comes to the workplace and when people have nothing good to say, they typically make up some bullshit comment such as "Living the dream!" Too many people accept the current work environment as the status quo, but Wayne knew it was not okay to be treated so poorly. Profits over people, numbers before names, seems to be the way companies run things.

---

[15] Weinzimmer/McConoughey, *The Wisdom of Failure* (2012).

[16] *Harvard Business Review*, April 2012, https://hbr.org/2012/04/the-real-leadership-lessons-of-steve-jobs.

Over Wayne's twenty-year career, he sat in on countless strategy and planning meetings, which gave him a greater appreciation and understanding regarding the importance of the numbers. If the numbers—that is, revenue or profits—are not achieved, then the business fails, and people lose jobs. He understood the importance of the numbers, but also knew that numbers alone would not make a business successful.

The million-dollar question for Wayne was, can a leader be successful, wealthy, and dominant in business while still loving his or her people?

Jim Rohn once touted that we get paid for bringing value to the marketplace. Executives running organizations certainly deserve the salary they are paid for the work they do and the value they bring to the marketplace. When the work and value they bring to the marketplace become subpar and they no longer hit their numbers, do they point the finger at their employees rather than themselves?

Could it very well be the reason the numbers, or profits, were missed was the lackluster leadership? The employees are following the orders from management. They are doing the job they were assigned. When things fail and the wheels fall off, it is rarely those in positions of leadership whose heads roll. Rather the employees bear the brunt of the punishment. Yet, all they were doing was executing the business plans and directions instituted by leadership. The finger is pointed at the employee rather being pointed at leadership. If you fire the employees and leadership continues making the same mistakes, you will have constant turnover, poor results, and an actively disengaged workforce, all because of loser leadership.

Words to Lead By

Q: Are you a true leader or just a manager? How do you know? Are you willing to allow your people to grow? Do your people reject job offers because they love where they work, their work, and your leadership? Are you willing to support your people even in the event they are looking to work somewhere else? But first you've got to ask yourself why they are looking to work elsewhere.

Unlike management, leadership cannot be taught, although it may be learned and enhanced through coaching or mentoring.
—*The Business Dictionary*

♟ You've Got to Play the Game

> I don't play games. Games are for children.
> Business is not a game. I'm looking for
> strategy and leadership, not child's play.
>
> —*Anonymous*

Earlier in the year while at the national sales meeting during the first week of January 2017, Wayne stood in the atrium outside the conference room of the Florida resort. Staring out at the clear blue sky above that stretched across the Atlantic Ocean as far as the eye could see, he spoke with Patrice about a few work items they were working on, which led into yet another conversation about their mounting frustration with the abysmal way Ned, Corey, and Carl were running things.

"I believe they're trying to protect their positions in the company," Wayne said.

"What do you mean?" Patrice asked.

"Or maybe I should say they're trying to validate their positions. Either way, it seems like they're insulating their positions in the company by surrounding themselves with managers and employees who do as they are told without questioning the work they were asked to do or how it impacts the overall effectiveness of the business and the morale of colleagues. Look at who they are surrounding themselves with: Hank, Elaine, Fiona, and Darlene."

"Yep, I see that," Patrice said.

"Think about it. When someone is in a job that they never thought possible and is being paid more than they've ever been paid before, why would they jeopardize it by calling a spade a spade? They're not going to push back and challenge Corey or Carl, but rather they'll accept it as it is because they don't know any better, and they do not want to screw up what they have. How many people are afraid of speaking their mind out of fear of retribution or possibly losing their job?"

Patrice chuckled. "I can't afford to lose my job."

"Hey, I didn't speak my mind until I saw Ned pushing people around. I began speaking up because I knew I could and no longer cared to see colleagues treated poorly just because a manager has a title and power to get away with awful behavior. But when it came to Corey and Carl, I stepped back again. I don't like the way they operate. It's bad energy, and they're very demeaning. Even when you speak honestly and offer suggestions for improvement, they handle it poorly, retaliate, or sometimes simply ignore it. All I know is that I need to find another job. I can't do this any longer."

"You can't leave me here. If you leave, I'm going to kill you!"

"You will be one of the first ones to know when I leave. You should start looking as well."

"I have been, but where am I going to get another job that allows me to work from home? My health condition makes it difficult to get another job. I don't know if I'll ever be able to leave."

"What about speaking with Belinda and World Pacific Group? You used to work with her. She loves you. Why don't you give her a call?"

"I don't know. I like her, but I'm not so sure."

"Well, don't wait forever."

"Yeah, you're right. The sales numbers have been steadily increasing, we are launching new products, and we are the top carrier in many of our firms, so things are good. Although I am tired of getting yelled at for stepping in and helping to clean up the messes created by sales ops and marketing."

"I agree. Things look great on the surface. Even to Skip Armah, things look perfect! This is what was presented to Samurai Life when they purchased Pigeon Financial. They don't see the awful morale and abhorrent management. This isn't something that can be captured in black and white in the numbers and profits. And they aren't going to jeopardize their success by acknowledging the growing dysfunction and disconnect within the entire division. They will sweep it under the carpet if they can. Although Ned was never the ideal leader, I will say he was all we had and the only glimmer of hope we had for change. Now that seems to be gone. Corey and Carl have been politicking the entire time, pushing him out."

When Wayne started with the company, Ned oversaw the entire division. Shortly thereafter, Chad was promoted to basically the same position as Ned. That signaled the beginning of the end, and Skip Armah, the CEO, was the culprit. Maybe because he saw Ned's volatile ways and couldn't afford to have him at the helm, he promoted Chad.

Skip was known to pit people against one another and then sit back and watch them fight it out. This led to a great deal of contention between Ned and Chad. Then Chad began moving up the ranks while Ned was slowly slipping down. All the while Carl and Corey were stepping on and over Ned to move up.

Wayne did not play these games and earned everything he worked for. He created a very successful career for himself, despite accomplishing it from a place of learned aggression and assertiveness. Deep down in business and life, he preferred to be kind, but when someone is kind, it is often viewed as a weakness. He did not want to fall in line with the crowd and lead in the same ways the assholes at Pigeon Financial did. He knew there was another way to lead, but it was not a fit for Pigeon Financial.

Repeatedly, Wayne heard from colleagues and read research from the pages of business books saying that in the business world, you have to play the game, you have to learn to swim with the sharks, and it's a dog-eat-dog world...Blah, blah, blah.

Wayne had many conversations over the years with the only person who could make a difference at Pigeon Financial, and that person happened to be Ned Desilent. It took a few years for Wayne to realize this, but deep down, Ned was an angel who had a difficult time allowing his angelic ways to shine through. Wayne believed that Ned learned to become aggressively assertive and, often, a complete asshole because he was groomed in the dog-eat-dog approach to sales and business.

Although he was very intelligent and understood the business in ways that created unique opportunities for Pigeon Financial, the problem was that Ned felt the need to prove he was the smartest man in the room. This often came at the expense of relationships and business. Ned was as graceful as a bull in a China shop. Wayne and his teammates often were in damage control mode having to clean up Ned's messes after meeting with accounts. It was like a child having to apologize for a belligerent parent.

After years of working with him though, Wayne began to understand and appreciate Ned's approach to business. Finally seeing through Ned's harsh exterior, or assholeness, Wayne learned to appreciate his passion for the business.

Wayne was given a glimpse into Ned's true side, which was that of a man with a big heart and the only one who seemed to truly care about the employees. Ned had a strange way of conveying his passion, which most people did not see because of his abrasive approach. It took time and many confrontations to get to this point.

An example of this was in 2015 when the relationship management team was in Bellevue for quarterly strategy meetings. After the day of meetings concluded, the team gathered for a team dinner at yet another fancy restaurant. Ned dined with them that evening, using it as an opportunity to lecture them about what the relationship management team was supposed to be doing for the sales division. He ranted about how the relationship management team did not own the accounts they covered, but rather they were ambassadors for the accounts. The irony of Ned's arrogant comment was that he, too, was an ambassador. He sure as hell did not own the accounts either.

Ned was so smart he often made comments that made him seem stupid. The longer Wayne worked in the industry, the more he encountered executives in positions of leadership, like Ned, who were too smart for their own good, often lacking common sense and emotional intelligence.

During dinner, Ned continued his passion-filled rant while Wayne and the team sat around the table in stunned silence and awe. They were intimidated, or more aptly stated annoyed, by his arrogance and couldn't get a word in edgewise.

Sharing his vision for the sales division, Ned demanded that Wayne and his peers follow his directive and messaging. After witnessing too many executives in positions of authority over the years demanding respect, abusing their authority, and pushing people around, Wayne felt compelled to speak up. Plus, when someone demands respect, it usually is a sign that they are not confident in their abilities and do not know how to lead. Respect is earned, and Ned had not earned it, yet.

Just because someone has a title does not give them license to be an asshole. Wayne was not speaking up out of disrespect but rather from a place of respect for himself and his colleagues. Knowing that Ned, Wayne himself, and the entire team were all mature adults, he felt everyone deserved the opportunity and respect to share their thoughts and insights without fear of repercussion.

After Ned made his idiotic comment about the team being ambassadors for their accounts, Wayne spoke up and challenged Ned.

"What are the divisional managers and national sales team currently doing to promote our message? How are the wholesalers communicating it to our accounts and advisors?"

"I am not sure what they are doing, but our messages must align, and it starts with you," Ned replied.

"Well, as the head of the retirement division and national sales, isn't it your job to know what your divisional managers and wholesalers are doing?" Wayne blurted across the table.

Everything went silent. Even Ned fell silent, which rarely happened.

Charlize spoke up, breaking the uncomfortable silence. "Wayne makes a good point. We have tried time and time again to get this done. Without the buy-in and support from national sales we will fall short again."

Amy, who at the time was the manager of sales operations and strategy, interjected to prevent things from going any further off the rails. "I think we need to collaborate with national sales to ensure that our messaging aligns. This is my takeaway, and I will reach out to the divisional managers to move things along."

Amy saved Ned from an uprising in response to his belligerent comments. Unfortunately, Ned did not return the favor a couple of years later when Amy was Nelson's successor as the head of relationship management. Instead of throwing himself in front of the bus to save her, he threw her in front of the bus.

This was just the beginning of a long, jagged relationship in which this sort of exchange between Ned and Wayne became a common occurrence. Ned would boast grand ideas in his rough-around-the-edges and arrogant style, trying to prove that he was the smartest guy in the room. On many occasions, Wayne spoke up, challenging Ned on his boastful words to keep his arrogance and ego in check.

Wayne frequently tried to get through to Ned, doing his best to get him to make a connection with his audience, rather than spewing statistics and big words like *Japanification*, *negative convexity*, *asset correlation*, and *risk-adjusted returns*.

In the summer of 2016, Ned and Wayne were in Raleigh-Durham, North Carolina, for an industry roundtable meeting, addressing the proposed DOL fiduciary regulations. Prior to the meeting, they met for a cup of coffee to discuss Wayne's concerns.

"For a company that prides itself in the numbers to ensure we hit our sales and revenue goals," Wayne stated, "it's an embarrassment to see the thousands of dollars you are throwing out the window every day because of lack of productivity and people simply not doing their work."

"What are you referring to?" Ned replied.

"I'm referring to the lack of leadership at the home office with the team. I am referring to the sales operations managers delegating their work to the internal relationship managers because they don't know what they are doing. They're taking advantage of the IRMs because they know the IRMS will do their work for them. I am talking about the sales ops team working whenever they choose and deciding whether or not they are even coming into the office for the day."

"Elaine is running the sales operations team and should be handing this," Ned replied.

"Well, that's another issue altogether in itself. A lot of this was instigated because Patrice works from home. They're acting like children because they can't work from home. But Patrice has legitimate health concerns and for ten years has received approval to work remotely. By the way, this is private information that from a legal perspective is none of their business. Ned, no one's there to manage the sales operations team or the internal relationship managers. It's getting out of hand. I understand that she needs to recertify each year, but the way Elaine and the human resources team handled it was abusive and a bullying tactic. You should be embarrassed by the way she was treated. Elaine reports to Carl, who is influencing her. Plus, she is responsible for the IRMs, who are technically under Corey. So, why does Elaine have two bosses? It makes no sense and looks like you didn't know what you were doing when she was promoted. Patrice has never done anything wrong other than represent this company the best way possible, maybe caring too much to a fault. She is the best IRM we have, and they treat her like shit!"

"As a company, we are legally required to have employees complete an annual recertification; otherwise, we open ourselves up to potential litigation."

"Ned, I understand, but the company is opening itself up to potential litigation based on the way they handled it."

"We're working on making some changes to improve things. Like I said, Elaine is running the team and should be handling it. Let me look into it."

Wayne and Ned grabbed their coffee and walked to the conference meeting room to kick off their meetings for the day.

In another instance during the summer of 2016, Wayne and Ned were in Florida at the Omni Resort for one of Bear and Bull Financial's annual sponsor meetings. Sitting outside the resort conference room, they discussed Ned's upcoming breakout session with Bear and Bull Financial's sales team.

"Ned, why are you here?" Wayne posed the question.

"What?" Ned appeared caught off guard by Wayne's question.

"Why are you here?" Wayne repeated.

"To talk about our sales team and our products as fixed income alternatives."

"Ned, there are fifteen other product companies here to speak to this same group of people about the same damn thing. What's going to make them remember you after fifteen other product providers speak to them? Ned, you have to be memorable!"

"Okay?" Ned appeared slightly confused by Wayne's comments.

"Don't just talk about negative convexity and risk-adjusted returns. Talk about why they need to know about it, why they need to work with us. Show them how to use their own technology, financial tools, and resources to identify opportunities to position our product. Connect Pigeon Financial to everything they are doing as a firm. Make it relatable," Wayne stated with conviction.

⟶◆⟵

Ned was a product of the kill-what-you-eat business world, where dogs eat dogs, you swim with the sharks, and the need to be right far outweighed the need to make a connection and move people. After five years of working with Ned, Wayne believed his advice and suggestions were beginning to resonate with him.

Wayne learned to love this man for his passion. More impressive was Ned's compassion for the people who worked for him. This was a side of the man that most people were not fortunate to witness.

Ned was always there no matter how often he and Wayne disagreed, how insane Ned's actions and words seemed, or how impassioned Wayne's pleas were to forge positive change within the company. He truly listened to Wayne's concerns and deep down wanted to improve the workplace, but there wasn't much Ned could do any longer because he was gradually being pushed out by Corey, Carl, and Chad.

Wayne challenged Ned when no one else would. He called him on his arrogance when no one else would. He was open and honest with Ned when no one else was. Well, no one else aside from Charlize. All the while, Ned showed his brilliance in crafting the story and message that carved the path for Pigeon Financial's success.

No one else in the company or the industry was doing what Ned was. It took a while for Ned's message to resonate with the sales team, their accounts, and advisors. Often, he lost people at "negative convexity" and the "Japanification of rates." His ideas and concepts were a little ahead of their time, as the industry was not quite ready to embrace fixed indexed annuities as a legitimate fixed income alternative.

The typical fixed annuity producer was not building fixed income portfolios and bond ladders, so his message did not resonate with them. The typical fixed income producer who was laddering bonds and building fixed income portfolios was not using fixed annuities as a part of their strategy, so Ned's ideas were lost on them.

Nonetheless, his approach was brilliant, and the sales force slowly began to embrace his ideas. The competition followed suit when they began plagiarizing his ideas, which is normal and expected in business.

It was Wayne's observation and belief that Ned was like that kid on the playground in middle school who was picked on. Yet, somewhere along the way, he learned to play the game by adopting the behavior of an obnoxious asshole to succeed in the cutthroat, greedy business world. It worked for Ned and countless other executives, so this approach to the business world was carried forward.

Having grown tired of witnessing executives and upper management pounding their chests and treating employees like shit, Wayne realized that he, too, had a voice and decided he was no longer going to idly sit by, allowing these assholes in positions of power to abuse that power.

Wayne felt very little would change despite the numerous times he spoke with Ned, Corey, and Chad about the problems within Pigeon Financial. Wayne felt the one person he could confide in was Ned, who was his only hope for positive change.

Wayne continued his dialogue with Ned intermittently, but gradually over time, Ned's authority to make any change deteriorated. Wayne even pleaded with Amy when she was in charge, but there was not much she could do, and then they fired her. Wayne continued pushing for change until it got to a point at which Wayne practically asked Ned to fire him.

In October 2017, Wayne was with Ned and Corey in Mount Laurel, New Jersey, for another week of travel and meetings with NA Bank. The following day, they would meet in New York for morning meetings with Bear and Bull Financial.

The Tuesday meeting with NA Bank was a three-and-a-half-hour partner review meeting in which they reviewed the entire relationship: sales, marketing, operations, compliance, technology, product—everything. Wayne sat through the meeting but felt completely lost. All his energy was depleted, and he felt sick to his stomach.

Afterward, they grabbed lunch at P. J. Whelihan's a few minutes from the NA Bank office building. Wayne gave Corey and Ned a ride to the restaurant. At the conclusion of lunch, Corey and Ned would take a car to New York for their meeting with Bear and Bull Financial the following day.

They walked into the restaurant to be greeted by the hostess who escorted them over to their table in the middle of the restaurant. They sat at the table in an awkward silence while Wayne formulated a way to have a conversation with Ned to let him know he had had enough of the bullshit and wanted to part ways. Wayne could have easily had the conversation with Corey, but he felt he could not confide in Corey. His only remaining hope for change was with Ned.

Wayne wondered if he was gradually becoming a part of the problem. All the negative energy from the toxic work environment was wearing on him. He was miserable, and it was now reflected in his work. Unexpectedly, Corey excused himself to go to the restroom. Wayne jumped at the opportunity.

"Ned, thank you for everything you have done for me over the years." He looked over his shoulder to make sure Corey was out of sight. "I just can't do this any longer. I am tired of the deceit, lack of support, and lack of action. I often hoped that I'd get a call from you or Corey with an offer to leave the company."

Ned's face sank, and his complexion became a pale white. "What are you talking about?"

"The entire team and department have gone downhill. I'm tired of Fiona and Elaine disrupting things and wreaking havoc. I'd much rather work somewhere else where my efforts are appreciated. After I created the three proposals, you guys did nothing! I just want out. I have no idea anymore what you guys want from me or the team.

Who the hell is in charge? Is it you? Is it Corey? Carl? Chad? You're all acting like a bunch of fucking kids."

The look of worry on Ned's face spoke a thousand words. He was about to speak when Corey returned to the table. Things fell silent again, and lunch dragged on until Ned paid the bill. They slowly meandered awkwardly out of the restaurant.

Their car to New York was awaiting them outside the restaurant, and they walked to Wayne's car to grab their luggage. Corey grabbed his suitcase out of the backseat, shook hands with Wayne, and walked over to the car. Ned waited for Wayne to open the trunk so he could grab his bag. When they walked around to the back of the car, Wayne grabbed his luggage and placed it on the ground. Ned's transition lenses began to darken in the sunlight, but Wayne could still see the concern in his eyes. They shook hands and embraced.

"Can you sit tight? Give it a little longer. We will work things out for you."

Wayne knew Ned wanted to help. "Sure, Ned, but what choice do I have?" Wayne had heard those same words from that asshole Fred at Doe Financial, who eventually turned his back on the entire team.

Ned walked over to the car, slid inside, and closed the door behind him. The car cruised off to New York. Wayne felt good about laying that on Ned so he could stew over it with Corey on their two-hour car ride to New York.

Wayne took the train the following morning to join Ned and Corey in New York for their meeting with Bear and Bull Financial. He grabbed a coffee from the Starbucks across the street and met Ned and Corey in the lobby of the building complex at Bryant Park.

They took a few minutes to chat before their meeting, and like the day before, for the slightest moment, Corey walked away. Ned spoke up. "I spoke with Corey about our conversation yesterday. He's fully aware of your concerns and will do his best to make sure things work out."

"Thank you, Ned. I appreciate it." Wayne genuinely appreciated Ned's support but was not buying it. After all this time, nothing had happened, and deep down, he felt Ned's words were an empty promise and nothing would result, once again.

During their hour-long annual review with Bear and Bull Financial, Wayne began to feel sick to his stomach, like he did the day before. He didn't want to play the games any longer. If this was the game to be played, Wayne no longer wanted any part of it. He understood and appreciated the strategy and negotiation that applied to his accounts and clients but having to play this apparent game with his colleagues was bullshit. It was more of a child's game rather than a game of strategy, execution, and success.

As the meeting concluded, they shook hands with the Bear and Bull Financial management team and went on their way. Together, they rode the elevator down 31 flights to the lobby of One Bryant Park. After exiting the elevator, Corey walked ahead through the revolving doors outside to hail a cab for their ride to the airport.

For a moment, Ned and Wayne remained behind. "Wayne, can you hang tight. We should have something for you in the next month or two."

"Yeah, okay, Ned. Thanks," Wayne responded. "I appreciated what you are doing."

This had dragged on for too long, and Wayne no longer knew what to believe. All he wanted to do was to catch the train home. They shook hands, and Wayne began his walk to Penn Station.

Words to Lead By

Q: What is this apparent "game" that we are supposed to play in the business world?

It is not a game when you mess with people's livelihoods. It is not a game when you wreak havoc within the organization.

Do people go to college and pursue a major with a belief that their career is going to end up being a game?

You Must Prove that You are the Right Person for the Job

Their greatest fear is that somebody working near them might challenge them or show them up for being a dimwit! Ego is stronger than fear of business failure.

—*Liz Ryan*

It was now early December 2017. Wayne was in Bellevue, Washington, once again for a day of meetings on Wednesday and an all-employee meeting on Thursday. Wayne asked Ned to grab coffee with him so they could discuss the mythical promotion to find out what was going on.

They agreed to meet first thing in the morning at the Starbucks in the office building next to Pigeon Financial. Ned and Wayne ordered their coffees and grabbed a seat in two big leather chairs in the atrium. The atrium was a few steps down from the Starbucks. If anyone passed by, they could have easily heard what was being said.

"The best salesperson doesn't always make the best leader. Although you are our best relationship manager, that doesn't guarantee you will be a good manager," Ned said to Wayne. "You still need to prove to Corey that you will be a good leader."

"I agree. Sometimes the best salesperson doesn't make a great leader." Wayne processed Ned's words, not exactly sure how he was supposed to take his comment. Ned wasn't the greatest leader. His idea of leadership was being the smartest guy in the room and making others feel inferior. Ned's point was taken because Ned was neither a sales guy nor a relationship manager. Wayne finished his thoughts and responded, "Ned, I already display strong leadership characteristics with the relationship management team, the sales team, and our accounts. Maybe you could help me understand what your definition of a good leader is because I am not so sure our definitions are aligned. I am hearing you say that I need to be a strong leader. I don't disagree, and I've already proven my leadership capabilities. If Corey is looking for someone who will get in line and who does as he says, abiding by his bureaucratic, authoritative, self-serving leadership style, then you've got another think coming. If he wants someone who leads the way he does, then I am not interested. Thanks, but no thanks!" Wayne's comments were abrasive but honest. He was no longer buying it and spoke up for himself and his peers. If he was going to follow in their footsteps and embrace their leadership style, then he did not want the promotion.

"Wayne, I don't believe Corey wants you to be like him."

"Are you sure, Ned? Have you ever asked him?"

"Let me put it this way. In this management position, you must be willing to compromise. For example, if you believe purple is the best color and you emphatically state your case for purple, but Corey and the management team decide red is the best color, then you are going to have to cut your losses, concede, and agree with their decision that red is the best color and support everything red."

"Ned, I will try not to be offended by your comment."

"Why would you be offended?"

"Because I have been telling your damn red story all along. I have supported all of management's decisions and conceded on every occasion. Your comment is ignorant. It tells me you haven't been paying attention. Everything you have proposed over the years, I made work. I've improved it! I've done the same with Corey and his bullshit product scripts. Come on, Ned, this is child's play and an insult to the wholesalers and our team. So, please tell me where this is coming from. Regardless, if they decide on red, I will comply and support their decision just as I always have. And you know what else? They've made some pretty stupid decisions, decisions I supported despite how amateurish they were."

Ned nodded. "Okay, fair enough. Look, Wayne, you need to convince Corey that you are the right man for the job."

As Wayne confided in Ned, seeking his guidance and support, it became increasingly clear that Ned no longer had any pull or authority. His position of power and influence was fading. At that point, it was clear that Carl, Corey, and Chad were calling the shots. Ned was being pushed to the sidelines.

Wayne tried to maintain his cool but could not hide his growing frustration. "Ned, you and Corey have been talking to me about a promotion for three years. Every time I speak with you about it, you tell me to give it a little while longer. For three years? Come on! Nothing has been done to address the mounting issues and inefficiencies! Do you have a job to offer me or not?"

"Wayne, all I am saying is that you need to convince Corey you are the right guy for the role. I support you and want you to get the promotion, but you have to convince Corey," came Ned's response—a response that had no backbone.

"After all I have done for this company! After all I have done to bring Pigeon Financial from a nobody product carrier to the number-one indexed carrier at Chariot Horse Advisors! And the work I have done at DOL Financial, Bear and Bull Financial, NA Bank, and all the other accounts! Ned, I have done a fucking stellar job. It's not my nature to boast or brag, but I am good at what I do, and I've done a fucking excellent job for this damn company!'"

"Yes, you have, Wayne, and I am grateful," Ned replied, nodding his head with a look of fear.

"You've been leading me on for three years, blowing smoke with your empty promises of a fucking promotion and things getting better around here! Although sales are still strong and our success continues to grow, everything else has turned to shit. The morale sucks. People want to leave, but it's tough to land a job anywhere else, so they are stuck accepting this demoralizing shit show of a workplace. Do you really want to be remembered for that?"

Ned paused for a moment to process what Wayne was saying. "Of course I don't."

"Whether you like it or not, Ned, that's exactly what's happening. The workplace should *not* be so toxic! Especially when most of us spend sixty to eighty hours a week on the job, away from home and away from our families. I don't need to convince him of anything! You are out of your fucking mind!" Wayne's words echoed through the atrium as he continued his emotion-laden rant, "Whatever it is you are selling, I no longer want it. Even if there really is any opportunity to lead the team, I don't need to convince anyone that I'm the right person for the job. On the contrary, you need to convince me that I even want the fucking job! I have proven myself repeatedly. What else is there for me to prove? You are out of your damn mind!"

Ned sat in silence with a stunned look on his face while Wayne continued his onslaught, "I'm tired of the games, Ned. If there really is a job, you can fucking keep it!"

"Listen, Wayne, your points are valid, and I don't disagree. You are the best relationship manager we have. I am grateful for your work and what you've accomplished for the company and me. But can you please rethink this? Is there anything that would make you reconsider?"

"No!" Wayne replied without hesitation.

Ned persisted, "Wayne. Come on. Think about it."

The blood flow returned to Wayne's head as he regained some of his composure. "Ned, we've had this same conversation too many times to count, yet things continue to get worse. The team is burnt out and beyond frustrated. Corey is not providing any guidance, making things more difficult for the team. We can't even scratch our own asses without his approval. It's nearly impossible to get things done or simply move things along without Corey and Carl's approval."

"Can you think about it first? You've worked so hard and have been pushing for this opportunity." Ned paused. "Is there anything that would make you change your mind."

Seeing the deep concern on Ned's face and hearing the integrity and honesty in his question, he replied, "You. I'd do it for you."

Wayne did not really know where the words came from. His compassion for the people he worked with and desire to institute positive change made him concede.

"Schedule time to speak with Corey about this as soon as possible. Let him know you are the right man for the job."

"Okay," Wayne replied.

They stood up, shook hands, and walked together back to the office.

It was in that moment when Wayne realized how much Ned really cared, but it was too late. Although Wayne said he would do it for Ned, it was going to take a miracle for Wayne to get his spark, energy, and passion for the job back.

Wayne sent Corey a text message to meet the following day, and they scheduled time to meet at seven o'clock the following morning for breakfast before the all-employee meeting.

Wayne didn't look forward to meeting with Corey. He felt like his soul had been sucked from him. He no longer cared. He no longer showed emotion. He was just going through the motions, but with no energy or enthusiasm, sort of like the actively disengaged who go to work with no purpose or energy for their job.

Wayne had felt this before in prior jobs, and when it got to this point, he was not the sort of person to just show up and collect a paycheck. For Wayne, there was more to it than just a job. It had purpose; it was an opportunity to become better professionally and personally, both for himself and his colleagues.

This was clearly not Corey's or Carl's intention. Their intention was in gaining more power and authority so they could step on and over people while the pride and confidence of employees were driven into the gutter.

As usual, he had a good idea how his meeting with Corey would go with the usual emotionless, robotic questions. This should have made it quite predictable for Wayne, sort of like having the opponent's playbook, but it would not unfold that way.

Going through the same dialogue, the same rote questions and responses from Corey over and over again year after year without any action being taken became very tiresome and frustrating. It felt like yet another "Asshole's Fable of the Company Who Cried Wolf."

The next morning, Wayne met Corey in the restaurant of the Marriott for breakfast before the all-employee meeting. Immediately upon sitting down, Corey hit Wayne with one of his usual bullshit questions: "Uh. So, Wayne, tell me what your definition of relationship management is."

Although Wayne knew what Corey's questions would be, he could not help but be annoyed by his repetitive and robotic approach. *Are you fucking kidding me! You keep asking me the same damn question every time we discuss this. Have you been paying attention to anything we've discussed over the past three years?* Collecting his thoughts, Wayne regained his composure to snap out of his daydream and responded, "Well, Corey, I am not really sure anymore. Relationship management is the face of the organization for our clients." Wayne's reply lacked any emotion. He felt sick to his stomach, hearing Corey ask the same damn questions. It was clearly laid out and discussed in the roles and responsibilities proposals Wayne put together.

Wayne replayed Arnold Schwarzenegger's words about standing on the shoulders of giants, leaders and mentors who supported him on his journey. But, at Pigeon Financial, it was quite the opposite. The team carried Corey and Carl on their backs while they left the team tired and beaten. That was not real leadership. That was mindless, self-serving tyrannical leadership.

Corey proceeded to share his definition of relationship management: "Well, Wayne. Uh, let me tell you what I think relationship management is. Relationship management is the automation of systems and processes for national accounts …" Corey rambled on.

This infuriated Wayne so much that he was unable to concentrate. He did everything he could to prevent himself from jumping across the table and smashing his fist into Corey's face. "Makes sense," Wayne commented.

"Cool. Uh, what do you think the critical components of a successful relationship management team are?" was Corey's next question, and Wayne realized that he was being interviewed.

Is this fucker interviewing me? Wayne thought to himself. Unbeknownst to Wayne, he had sat down to an interview that morning. Maintaining his composure once again, Wayne responded, "Corey, a successful relationship management team collaborates with the departments to meet and exceed the division's goals and objectives. This collaboration includes and is not limited to clients, sales operations, marketing, and national sales. This collaborative approach ensures the successful implementation of Pigeon Financial's goals and initiatives for our clients and sales force. At the end of the day, relationship management is the face of the company and is ultimately responsible for the overall success through a well-orchestrated approach," Wayne responded in a robotic, disinterested fashion, mirroring Corey's personality style.

"Cool. Uh, here is what I think the critical components of a successful relationship management team are …" Corey droned on in his monotonic, robotic style again.

"Sounds good, Corey. That makes sense." This was becoming Wayne's go-to reply when he lost interest but had to appear as though he was still engaged in the conversation. A few years before, his response would have been one of enthusiasm, excitement, and action. Wayne was dead inside. He sounded like every other employee who eventually gives up, joining the actively disengaged, no longer giving a shit, those who are there to collect a paycheck and go home.

"What's the problem? You seem upset." Corey looked up toward Wayne.

Wayne could not maintain his composure any longer yet still attempted to remain as emotionally neutral as possible. "Nope, fine, Corey …" Wayne paused. "I clearly defined the role of relationship management for you in the three proposals that I created for you over the past two years. Not to mention the countless calls and meetings over the past few years in which we discussed the same thing. I have serious doubts that you are even paying attention to any of this.

Why do you keep asking the same questions and still haven't done anything about it?" Wayne continued, "Sorry, but let me correct my prior comment. I'm not fine. In fact, I am very disappointed. Going back to the first time we reviewed the proposals in Charlotte, you asked the same questions you are asking today, the same questions that were addressed and answered in the proposals. Come on, Corey. Is this a game to you? Do you find enjoyment in your mindless way of management? Show a little consideration and respect for me and the team. I'm tired of wasting my time."

"Wayne, I read the proposals. That's the way I handle meetings by asking questions," Corey responded with a tone of irritation. Wayne could see Corey about to lose his shit. "Is there something I should be doing differently?" Corey asked.

"Well, yes. I would like to provide honest feedback without you retaliating."

"What do you mean, Wayne? I don't think that's fair. I am open to hearing your comments. I just asked for your feedback, didn't I?" Corey replied with a tone of frustration.

"Really, Corey? I gave you my honest feedback just a moment ago, but your retaliatory response made it very clear to me that you aren't listening but instead taking offense because my comment clearly pissed you off. Don't ask these questions if you are not ready to hear the truth. You ask the same damn questions over and over again and do nothing with it."

"Wayne, I think you need to step back a moment," Corey replied, doing his best to remain calm.

"No, I don't, Corey. You are the one who needs to take a step back. You keep asking the same questions as though that's enough. Stop asking the same damn questions and checking your fucking boxes. How about you do something instead. You asked that same question a couple of years ago, when I mentioned names before numbers and Rule Number Eight from *The Energy Bus*, to love your passengers. This company has gone downhill from a morale standpoint. The energy in this place is awful—at the home office, on our calls, and in our meetings. It's clearly affecting our work and the work of the division. Fortunately, you have a group of professionals who care enough to make sure the company succeeds despite your ignorance. The relationship management team, along with the wholesalers, have so much pride that they won't allow themselves to fail regardless of the incompetence displayed by you and the so-called leadership in this company."

"What do you mean, Wayne? Give me an example. Who is saying this?" Corey abruptly responded. He was clearly flustered.

"Everyone, Corey! They don't mention it because they're tired of your continued ignorance of the issues, and even worse, they're afraid of getting into trouble for speaking up."

"Who?" Corey asked.

"Come on, Corey. All of us! Me, Charlize, Melanie, Patrice, Adam, Jean. The entire team, Corey! Don't you see it? What the hell happened? You have become so unreceptive to feedback and ideas from the team. This is a complete one-eighty from a few years ago."

"I haven't heard this from anyone, Wayne!" Corey firmly stated, becoming increasingly angered.

"Of course, you haven't. Like I said, they've gone silent. Even despite our continual expression of concern about the morale and dysfunction, you somehow disregard it. Come on, Corey! I, for one, have voiced my concerns, and so has Charlize. And when you tell her 'it isn't any worse than other companies,' that's a goddamn cop-out. It is worse than other companies. Why are you settling for average? Who wants to be like everyone else, especially if it's as disconnected as Pigeon Financial? I'd hope you had greater aspirations for yourself and the company. If it were me, I sure as hell would want my company to be better than the industry average. If we weren't at the top, I would want to know why. Yet here we are, having the same conversation with no action."

"Come on, Wayne. That's not true."

"Do you really believe that, Corey? You can call it what you want. What about the way Patrice was treated when she was asked to recertify her work-from-home status? All the years in this business and of all the shitty things I've witnessed, this one took the cake!

You should consider yourself lucky you don't have a lawsuit on your hands. The way it was handled was atrocious!"

"That's enough, Wayne!" Corey retaliated. "Patrice was asked to recertify her work-from-home status because it's a requirement by law, and the HR team had to receive the certification."

"Look, Corey. I get it and understand the HR team needs her to recertify every year. But the way it was handled was an embarrassment. She's worked here for more than ten years, and this was the first time her work-from-home status was handled in this fashion. Nothing changed other than Elaine's abrasive approach, which I believe was influenced by Carl and Fiona. Elaine was in over her head. She didn't know how to properly approach this, nor did she have the confidence or clarity to see through Carl's deceptive ways. Open your eyes, Corey. Fiona started her own work-from-home schedule without medical clearance or managerial approval. She did it out of spite, and there was no one there to tell her otherwise. All of this happened because you lost control of the sales ops team and lost sight of the relationship management team. Patrice should not be the one being persecuted here. You handled this poorly. By the way, how do you explain the work-from-home status, or remote work, for Jake in product and Ethan on the life insurance team? They decided to relocate and were granted permission to work from home without legitimate reasons other than they didn't want to commute to the office any longer. Yet, you chastise Patrice, despite her legitimate and often life-threatening health issue. You should be ashamed of yourselves." Wayne paused. "What about the time you approached Charlize privately, accusing her of monopolizing the team calls, and you told her to stop speaking on the calls?"

"Yes, I did because I wanted the rest of the team to have an opportunity to speak," Corey retorted.

"I have news for you, Corey. It's not because Charlize monopolizes everyone's time. No one speaks on the calls anymore because you shut us down. Leaders who don't listen will eventually be surrounded by people who have nothing to say. The irony of your ignorant demand of Charlize was after she heeded your words of advice and toned down her comments, on the next team call, you immediately approached her privately afterward and grilled her about why she was so quiet. You don't even see the absurdity of your comments!"

"Okay, Wayne. That's enough! You need to put these things into perspective. You haven't considered what the teams have on their plates and what they are responsible for."

"Really, Corey? Perspective? I put things into perspective, and what I see is a company off the rails. You and Carl are out of control. Yet, we are making you look good because we cannot bear to see the retirement division fail. We keep cleaning up the mess, while you continue to sit pretty on your perch, reaping the rewards from our efforts. And when we make any mention of it or express our concerns, you become retaliatory. The entire team has become silent, and it's not because of Charlize. The only person who speaks up any longer is Charlize because Charlize can't help herself. Despite growing tired of the neglect and disregard for the team, she keeps pressing on. Thank goodness for her, though. The rest of us no longer have anything to say to you."

"Wayne, hold on. What are you talking about? No one has brought this to my attention." Corey interrupted. Wayne saw Corey losing his patience and becoming more enraged.

"Well, Corey, thanks for proving my point. When you ask me what I am talking about, it simply confirms that you are not paying attention. You have your head so far in the clouds you cannot see anything else. The team calls are one-sided and have become more of a dictatorship. Yeah, you open it up for questions, but we remain silent because we're tired of the dysfunction, the inaction, and the disrespect. On the rare occasion when we speak up, your response is demeaning, and you are clearly annoyed. The morale of the team is pitiful. The IRMs are tired of doing the SOMs work. We are tired of cleaning up all the mistakes. We are tired of getting our wrists slapped for doing our job. The entire time we've made it very clear what our concerns are and even offered to help by providing suggestions for improvement, yet you do nothing about it. As I have previously mentioned, you have to love your people, and you clearly don't. It appears you love the numbers far more than the people. We, the people, are the ones who make the numbers possible in the first place."

"Uh, Wayne, it is clear we are not seeing eye to eye," Corey responded, doing his best to contain himself. "You need to be objective. Have you considered what Elaine's responsibilities are and our responsibilities as a company?"

"Yes, Corey, I have been objective. I am doing my best to understand Elaine's responsibilities, the company's, and even yours. But you've lost sight of your responsibility as a leader. You've lost sight of the deplorable way your employees are being treated. I am beginning to believe you condone this deplorable approach to management. This is not limited to Patrice; there are plenty of employees who are fed up, but they just won't speak up because they're afraid."

"Who are you talking about, Wayne?"

"Do I really have to tell you who? You've got to be kidding! What about Mary? She's been treated like shit, and so has Jean. Even Adam is tired of the lack of guidance on the team. Quite frankly, I believe you have a far greater issue on your hands."

"Where is this coming from?"

"Come on, Corey, don't do that with me."

"Do what?"

"Act like you don't know about it. Mary is a ticking time bomb, a time bomb you guys created."

"Wayne, you are overstepping your bounds."

"Am I really, Corey? The employees of this company, at least in this division, are managed in an unprofessional and demeaning fashion. We all see it, but very few are willing to confront you about it."

"Okay, Wayne. That's enough!"

"For today, it's enough, but you can't dispute what I am saying. All you have been able to do so far is tell me to put it in perspective and be objective. The problem is bigger than Pigeon Financial, and comparing it to another company is a cop-out. You should strive to be better than that. Just because the morale at other companies is in the shitter, like it is here, doesn't make it right! So, stop condoning your atrocious behavior because everyone else is acting like an asshole. You sound like a kid telling himself that his bad behavior is permissible because all the other kids are acting like assholes!"

"You've given me a lot to think about, and I want you to think about what you have said this morning. We will need to continue this discussion at another point. We have to get to the all-employee meeting. I will have Deanna schedule another time for us to meet."

"Okay. Thanks, Corey."

They got up from the table and walked together through the streets of Bellevue in silence for a few blocks to the all-employee meeting at the Westin Hotel.

Wayne had quite possibly destroyed any opportunity for a promotion and felt like a dead man walking. Any semblance of joy, passion, and enthusiasm for work had finally been sucked out of him. He had endured long enough, after six long years at Pigeon Financial. This was the beginning of the end.

Wayne knew it was not like that everywhere, or at least it should not be like that everywhere. He knew there were great companies with excellent leadership who treated their employees right. Wayne realized that he, too, needed to change his perspective for things to improve. Being continually sucked in by the negativity made it much easier to overlook the positives. Sort of like names before numbers, he needed to find a healthy balance by strengthening and honoring the positive while improving the negative.

Wayne and Corey arrived at the Westin Hotel. They rode the escalator to the second floor of the hotel where the meeting was being held. On the way up the escalator, Wayne sent a text message to Charlize to see if she was already at the meeting to let her know he was on his way. Upon reaching the second level, Wayne and Corey went their separate ways.

Dozens of employees were buzzing about, grabbing coffee, water, a snack or taking a bathroom break and chatting before the meeting commenced. When Wayne met up with Charlize, he shared the dialogue from that morning with Corey and the day before with Ned.

Words to Lead By

Q: Are you able to see past your ego and the numbers to see your people?

> Their greatest fear is that somebody working near them
> might challenge them or show them up for being a
> dimwit! Ego is stronger than fear of business failure.
> —Liz Ryan

# Love Calls, but Hate Would Have You Stay

Love calls, but hate would have you stay.

—*A Course in Miracles*

December 2017 and the holidays were near with the New Year right around the corner. The national sales meeting, which was scheduled for the first full week of the year, was approaching. This meant Wayne would spend yet another holiday stressing about the meeting rather than relaxing and enjoying time with his family.

There was good news on the horizon though. The job opportunity as the head of relationship management finally manifested! The bad news was that Corey posted the job rather than promoting Wayne. This was not exactly the way Wayne had been led to believe it would happen—after three years of the bullshit, after proving himself, after creating the roles and responsibilities proposals, after all the success he and the team had created with their accounts.

Wayne was the fool for assuming he could earn a promotion by being offered the job without having to interview for it—although it felt as though he had been interviewing for the job for more than three years. *I guess that's what my brother meant about playing the game. Well, the hell with the game! If this is how fellow teammates and players are treated, then I no longer care to play. This is bullshit!*

When she saw the job posting, Charlize immediately called Wayne. They spoke about what was going on, why Wayne did not receive the promotion, and whether either one of them would apply for the job.

Charlize remained firm in her stance and wanted nothing to do with a management job at Pigeon Financial. She reminded Wayne that when Nelson and Amy were in the role, they practically walked into the job. It was not posted for anyone else to apply, and neither one of them were subjected to an interview process. They were basically handed the job.

This did not make Wayne feel any better. He still wanted to pursue the job despite the obvious signs that he should consider otherwise. To add to his angst and frustration, Wayne begrudgingly prepared for the national sales meeting. In the past, Wayne would have easily welcomed the opportunity to spend his holiday planning for a national sales meeting, but this was no longer the case. In fact, it ruined his holiday. Wayne did not want to be there and certainly did not care to begin his New Year in the company of Carl and Corey.

On Tuesday, January 9, Wayne arrived at the national sales meeting in Scottsdale, Arizona. Scottsdale was one of his favorite places. He and his wife had lived there many years prior in 2002.

He met up with his teammates outside the conference room. They talked among themselves about the holidays while greeting the wholesalers as they arrived. Many of the wholesalers expressed bewilderment at the job being posted and expressed their regret for Wayne not receiving the promotion. They knew he earned it and wanted to see him get the job.

The energy at the meeting that year was off more than the usual misaligned energy. Everyone wanted to know what was going on. The wholesalers scoffed at Carl now in the role as the head of national sales. They joked about how awful he was as a leader, clearly holding very little respect for him. They spoke about prior national sales meetings and the drunken antics Carl pulled and joked about what bullshit antics they expected from him this year.

There were whispers about Chad recently being passed up for the CEO role. They reminisced about prior national sales meetings when Ned jumped on top of the table, ranting and raving while throwing papers, trying to motivate the team. They talked about Wayne being passed up for a promotion as the head of relationship management. Practically everyone expected him to receive a promotion, but to everyone's surprise, Corey posted the job, putting

Wayne through more of the same bullshit and mind games. What came as an even bigger surprise was Ned's new position as the head of channel distribution. This was a newly created role and division that seemingly came out of nowhere and appeared to be another step toward pushing Ned aside.

Wayne decided not to apply for the job, although deep down, he still desired the opportunity. During the second day of the meeting, Corey sent Wayne a text message, asking if he had applied for the job. Wayne was at a loss for words and incensed by Corey's ignorance. Having grown tired of the games, he did not respond. Deep down, he wanted to tell Corey to go fuck off, but he knew he had to respond at some point.

A few minutes later, Chad sent Wayne a message suggesting they meet that afternoon. This was in response to Wayne's message to Chad leading up to the national sales meeting, asking that they set up time to speak. They agreed to meet that afternoon at two o'clock, which gave Wayne some time to delay his response to Corey.

Wayne and Chad broke away from the afternoon business sessions to meet outside in the courtyard where the group had had lunch an hour prior. The tables were empty, and the sun shone brightly down as they spoke. Chad's demeanor had changed from their many conversations before. Over the years working together, he had always been open, honest, and supportive of Wayne, but this time, he seemed off; something was different. Chad's words and tone had changed, sounding vague and more corporate.

The rest of the dialogue was a smattering of vague bullshit and empty words. "Is this about the job being posted?" Chad asked Wayne.

"Yes, it is," Wayne confirmed.

"I assume you are upset because you didn't receive the promotion."

"Yes, I am, Chad."

"Well, Wayne, you shouldn't be upset about it. You are good guy, and I am sure if you apply, you'll do well in the interview process."

"Chad, can you explain to me why you posted the job after all of the effort I put into this role over the past three years? Why, after creating the roles and responsibilities proposals, clearly outlining the job detail for relationship management and sales ops? Why, after all we did as a team coming together to create all this success despite a complete absence of leadership? I have the team's support. They know I deserve the job. Even the wholesalers want to know why I wasn't promoted. Please explain that to me."

"Listen, Wayne. I didn't get the CEO job. Am I disappointed? Yeah, of course, I am. But I am not going to allow that to stop me. I am going to look at the opportunities I have in my new role as the head of the retirement division and life division. I am looking for the positives in this, and you should as well."

You're such an asshole! The words came to Wayne's mind. *You can't compare my situation to yours. I'm well qualified and have earned the promotion, while you are certainly not CEO material. At least not yet.*

Another irony of Chad's ignorant comment was that, despite not getting the CEO role he was promoted to run both the retirement and life divisions. He was in a position with more power and authority than before. It was easy for him to sit back and tell Wayne to look for the positives, while he sat pretty with a promotion, one he did not interview for.

You son-of-a-bitch! You have the balls to compare my situation to yours! You ignorant asshole! Don't sit in front of me and cry your sob story. You're not CEO material! You're the executive vice president of two sales divisions, and you are hung up on not getting the CEO role? Douche bag.

Wayne was well qualified for the promotion he was seeking. It was all but expected that he would get the promotion. In contrast, Chad was not ready. He was not CEO material, at least at that point in his career.

"Well, Chad, I am upset. Do you really expect me to continue the games you guys are playing and apply for this job to continue down this path? I don't think that's going to happen. For the six years I've worked here, you've been dangling a promotion in front of me, and then you spit in my face and post the job? Come on, Chad."

Chad babbled some more corporate bullshit lines. "Look, Wayne. You're talented. We are growing. With Ned's new role, there might be an opportunity for you. I want you to think about new roles, new areas where we can use your expertise. Run them by me so we can discuss them. There might be something out there for you. Don't let this frustrate you. Like I said, I'm not going to allow it to frustrate me despite wanting the CEO role."

Wayne remembered the first time he had met Chad at the 2012 national sales meeting, which happened to be in Scottsdale, Arizona, as well. Chad stood in front of the entire sales division, fielding questions from the group. Wayne was blown away by his honesty and willingness to speak with the group. No questions were off limits. Wayne and his peers respected that about Chad—but not anymore; Chad's demeanor had turned corporate with no emotion.

"Okay, makes sense," Wayne said, which sadly had become his go-to comment. Wayne stood up and shook hands with Chad. "Thanks, Chad."

They walked back into the conference room to join the business session. Their conversation during the national sales meeting was one of the last times Wayne spoke with Chad.

Words to Lead By

Q: Do you remain in a job, or career, because you are afraid to make a change? What makes you stay and remain stuck versus finding the strength to move on?

☹ Pain is a Wrong Perspective

Change happens when the pain of staying the same is greater than the pain of change.

—*Tony Robbins*

Being creatures of habit, we typically do not know there is another way of living our lives or pursuing another career until it's too late or we find the strength to make positive change in our lives. It is a natural part of human existence; most never make any real change in their lives because they are afraid to, or the pain has not yet become so extreme that they are forced to break free by making a change and altering course.

This is analogous to the boiling a frog fable. If you place a frog in boiling water, the frog will jump out to safety. On the other hand, if you place the frog in tepid water and slowly bring the water to a boil, the frog will not perceive the threat and will gradually be cooked to death. Yecch!

Like the frog, Wayne and his colleagues were slowly being boiled to death in a toxic work environment. Thankfully, Wayne noticed this and jumped out before it was too late. Unfortunately, many others remained in the boiling pot of toxicity under the illusion that they had no other choice and that it was like that everywhere.

Working at Pigeon Financial had become quite a farce. Employees were deferring their own work by delegating it to other colleagues. This was not delegation executed properly but rather an abuse of colleagues and avoidance of work duties because they knew someone else would do their work for them. The continued lack of competent management and, at times, no management whatsoever meant no one in a leadership capacity was there to ensure the work was being completed properly.

The absence of leadership was astonishing. Corey, Carl, Ned, and Chad were constantly trying to sabotage one another. No one was there to lead the teams and hold the employees accountable for their work. Wayne and his teammates could not allow the work to remain unattended, so they completed the work that was neglected by other employees and departments.

Another misstep was an absence of proper training. If an actual training program had been deployed, the efficient and effective workflow upper management was striving to achieve would have been accomplished.

The teacher left the classroom. This absence of management contributed to a free-for-all. People did whatever they wanted or, in this case, very little. Some worked from home; others called out sick on a regular basis or created their own work hours and got away with it! No one was there to mind the house.

Wayne and his teammates did their best to keep management apprised of the situation on numerous occasions. Ultimately, very little to nothing was done to address or remedy the issues. The constant upheaval, lack of leadership, and lack of collaboration with management at Pigeon Financial contributed to things erupting around them. Wayne and his teammates had to take things into their own hands, guide the division, and clean up the mess left behind by upper management because of the lack of leadership.

Wayne sat at the kitchen table of his home talking with his wife. "After that anger-filled conversation the week before Christmas, I was afraid that it would be the last one. Well, at least for a little while," he confided. "Deep down, I hoped that we would pick up where we left off at some point in the future, but I really wasn't sure if that would ever happen. I needed to walk away and walk on my own for a while to figure things out."

"You didn't yell at her, did you?"

Wayne took a sip of his coffee, paused, and muttered, "Yes."

"Why? She is wonderful. Why would you treat her like that?"

"Hold on a second. Let me explain." He sat back in his chair. "When I am yelling, she knows it is not directed at her. In a way, it is a cleansing for me. She knows how to push me by asking the right questions and saying the right things. It is as though she instigates me, which brings my frustrations to the surface, allowing me to express and release them. This helps me realize that my anger is unwarranted. It is unwarranted because I totally misinterpret what she says. She's helping me see that my perspective is wrong, which allows me to see things more clearly. I am not sure if that makes sense."

"In a way, it does. I just don't understand why you're so upset," Sue said in her usual matter-of-fact style. She was an excellent grounding source for Wayne, allowing him to see when he was being irrational and complicating things.

"Yeah. I don't either, but for some reason, I'm pissed off. It seems difficult for me to just let it go. That's why I am working with Marianne to let go of the bullshit. I spent too much time chasing success and searching for my salvation in the approval from other people and even through work."

"But you are successful, Wayne."

"Yeah, thank you. But I don't feel that way. Something's missing."

"What could be missing?" she asked, taking a sip of her herbal tea.

"I don't know. It's sort of like I won't be satisfied until I feel as though I've arrived. Whatever the hell that means."

"But you have. Look at all that you've accomplished!" She could not comprehend where her husband was coming from. She stood up from the kitchen table and walked over to the sink to fill her water bottle.

"Yeah, but I don't feel it."

"Do you remember what you always tell me?"

"No, what?"

She walked back over to the kitchen table and sat down. "If you look for approval in the eyes of others, eventually someone is going to disappoint you."

"Yes, that's Abraham-Hicks." Wayne sighed. "I allowed myself to be disappointed for far too long. Especially in my career, I was looking for the approval of my bosses and even my colleagues, never taking pride in what I had accomplished."

"I still don't understand what's so difficult. What did you get into an argument about anyway?"

"It was about work. I'm tired of the bullshit from Corey, Carl, Ned, and Chad."

"Why can't you just ignore it and do your job?" Sue stated matter-of-factly, again.

It drove Wayne crazy when his wife was so up front and to the point, but he knew she was right. He just needed to remember Rule Number Six, to not take himself so Goddamn seriously!

"I wish I could ignore it and mindlessly go to work, but I just can't. I feel sick to my stomach whenever I have to go to a meeting. My jaw tightens, and I feel a lump in my throat whenever I have to get on another conference call."

"You expect too much out of people and yourself," she commented. "Just do your job and deal with it."

"I can't!" He broke down. "If I stay, I will continue my successful career, and I will make more money than ever before. Everything on the outside looks perfect, but I feel like I am dying on the inside. I'm sure all of this sounds crazy."

"Well, it does! Have you lost your mind?" she barked in frustration, losing her patience with Wayne.

"Yes, at times, I feel like I have. Working for this company is like a cancer slowly killing its host. I feel like I am slowly dying from the self-serving assholes in upper management who contribute to the toxic and demoralizing work environment. I'm sorry. I can't explain it."

"Well, neither can I. If you can't explain it, how can I understand it?"

"I believe there are those of us who feel we must suffer and struggle to be worthy of anything and feel a sense of achievement. I am one of them," he shamefully commented. "You know the saying 'No pain, no gain,' right?"

"Of course. Who doesn't?"

"What if I told you this wasn't true?"

"I would say that's a load of crap. Show me!"

"Exactly! You and almost everyone in the world agrees with those words. We believe that if we don't feel any pain or suffering, then we will not be successful, nor will we deserve it. On the other hand, what if you embraced the belief that you can be successful and deserving of wealth without having to work hard and struggle? Basically, shift your belief, or perspective, from 'no pain, no gain' to 'gain without any pain'?"

"Nah! That won't work," she remarked with skepticism. "How's that possible?"

"Have you ever known someone who seemed to have it all, money and success, and everything seemed to come easy for them?"

"Yes, I can think of a few people."

"That's an example of gain without any pain. But most people despise those who have everything without any pain or struggle. That is what I am talking about. It's a reframing of our perspective. We ditch the belief in our apparent need to suffer, our apparent need to feel pain, struggle, getting it wrong and losing to gain or succeed. We shift our perspective from what we perceive as painful moments and instead see them for what they truly are: learning and growing opportunities and experiences."

"Sometimes you make absolutely no sense. Whatever it is you are talking about, it's not possible," she challenged him.

"Stay with me. Think about our daughter's growing pains. To grow, our body must transform and go through these 'growing pains,' right?"

"Yeah."

"It's a necessary pain. But is it really a bad thing?"

"No, not really. It's our body growing, becoming stronger, healthier, and so on."

"Right! But why do we consider it 'painful'?"

"Because it is!"

"But if we shift our perspective from fearing the pain to welcoming it, things might change. We know it is a good pain.

It's something that allows us to grow, to become stronger. So, we shouldn't fear it."

"Huh? There you go making no sense again!" she prodded him.

"If we understand our growing pains as a wonderful thing, we may no longer consider the pain an awful thing ..."

"But wouldn't that support the idea of no pain, no gain? Because if we see these growing pains as positive learning or growing experiences, won't we believe that we must feel pain to gain?"

"Hmmm," he mumbled. "Yeah, I guess you're right, but that's a good example of perspective. If we choose to believe the pain is required to gain and grow, then we will believe there is no other way. All I am saying is that there is another way. Plus, the saying 'no pain, no gain' speaks to physical pain. For example, exercise, weightlifting, physical fitness, and so on. Somehow, along the way, it became associated with our job, life, and career. For example, why do we fear failure and often consider failure as painful?"

"I don't know, but I rarely fail." She smirked in her confident and determined manner.

"True. But we are not talking about you," Wayne said facetiously, rolling his eyes. "We are talking about the regular people among us who are not as talented as you," he played along. "Most people feel pain from failure because we have been taught to perceive it that way, versus seeing it for what it truly is."

"Which is?"

"Our greatest teacher! Without it, we would not succeed. All I'm saying is that it doesn't need to be so painful; there doesn't need to be so much struggle, so much sacrifice to be successful, happy, and wealthy."

"Well, if that exists, sign me up. I want some of that."

"If we learn to embrace failure and all of these apparently painful things as growing and learning opportunities, rather than struggle and suffering, maybe life would change as we know it."

"Okay. You had me, but then you lost me again. By the way, I am happy and don't need to change."

"All I am saying is, personally, I'm learning that I don't need to create pain and suffering, or believe in it, to be successful or wealthy. So, what I perceive as failure is a wrong perspective. Instead of feeling like a failure, I see it as an opportunity to grow and become better because I won't make the same mistake again. No fear."

"Why do you find it so difficult to be happy?" she mocked him.

"That is what I am trying to figure out. But is anyone really happy anyway?"

"There's nothing to figure out. Just be happy for fuck's sake!" she exclaimed.

"I am working on that. I realize that all this emotional and mental pain doesn't exist. Physical pain does exist, although it doesn't have to if we train our minds properly. This is an entirely different discussion for another time."

"It sure is!" she moaned. "Can I go now?"

"In a moment?" Wayne asked apologetically. "What if your life drastically changed for the better and the same things you desired all along—success, wealth, prosperity, health, and so on—all came to you with little effort? Would you believe it? Would you think you deserved it, considering you didn't work hard to get it?"

His wife glared at him. She sat in silence, which meant she was done with the conversation. Wayne continued, "Things that we think suck or are awful or shitty don't necessarily have to be if we change our belief system and understanding of them. We can feel gain without the pain. Because the pain is really a teaching or learning opportunity rather than something awful. This is one of those 'I'll believe it when I see it moments.'" Wayne gestured air quotes by raising his hands in the air and holding his index and middle fingers up like rabbit ears. "So, most people continue living their lives in pain, struggling and suffering because that is the way they believe it's supposed to be."

Still no response from his wife. Although she was physically sitting there in front of him, it appeared as though she had moved on mentally. Wayne continued his diatribe, "You must suspend all doubt and actually believe what you want before you see what you want. Most of us will only believe things when we see them; therefore, we are less likely to break through any limiting beliefs."

"Okay. I will take your word for it because you are talking about things that I don't fully comprehend," she interjected. "You really have done a great job. I do see the positive changes in your mannerisms and how you approach things."

"The problem is that all of these bullshit antics still occur in the workplace, which is not segregated to only Pigeon Financial. This sort of toxic, self-serving behavior is rampant in most companies. I'm tired of hearing bullshit comments like 'It's like that everywhere,' and 'the grass isn't always greener.' All that does is excuse and condone the shitty behavior by executives and upper management who run these companies into the ground. It shouldn't be this way!"

"I can't argue with you there. I am so glad I'm no longer in the corporate world. I don't envy what you are doing, but I honor it and am amazed by what you have accomplished."

"Thanks. All I want to do is give a voice to people who believe they don't have one. I am tired of seeing all the self-serving and mindless assholes who run these companies treat their employees like pieces of garbage. I am still trying to understand it and make peace with it, but there are times when I want to scream, 'Fuck you!' and tell them to go screw themselves."

"Ahh, there it is." She smiled. "That part of you does have to go. That's scary."

"Yeah, yeah. Thank you for keeping me grounded. I love you." He approached her with a kiss and loving embrace. "I need to understand why employees feel like they don't have a voice in the workplace. Is it possible for employers to love their people? I would really like to find another job where I am valued and don't have to deal with ignorant and incompetent leadership."

"But hasn't Pigeon Financial shown that they value you with the signing bonus, the Relationship Manager of the Year Award, and the stock ownership? Don't screw it up. You still have to support our family."

"I know. Thanks for the reminder."

Words to Lead By

Q: How do you make real change in business and life?

Change happens when the pain of staying the
same is greater than the pain of change.
—Tony Robbins

Pain is a wrong perspective.
—*A Course in Miracles*

⚠ No Risks in the Absence of Fear

> The way human nature is, we're never really calculated
> about our entry points. We're never really thoughtful
> about where we give in and what we are really risking.

— *Paul Tudor Jones*

Wayne took a three-month hiatus from working with his life coach, Marianne. He needed to take time to reflect on things and walk on his own. There was not much more Marianne could do for him at that point.

Since their last conversation in December 2017, a lot had transpired. Wayne applied for the job as head of relationship management, and in February, he accepted the job offer from Corey. But it looked as though it was too little too late. Continuing to witness the dysfunction and deceit, he no longer cared to work alongside Corey, Carl, Ned, and Chad. He had been depleted of all and any desire for his work and had grown tired of playing the games.

It was now March, and Wayne was speaking with his wife about his reunion with Marianne.

"So, how did your call with Marianne go?" Sue asked.

"It was good, like we never skipped a beat," he replied with a spark in his voice.

"How long was it since you last spoke?"

"About three months."

"What did you talk about?"

"Trying to summarize what had transpired over the past two thousand hours of my life in a one-hour conversation with Marianne wasn't easy, so I jumped right into everything."

"Like what?"

"Mainly my career and how tired I am of all of the bullshit."

"But you just got promoted. How can it be bad?" Sue asked, unaware of her husband's continued frustrations.

"How much time do you have? I don't bog you down with these things because I don't want you to worry or stress out about all of the shit that I stress about. Two stressed parents are not a good combination, although one stressed parent and one happy one is a slightly better scenario."

"Yeah, but I do like to know how things are going for you at work. I just worry when I hear how stressed you are."

"Okay. But please tell me if it's too much or you're sick of hearing about it. This is going to be a long one. If you need to walk away, I will understand."

"Sounds fair," she replied as she took a sip from her water bottle.

"Like I said, it was as though we had never skipped a beat, which is a wonderful thing about working with Marianne. We mainly talked about my promotion and the other job I interviewed for."

"Oh yeah, what happened with that job? That was with the technology company, right?"

While pursuing the promotion at Pigeon Financial, Wayne was also looking at other opportunities outside of Pigeon Financial. But landing another job when someone spends well over sixty hours a week at work constantly on the road with colleagues proves to be difficult.

The good news was that Wayne had been contacted by a headhunter for a national accounts job with an upstart FinTech company. He secured a Skype interview with the president of the company, who asked Wayne why he was pursuing the role and if he was concerned about the risk he would be taking by going with a start-up company.

Instead of focusing on the risks associated with leaving, Wayne considered what the risks would be if he remained at Pigeon Financial. People don't leave companies; they leave management. And when the leadership is deplorable, they run for the exits, often without a plan.

Wayne did his best to foresee questions he would receive from friends, family, and peers by thinking of man, or human beings in general, and taking away ego and fear of failure and judgment. Fear is of the ego, and the ego's foundation is fear; they are one and the same. Understanding that 99 percent of the replies and comments would emanate from the ego and a platform of fear made it easy for Wayne to foresee the reactions and comments he would receive: *What will happen if I make less money? What will happen if it doesn't work out? Why would I leave my current career? Why take the risk of nearly starting over and with an upstart? What will my family think? What if this is as good as it gets?*

This triggered thoughts about the movie *As Good as It Gets* with Jack Nicholson, Helen Hunt, and Greg Kinnear. In a scene from the movie, Melvin Udall was leaving his psychiatrist's office when the receptionist asked him, "How do you write women so well?"

Melvin Udall's response was, "I think of a man, and I take away reason and accountability."

That was how Wayne approached his decision to leave Pigeon Financial. He thought of a human being and removed fear and ego. This made his decision crystal clear. He also realized that there are no risks in the absence of fear.

The character Melvin Udall had a flawed perspective of the world. He was cruel, rude, sexist, judgmental, and downright ignorant. His behavior and actions represent the boss or manager who acts like an absolute asshole. You know the one; we have all had a boss, manager, or coach like Melvin Udall, someone who treats their employees like shit while no one does anything about it, until an angel arrives.

The angels in this case were Carol (Helen Hunt's character) and Simon (Greg Kinnear's character). Their ability to understand and forgive allowed Melvin Udall's inner angel to sing. We are all angels hiding behind an egotistical veil of being right, a need to win, fear of failure, on and on. The movie simply represents our ability to change our perspective, allowing us to change our life and career for the better. In this case, it was about removing our egotistical and fearful tendencies, which turns us into assholes. Although being an asshole may appear to work in the moment, it is tragic over time.

It did not make much sense for Wayne to pursue the job with the FinTech company. All things pointed to remaining at Pigeon Financial, but when pulling back the curtain to reveal the shit show behind the scenes at Pigeon Financial, Wayne knew it was time for a change.

If he made a change, the biggest challenge would be the worry and angst over whether it was a huge mistake. This is what keeps most people stuck in the same miserable patterns and not taking risks. This is what kept Wayne stuck and influenced his decision to accept the promotion. The fear of not taking the promotion and the fear of what he would lose by walking away kept him stuck despite the deplorable way Chad, Corey, and Carl ran things.

He thought long and hard about his decision, realizing he would rather take the risk of resigning instead of remaining at Pigeon Financial, continuing to work alongside those who stood on and stepped over the bodies and souls of others to get ahead. He preferred to succeed in his career and life because he stood on the shoulders of giants and knew deep down that his life was built on the foundation of parents, coaches, and teachers, of kind souls who guided him with honor, respect, and dignity.

If Wayne learned to properly plan for change, or risks, he could then make a totally imbecilic move and still be successful. Wayne had taken plenty of risks in his life, and his decision to resign would be one of them. He understood that his approach to risk control, or risk mitigation, had always been questionable at best.

As Paul Tudor Jones said, "The way human nature is, we're never really calculated about our entry points. We're never really thoughtful about where we give in and what we are really risking." Wayne especially needed to be thoughtful about what he was risking and to become more aware of his entry points.

The expression "if at first you don't succeed, try, try again" is a great one that speaks to persistence. But apparently the definition of insanity is doing the same thing over and over again and expecting different results. Therefore, if at first, we don't succeed and we try, try again or do the same thing over and over again, doesn't that mean we are really destined for failure and insanity?

The book *The Wisdom of Failure* (Weinzimmer/McConoughey 2012) does an excellent job of speaking to this. Too often, executives decide on a project in which they invest the company's money, the shareholders' money, and the employees' time to develop. When it doesn't work out, they try and try again, spending more time and money on the same project. Eventually, they reach a point of no return because their ego and pride are now at stake. This is a difficult position to be in because if they stop what they are doing, they are in effect admitting to failure. So, instead of conceding and cutting their losses in the short term to try a different approach, they continue doing what they have been doing, destined for failure.

If we are honest and set our ego and pride to the side, failing is not possible. Failing is really a synonym in disguise for learning. The Japanese proverb "Fall down seven times; stand-up eight" is an excellent understanding of failing.

Humans have an inherently strong will to live, or to stand up. For many, it may be a struggle to stand up, but eventually we do. Once we are standing, we either play it safe so we never fall again, or we take on new endeavors and risks to become better.

When we understand our fears and failures by learning from them, we can chart an entirely different course. As Henry David Thoreau said, "If one advances confidently in the direction of his dreams, and endeavors to live the life that he has imagined, he will meet with a success unexpected in common hours."

Wayne was taking a risk because he didn't want to die with his music still in him.

Words to Lead By

Q: As a leader, do you remain stuck, complacent, because you are afraid to make necessary changes in your business approach? As an employee, do you remain stuck, complacent, because you are afraid to make necessary changes in your life and career?

Like everyone, to get where I am, I stood on the shoulders of giants. My life was built on the foundation of parents, coaches and teachers; of kind souls who lent couches or gym back rooms where I could sleep; of mentors who shared wisdom and advice; of idols who motivated me from the pages of magazines (and, as his life grew, from personal interaction).

I had a big vision, and I had fire in my belly. But, I would never have gotten anywhere without my mother helping me with my homework (and smacking me when I wasn't ready to study), without my father telling me to "be useful," without teachers who explained how to sell, or without coaches who taught me the fundamentals of weightlifting …

So how can I ever claim to be self-made? To accept that mantle discounts every person and every piece of advice that got me here. And it gives the wrong impression—that you can do it alone.

—Arnold Schwarzenegger
(Ferriss, *Tools of Titans*, 2016)

Five to one means I'm risking one dollar to make five. What five to one does is allow you to have a hit rate of 20%. I can actually be a complete imbecile. I can be wrong 80% of the time, and I'm still not going to lose—assuming my risk control is good. All you've got to do is just be right one time out of five. The hard part is that that's not how we invest. The way human nature is, we're never really calculated about our entry points. We're never really thoughtful about where we give in and what are we really risking.

—Paul Tudor Jones (Robbins, *Money*, 2014)

Walk Away from the Other 97 Percent!

> Leaders who don't listen will eventually be surrounded by people who have nothing to say.
>
> —*Andy Stanley*

Wayne continued his conversation with his wife, "I am tired of conceding and putting my life on hold to remain with the 97 percent."

"Now what are you taking about? What the hell is the other 97 percent?" she asked.

Their gray cat, Andy, jumped on the kitchen table in front of Sue and began nosing around for a snack.

Wayne heard the relaxing tremble of Andy's purr as he continued speaking. "Jim Rohn is a business leader who I've been listening to for years. In his *Challenge to Succeed* training course, he talks about the 97 percent. Listen to this." Wayne picked up his iPhone. "Hey, Siri. Play Jim Rohn *walk away from the 97 percent*." Jim Rohn's one-of-a-kind voice began to echo from the speaker of his iPhone.

> Here's what I'm asking you to do. Walk away from the 97%. Don't use their vocabulary. Don't use their excuses. Don't use their method of drift and neglect. Won't even walk around the block for their health. Won't even eat an apple a day. Won't even take the time to refine their philosophy for a better life. Walk away and join the 3%.
>
> Once you look back on it you will never turn back. You will never go back to the old ways and the old language and the old neglect.

In America 5% of the people are independent. 95% are dependent. I'm asking you take charge of your own life. Take charge of your own day. Don't have days like most people have, you'll wind up broke and poor. Pennies no treasures. Trinkets no values. Change it all. (*The Challenge to Succeed*, Disc 2, "Walk Away from the 97 Percent")

"Yes, I received a promotion! But it's not as exciting as I had hoped. From an ego standpoint, it's awesome. I have a new title, a pay raise, and a huge opportunity ahead of me. But from a mind-set and health standpoint, this is a death sentence. I've been talking with Ned and Corey about a promotion for three years, and they kept playing games and dragging their damn feet. The longer this continues, the more fucked up everything is becoming. I am the fifth manager in six years for the relationship management team. Uh, if that's not a sign of something wrong, I don't know what is."

"Yeah, I guess. But you have a good job, and who gives a shit how many managers you guys have had?"

"I know I shouldn't say this, but I'm going to. When you got sick, what happened? How did you get sick? You've said that you believe the combination of bad diet, stress, and overexertion contributed to it. I am sorry, but I'm not going to risk my physical health for this damn job because my mental health is already fucked up from working at Pigeon Financial. I busted my ass for them. They kept promoting other people on other teams, and all the while, Ned and Corey kept hinting at this promotion. For three fucking years, they kept promising that things were going to get better. For more than three damn years, they played mind games, dangling this promotion in front of me, and then they didn't promote me? After three fucking years of preparing for this and leading the team, they put me through the stinking interview process? That's bullshit! I am so burnt out. I accepted the promotion because it was the thing to do. I should have just remained where I was and not pursued the promotion." Wayne paused.

"I am sorry," his wife interjected. "I had no idea how you felt."

"I didn't tell you because I didn't want you to worry, but I can't take it any longer. Crap! This is an awful feeling! I can no longer put up with the self-serving management. We have no guidance; the teams receive no training, and we are treated like shit for doing our fucking job while we clean up their mess because no one else will. It's at the expense of the employees' morale and my sanity. Right now, I find it difficult to suit up each day and go to work. I despise who I've become. I despise the way upper management runs this company. We gave our heart and soul to the company, and they neglected us. Ignorance, ego, and idiocy is a bad combination, and this company has it in spades." Wayne paused to take a sip of water. After placing the glass down on the table, he wiped his mouth with the back of his hand. "Sorry, but I had to get this off my chest."

"It's okay. I'm just sorry that you feel this way, and I'm worried. I'm worried about you and what you're thinking about doing," she said in a concerned tone.

"So, when I reunited with Marianne in March, she expressed her excitement for my promotion and all of the wonderful things I had accomplished. But unfortunately, I was still frustrated and miserable dealing with the lies and bullshit from upper management. Nothing's really changed. Yeah, I have a new job. But all that means is that I'm now knee deep in the shit show they created and unable to find a way out. Thank you for listening." Sue remained silent while Wayne continued, "The more I talk about working for this company, the more my gut and my heart tell me I need to move on. The more I think about all the flawed and fucked-up ways they run things, how they protect their positions by surrounding themselves with people who are order takers rather than thinkers, the more I realize I need to walk away. But I won't because of fear. Fear that I will never find another job. Fear that I'll make the wrong decision by leaving. Fear that I'll be a failure. Fear that I'll disappoint you and let so many people down. But I no longer have anything to say. This fucking job sucks! Leaders who don't listen will eventually be surrounded by people who have nothing to say. That's what's going on. We no longer have anything to say—myself, my team, and even the wholesalers. I can feel my jaw tightening and my teeth grinding together the more I talk about it."

Andy jumped down from the table and meandered off into the living room.

"What does Marianne have to say about all of this?" Sue asked.

"She does her best to guide me based on what she knows about my life. I mean, she only knows what I tell her, and I can't tell her everything in a sixty-minute conversation. So, she addresses whatever I bring up, which most of it is about my frustration with work and my desire to be happy."

"You know, no one ever really does what they want," his wife said as a reality check for Wayne. "I mean, we all have to work and provide for ourselves, our families, and so on."

"That's something I just can't accept. It doesn't have to be this way, but for some reason, we believe we must work at a job and put up with managers who suck at their job and treat their employees like crap because that's 'the way it is.'" He gestured air quotes with his hands. "That is why I call bullshit! Maybe I just don't quite understand it, but there has to be another way.

"Each time I expressed my desire to leave the company and find my own path, Marianne continually said that I should stay. At least that was what I was hearing. Remaining there, it would put me in a position to uplift and inspire the people I worked with. Again, a sort of win-win-win for all: myself, my employer, our accounts."

"I like that idea. That makes sense," she said as her face lit up.

"But, for some reason, each time I heard the suggestion from Marianne that I stay, I felt more resentment and anger. I just can't get past the feeling of emptiness inside and worthlessness when I have to go into a meeting or jump on a call with Corey, Carl, Ned, or Chad. It is like I am back in fucking middle school. These guys are like eighth graders pushing the sixth graders around. But, unbeknownst to them, there is another world out there, much bigger than middle school, and it will fucking eat them alive. These idiots think they are big shots in their little world, and they better check their egos at the door because when they get to high school and college, they will be at the bottom again, and the upperclassman will see through their bullshit. The kids who are treated like shit end up feeling like there's nothing they can do. So, they end up dreading school because they don't want to put up with the assholes any longer. They lose all desire for school and end up despising a place where they should thrive. That is the childish crap I deal with but in a corporate setting with apparently mature adults! Like the kids who were treated like shit and wanted out, I no longer care to work for Pigeon Financial. Yet all I chose to hear from Marianne was her insistence that I stay. I stayed because that was what I was supposed to do. Get in line, do my work, and do what my boss tells me to do even if deep down I know it's wrong. Don't speak up. Don't share your thoughts. Just stay in fucking line. Sorry, but I am in the wrong damn line!"

"I am afraid to ask, but you mentioned when you got the promotion you didn't feel that good about it. What does that mean?" Sue's voice trailed off as she posed the question.

"Well, this is where you and I won't see eye to eye. I apologize for this, but I want to be as open as possible about this without freaking you out."

"Okay?" came her anxious response. "Now, I'm beginning to freak out!"

"You've heard stories when someone takes a leap of faith?" he cautiously asked.

"Yeah."

"Well, this just might be one of those times," he continued.

"Okay, I already don't like the sound of this," she said with a tinge of fear and anger in her voice. "Don't tell me you are going to go off and write your fucking books."

"Well, sort of."

"Come on! We can't do that!" came her retaliatory response. "Can we?"

"I don't know. But a good friend of mine was telling me about some of the changes he was making in his life and career."

"Who are you referring to?"

223

"Nick, Tanya's boyfriend."

"Okay. What's he doing that has anything to do with what you're doing?"

"Nothing. Just listen. He just left Bluefin restaurant because he was tired of the bullshit from management, and it was stressing him out. One of his customers is a manager at a local gym. He came in for dinner and offered Nick a job as a CrossFit trainer. He started the job a week later. He's taking a leap of faith by leaving the restaurant business to be a full-time trainer, but—"

"Let me guess," Sue interrupted. "He's making much less money."

"Yes."

"And he doesn't have a family to support. He's not even married. How's that the same?" she retorted in anger.

"I'm not saying any of it is the same. I am just trying to figure out what the hell I'm supposed to be doing."

"You're supposed to be a husband and father. You're supposed to make money to support this family. *Your* family!"

"Yeah, yeah. Point taken," Wayne grumbled. "Well, for what it's worth, Nick said it was a true leap of faith. My response was that there are no leaps of faith unless you believe you need to leap. I saw it as just another step on his amazing journey and belief, a deep belief in himself that no one can shake or will shake. I suggested he take his step because the next one will be even more amazing. There are lots of steps in front of him, and he might as well enjoy them."

"That's pretty insightful. Why are you telling me this?"

"Uh, because I need to take a leap of faith."

"Uh, no you don't!"

Wayne continued to reflect on his conversation with Marianne, while Sue grew even more concerned about his unhappiness.

<hr>

"You keep telling me to stay, and I haven't heard you say once that I can go. Why the fuck do you keep telling me I have to stay?" Wayne barked over the phone at Marianne. "You tell me I need two years' of income saved up before I can make a change. Where is that coming from? All that is, is fear speaking," he pleaded. "If you truly believe in the abundance of the universe and that everything always works out, then please tell me where this bullshit is coming from?" His rant continued, "Who the fuck said I must have two years' of income saved up? Who the fuck has two years' of income saved? I sure as shit don't. All I hear in your words is fear! I have made changes like this before with nowhere close to two years' of income saved. At the most, I had maybe three months' tops, and I made it work." He couldn't stop. "This is bullshit, and all it is, is fear. Plus, what does it matter in the end? When I'm gone, I won't have any of my wealth to take with me, nor will I have any of my doubts or debts. It doesn't fucking matter!"

"Wayne, I never once said you couldn't leave. I don't know where this is coming from," Marianne lovingly replied, unfazed by Wayne's viral assault.

"That's bullshit! You have never once said, 'Wayne, it's okay. You can leave. It will be all right.' All I hear you saying is that I have an opportunity to lead and uplift the people at work. You keep sending me messages that I can't leave, that I am supposed to stay there. What the hell is that! Why haven't you said, 'Wayne, all things are possible. No matter what you do, it will all work out for you.' What the fuck!"

"Wayne, I am sorry. But I never said you had to stay. I think this is what you are choosing to hear. You can choose to do whatever you want," she patiently continued.

"Whatever," he said with an emotionally absent reply. "I'm tired, Marianne. You keep telling me that I have an opportunity to lead in this company, but I am tired. I am tired of my job. I love what I do, and I am proud of what I accomplished for myself and this company, but I am fucking tired. This job sucks the life out of me. The people at Pigeon Financial are killing my soul and sucking the life out of me. I don't know how this happened, but I hate my job. I'm tired of fighting everyone. I have no passion for it any longer. Plus, what is the point of my job? Nothing! All this company does is fight and compete out of their own fucking fear and ignorance. Nothing beneficial for my career or life has come from working here, other than learning what *not* to do! I'm tired. I fucking hate this job and the assholes running this company! They should be running it, but instead they are fucking ruining it! I thank you for your love and guidance, especially your patience. I understand what is going on here, and whether you know it or not, you are playing the role of my mother. All this safe and don't take any chances bullshit! She would say the same exact thing you are saying, 'Be safe, save two years' worth of income, have another job lined up, and then you can go."

"Ahh, the Divine Mother," Marianne commented.

"No! Not the Divine Mother, my mother." Wayne chuckled in response.

"Hmm. What do you mean?"

"My mom would say something similar. That's what parents do. All I'm looking for is someone to tell me it's okay." Tears began to trickle from his eyes. "Then I can go. I know ultimately that I'm the one who needs to give myself permission. I can no longer afford to live my life waiting for someone else's permission. I need to give myself permission, but I'm afraid." Tears continued to rain down his cheeks in an emotion-laden rant. "I need someone to tell me it's okay."

"Oh, sweetie, you know I love you and you can do whatever you want. You can go. If it's that awful, you can go. I didn't realize it was that bad," she replied in her usual loving manner.

"Thank you. That's all I needed. Look, I hate my job. It's no longer rewarding for me. I truly loved working there for the first few years. But, after that, I began to see their true colors. I even tried to get fired on a few occasions. I spoke my mind with upper management many times, expressing the need for them to care for their employees and address the toxic environment that was growing out of control. I still don't understand how companies can treat their employees like shit and get away with it. I spoke my mind again and again, and for some reason, the universe kept me there. I'm now at a point at which I can no longer go on. I despise my work; my confidence has been shattered because of these assholes. I am so far gone that I'm no longer doing any work. They don't even notice! It really isn't fair to me, nor is it fair to the company or my team members."

There was silence on the other end of the line.

Wayne continued, "If my path in this life is suffering, then I want to choose my suffering. I guess my choice to suffer will be by stepping out of line. I am not going to stand in line any longer. For most of my life, I stepped out of line, and when I did, almost everyone had something to say about it. They wanted me to get back in line. Fuck that! What's the point—to be born, go to school, work, start a family, retire, and die? That's just a sad statement. Is that the point of life? If so, then fuck it! I am getting out of line. There's more to life than working for self-serving, demeaning management. I will choose my own suffering instead of suffering at the hands of mindless leaders. I've thought about this more than I care to admit. I thought about all the dire results that could come from my decision to leave, and I challenged each one. I challenged my fears. And you know what? They're all illusions. They don't exist! If I leave my career, here is what my ego, or subconscious, is telling me: that I am leaving the only job in the world for me. Out of about 325 million people in the United States and quite possibly 175 million jobs, how is it that my ego is telling me that there are no other jobs for me? If I were to leave my job, fear is telling me that I am going to die, and there are no other jobs for me. Out of 175 million jobs! Is my job the only one in existence; really? That's how the mind works. This is how fear is apparently keeping me safe, in misery. This is how fear keeps most people in line. I choose to see the other 175 million plus job opportunities. I keep waiting for a sign to move on. The problem is that they've been appearing all over the place, yet I still keep ignoring them out of fear, and my ego is telling me to stay. I don't have a plan right now, although I have been planning this for years. I do not have another job lined up because this company has fucked me up so much that I don't want this job any longer and I don't know if I can work anywhere else. By working in the corporate world, I have become a sheep in wolf's clothing—more like an angel in asshole's clothing.

And I am apparently working in a dog-eat-dog world where you must be able to swim with the sharks and eat what you kill, blah, blah, blah. Falling victim to the herd mentality, I have made poor decisions and even treated other people poorly along the way. I don't agree with this. Receiving the promotion quite possibly put me in a position to make the positive changes I desired, but it became clear I won't be able to pull it off. It didn't work for Nelson. It didn't work for Amy. How the fuck would it work for me? The old saying goes, 'If you can't beat them, then join them…'" Wayne paused and then continued, "Or just leave."

Marianne apologized for not knowing how awful things were for Wayne and gave him permission to go. Once again, their conversations halted, and Sue remained deeply concerned about Wayne's stress at work.

Words to Lead By

Q: As a leader, are you truly able to listen to your people?

Leaders who don't listen will eventually be
surrounded by people who have nothing to say.
—Andy Stanley

Imposters and Posers

> Where good leadership is needed, poor
> management is there as an imposter.
>
> —*Warren Bennis*

It was a beautiful spring day in May 2018. Wayne walked into his favorite coffee shop, Burlap and Bean, and was immediately greeted by the aroma of freshly roasted coffee beans. There was something about the smell of freshly ground coffee beans that filled his heart with joy. He was meeting his friend Betsie for coffee.

He ordered his usual dark roast coffee with a splash of soy milk. The coffee at Burlap and Bean was probably the most caffeinated coffee he had ever had. A couple of cups would supercharge his day. He walked over to grab a table located alongside the wall.

"Hey, Wayne!" He heard his name called out.

His friend Betsie was waving, trying to get his attention. Wayne's face lit up.

"Hey, Betsie! How are you?" he greeted her.

"I'm doing well. It's great to see you. I ordered you a cup of coffee," she said.

"Thank you for the coffee! This is perfect." Wayne sat down, placing his cup on the table. "I won't have to get up from my seat to order a refill." He smiled as he took a sip of his coffee.

"So, how have you been? What's going on in your life?" Betsie asked.

"You know, Betsie, while on the way here, I was thinking about whether or not my parents brought me up the right way."

"Wow! Really? What do you mean?" she replied, caught off guard by Wayne's comment.

"Well, I'd like to think my parents brought me up the right way. They taught me to be honest, to always give it my best, to work hard, and to treat others with respect."

"Yes. That makes sense, and it appears they did a pretty good job."

"Thank you, but I'm not so sure. I am grateful for the guidance from my parents and grandparents, but I feel as though it's a lie. I've worked hard, I've been honest and have treated others with respect, yet these values seem to elude the leaders at Pigeon Financial. It's so bad that I often feel as though I need to start doing what they are doing—lying, cheating, and treating people like shit so I can get ahead to the next level. The old saying goes, 'If you can't beat 'em, join 'em.' I seriously question whether or not my honesty and strong work ethic is what is preventing me from moving up to the next level."

"Unfortunately, many of them don't care," Betsie added. It can be quite disturbing to see people like this in positions of power. All too often, they're ignorant of any internal conflict, lack of support, and camaraderie at the home office."

"Yep, that's it! I just don't understand. I'm tired of working my ass off and doing what's right for the company, for my clients and the wholesalers, to only be pushed aside by management because of their ignorance and unwillingness to listen," Wayne quipped.

"It's funny you said that. I recently read an article from Liz Ryan in which she said that in healthy companies, people debate issues. They know that smart people won't always agree. They expect dissent around any big management decision, and they keep the lines of communication open. They don't silence people who disagree with them. There definitely is some sort of compromise when you are in a position of management, or leadership, in which you must set aside what you innately know is right for what is the best for the company and leadership—even when it means neglecting employees and hurting them personally and professionally."

Wayne grabbed his iPhone, tapped the *Notes* icon, and scrolled through his notes. He began reading, "'For most organizations, management is common, and leadership is rare. All too often, where good leadership is needed, poor management is there as an imposter.' That sums up Pigeon Financial!

"I read that in the book *Launching a Leadership Revolution*. My friend Gary introduced the book to me and even suggested we read it simultaneously and discuss each chapter. Sort of like a study group."

"Did you?" Betsie asked.

"Well, at first, I scoffed at the idea because it was something I had never done. But it turned out to be very beneficial to hear someone else's perspective. I believe most employees who wish to move up within an organization fly under the radar, unable to do so because of immature and inept management. And those at the top in positions of leadership are ignorant to it either because they don't know or don't care to know. Plus, if you aren't in the 'boys' club,' then you have little chance of joining the ranks no matter how hard you work."

"Good point, although it isn't necessarily the fault of the leaders at the top. Often they do not see what's going on within an organization and that is why—"

"They have management, right?" Wayne politely interrupted.

"Yes."

"But if management is inept and treats their employees like shit, executive leadership remains unaware either because they are too far removed or because their management team simply ignores it, allowing the shit show to continue unabated."

"Well, I am not so sure about that ..."

"Come on, Betsie! Are you condoning the deplorable behavior of management at these companies?" Wayne exclaimed. "Now, I'm not saying this applies to every company. But there are far too many companies like this. For example, Pigeon Financial! And most employees just deal with it because apparently it's like this everywhere."

"Wayne, I am not disagreeing with you. I champion your efforts, but I am just vetting the idea to get a better understanding where you are coming from."

"Someone needs to reveal the assholes who poorly manage these companies so they can be removed. Someone needs to step up and teach management that it is okay to love their people just as much as they love their profits. I mean manage your profits while embracing your people. It's not that hard to do."

"But it gets lost in translation."

"Yes!" Wayne exclaimed. "Say an executive truly intends to institute honesty, transparency, and integrity. If their management doesn't embrace any of it, these core values are doomed from the start."

"Yep! It's sad. Someone needs to be held accountable, but it's as though these managers are unable to have any independent thoughts. Rather they just take orders. They're awful at executing those orders. They're not properly trained by management and therefore don't know what their core responsibilities are. If there seems to be an issue, rather than solving it, they just let it continue. They don't act on it because they weren't given permission by their manager. Despite being grown adults, they act like fucking children waiting for their mommy or daddy to give them permission to think. They should be able to decide on their own, but they can't. I'm tired of working for these assholes who are ruining these companies. Oops!" Wayne chuckled placing his hand over his mouth with a look of surprise on his face. "I meant to say 'running.' Did I say 'ruining'? And what do most people do about this shit show? Nothing! They go back to their miserable job, hating it while continuing to put up with all the bullshit, because they believe there is nothing they can do about it. And it's like this practically everywhere!"

"Okay. You're right about that." Betsie paused, taking a sip of her tea. "Plus, there are very few people who express their concerns or reveal the truth about the workplace because they're afraid of retribution and retaliation."

"Exactly! That's typically when the workplace grows increasingly uncomfortable and people go silent. Another thing that I believe leads to this assholeness in the workplace—"

"Did you just say 'assholeness'?" Betsie interrupted.

"I sure did." He smiled.

"Is that even a word?"

"I don't think so. At least it wasn't up until now!" Wayne laughed. "I believe this constant restlessness and stress of chasing success contributes to this assholeness. I am tired of working for an employer whose approach is to focus on what's wrong!" he expressed in frustration. "They spend their energy focusing on what everyone is doing wrong, even reprimanding employees for speaking up and sharing productive ideas and opinions for the betterment of the organization. If this is the way a company manages and leads, then I'm not buying what they're selling."

"Plus, what does that say about how employees learn to work and manage?" Betsie interjected.

"Precisely!" Wayne's face lit up. "They're teaching their employees to manage like an asshole, continuing their toxic and distrusting ways. This creates a domino effect of shitty work experiences that spiral out of control. These assholes in upper management are all considered successful, but what type of success is that when it's achieved at the price of their employees' confidence and pride?"

"I hate to say it, but I understand how you feel."

"I believe it's learned, and we can break the cycle. Here's an example. It's a little strange, but you'll get the point."

"Okay?"

"You know I used to have season tickets for the Philadelphia Eagles about twenty years ago when they still played at the Vet," Wayne went off on a tangent.

"You had season tickets? Wow!"

"Yep, but I stopped going to the games and gave my tickets to a friend."

"Really? You just gave your tickets away? Why?"

"Because I was tired of all of the assholes in the stands. But a few years ago, I gave it another try. I was at the Seahawks' season opener against Green Bay the season after the Seahawks won the Super Bowl. It was such a great experience that I wanted to give the Eagles another try, so I bought tickets to a game, which just so happened to be against the Seahawks. There is something about experiencing thousands of fans flowing into the stadium in a sea of Eagles' green. It's pretty amazing. The energy and the excitement are powerful."

"Yep! There's this energy when you're at a pro football game, both bad and good energy though."

"Unfortunately, an Eagles' fan stood up and started chanting, 'Asshole! Asshole! Asshole!' for no apparent reason. I was immediately reminded why I stopped going all those years ago. For whatever reason, this fan felt it necessary to stand up and chant, 'Asshole!' over and over again. I remember saying to my wife, "Look at that idiot!" when it dawned on me that this assholeness was all this guy knew. He was probably a fan who grew up going to the Eagles' games watching his friends or quite possibly his parents standing up and chanting, 'Asshole. Asshole! Asshole!' Why? Was it necessary? Making it even worse was the fact that nothing provoked this idiot to do so other than the fact that he knew of no other way to behave. So, if this idiot is taught that chanting 'asshole' is cool and is the thing to do while at an Eagles' game, then a tradition of assholeness begins and is carried forward from generation to generation, season after season, seemingly with no end in sight. Unfortunately, Eagles' fans are known for their stupid antics and being assholes because of this learned behavior of assholeness."

"Humph. That's just sad. So, what does that have to do with work?"

"Sorry, I digress. But there are parallels. You see, in the business world, if management is inept and teaches employees the way of the asshole ..." Wayne smiled. "Then their employees will embrace it because that is what they were told, and now it's all they know. Despite how idiotic it is and how it makes them behave like fucking idiots, they do it anyway because everyone else is doing it. This tradition of management by assholeness is learned, thus beginning a tradition in the workplace because they know of no other way—"

"And because everyone else is doing it," Betsie interjected.

"Yes! Herd mentality," Wayne stated. "I am sure Eagles' fans will start chanting, 'Asshole,' when they read this. That's okay. I forgive them for they know not what they do."

Words to Lead By

Q: Do your people respect you as a leader because you earned it or demanded it?

Many would-be leaders are in it for the wrong reasons. Many people are interested and strive to be in leadership because of what they imagine it can provide for them. Some of those provisions they think will be there are the following:

1. Power
2. Control
3. Perks (i.e., money)

The life of a true leader is actually quite different from those expectations. The life of a leader involves:

4. Goals: Having a mission for your team or organization is the best reason there is for wanting to be a leader.
5. People: helping other people be more successful or empowering others!
6. Responsibility of leading others

See, leaders lead for the joy of creating and fulfilling something bigger than themselves.

☺ Fu*k Success

A quiet and modest life brings more joy than a
pursuit of success bound with constant unrest.

—Albert Einstein

Wayne and Betsie spent the rest of the afternoon in Burlap and Bean, enjoying their coffee and conversation. A group of regulars from the Townhome Retirement Community across the street arrived for their usual afternoon card game.

One gentleman in the group had a loud, boisterous laugh. His laugh was so loud it caused Wayne to jump out of his seat. Eventually, it became infectious, and Wayne would chuckle every time he heard the guy's laugh.

"My entire life, I relentlessly chased success. I studied it, fought for it, and competed for it," Wayne continued his conversation with Betsie. "I mindlessly chased after it time and again to be left with the feeling as though I came up short. In a way, I was driving myself crazy pursuing it. I would often display these traits of assholeness, which were incited by my mindless and restless pursuit of success. Despite making more money every year and receiving numerous promotions, I felt as though I always arrived just short of the finish line of success. So, I continued my pursuit, finding myself feeling even more lost, frustrated, and tired. Something had to change."

"So, what did you do?"

"I stopped chasing it."

"Stopped chasing success? I'm confused."

"Don't be. I stopped chasing success and decided instead to say, 'Fuck success!'" Wayne proclaimed.

"What did you just say?" Betsie replied with a look of surprise and shock.

"I said fuck success! I'd rather be happy!" he firmly stated with a grin.

After a long, uncomfortable silence, Betsie looked around to see if anyone had heard what Wayne had just said, but no one heard him because the guy playing cards let out one of his boisterous laughs and nothing else could be heard above his laughter. With a whisper, she leaned toward Wayne. "What the heck does that mean?"

"Humor me and ask Siri what success is," Wayne said with a smile.

"Okay? Hey, Siri, what is success?" Betsie went along with Wayne's request.

"Victory. Term that applies to success. The term victory originally applied to warfare, and denotes success achieved in personal combat, after military operations in general or, by extension, in any competition ..." Siri's' reply echoed.

"How about this?" Wayne smiled. "Hey, Siri, what is the definition of success?"

Siri's voice recited the following words, "Success means the accomplishment of an aim or purpose."

"Now, read the rest of the definition," Wayne said as he handed his phone to Betsie.

Leaning forward, she grabbed the phone to read the text on the screen, "'The attainment of popularity or profit, a person or thing that achieves desired aims to attain prosperity, (archaic) the outcome of an undertaking, specified as achieving or failing to achieve its aims.' Okay, that's the definition of success." She leaned forward again and asked, "But why did you say, 'Fuck success'?"

Wayne smiled and proceeded to read several definitions of *success*. Upon finishing, he asked, "Do you see a recurring theme?"

"Yeah, success means you have attained great things, like money, a home, career, and so on."

"Yes, precisely! But what's missing?"

"Uh, I don't know?"

"Success is generally focused on the attainment of goals. In the business world and life, most people consider success as the attainment of status, titles, power, wealth, nice cars, a big home, the latest iPhone, flat-screen television, and all the things that apparently make us happy. It's just fuel for the ego. It can be very stimulating but is also a fleeting moment of ecstasy until we feel that we must have more."

"Interesting. I never thought about success that way. So, success is a product of the ego?"

"*Yes*! That's it!" Wayne exclaimed loudly, sitting back in his seat while onlookers glanced in his direction. "The stinking ego." He smiled. "The one thing that's missing from the definition of success is the attainment of a modest life, peace with oneself and the world. Or shall I say *enlightenment*? There is absolutely no mention of that in the definition of success! My realization was that despite all my striving and apparent success, I was really dying inside. I did not have any sense of peace with myself and sure as heck not with the world. Feeling very little semblance of true success and being unable to honor myself for my achievements, there certainly was no way I could honor anyone else's success." Wayne paused to take a sip of his coffee. He was surely caffeinated at this point and didn't need any additional fuel for his excitement and energy. "You know, Albert Einstein even said, 'Fuck success'!"

"Okay, Wayne. Now you're being ridiculous," she interjected out of embarrassment because Wayne wouldn't stop saying the f-word.

"Really, you think I am being ridiculous?" He smiled.

"Well, did he really say that?" She smiled back, pressing Wayne for proof.

"Of course not! At least not in so many words," he said with a sly grin. "Although, I believe his words can easily be interpreted as such."

"Okay. What are you referring to now?" she asked and took a sip of her tea.

"Do you remember reading the headlines regarding a note that was written by Albert Einstein nearly a century ago that recently sold at an auction?"

"Uh yeah, I vaguely recall," she continued. "Wasn't it a note that he wrote to a bellhop or courier or something along those lines?"

"Yes! That's the one. It was 1922. Albert Einstein was on a speaking tour in Tokyo when a courier delivered a message to him at the Imperial Hotel. Upon realizing he didn't have enough change to tip the courier, Einstein scribbled down some life tips instead. His words of wisdom, or advice, were as follows, 'A quiet and modest life brings more joy than a pursuit of success bound with constant unrest.' He also wrote down the following, 'Where there's a will, there's a way.'"

"Nearly a century later, in 2017, that note sold for over one and a half million dollars! Listen to his words, 'A quiet and modest life brings more joy than a pursuit of success bound with constant unrest.'"

"Okay. That makes sense. But I'm not sure what you're getting at."

"In essence, what Albert Einstein was saying in his million-dollar eloquence, genius, and proper manner was 'Fuck success'!" Wayne smiled and took a sip of his coffee. "A quiet and modest life brings more joy! Rather than a pursuit of success bound with constant unrest—or shall we say stress, anxiety, anger, dis-ease, sickness, sleepless nights. Should I go on?"

"Uh, no need," she conceded. "Although it is a little brash, I can appreciate what you're saying."

"The definition of success is flawed because there is absolutely no mention of happiness, heightened awareness, or joy, but rather it is based on the ego's ultimate goal, which is to defeat everyone and attain materialistic things, basically greed. So, I have to ask how in the world is it possible that there is no mention of mind-set in the definition of success?"

"Uh, I don't kno—"

Wayne continued his diatribe before Betsie could answer, "What about considering success as the attainment of a positive, loving, and abundant mind-set? Why isn't success defined as the attainment of a life fulfilled and embracing a deep love of everyone and everything?

Why is the attainment of a heightened awareness or enlightened way of living absent from the definition of success?"

"Well, I really don—"

Wayne interjected once again before Betsie could answer, "Another aspect to the 'fuck success' theme revolves around all of the assholes who are successful, in particular, the jerks who stepped on people and over people to get ahead. Who wants to be known for that type of success? I'd rather be happy! You know, Siri's initial definition of success unfortunately is an accurate depiction of how most people live their lives and careers; 'victory applied to warfare, and denotes success achieved in personal combat.' Seriously? Warfare and combat? Are people commuting to war and combat every day of their lives?"

"Sometimes it feels like it," Betsie quickly interjected. "This is a valid question to pose. I'm not sure everyone feels that way, but I have to say you have my attention. What I hear you saying is the idea of success feeds the ego and does not speak to the overarching aspect that gives life true meaning, which is love."

"Exactly! I believe that the leaders and managers at Pigeon Financial and other companies cannot find it within themselves to lead with love while still being considered successful by the modern-day definition of the word," he pleaded.

"It certainly is possible, but it has proven a difficult task to accomplish in this modern era," she agreed.

"Very few people have attained this type of success—although there are those exceptional few I believe who have met with success while embracing the ability to love their people, remaining modest and living lives filled with joy: Jim Rohn, Zig Ziglar, John Maxwell, Tami Simon, Louise Hay, and Marianne Williamson."

"You know, I never thought about it that way."

"What I'm trying to understand is why I feel like people fear failure. It's as though they're running from death. Instead, they should, myself included, be running toward living, running toward happiness and real success," Wayne deplored. "If we knew death and failure for what they really are, we would no longer run from them. What if our perspective of failure shifted from a devastating and miserable end to a new beginning or a continuation of our journey? Life as we know it would change. Success as we know it would change."

"Huh? What are you saying?"

"Suffering defines the human experience, but it doesn't have to be that way. Most people do not realize that suffering, struggling, and failing can be an empowering teacher that contributes to success in life and business. It pushes us to evolve. Ultimately, we become better when we can accept our failing as a necessary ingredient on our path to success. Unfortunately, most people believe that we must work our fingers to the bone and suffer to be successful or to find meaning from life. This was something I believed for the longest time, but I know now that it's not necessarily true—although I will concede and admit that suffering and pain are wonderful teachers," Wayne continued. "The more I struggled, the more I succeeded; therefore, it seemed logical for me to surmise that stress and struggle lead to success. The conundrum with struggling and always feeling the need to work hard is that it seemingly has no respite or end. Too many people work and chase success in the hope that they will achieve this apex in life at which they no longer struggle and will finally be able to enjoy life. Unfortunately, for most people, they never reach that apex because they either don't enjoy their work or in some cases don't enjoy life. Most people find it very difficult to let go and allow life to flow. In other words, most of us believe we need to control everything in our lives. But the more people try to control and grasp onto the things they acquire in life, the more stressful their lives become. This wreaks havoc in their world, and they have no clue they are doing this. Even worse is when they remain blind to the fact that there is another way. The more we get, the more difficult it is to let go because we define ourselves by the things we get in life. So, letting go freaks us out! Have you read the story *The Death of Ivan Ilyich*?"

"I can't say that I have."

"Well, make sure you check it out. Although it was written over a hundred years ago, it is just as relevant today as it was then."

"So, how did you figure it all out? When you still get caught up in the bullshit, how do you fix it and remain aligned?" Betsie asked in earnest.

"It occurred gradually over many years until suddenly it happened. I had an awakening, if you want to call it that. Maybe a heightened awareness."

"Okay. But how do you still remain focused and at ease?" she persisted, seeking an answer.

"It's more about the journey than the finish line," Wayne quickly replied. "We spend our lives chasing after so many things that we rarely enjoy the journey. If we don't believe we are enough, then we will never have enough. And when we have enough, the question begs, are we able to enjoy what we have, or are we worried about protecting it and getting more? Finding acceptance within ourselves versus looking for our salvation, or acceptance, outside of ourselves in the form of titles, money, and possessions is the key. But we must be brave enough to change it."

"Are you saying we don't need money and possessions? Because you lost me there," Betsie asked.

"Nope! Good point though. I'm not saying we shouldn't have money and things. Life would be boring. But what I am saying is not to attach our identity to these things."

"Okay, I was worried." Betsie chuckled and took a sip of her tea.

"How often do you hear people bragging about all of the stuff they have—their job, their house, their car, and all of that bullshit?"

"Well, all the time. But, Wayne, what else would we talk about?"

"Nothing, except maybe the joy we experience. Or we would listen more." Wayne smirked. "Maybe we would hear what people have to say. Maybe we would learn something new and exciting instead of having to be right or feeling inadequate because someone else has more than we do. When someone boasts about how much they have, what happens? We typically feel that we have to boost our ego by bragging about what we have," Wayne answered his own question. "If our perspective is one of needing to have everything, basically greed, will we ever be satisfied? By the way, greed is really a fear of loss, meaning our perspective is a poverty mind-set, or of not having enough. There is a difference between a mind-set of greed and a mind-set of abundance. What about people who have attained wealth, status, celebrity, and all of the possessions that apparently define happiness and success? Are they truly happy? Do they really believe they have enough and are enough? I am not making light of the seriousness of this, but what the heck happened to Anthony Bourdain and Kate Spade? They were considered successful, yet they committed suicide!"

"Yep. Even Robin Williams."

"Shit, what about the college admissions cheating scandal? Actress Lori Loughlin, who lives in a thirty-five-million-dollar home, felt the need to pay half a million dollars in bribes to get her daughters into the University of Southern California as crew athletes even though neither one ever participated in crew. This is conjecture, but they apparently had it all and yet felt the need to misrepresent themselves. Why? Was it because they were afraid that they and their children were not enough because someone else had more? Did these apparently successful parents fuck up their children's lives because they were empty inside despite having everything?"

"Didn't Felicity Huffman and her husband falsely inflate their daughter's college entrance exam score by paying a test monitor to correct her wrong answers?"

"Yes! Jim Rohn said, *'The greatest, most devastating unhappiness is to be unhappy with yourself.'*"

Words to Lead By

Do you wish to rise? Begin by descending. You plan a tower that will pierce the clouds? Lay first the foundation of humility.
—Saint Augustine

> The greatest devastating unhappiness is
> to be unhappy with yourself.
> —Jim Rohn

From the Story of Judas as told by Jim Rohn:

"Judas got the money!"

You say, "Well that's a success story."

"No! No! It's true thirty pieces of silver was a sizable sum of money. But it was not a success story. His name was Judas. Doesn't that ring a bell? It makes all the difference in the world. Judas got the money! Here's something interesting about the story of Judas. After he got the money, he was unhappy."

Someone says, "Well, if you had a fortune in your hand, why would you be unhappy?"

"And here's the key, he was not unhappy with the money. He was unhappy with himself. Here's a key phrase, the greatest source of unhappiness is self-unhappiness. It's not from outside, the things that make us unhappy. The greatest devastating unhappiness is to be unhappy with yourself."[17]

Definitions of Success

Success: "1) obsolete: OUTCOME, RESULT 2) a: degree or measure of succeeding b: favorable or desired outcome. also: the attainment of wealth, favor, or eminence" (*Merriam-Webster*).

Success: "1) the favorable or prosperous termination of attempts or endeavors; the accomplishment of one's goals. 2) the attainment of wealth, position, honors, or the like. 3) a performance or achievement that is marked by success, as by the attainment of honors: The play

---

[17] Chris Brady and Orrin Woodward, *Launching a Leadership Revolution: Mastering the Five Levels of Influence* (2005).

was an instant success. 4) a person or thing that has had success, as measured by attainment of goals, wealth, etc." (Dictionary.com)

Success: "the achievement of something that you have been trying to do. 2) Success is the achievement of a high position in a particular field, for example in business or politics. 3) The success of something is the fact that it works in a satisfactory way or has the result that is intended" (*Collins Dictionary*).

 # Gradually and then Suddenly

> "How did you go bankrupt?" Bill asked.
> "Two ways," Mike said. "Gradually and then suddenly."
>
> —*The Sun Also Rises* (Hemingway 1954)

Wayne finished his cup of coffee, slid his laptop into his Tumi backpack, and threw it over his shoulder. "See ya, Alannah," he said to the barista.

"Bye, Wayne. Have a great day!" Alannah replied.

Wayne strolled out the front door and walked to his car. Looking at his phone, he noticed the time was 12:11 p.m. EST on Tuesday, May 8, 2018. He opened his car door and sat in the driver's seat. Pulling the car door shut, he stared straight ahead, as though in a trance. He was lost in his thoughts about what would soon transpire.

"Well, here goes nothing," he mumbled out loud. "I don't know how to say this, Corey. Thank you for the opportunity, but I …" Wayne practiced what he was about to say to Corey at 12:30 p.m. "No, that's no good. 'Corey, it's been a privilege to work with you' … No, that's a fucking lie. 'Corey, thank you for your time. There is no easy way or right time to say this, but I am resigning.'"

Wayne's phone rang. It was Corey, calling for their scheduled 12:30 p.m. call.

"Hey, Corey. How's it going?" Wayne answered.

"Uh, hey, Wayne. Things are good. How about you?"

After they finished with the bullshit pleasantries, it was showtime.

"There is no easy way to say this or the right time or place. I am resigning from the company …" Wayne held his breath. He couldn't believe it had come to this after the hard work and effort over the years to establish Pigeon Financial's brand and success, after all the time and effort he had put into creating the roles and responsibilities proposals, but something had to give. After a week of allowing it to settle in—preceded by sixty-nine weeks and one day—he knew it was the right time, the right place, and the right way. The million-dollar question would soon be, should Wayne have secured his next job before resigning?

After a brief pause, Corey responded, "Okay. Why are you leaving?"

"There is no easy or concise way to say this. It happened gradually and then suddenly. I just don't feel I can be successful in my role. There are too many disconnects that haven't improved in the six years I have been here."

"Is it your new manager role? Is it pay? Is it me? Did I do something wrong?" Corey asked in his usual robotic style. If Corey had paid attention to Wayne's and his colleagues' pleas for change over the last six years regarding the dysfunction, the low employee morale, and the toxic work environment, he wouldn't have had to ask such ignorant questions."

"Yes, it's you! You fucking idiot! Wake the fuck up!" The words roared from Wayne's mouth. "What have I been urging you to do for six years now?" Wayne snapped out of his daydream, took a deep breath, and spoke. "Well, I don't know. It's not the role; it's not pay. I just can't put it into words," Wayne conjectured with a bullshit response.

Considering Corey hadn't heard the message and cries for help up to that point, Wayne knew he probably never would. Deep down, Wayne wanted to be honest with Corey and share his true feelings, but knowing how poorly Corey handled honest feedback, Wayne steered clear of the truth. Plus, he wasn't looking for a fight, so he did his best to make peace with it. It was time to move on.

"Were you thinking about leaving before you received the promotion or after?" Corey quipped in response. "We put a lot of time, resources, and effort into your new role, and I wish you would've let me know." He tried to lay the guilt on.

"Yes, it was long before the promotion. One year, four months, and six days to be precise since you love your fucking metrics so damn much!" Wayne snapped out of his daydream again and replied, "It was after I received the promotion."

Of course, Wayne held back, refraining from letting Corey know how disappointed he was. Plus, he firmly believed that discussing it at this point would have been fruitless. After allowing everything to settle in, it was crystal clear that Corey did not know how to connect with people; he lacked emotional intelligence and the human connection needed in sales and life was absent.

Corey projected his anger upon Wayne, but Wayne no longer bought into Corey's ignorance and robotic interrogations. Corey asked questions but did nothing with the answers—probably just entered it into a spreadsheet and called it a day.

Wayne could have very easily responded to Corey's accusatory questions with attack and retaliation or let him know how disappointed he was in Corey's leadership and how poorly he handled the entire situation, but he chose not to. What purpose would that serve at this point?

He remembered the old saying "If you can't beat them, join them," or if you choose not to follow the herd to a slaughter, knowing it need not be this way, there is another option. That option is to walk down another path. So, Wayne did and resigned.

Wayne sat in stunned silence and awe at what he had just done—even more at the way Corey had handled it. Of course, doubts and second thoughts started jumping around his mind. To assuage these thoughts, he reflected on the events that had led up to his decision.

Although he had accepted the job offer in February 2018, the momentum from the negativity and disconnect between Corey, Carl, Chad, and Ned spiraled out of control. This helped nudge Wayne to resign because he realized there was not much he could do to improve things. One of his regrets was not negotiating for more. Upon accepting the job, he did not negotiate for more money or request to have the external and internal teams report to him, which he should have. The negotiations were something he looked forward to. They allowed him to challenge and ask for more, but this time, he didn't. He was done, no longer caring to stand up for what was right because of the constant resistance from Corey, Carl, Chad, and Ned.

The night he accepted the promotion, he lay awake in bed with his eyes wide open while he replayed everything in his mind. "Fuck! I should have pushed back and asked for more instead of just giving in!" Wayne mumbled under his breath.

"What?" His wife was awakened by Wayne's tossing and turning.

"Oh, nothing. Sorry. I was just thinking about work. Love you," he whispered to his wife. "Ahh, that's it! I can ask Corey for more money for the team," he mumbled out loud.

"Wayne, what are you doing? Get some sleep," his wife whispered.

"Okay. Good night." Wayne fell fast asleep, resting on the idea that he would ask for more money for the team.

The next day, Wayne called Corey and proposed they deploy money to the team in the form of raises or bonuses. There had always been a way of finding additional funds for pay raises and bonuses for the team. But Wayne was met with disappointment when Corey gave his usual response about not having the budget for pay increases or bonuses. Corey then made a comment about Wayne's promotion not being in the budget, but they made it work anyway. This came as a surprise, considering the numerous discussions he had had with Corey and Ned over the past few years to plan for it. Wayne doubted what Corey was saying, especially since they had somehow found the money in the budget to promote Elaine and Darlene.

The first thing Wayne was tasked with in his new role was to work on the account alignments for the team, which he had already been working on since creating the third roles and responsibilities proposal months before. The more Wayne became involved in the day to day with Corey and Carl, the more he realized that any hope for positive change was a pipe dream. In addition, it became clear to Wayne that Carl had hired Elaine and Darlene to protect him and support his self-serving agenda.

During the last week of April 2018, while in Bellevue at the home office, Wayne arranged time to meet with Darlene to discuss working with the internal relationship managers. Wayne walked into the building lobby, grabbed a cup of coffee at the café, and sat down at a table situated in the corner of the seating area outside.

When Darlene arrived, Wayne stood up from his chair to greet her. The first words out of her mouth were a demand that she be included in every conversation, meeting, and email Wayne had with the internal relationship management team. Next, she expressed unwarranted concerns about Patrice, seemingly on a mission to destroy her and repeal her approval to work remotely from home. Next, she hinted at Mary being a concern when she demanded that she should have a say about the account alignments and which accounts were to be assigned to Mary.

It seemed as though Darlene was there for one purpose, to protect Carl from retaliation and help him gain more control and power. She certainly was not there to improve the workplace. In less than a month's time, the more Wayne engaged with Darlene, Carl, and Corey, the more he regretted accepting the promotion.

Wayne was gradually losing any semblance of trust working with Corey. And having to put up with the games Carl and Darlene were playing was too much for him to accept. Their motivations were not in the best interest of the employees or the company but rather themselves. Carl wasn't hiring the best people for the job but rather those who served his self-interests and would cover up his lies and mistakes.

Promoting Darlene to run the sales desk and the internal relationship management team was another poor decision. This was not just Wayne's opinion but that of the entire team, as well as the sales force. Adding the fact that Carl was sleeping with Darlene made things even worse.

With the organizational structure of other companies as a baseline to build from, it became apparent to Wayne that Pigeon Financial's approach from an organizational standpoint did not align with the rest of the industry. This is not necessarily a bad thing, if it is approached the right way rather than from a self-serving power grab to insulate poor leaders from being exposed.

Working with Corey and the team, Wayne sought the best account assignments that made the most sense without too much disruption to the team and their accounts. Upon approval of the final alignments, Corey gave Wayne the thumbs-up to announce it to the team.

Despite Corey's executive position and the relationship management team reporting to him, which meant it was his responsibility to oversee and approve the team and the account alignments, Darlene nonetheless felt the need to express her disapproval.

When Corey gave the internal relationship management team over to Darlene, despite Corey still overseeing the entire relationship management team, it was yet another one of his mindless mistakes. Remember, prior to Darlene, Elaine was tasked with running the internal relationship management team who reported to Carl.

Wayne had always been one to go along and allow others to voice their opinions, even when they griped and bitched because he always believed there was a way to work things out. Sadly, he quickly came to see that in working with Carl and Darlene, this approach would no longer work. Wayne could not afford to give them an inch because they would take a mile.

Now, Darlene reported to Carl as the manager of the sales desk. She also reported to Corey as the manager of the internal relationship managers. Wayne and his fellow external relationship managers continued to report to Corey, not Carl or Darlene.

Darlene was in over her head; she had no idea what she was doing regarding relationship management—similar to Elaine's predicament when she was promoted. The two should never be combined. Sales and account management (i.e., relationship management) do not mix. You are asking for trouble when you provide a sales team with access to confidential account information, such as revenue sharing, marking allowances, sales agreements, and product approvals.

Sales professionals are excellent at what they do, and when given a task, they typically excel. The problem is when they have information that is sensitive and not intended to be shared quite yet, they cannot help themselves, and they often let the cat out of the bag. This is not a complaint about sales professionals but rather an applause of their tenacity and ability to go after business with the information they are provided.

It is not advisable to have one person manage both the internal sales team and the internal relationship management team. You are asking for trouble, unless that individual is good at the job and he or she knows how to keep the two separate when necessary. This was not the case with Pigeon Financial.

Corey's explanation for his decision was that the internal relationship management team needed a manager at the home office to support them. Plus, since the team provided the internal sales desk with firm intelligence, sales campaigns, and product information, from that standpoint, Corey and Carl decided both teams should report to Darlene. On the surface, the idea made good sense, but once you delved deep into what the internal relationship management team did and how they needed to remain separate from the internal sales desk, it was clearly an awful decision.

You do not manage relationship managers the same way you manage wholesalers. This was a problem at Pigeon Financial; leadership did not know how to keep the sales aspect separate from account management. They provided too much information to the sales force and gave them access to information that simply should not be in the hands of the sales team. Sort of like asking a seven-year-old to keep a secret—it is not going to happen. This only created problems. When a wholesaler blabbed about the details of a new product that was not approved for sale by the account, it was a train wreck waiting to happen. As the saying goes, loose lips sink ships.

Another big challenge Wayne foresaw was Carl and Corey's intent to automate the activities of the internal relationship managers just like they were doing with the internal and external sales team. Automation was their vision for practically everything. It appeared that Corey's intent was to automate and metric everything, thus removing the "relationship" aspect from relationship management. But this is a difficult task for relationship management and was one of the reasons Wayne continued to press Corey about his definition and view of relationship management, especially when creating the roles and responsibilities proposals.

During that same week, while in Bellevue, Wayne schedule one-on-one meetings with Elaine and Darlene to hopefully clear the air by bringing the toxicity and dysfunction to the surface so they could move forward.

His first meeting was with Elaine who no longer managed the internal relationship managers. Hmm. Wonder why? Well, Wayne got right to it. "Elaine, there is this impression that you don't like the relationship management team very much, and the relationship management team doesn't like you much either. I'd like to clear the air so we can move forward and work together."

There was silence. Elaine didn't say a word. Wayne elaborated, "You have done a great job with the Bear and Bull Financial sales operations team and received excellent ratings on their partner scorecard."

"Thank you."

"Bear and Bull are easily one of the most demanding accounts. To receive such high ratings is a tremendous job well done. You deserve to be acknowledged for your great work."

"Thanks, Wayne. Well, they sure aren't the easiest to work with, but the team did a good job working with them."

"This is an area we should leverage. We should promote that fact that you have done such a great job with their operations team. We need to make sure their sales division knows what a great job you have done as well. On our next visit to their sales desk, you should come with us for the sales desk training so we can introduce you to their sales team and review unit."

"I'd like that."

"Let's bookmark that and plan on you joining us in the next quarter or two. I believe we can do a better job of working together as a team to make all of us more efficient and hopefully improve our effectiveness so team members will find their work more rewarding."

"I agree. We need to improve how we work together. I am very happy to work with you and the team on that."

Yes, he could have used a better choice of words and approach, but he was fed up with the ignorance of the issues hidden underneath all the lies and the bullshit. So, he felt it necessary to bring it all to the surface, which seemed to work in his meeting with Elaine. She didn't deny anything or act as though Wayne was out of line with his comments. They connected, and Wayne believed she truly wanted to work together to improve things. Plus, now that she was no longer reporting to Carl, she began to see through his bullshit and lies.

Wayne and Elaine concluded the meeting cordially. He intended to have the same dialogue in his next one-on-one meeting scheduled with Darlene. He felt pretty good about it since things seemed to work out fairly well with Elaine.

When Wayne arrived in the conference room for his meeting with Darlene, Fiona was with her. This was unexpected and caught Wayne off guard. He had cause for concern, considering Fiona was one of the main culprits behind the negativity and toxicity between the teams, which started when she worked on the sale operations team.

The moment he saw Fiona, he knew there was going to be trouble. He should have bitten his tongue and not posed the same question to Darlene and Fiona that he posed to Elaine, but he felt compelled to bring it to the surface. Plus, deep down, he knew he needed to plant this seed to see whether or not Darlene and Fiona would understand and be willing to move forward.

After they had exchanged greetings, Wayne jumped into it as he had done in the prior meeting with Elaine. "There is this impression that you don't like the relationship management team very much, and the relationship management team doesn't like you much either. I'd like to clear the air so we can move forward and work together." The moment the words came from his mouth, he knew he had made a huge mistake.

After a moment of silence, Fiona spoke up. "I am not sure what you are talking about. I don't have a problem with the teams. We work well together," she commented in her usual bullshit facade with her charming smile and sweet-sounding voice. This was how Fiona operated by acting sweet as pie on the surface while underneath she was ugly and vindictive. Wayne could see the resentment in her eyes and in that moment knew she was going to cause trouble.

"Okay, good to know," Wayne replied, despite knowing Fiona's ill intentions.

"We're good," came Darlene's reply.

"I just want to make sure we clear the air. If there are any concerns or issues between the teams, we need to get them behind us so we can move forward." The moment was awkward. Wayne knew Darlene and Fiona were not forthcoming, especially considering Darlene had targeted Patrice earlier in the day when he met with her.

When Fiona worked in the sales operations management team, she created much of the dissent on the team and targeted Patrice because she did not like that Patrice worked from home while the sales operations team had to come into the office. Plus, Patrice was excellent at her job and was not shy about expressing her concerns about the chronic dysfunction and disconnect on the sales operations team, and Fiona did not like it.

Wayne proceeded with the meeting, and they discussed project management, product launches, and ways to improve things with the teams. It was very much surface talk with catty smiles and bullshit comments. The meeting finally came to an end, and they went on their separate ways.

Wayne did not stick around. He quickly expressed his thanks for their time and walked out. Walking over to see Patrice and the rest of the team, he mumbled to himself, "Fuck! That was a goddamn train wreck." After visiting with the team, he was going to take a quick breather before they all met for dinner that evening.

He replayed the day's meetings in his head. He slightly regretted what he had said, but he still stood by his convictions that things needed to change for the better. *I know Fiona and Darlene are going to bring this up to Carl and Corey. I just know it. Now I'm fucked. They are going to blow it out of proportion. Elaine might complain, as well, but I doubt it. She is starting to see the light. But Fiona will absolutely stir the pot, and she will bring Darlene with her. Fuck it! If that happens, then I know it is time to move on, and it confirms that things are as messed up as I think. This will be my confirmation that I need to move on.*

The following week, Wayne was at the airport in Charlotte, getting ready to board his flight when his phone rang. It was Corey, and Wayne knew exactly why he was calling. It was only a matter of time before he got a call from Corey about his comments in his meetings with Elaine, Darlene, and Fiona.

In a strange way, looking back on it, it was as though Wayne had sprung a trap. Knowing Darlene and Fiona were at the root of all the constant trouble in the division, he believed they would approach Carl with their version of events in an attempt to target Wayne. Next, Carl would have a conversation with Corey about Wayne's comment and then *ring, ring, ring* a phone call.

"Hey, Corey. How's it going?" Wayne answered.

"Hey, Wayne. Uh, do you have a minute?"

"Yes. What's up?"

"Uh, I just got done speaking with Darlene and Fiona about your meeting last week."

Butterflies fluttered around in Wayne's stomach as he anticipated what was about to happen next.

"What did you say to them in your meeting last week?"

Wayne wanted to hear it from Corey first before he spoke about the meetings and what he intended by his words in the hope of addressing the disconnect and bringing the toxicity to the surface. "What are you referring to, Corey?"

"Did you tell them you and the relationship management team didn't like them? You can't tell them that you don't like them or that they don't like you. What were you thinking? You must be smart about what you say. If they go to HR about this, you could end up in hot water, especially since you are dealing with women, which is always a sensitive subject and dangerous ground. Plus, the shit we are dealing with when it comes to Mary isn't good, and this doesn't help."

Wayne listened as patiently as he could to Corey's accusations of his apparent inappropriate behavior, all of which were one-sided, based on Darlene's and Fiona's comments. Corey did not give Wayne a chance to voice his side but rather immediately made accusations against him before knowing the full story. This was exactly what Wayne had anticipated and expected from Corey.

The longer Corey barked at Wayne, the more it infuriated him. There is no doubt that women in the workplace deserve respect, but this had nothing to do with gender. Wayne would have voiced those same words to anyone, male, female, white, black, brown, green, or blue. And he had always voiced his opinion to Amy, Corey, Ned, and Chad, but that was never an issue. Wayne had great relationships with Charlize, Patrice, and the rest of the team.

The irony of Corey's concern was the simple fact that Carl had been getting away with harassment toward women and men for years, yet no one seemed to approach him and reprimand him. If Wayne's comments were intended as harassment, he would have happily admitted it and apologized.

Wayne even spoke with his female counterparts about hiring an attorney to file a sexual harassment suit against Carl. They decide against it fearing that they would lose their jobs or possibly worse. His sole intention was to bring the disconnect and hatred to the surface, especially since no one else was willing to do it and no one had done so up to that point. It would have been swept under the rug as it always had been, so Wayne felt obliged to address it. Otherwise, the lies and deceit would have continued unaddressed.

Wayne understood and appreciated the importance of fairness in the workplace and abided by it, but Darlene was not being fair with Patrice, and she was not being fair with Mary. Elaine did the same thing to Patrice, until she no longer reported to Carl, which opened her eyes to his malicious ways. There was no effort to rise up and heal, but rather they hid, covered up, and buried things.

Wayne took a deep breath, unmuted his iPhone, and responded, "Corey, I understand and admit I could have chosen my words more wisely."

"Uh, yeah."

"But something needed to be said. The dysfunction and disconnect between the departments need to be addressed."

"But you didn't need to tell them you hated them, Wayne."

"Excuse me?" Wayne's patience ran out. "Did you once even consider my side of things? Instead, you open this conversation accusing me of something when you do not know the full story. Did you even consider asking me what I said?"

"Uh—"

"No. You didn't. Not once did you ask me what transpired. You accused me from the moment I answered the phone. I'm sure even before you called me this was your intent."

"Uh, well, Wayne, did you tell them you hated them, and they hated you?"

"No, Corey, I did not!" Wayne snapped back in frustration. The people in line waiting to board their flight popped their heads up, looking at Wayne.

"Then what did you say!"

"Corey, I met with Elaine before meeting with Darlene and Fiona. I said the same thing to Elaine as I did to Darlene and Fiona," Wayne firmly stated. "Which was, 'There is this impression that you don't like the relationship management team very much and that the relationship management team doesn't like you much either. I'd like to clear the air so we can move forward and work together.'"

"Uh …" Corey paused. "Why didn't you tell me that was what you said?"

"Because you never asked! Not once did you give me an opportunity to tell you what happened. By the way, who mentioned this to you?"

"Fiona and Darlene."

"Is that it? What about Elaine?"

"Uh, no. Elaine didn't say anything."

"Let me tell you something, Corey. I knew we were going to have this exact conversation. Darlene and Fiona are trouble, and they are looking to cause more trouble. The moment I made that comment, I knew I'd be talking with you about this. I said the same damn thing to Elaine, and did she complain?"

"Uh, no."

"Of course, she didn't because she knew exactly what I was talking about. She's ready to clear the air and move forward. But Darlene and Fiona are looking to cause trouble. I had a feeling they would make a scene about this. That's what they do, and you're buying into it. Plus, Carl is constantly in their ear and is the one responsible for this mess just as much as you are!" Wayne's voice rose above the gate attendant announcing the boarding groups. Passengers looked over at Wayne.

"Okay, Wayne, you need to calm down. You should have told me what you said—although there is still some damage control that needs to be done here."

"And you should not blindly accuse me without asking exactly what happened. You blindly took their word without asking anyone else, without asking me. You're damn right! There is so much damage control that needs to be done, and it's certainly not because of me! This place has been damaged for years, and you don't see it because you're the culprit. I'm just calling it out and trying to fix it. This is not the way the workplace is supposed to be. You need to get your head out of your ass."

"That's enough, Wayne!"

The last boarding group was announced over the PA system. "Okay, Corey. I have to board my flight now. Thanks for hearing my side of it. I'm glad I can rely on you," Wayne said facetiously and walked down the tarmac onto the plane. He was shaking as he took his seat, clearly rattled by what had just transpired despite knowing it would come to this.

To make things worse, it was now clear that Carl controlled the narrative. He dictated what Darlene and Fiona said and did while they reported everything back to him.

The straw that broke the camel's back came when Wayne announced the new account alignments to the relationship management team. As previously mentioned, Wayne worked closely with Corey regarding the alignments. That same day, when he announced the new alignments, Wayne received an angry email from Darlene expressing her disapproval. He tried to reason with her via email. In general, that typically never worked well and was not going to work with Darlene.

So, he picked up the phone and called her. The past several times he had called, she never answered, and her voice mail was full. This was a sign that she was overwhelmed and in way over her head. If you are in financial services and running a sales desk, your voice mail better not be full! You should pick up the phone every time. It is just the way business should be done. Not with Darlene, she was of the complete opposite mind-set.

In sales and relationship management, being available and responsive is a very important quality to have. This was another thing that Darlene failed at miserably. But when she wanted something that benefitted her, she was always available. This time, when he called, much to his surprise, she answered.

Wayne suggested they speak rather than go back and forth with emails. She remained stubbornly persistent in her stance, feeling as though she had been disrespected, and the new account alignments had to change. Based on her comments, Wayne quickly saw Carl's influence at work. They feared Mary because she was a ticking HR time bomb, which made things worse.

Wayne had had enough of Darlene's belligerent comments and demands. He suggested they arrange a call with Corey and Carl to resolve her conflict. The call was scheduled with Corey, Carl, and Darlene on Thursday, May 3, at 3:00 p.m. East Coast time.

Wayne was in Jacksonville, Florida, finishing up his meetings with the Bear and Bull Financial sales team and central business review unit. Wayne took an Uber to the airport and made it through the security checkpoint in time for the three o'clock call. When he dialed in, he placed his phone on mute to avoid the background noise. He heard a few beeps on the line, which indicated the others were dialed in for the call.

"Uh, Corey here." Corey broke the silence.

"Hey, Corey. It's Carl. What's up?"

Wayne unmuted his phone. "Wayne's on." He then muted the line again.

"Darlene's here."

With everyone on the call, it was time to kick things off, but it was silent. Wayne opened things up, providing the background and the reason for the call to address Darlene's issue with the account alignments. Carl immediately chimed in, defending Darlene. Darlene followed suit, expressing how offended and insulted she was that she was not consulted regarding the team alignments.

Up until that moment, Wayne believed Corey was in cahoots with Carl, but this call would change everything. Corey apologized to Darlene and Carl for not including her in the discussions. He proceeded to explain that he and Wayne worked very closely to create the alignments that were best for the entire team and their accounts.

Carl chimed in, challenging Corey. "You don't have the final say. Darlene oversees the internal team, and she decides which accounts her team works with. Darlene reports to me, and I have final say when it comes to the internal relationship management team."

At that moment, the ugly truth was revealed. It was clear that Carl was behind all of this, and he would not bat an eyelid about throwing Corey under the bus just as he did with Ned, Amy, and Elaine.

"Carl, the accounts are assigned to the external relationship managers and their accompanying internal relationship managers. I don't believe you have the final say about this."

"Oh, but I do. We need to make sure we get the alignments right. We cannot afford to give Mary too many accounts. If we do, it will look like she is being picked on or targeted. But we also can't afford to give her too many tier four and five accounts. She will feel like she is being pushed to the side," Carl opined. Tier four and tier five accounts were the smallest accounts. They did not produce much business and did not require a great amount of attention. They were the easiest to work with and were not as important as the tier one and tier two accounts.

In preparing the account alignments, Wayne had open and honest conversations with each of the IRMs about the account alignments. He shared what he was looking to accomplish in an open and honest dialogue with the team, which apparently was considered taboo. Honesty and transparency are core values plastered across a company's "About Us" pages, but when it comes to being open and honest, companies often fall short of abiding by their own guiding principles and core values, which was where Pigeon Financial was headed.

Every internal relationship manager on the team had a slight edge of skepticism, not believing any positive change was possible. It was clear Mary was on the fringe. She was initially hired by Pigeon Financial for her expertise in bond strategies and fixed income portfolios to help solidify Ned's message as a fixed income alternative.

Working in relationship management was clearly not a role suited for her. Wayne realized she was placed there because no one else wanted to deal with her. This was because of an altercation Ned had with her years before in which he publicly humiliated her. Ever since then, she had been tossed around from one position or department to another over several years.

Wayne sensed her hesitation when he met with her a few weeks prior. She even scoffed at the incompetence of management when they met. She clearly had her guard up and was not very trusting of Wayne despite his doing his best to seek her input regarding the account alignments and attempt at improving morale.

When Carl and Darlene went after Corey on the call, he was sick to his stomach. Even though Wayne and Corey did not see eye to eye, Wayne was not the type of person or business professional who would blatantly attack a colleague the way Carl did. Carl was determined to get control while continuing to demand that Darlene be included in everything with the internal relationship managers and that she should be a bigger part of relationship management.

Corey was surprisingly at a loss for words; then his frustrations came to the surface when Carl pulled one of his power plays. They ended the call by agreeing to disagree, and Darlene ended up with more influence than she should have had. This was the final chip to fall. The Pigeon Financial shit show was beyond repair, and Wayne deeply regretted ever accepting the promotion.

The irony with all of this was in Pigeon Financial's core values: "We do what's right every time—Integrity. Honesty. Responsibility," which have since changed as of this writing. Carl had no integrity to speak of. Darlene, Fiona, and Corey weren't far behind. As far as honesty was concerned, Carl's continual lies made Pigeon Financial's core values laughable.

The only way Wayne saw anything changing would have been for Chad, Corey, and/or Carl to leave. But Wayne did not see that happening at any point soon. It was not something worth waiting for.

Carl and Corey had been like a cancer running rampant in a body, ravaging all the healthy cells (i.e., employees) it came in contact with. They took Darlene and Fiona with them. The problem with cancer is that when it eventually conquers its host, the host dies. Cancer is so stupid that it will kill every healthy cell in its path, eventually killing the host and ultimately itself. Corey and Carl are like a cancer killing Pigeon Financial to ultimately cause their own demise.

What is even worse is when leadership and management know the cancer (i.e., dysfunction, toxicity, and negativity) is there, yet they are not willing to acknowledge it or do anything about it. This ignorance mitigates any opportunity for treatment, which would allow the host to return to a healthy state. The cancer runs rampant like Carl, Corey, Chad, and even Ned, wreaking havoc, creating chaos and conflict within the company.

Nothing was going to change until the cancer was removed or healed; Corey and Carl were the most dangerous. Ned, although the only one who truly cared about the employees, was still a little volatile. Chad could have been a better leader if he had matured and had better people surrounding him.

During the national sales meeting in 2018, the entire sales division gathered in the conference room at the Scottsdale Resort at Gainey

Ranch. Carl stood in front of the group, speaking about their focus on the independent broker/dealer channel for the coming year. "We have invested a great amount of time and money in the independent channel expansion for this coming year …" Carl hesitated. The fear and doubt that crept in was visible in his expression and audible in his voice. He continued, "This is critical to our success, your success. Look around the room. Come this time next year, some of you will no longer be here. If you don't execute on the channel expansion in the independent channel, you will be looking for a job."

Wayne stood in the back of the room while Carl's mindless words echoed through the meeting room. Then a gasp came from the group followed by silence. Everyone looked at one another in disbelief at what they had just heard Carl say. Slight chatter ensued among the group in disbelief at Carl's arrogant comments and his lame attempt to motivate the group.

They tried their best to refrain from bursting out in laughter at Carl's attempt at demanding respect. When someone is bold enough to utter such words, he or she damn well better be prepared to deliver the message with absolute certainty, confidence, and conviction.

The group saw through Carl's bullshit. He was more of a farcical character out of the hit television show *The Office* rather than an actual business leader. Dwight Shrute, the dope that he is, stands in front of the entire team at the annual conference and utters those same words: "This is critical to our success, your success. Look around the room. Come this time next year, some of you will no longer be here. If you don't execute on the channel expansion in the independent channel, you will be looking for a job."

The conference room bursts out in a loud roar of laughter. People laugh among themselves at the absurdity of Dwight's comments. Their laughter fills the halls of the building as they head to the bar. Fellow colleagues slap one another on the back, sharing a laugh at Dwight's expense. They raise their drinks and make a toast to the independent channel expansion, mocking Dwight, or Carl in this case. The scene shifts back to Dwight, or Carl, standing on the stage, abandoned, all alone, and then fades to black.

A couple of years prior, at the midyear meeting in Washington, DC, Carl blabbed to Wayne and the relationship management team about how great he was at building teams. Shannon was still new to the team and had not yet had the pleasure of seeing Carl in his element.

Ned, Corey, and Carl spewed their rhetoric to the team. When it came time for Carl to speak to the group, they smirked at one another, knowing what was in store. Carl told a grandiose bullshit rah-rah story about the campaign for the upcoming product launch and was not bashful about boasting how great he thought he was.

Carl sat at the head of the table and said, "I am great at building teams. I was successful at building teams when I worked for Relliantz Life, and I've continued my success here at Pigeon Financial with the sales operations team."

The words oozed from Carl's face with his usual facade of confidence while the team looked on in disbelief. Melanie snorted to stifle her laughter. No one said a word, hoping the meeting would end quickly and Carl would be on his way. Finally, Carl finished his boastful self-promotion, stood up, and left the meeting room to head to the general session. The team remained seated while waiting for the door to close behind him.

The moment they heard the click of the door closing behind Carl, the group let out a roar of laughter.

"What an asshole! Did he really just say that?" Jean said in disbelief.

"That's the biggest load of crap I've ever heard," Melanie gasped. "Please don't tell me he was serious!'"

"Shannon, we apologize for our behavior, but if you haven't noticed Carl is full of shit and Corey isn't far behind," Charlize commented.

"I think he makes up half the shit he says," Wayne said. "By the way, anyone can build a team. The difference is whether you can get the team to come together to get the work done. That is an entirely different thing and a sign of a good leader."

"It's clear he's building his team made up of people who take orders, do whatever he says, and do not challenge him. This keeps him in a position of power!" Charlize stated in frustration. "It's not that difficult to find bodies to fill the roles. He has absolutely no leadership skills and very little respect from the team and sales division."

Words to Lead By

Q: Are you ignoring the toxic behavior in the workplace? Can you even identify the toxic behavior? Does it emanate from your management style and approach?

"According to new research from Fierce Conversations, employees say toxic behavior continues to be ignored by company leadership and wreak havoc in the workplace. Why is this happening?"[18]

---

[18] Fierce Survey: Toxic Workplace in 2019, https://fierceinc.com.

 # The Sun Also Rises

If you can't beat them, join them ... or chart an entirely different course.

—*T. E. Corner*

Wayne had not communicated his resignation to his colleagues yet. He was still digesting what had transpired and figuring out his next steps. He had fought so hard for so much over the past six years and, also, gave up a lot.

Allowing his heart and emotions to overpower any logical thinking, he did not have a solid plan in place, other than getting on with his life and as far away from the toxicity, deceit, and dysfunction as possible.

Wayne's first call was to Charlize. "Hey, Charlize! Are you on the road today?"

"I am heading to Atlanta to meet with EclipseTrust Financial and then on to the golf tournament. What's up?"

"I wanted you to be one of the first to hear. I tendered my resignation this week."

"Wayne! Really? What happened?"

"I gave my notice to Corey on Tuesday and let him know that I would work as long as they needed me, but he said my last official day will be on May 18."

"I can't believe it! Although I don't blame you. As I have said before, never in my career have I worked for a company that is so disconnected, untrustworthy, and blatantly ignorant of their employees. This management team is deceitful and the cause of all the turmoil here. I'm tired of their micromanaging and have never felt so undervalued as an employee in all my years of doing this! Oh, would I love to leave, but at this stage of my life and career, I can't start another job."

"That's why I'm leaving. I just can't put up with the dysfunction any longer. Honestly, I don't see it ever improving."

"As long as Corey, Carl, and Chad are running things, nothing will change. By the way, I don't think we had a chance to talk about the management training class you attended a few weeks ago. Not that it matters now, but I am curious to hear how it went."

"You know, to my surprise, it was pretty good."

"Seriously?"

"Yep. But it was also a tipping point with my decision to resign. At first, I was impressed with the training class. They touted the company's culture, core values, and guiding principles. It was good to hear about the new initiatives with Karen now at the helm."

"Yeah, but that is all HR bullshit. Their guiding principles are laughable, considering Carl, Corey, Ned, and Chad don't embrace any of it. Integrity? Come on! Honesty, transparency. Ha!"

"No argument from me, but with Karen at the helm as the new CEO, I'd like to believe that positive change is on the horizon."

"I don't think it's possible. If she doesn't see what's really going on, this shit show will continue. Even worse, what if she's as devious as the rest of management?"

"Well, then there's no hope. Call me naive, but I'd like to believe she's the only hope for any positive change. When she spoke to the training group, I thought it was a good sign. Of course, the following day, I had to break away from training to join Corey and Carl for an executive update meeting with Chad. Immediately, when I walked into the room, Carl blurted out, 'Hey, Wayne. How was Me Too training? Do you feel included?' That did it for me. Knowing how much he has lied and the number of women he's propositioned, I had heard and seen enough."

"Did he really make that 'Me Too' comment?"

"Yep."

"What an asshole! Shannon, Melanie, Jean, and a few others have said that he's made sexual advances toward them," Charlize said with fire in her voice. "The parties he threw during the national sales meeting this year and last year were atrocious. He said some salacious things and propositioned one or two female employees. Ask Melanie; she'll tell you. Even the disparaging things he said about the wholesalers was an embarrassment! I felt awful for Dave Smith. He was trying his best to get the Southern California wholesaling job when Carl unabashedly made comments about Dave being a joke and would never wholesale because he wasn't wholesaler material. After that, he blathered on saying some pretty shitty things about a few other wholesalers. At that point, we all left. The next morning, he woke up to a shit show and was on a mission to cover up what he had done the night before. He approached me, Melanie, and Jean, pleading with us to keep quiet and even threatened a few of us to keep quiet."

"Yeah, I heard the same story. I'm sure you can appreciate why I was so incensed by Carl's ignorant comments. Someone needs to speak up about this."

"People have, but the HR team is covering up for him."

"I can put on a bullshit corporate facade but only for so long. I didn't want to be a part of it and didn't see any way around it other than leaving. Plus, it dawned on me that I was going to be spending most of my time with these guys. That was when I realized I knew I was fucked. In the brief two months I had been in the new role, it was crystal clear to me that it was time to move on. It's an embarrassment, not only to Pigeon Financial but the corporate world and the industry. Sadly, no one seems to give a shit. And if the few who do care speak up, they are outcast or silenced."

"Corey has said some ignorant things to me over the years, but what can I do about it? I am not going to start over at another company. I am too old for this shit. I am going to have to tough it out a little longer until retirement."

Ned was the only glimmer of hope for change, but he was no longer in a position of influence. This all started when Skip Armah promoted Chad to a similar position of power as Ned. Corey and Carl then began politicking to push Ned out.

When Wayne was hired, he walked into the middle of the disconnect, which was the beginning of Ned's descent and Chad's rise to the top.

"Now look at Ned! You do know that they didn't even tell him about his recent demotion, right?"

"What?"

"At the end of the year, they sprang it on him! Unbeknownst to him, they created this new distribution channel or division and told Ned he was in charge of it. There's no one else on the team. Just Ned."

"Thinking about it, I'm not surprised! You know he's been asking me for help since he started the new role," Wayne interjected. "I don't think he has a team or any support. When I spoke with him a few weeks ago, he mentioned that he was working for us. He needs us more than we need him. After everything he did for the company, giving our product a voice with advisors and positioning it as a part of a fixed income portfolio, they took it all away from him." Wayne continued, "While at the home office for management training, I had a meeting with Ned and Corey. I sat there watching Ned drown doing his best to figure out his role, sharing his ideas with us, looking for ways we could support one another. The entire time, Corey had his head down in his fucking laptop, checking emails, apparently working on something more important. He would look up every so often as though he was checking to see if Ned was still there. Then he just stood up in the middle of the meeting and walked out. He had Ned by the balls!"

"Really?" Charlize responded in astonishment.

"I can't make this shit up," Wayne replied.

"I have never witnessed so much incompetence and backstabbing in my life. My husband gets tired of hearing me talk about it, but I have to express it because I often feel like I am losing my mind. Now he avoids any conversation about work because it is so depressing and frustrating. He wants me to leave, but I just can't."

"I wish there was another place we could work together. We have such a good team and would do so much more if we had the right leadership. Corey acting the way he did during that meeting was so disrespectful—although Ned had it coming because he did the same thing to other people."

"You're right. Ned carved his own path. But once you peel the layers of arrogance away, Ned was the only one who truly cared about the employees. Despite his arrogance and having to be the smartest in the room with his rough approach and poor communication skills, he was truly the one who created our messaging and opened the doors to new ways the industry looks at indexed annuities, and, yes, he had our best interests at heart," Charlize passionately stated. "Adding salt to the wound, Carl was Ned's confidant before Chad was promoted. Carl worked the angles with Ned to put himself in a position of gaining more authority and control—"

"And he did exactly that. Now look where he is. All of this happened right before our very own eyes and no one stopped it," Wayne commented.

"When Chad was promoted, Carl immediately threw Ned under the bus and began playing Chad. I will give the man credit for playing the game! He is good at manipulating people and saying the right things to gain favor with leadership."

"It was always very awkward having to explain our organizational structure and hierarchy to clients. It was the one question I despised getting. 'So, who's in charge, Ned or Chad?' I would give them a bullshit answer about the company growing and the divisions expanding as explanation for having two people practically in the same position. I would do this until they shrugged their shoulders and said, 'Okay, if you say so.' We would smile and move on to the next agenda item in our meeting."

Charlize continued, "In short, this was our way of agreeing that it was messed up without having to actually utter those exact words. You see, the thing is that these companies, our accounts, really don't give a shit how messed up we are as long as our sales keep flowing, and they meet their sales numbers, which means the revenue keeps flowing in. Everyone gets paid. They're happy, so no one gives a shit how fucked up everything is."

"I never really liked having to answer that question either. I would skim over it whenever I could, although on occasion I would outright admit to clients that it didn't make sense. They saw it, but as you mentioned, their number one concern was business, and if business was good, any concerns about the organizational structure were brushed under the rug.

"Ned and I certainly didn't see eye to eye in my first couple of years," Wayne continued. "He was, and still is, rough around the edges. His communication style was jagged, but I am happy to say that it has improved, which I never thought was possible—"

"He's a goddamn bull in a china shop and hard to handle, although a brilliant man who has an amazing vision. I lost count of the number of times I had to do some sort of damage control after he was in front of our clients. It has become something I incorporate into every meeting. And after all this time, I'm still not used to it," Charlize continued.

"Tell me about it. It's always a battle with him," Wayne said with a sigh. "He always has to show that he is the smartest guy in the room and often was."

"I'd say he was the most intelligent guy in the room, maybe not the smartest because he was outsmarted by Carl and Corey."

"Before they fired Amy, I had Chad's ear. I wanted him to do something about the dysfunction and absence of guidance. Even with Amy at the helm, she was in over her head and was letting our team slip. I didn't have the entire picture though. I wish I saw how overworked she was. I could have chosen my words more wisely when speaking with Chad."

"Look, Wayne, it really didn't matter what you did or didn't do. They set her up to fail," Charlize stated.

"I truly thought she didn't care and brushed aside the mounting problems," Wayne said with a tone of regret.

"She did it to herself. She wanted to have it all, just like Corey. She wanted to run our team and be the heroine who saved Pigeon Financial's relationship management team, but she didn't know anything about running relationship management. She was destined for failure. Not having the support of Chad, Corey, Ned, and Carl didn't make things any easier for her. The final straw was Bear and Bull Financial. After they didn't approve the Pension Pledge Indexed Annuity, apparently Chad blew his top, which led to Amy's firing."

"Yeah, Bear and Bull Financial is the most difficult client I have ever worked with. But I had no clue they were the reason for Amy's firing."

"Well, apparently after the numerous attempts at getting the product approved by Bear and Bull Financial, Chad lost his shit. He gave Ned an ultimatum and threatened that one of them was going to lose their job over this, and it was either Ned or Amy. So, Ned looked out for himself, and Amy was fired."

"No shit!" Wayne gasped. "Really?"

"Yes," Charlize replied. "I mean, do you think Ned was going to fire himself?"

"Thinking back on it, it was clear that Ned was under a lot of pressure. He griped, moaned, and yelled at the Bear and Bull Financial team on multiple occasions, often sounding like a whining child who wasn't getting their way. He would cry a sob story about how much money we invested in them, and they owed us. I advised Ned and Amy to take the high road by not bitching and moaning, which the majority of the other product partners did. I urged him to do what no other partner would, which was to take the high road, accept their stance, and foster a relationship. We could come together in partnership to support their efforts and gain a better understanding of their challenges, their workload, anything that would make it easier and open doors for us.

"Of course, that didn't happen, and I apologized for Ned's behavior. I had a private conversation with Christine, who was my counterpart at Bear and Bull Financial to apologize for Ned's behavior."

"You don't have to tell me; he does the same thing with my clients," Charlize said in frustration. "It got to a point at which clients would come to me before Ned. On multiple occasions, I had clients laugh at the absurdity of his behavior. So, what's next? What are you going to do?"

"I don't know. You mentioned it took Amy nearly a year to recover from working here. I think it will take me longer. I hate to say this, but I have no desire to do this any longer. I am so jaded and traumatized by the way this place runs things and how poorly they treat employees."

"Amy was devastated," Charlize commented. "But once she left, the healing process began. Her health improved, she lost weight, and she spent time with her husband and kids. Despite it taking nearly a year for her to recover, it provided her with a new perspective, which allowed her to realize how awful it really was working here."

"I will definitely need to give it time. This will be a gradual healing process until suddenly I'll be ready for my next step. But, for now, I need to wash my hands and mind of this place."

After he spoke with Charlize, Wayne made a call to Patrice. They had been very close and often spoke about the dysfunction at Pigeon Financial and their shared desire to leave, so when he gave her the news, it came as no surprise to her. She was saddened by the news but happy she had the opportunity to work with Wayne.

Words to Lead By

Q: Has your leadership training, or absence of leadership training, failed you and your people?

"Sometimes we are failing so slowly, we think we are doing fine. Your business may be failing, one pointless conversation at a time. Do you struggle with missed sales targets? Are employees texting under the table during meetings? Do your high-level projects stall out?"[19]

---

[19] "Five Conversations You Need to Start Having Today," https://fierceinc.com.

🧠 I Healed

> The body cannot heal because the body cannot make itself sick. It needs no healing. Its health or sickness depends entirely on how the mind perceives it, and the purpose that the mind would use it for.
>
> —*A Course in Miracles*

After speaking with Charlize and receiving numerous calls from colleagues and even competitors, Wayne felt good about his decision. He felt good about the relationships he had established over the years, which were reflected in the kind words shared by many.

Speaking with his friend Gary about life and career always gave Wayne a different perspective, a perspective of appreciation and seeing things for the best, no matter how difficult. Of course, breaking the news to Gary wasn't easy because he was not the one to hold back his thoughts and true feelings. This often upset Wayne, but it was helpful, and he always appreciated his honesty.

It was time for Wayne to heal and move on with this life. A few months after resigning, he spoke with Gary again in one of their regular Friday night conversations. "I experienced my own healing after I resigned from my job," Wayne said.

"What?"

"For about an entire year prior to my resignation, I had two cuts, maybe you'd call them wounds, that wouldn't heal. Less than a month after I resigned, they miraculously healed!"

"What sort of wounds are we talking about?"

"I had a bruised toenail. Actually, I believe it was dead. The other was a cut, or abrasion, on my forehead. So, the big toe of my right foot was black and blue, and the toenail looked dead, but a new one wasn't growing."

"Well, you do know that it can take up to a year for a toenail to grow, right?" Gary stated.

"At the time, I didn't realize it, but once it healed, I looked up how long it typically takes for a toenail to heal. Either way, my toenail appeared stuck as though it wasn't healing at all. You know when a new toenail is growing, you can see the new nail pushing its way up at the base of the toenail?"

"Yes. It takes a long time."

"When I ran the Media Five Mile Race about fifteen years ago, I ran with shoes that were too small. Long story short, my big toenail died. It hurt like a son of a bitch! I mean it *really* hurt! Eventually, it fell off and a new one grew. But it certainly did not take a year; it didn't even take six months. This time, it was different. It was clear the toenail was dead, and for several months, a new one didn't seem to be growing. Then I resigned from my job, and less than a month later, the dead toenail was gone."

"Hmmm. Interesting," Gary responded with a tone of doubt.

"You think I am crazy?"

"Nooo."

"Well, let me tell you about the cut on my forehead," Wayne responded.

"Okay."

"This one is even more intriguing and one that worried me. It started as a little scratch on my forehead, right in the middle. It healed and scabbed over. When the scab fell away, the cut reopened. Instead of fully healing, it would scab over again. The scab would fall away again, revealing the light-pink delicate flesh of my forehead. It bled lightly until it scabbed over again. Once again, the scab fell away, revealing the light-pink delicate flesh of my forehead. This cycle repeated itself week after week, month after month for nearly a year."

"Yeah, that's strange. It should have healed itself in about a week," Gary interjected.

"Exactly! But it didn't show any signs of getting better. It was about the size of the fingernail on my pinky finger, but it was slowly getting bigger and a little worse each time. I know it was there for at least eight months because I have a picture from the summer prior, and the cut was very visible. Compared to my toenail, this was really strange!"

"Did you go to the doctor to get it checked out?" Gary asked in his usual logical way.

"Come on, Gary!" Wayne chuckled. "Of course not. After a while, I became self-conscious of it though. I would always catch myself picking at it. While in Florida for a business meeting, I was talking with our eastern divisional sales manager when I noticed his eyes breaking away from mine to stare at the cut on my forehead."

"Dude, you need to get that checked out."

"After that, I hurried back to my hotel room to look at it. I even took a picture of it while I was riding the elevator back to my hotel room. Deep down, I knew what prevented the cut from healing."

"What was it?"

"Work. Well, more aptly stated, stress from work. It was all the stress and anxiety that had built up. It was my damn mind-set. I loved my job and thoroughly enjoyed the work. The stress I am referring to is the stress from an overabundance of toxic energy and the downright shitty management at Pigeon Financial. I believe this was what prevented the cut and my toenail from healing. I even have a scar on my forehead where the cut was. Whenever I look in the mirror, I am reminded why I resigned."

"Whew! Dude, I don't know what to say or believe."

"I am as amazed as you. Think about it, I resigned on May 8, and my official final day was on May 18. Take a guess when the cut healed?"

"No clue."

"June second!" Wayne enthusiastically replied. "Fifteen days after I left, both the cut and toenail healed! All I am saying, Gary, is that you cannot ignore that fact that illness is also attributable to nonphysical factors like stress, anxiety, and a negative mind-set. Our thoughts are just as powerful, if not more powerful, than physical causes of disease and illness."

"I follow you, but at the same time, I am a little skeptical." Gary sighed. "I am going to have to let this sit with me so I can make sense of it."

"Listen, Gary, you know I wouldn't make this up. I am a living example of the mind-body connection. Louise Hay, who published the book *Heal Your Body*, over forty years ago, back when you and I were in first grade, discussed the connection between the mind and body, as Dr. Wayne Dyer, Eckhart Tolle, and many other spiritual leaders have. I am a living example of what they teach," Wayne continued. "Although it may not be nearly as dramatic or amazing as Anita Moorjani's story in *Dying to Be Me*, it can't be ignored."

"I've heard of Dr. Wayne Dyer. The others don't ring a bell, but you certainly have my attention though."

"The approach to medicine is to attack and destroy. Western medicine is not about finding a cure but rather identifying the disease and destroying it. We cut; we attack and remove rather than understanding, healing, and nourishing the body. We do the same thing in business. People have been taught to attack, to eat what you kill, to swim with the sharks, and so on, rather than understand people, their mind-set, and help them grow to become better."

"Well, what about mentorships? I have always had a mentor, and it worked."

"Mentorship is a great idea, but if the mentor has been taught to attack and annihilate rather than lift one up, this is where I will have to challenge that approach. If you can ride on the shoulders of giants, then the mentorship program is far more beneficial. Instead of teaching you to step on and over the shoulders of others to become successful, the good ones allow you to ride on their shoulders while showing you the way." Wayne continued, "There is a growing community of people who agree that disease is caused not only by toxic foods but also toxic energy, such as stress, anxiety, negativity—basically, fear or a negative mind-set."

"I believe you're right," Gary commented. "Stress and anxiety without a doubt contribute to cancer and other illnesses."

"Even more controversial is what I believe the cure is, which spits in the face of modern medicine. Considering you are in the pharmaceutical industry, I am curious what your thoughts are," Wayne said. "This is a growing elephant standing in the middle of the waiting room of life that can no longer be ignored. The more it's talked about, the more we hear real-life stories of survival. The more people who come out and speak openly about this, the less likely society will be willing to brush the truth aside.

"Take my wife's situation. Although heredity played its part when she was diagnosed with stage-four non-Hodgkin's lymphoma, it was her belief that the cancer was triggered by poor diet, excessive physical exercise, and stress from her career. All converged into a perfect storm, allowing the cancer to thrive."

"Hold on, Wayne," Gary interjected. "You're saying it was hereditary?"

"Yes and no. We inherit our parents' traits through DNA."

"Okay, I believe that."

"My wife's great-grandmother died in her early thirties apparently from pneumonia. When my wife was diagnosed with non-Hodgkin's lymphoma, her initial symptoms looked very much like pneumonia. Considering there were not nearly as many forms of this type of cancer in prior generations made it difficult to detect it, so illnesses like non-Hodgkin's lymphoma were misdiagnosed as pneumonia. In addition, there weren't nearly as many methods of treatment. Luckily, she caught it in time and found the perfect oncologist to treat and eradicate the cancer. The many advancements in the field of medicine have brought more treatment options and methods of early detection, which were not available to her great-grandmother. Plus, we were blessed to have found the greatest doctor we could have ever asked for. He provided the perfect treatment and approach to heal my wife, but I believe he did not cure the disease. Or, to put it another way, he didn't find a way to prevent it from manifesting again. He killed the cancer, or rid it from her body, which was amazing, but as far as a cure, chemotherapy and radiation therapy is not a cure. Rather, a cure can be found by changing lifestyle, diet, and nutrition. My wife changed what she consumed by removing toxic foods and removing the toxicity of stress by choosing a different direction in her life. She took it upon herself to ensure her body would no longer be conducive for the disease to thrive. Sue's previous lifestyle created the ideal situation, or terrain, for cancer to thrive. A tree will not grow from a seed in an environment that is not conducive for it to thrive. When it comes to cancer and other diseases, this is very similar."

"Okay. I follow," Gary commented. "Believe it or not, I am on the same page with you. I agree that both physical and mental stressors contribute to illness. But we want to always consider heredity. As you mentioned, I believe we inherit, or are predisposed, to diseases that our parents were exposed to. So, do I hear you saying that we can prevent these hereditary illnesses from happening?"

"Yes. I believe we can also disinherit these disease traits. To put it another way, we can disrupt apparent inherited diseases by breaking the cycle in a good way."

"Huh?"

"Our children inherited our physical features and even personality traits, right?"

"Yes."

"And we also learn by example, we learn from our parents and our environment. If we change our learning and environment, even our perspective of disease, then our inheritance can change. Maybe more importantly, when we change our perspective, or belief system, to one focused on health rather than sickness, the world we once saw changes for the better, and now anything is possible.

"My wife's survival is twofold. First, she removed the disease by choosing the only cure she knew of at the time, which was chemotherapy and radiation therapy. She broke the cycle of her inheritance by changing her environment and changing her belief system, ultimately changing her perspective. This was done through an improved diet, which is based on living an alkaline lifestyle. Plus, the removal of bad stress from her life has also been a critical factor as well. Therein lies the cure. This is a very general overview. I'm not getting into the details of the research, although this knowledge is not new by any means. It has been practiced and readily available for decades, even centuries. It just has not been adapted by the masses and therefore has been disregarded. You should read *The Biology of Belief* by Dr. Bruce Lipton.

"Even the pharmaceutical industry is threatened by this because in effect it mitigates the need for drugs and even vaccines, which in the long run could threaten the pharmaceutical industry. Talk about putting profits before people! In short, physical and mental health are equally important to our overall wellness. Many people have a difficult time accepting this, but more are waking up to the possibilities. Often when they do, they're still reluctant to change their lifestyle because we're creatures of habit and most have not been trained to think this way."

"I am with you, brother!" Gary enthusiastically replied. "Even though I sell pharmaceuticals, I understand what you are talking about. Many of the pharmaceuticals mask the illness rather than cure it, and people take far too many prescription drugs."

"I almost forgot why I got on this topic in the first place," Wayne commented.

"Oh! There's more?" Gary chuckled out of curiosity.

"Of course! You know I always have something to keep you on your toes."

"Yes, you certainly do!"

"Have you ever read Anita Moorjani's book?" Wayne asked.

"Nope, never heard of it. What's it called?"

"*Dying to Be Me.* The CliffsNotes version, she had end stage cancer, and while in the hospital, she died. The doctors confirmed her death, but she had one of those near-death experiences. When she returned to life, she was no longer in pain, and her cancer was gone! The cancer disappeared, yet the doctors would not accept it. Instead, they kept on searching for the cancer, determined to find it. They continued performing tests and searched for the cancer because they thought it was impossible for it to just vanish. Plus, they were so stuck in their ways by what they were taught that they were determined to locate it somewhere in her body because they had to administer the chemotherapy regimen they had prepared for her. Just like war, we identify the threat and want to annihilate it."

Wayne grabbed the book from his bag, opened it to the page that had been bookmarked and began reading.

> The doctor came into my room with a whole team of hospital personnel, looking concerned. Then he spoke: "We have the results of the bone-marrow biopsy, but it's a little disturbing."
>
> For the first time in days, I felt some anxiety. "Why? What's the problem?"
>
> My family members were in the hospital room with me, and all of them looked worried.
>
> "We can't find the cancer in your bone-marrow biopsy," he said.
>
> "So how is that a problem?" Danny asked. "Doesn't that just mean she doesn't have cancer in her bone marrow?"
>
> "No, that's not possible," the doctor said. "She definitely has cancer in her body—it can't disappear so quickly like that. We simply have to find it; and until we do, it's a problem, because I'm unable to determine her drug dose."
>
> So, the doctors sent my bone-marrow sample to one of the most sophisticated pathology labs in the country. Four days later, the results returned negative—there was no trace of cancer. I felt an overwhelming sense of victory upon hearing the news.
>
> Not to be defeated, the doctors then wanted to conduct a lymph-node biopsy to find the cancer.

"Sorry for all of the buildup, but I wanted to share that because it speaks to what I experienced with my healing—not remotely like

Anita Moorjani's experience, but the idea is along the same line of thought."

"That's a powerful story."

Words to Lead By

Q: Is your work killing you? Does workplace stress cause disease?

"If you have a cruel boss or rotten co-workers, beware. It may not be just your job that's on the line."[20]

---

[20] "Workplace Stress and Your Health," WebMD.com.

Blackballed

Go ahead. Follow your heart. I dare you.

—*T. E. Corner*

It was a Saturday in December 2018. Wayne, Sue, and their daughters were getting ready for a two-hour drive to Sue's brother's house to spend an early Christmas with his family.

"All I am saying is that I now understand that I can make big changes like my resignation with less chaos and suffering," Wayne said to his wife.

"Well, I wish you saw that before you decided to make the damn decision to leave," Sue said in frustration.

"I know, and I'm sorry. But if I didn't follow my inner guidance and summon the courage to face my fears, this downward spiral would have continued, and believe it or not, it might have ended up worse."

"Really? I don't think it can get much worse."

"Okay, I get your point, and I'm sorry. I'm sorry for putting you through this. This is the last time I make such a dramatic shift."

"You're damn right it is!" Sue exclaimed. "Because if you do this again, I am going to either leave you or kill you!"

"I know, and I am sorry, but I was not going to allow myself to wake up one day to realize that my life had passed me by because I was afraid to change and find a way to become better. Yes, how I went about it was fucked up. All of the shit I put you through was unnecessary.

"I want to express my gratitude for your patience through all of this, and I am truly sorry for any pain I caused," Wayne said, hoping his wife would understand.

"You know I love you, and I am doing my best to understand what you're going through, but I am still so damn mad at you! Why did you have to do it this way?"

"I didn't know any other way at the time. This sounds crazy, but my perspective was fucked up. I have been working on changing my outlook away from anger and attack toward love and forgiveness. This will allow me to make peace with myself and the assholes I worked with. It's clear I have a way to go and still hold on to remnants of resentment, but I'm doing my best to let go."

"Yeah, I can see that," she responded in a sarcastic tone followed by a smile.

"Would you stop?" he moaned in response to his wife's sarcastic comment. "You know what I mean."

"Yes, I do. I am just messing with you," she smiled.

"I still don't condone how they run the company and how they treat their employees. On the flip side of the coin, I too realize that this is a dual healing. The company will not heal unless the leaders heal or are removed. And I sure as shit wasn't going to heal until I changed my perspective or left."

"You certainly succeeded at leaving," she said, hitting him hard.

It was supposed to be a time of joy and celebration while on their way to see their cousins for the Christmas holiday, but an energy of doom and despair filled the air.

"Has your reputation been damaged?" Sue asked again. Tears flooded down her cheeks. Her eyes hidden behind her sunglasses, the tears streamed over her chin and down her neck. She gazed out the window. "You said nothing would change!"

———◆———

Wayne did in fact say those exact words six months prior. They were driving into Bala Cynwyd on their way to dinner at Bluefin Sushi. They were on City Line Avenue driving through Lower Merion, approaching the Saint Joseph's University campus. Bluefin was not too far past the campus in the heart of the local news broadcasting networks, ABC 6 Action News, NBC 10 Philadelphia, and CBS 3 Philadelphia.

The warm June evening sun emitted a blood-red hue across the horizon as it set. In a timid voice, he said, "Nothing has changed. I am the same person I have always been, but I was going down the wrong path, and something had to change. My job and the immense negative energy surrounding me at work. Nothing in our lives needs to change unless you believe it does."

"Wayne, how the hell do you expect me to believe that hocus-pocus shit?" Sue continued. "We have three daughters to raise. You cannot tell me nothing's changed when in fact everything has changed!" The shower of tears continued flowing down her cheeks, soaking her blouse.

Thoughts jumped around in Wayne's head. *Maybe she's right. The more she freaks out, the more doubt and fear creeps into my mind, where none existed before. All my belief in "All things possible" seems to be fading. Why is she making such a big deal out of this?*

He felt the past few years of his personal development and awakening of sorts suddenly turning to shit as his wife ranted about his huge mistake, how he fucked up her life, and how she had nothing left. All the progress he made with his life coach over the past several years was falling apart right before his eyes.

Thoughts of failure, worthlessness, and doubt romped around his mind. Then, in an instant, he decided not to allow the doubt and fear to creep in. *Fuck that! She's speaking from fear. Shit! She doesn't understand what I'm going through. I'm not going to die with my music still in me. No regrets!* "I'm sure you won't understand." Wayne spoke up.

"You're damn right I won't understand. I will never understand!" she roared.

"Look, I am trying to figure out what the fuck is going on. I'm working through this shit. If your comments are intended to help and make me feel better, well, they're not!"

"I don't give a shit how you feel right now. I'm the one who's upset and needs to feel better!" Sue screamed.

"Look, working at Pigeon Financial was a fucking shit show. I lost all confidence and desire in my ability to do my job and began doubting myself. Despite your intention to offer love and support, your questions feel more like an interrogation."

"Well, I do believe in you, and I wasn't being critical, but I am beginning to lose faith. I need you to tell me that everything is going to be okay!"

"It will be okay," he responded in all sincerity, but he just didn't know when. "I could apologize a million times and tell you everything will work out, yet it still won't be enough. Words are not going to ease your fears. I know you need more than that. You need to see something tangible that things are getting better, but I have nothing to offer at this point."

Wayne knew the biggest challenge was time. *A Course in Miracles* says, "Delay does not matter in eternity, but it is tragic in time." He had made a monumental change in his life, which seemed tragic to those close to him, but deep down, he knew nothing really changed other than how he saw the world, which would become much clearer for him.

"I saw this coming but did a poor job of preparing for it," he said, seeking her forgiveness and understanding.

"You sure did," Sue interjected.

"I'm finally learning that I don't need to create so much suffering for myself and everyone else when I desire change in my life. I can easily plan for it and ease into it without drama."

"No shit!" she interrupted.

"But that was all I knew for the longest time. By creating chaos and wreaking havoc, I believed it forced me to change. I'm finally seeing things clearly."

"You better fucking see things clearly. That was nearly the last decision you ever made."

"I had to make this change. If not, I would have continued down the same path of destruction. I had to change my perspective because the leadership at Pigeon Financial weren't going to take that step anytime soon, if ever. Even if they did change things for the better, nothing would've improved in my life or career until I changed," Wayne continued, hoping his wife would understand and forgive him. "Despite the fucked-up morale and deplorable leadership at work, I was making things worse because I was so burnt out and tired of all of the bullshit."

"You're damn right you made things worse!" she taunted him.

"Come on. I've told you I'm sorry and beg for your forgiveness. But I had to do it. I thought you'd understand, at least a little."

"Nope! I don't understand any of it!"

"This sounds drastic, but I could have continued doing what I was doing and ended up sick because of the mental and physical stress."

"Don't pull that bullshit with me, Wayne!"

"I am not pulling anything, but I want you to understand how bad it was," he replied. *She has no idea what I was dealing with,* he thought to himself. "Listen, I had a dead toenail and a cut on my forehead, both of which were not healing. The toenail was dead for a year, and the cut on my forehead wasn't healing. Actually, it was getting worse. This lasted more than eight months. The cut should have healed in about two weeks. Not eight months! Once I resigned, they both healed in a couple weeks. All I am saying is that I was not in a good place."

"I just wish you told me about how bad things were."

"I did over a year ago, a few days before the national sales meeting. If that wasn't a sign, I'm not sure what was."

"Sure, it was a message, Wayne. One that I wasn't ready for. I just wish you planned it better because you really handled this in the worst way."

"I know, and I'm sorry," he pleaded. "I often ask myself if I made a mistake."

"Really? You have to ask yourself that question?" his wife retaliated. "Allow me to answer it for you. Yes, you made a mistake. You made a fucking big mistake!"

"Now that's not helping," he replied. "Deep down, I know it was the right thing to do in order to make the real change I desire."

"What about our family? You have three kids to support."

"Thanks for reminding me." He sighed. "There was nothing I could do about the crumbling morale and growing toxicity at Pigeon Financial even in light of receiving the promotion. It was too much. Admittedly, I handled it poorly when making my decision to leave, but I have no doubt it was the best thing to do."

Going to the edge makes us stronger and allows us to break through barriers that otherwise were impenetrable. Clearing expressing these emotions in words in order for someone else to understand can be a difficult task. When they too are in the eye of the storm, where fear rules, getting them to see clearly and understand the importance of riding it out makes it even more challenging. But, when we allow the storm runs its course, clarity is always the result.

He was speaking in words of enlightenment and of a heightened awareness while she was speaking in words of fear, death, and despair. For practically his entire life, he understood the language of fear and anger that she was speaking, but he had found another way to view the world. He would not allow the fears of others, the expectations of others, to pull him back into the perceived depths of hell.

With each tear and gasp of fear, she pulled him back into the fear mind-set he had been escaping from his entire life. He kept asking for signs that all was well, and despite being offered signs practically every moment of every day, he was unable to see them. Deep down, he knew all was well, but he felt completely lost because there was no convincing his wife of that.

"I'm sorry" were the only words he could find. Although he wasn't sorry about what he had done, because it needed to be done, he was sorry for the distress it was causing her. Words could not convey his true feelings. Words were no good at this point because they were just that, words. She needed action. She needed something tangible she could see, something she could validate, but so far, he was coming up empty.

"Do I really have to go back to work? How much money do we have? Do you still have a retirement plan?"

Tissues were drenched in her tears as she wiped her eyes. Holding another tissue in her opposite hand, she blew her nose. A white cloud of tissues piled up on the floor of the car drenched in tears of frustration and fear.

"Our savings are gone. My retirement is practically gone," he responded. He wanted to feel sad about it, but he wasn't. It was just money, and money didn't mean shit in the grand scheme of things. Of course, for the rest of the world, this was a total disaster.

"You betrayed me. You lied to me. Now I have nothing! My parents are gone. I left my career to raise the kids, and now I have no skills to even get a job. I have nothing. I grew up with nothing my entire life, and I told myself I would never live that way again. I am at your mercy, and I don't like it. You better fucking fix this!"

There was nothing to say. What could he say? All and any apologies would not bring her to find forgiveness. Even though they sat beside one another only separated by the center console of the car, they were worlds apart. He couldn't reach her, and she couldn't reach him. His words were foreign to her, as her words of anger and fear were pulling him back into a place he no longer cared to be.

"Why can't you just go to work and do your job like everyone else? It's not that fucking difficult. You have to get a job!"

"I know," was all he could say.

"I don't think you do! Do you think your reputation has been damaged?"

"Yes! Everything is fucked up! What do you want me to say!" The words roared from his mouth. "You need to back off! You have no idea about the kind of shit I had to deal with at work! You never wanted to hear about it anyway, so how in the world can you have a damn clue when you never wanted to talk about it? I am not making light of the fact that we have three daughters to raise, but you have the best job in the world, and I think you hate it. All I hear are complaints about the kids. They are fucking kids. That's what kids are supposed to do. The house is a fucking mess. Can't you fucking clean the house? For fucking Christ's sake, you don't work, and I do. I know I am going to regret saying that. Don't fucking believe for one minute my job is easy, fun, or enjoyable. At least you are around people who love you always. They're not going to fire you because you might have fucked up or you might disagree or you lose your patience. You will always have a job and never have to be afraid your kids are going to lay you off, deceive you, or tell you that you are doing it wrong.

"You had cancer for fuck's sake! You had stage-four cancer and could be dead. Why the fuck are you so upset? This is nothing compared to what you've been through. Get off my fucking back!" Wayne roared in rage.

"Yes, my reputation is fucked. I can't get a fucking job. I have had so many conversations. I have spoken with so many people, but I cannot even get a fucking interview. Yes, I feel as though I have been blackballed. Yeah, I fucked up."

"Are you going to answer me? Do you think your reputation has been damaged?" his wife asked again.

Wayne's rant was in his head. "Thank God," he thought to himself. "I'm so glad I didn't say those things."

Then he spoke. "Yes, it feels like it. It's strange that I haven't been able to get people to call me back. Even connections I have known for years. Linda at Presidential Financial Group ghosted me after I spoke with her. I can't even get Jeff Sidecar to call me back."

"Can you call Pigeon Financial back and ask them to rehire you?"

"Are you out of your mind? Who the fuck does that? Hell no!" Wayne thought to himself. Then he responded, "No, I can't do that, and I won't do that."

"What about Ned Desilent? You said you had a good relationship with him."

"No. I am not asking him. Although I have been in touch with him and he has offered to help in any way he can. I won't do that. Plus, he has no leverage. They fucked him over."

Deep down, Wayne felt the reason he could not get a job or get anyone to call him back was because he didn't want one. He was not ready. He was so far gone that any belief he once had in himself was nowhere to be found. He was one of the best professionals in his line of work, but it was as though he was experiencing some sort of post-traumatic stress disorder syndrome and needed time to recover. He just could not shake it. Pigeon Financial was such a mind-fuck, and Wayne was not the only victim.

"Well, then what are you going to do?" she asked in as patient a voice as possible.

Wayne's eyes were laser focused on the road ahead of him. "I don't know. It is not like I'm doing nothing. I'm applying for jobs. I'm calling my contacts. I've been in contact with so many people, but it feels like a huge void where I cannot get a response from anyone other than rejection emails."

"What about your stepbrother? Have you called him?"

"No."

"Then call him."

"Okay. I will when I am ready."

Their oldest daughter, Abby, removed her headphones and in a quiet voice called from the back of the car, "Mommy, are you okay?"

"Yes, sweetie. I'm fine."

"Why are you crying?"

"It's okay. I am just having a conversation with your dad, and I felt sad for a moment. But I'm fine."

"You're not getting a divorce, are you?"

"No, sweetie," she replied. Looking over at Wayne, in a quiet voice, she asked, "Are we?"

"I don't know," Wayne replied although he thought it might be the best solution, considering how much Sue despised him right now for all the havoc he created.

"I could have stayed the course working in a very toxic environment. Sorry, but it's not just me. You can ask practically any ex-employee who worked for Pigeon Financial, and if they're honest, they will tell you it was a death sentence working there. You could even ask anyone who is still there, and they will tell you. Charlize will tell you. All I can tell you is everything will be fine. What I cannot tell you is when, and for that, I am sorry," Wayne repeated himself. He could do nothing to ease her fears other than get a job. But he was not going to get any job just to ease her fears. What good would that do? Working from a place of fear and desperation would be another death sentence.

He had to figure out his next step. He had to make peace with and forgive so much and so many people and himself. But when is it the right time? It is never the right time, and then it is too late! "You are not going to die with your music still in you," he heard the words of Dr. Wayne Dyer echo through his mind.

"I will get a job. Everything will be okay. That's all I can tell you, and I know it's not enough. I know that won't make this go away and ease your fears. For that, I am sorry. I am sorry for everything. I am sorry for the way I handled it."

"Okay. Then get a job."

"I will."

They rode in silence for the next forty-five minutes of their journey, but his head was loud and rambunctious with thoughts. The mosh-pit of his mind was insane with activity, and he wasn't sure he would make it out this time.

The conversations Wayne had with fellow employees after he resigned were those of love and support, some envious. The comments he received were "Take me with you!" "Let me know what I can do to help you out." "Thank you for what you've done. I am at Best Buy right now buying a new printer and paper. I am getting my résumé together and will be gone come October." "I don't blame you. I'd like to leave, but I just can't." "They're losing the only leader they ever had."

Ellen DeGeneres was blackballed by Hollywood, television, the media, and basically the world because she followed her truth. She followed her heart and was brave enough to reveal it to the world, and the world shunned her! For three fucking years, they shut her out. She was blackballed! And for what? Because she didn't care to remain in line with the rest of the world? Because she got out of line to find her truth? She got out of line for love, not anger, not hatred, but love, and she was blackballed.

Because she found the strength and courage to follow her truth, it allowed others to do the same. She broke down barriers of fear and judgment. Now she is beloved more than ever before. Wayne believed she didn't want to die with her music still in her. What if she never announced her truth? Where would she be now? Where would we be as a society?

If Wayne was blackballed for speaking his truth, if he was cast aside because he believed in loving your people, because he believed in Rule Number Eight to "Love your passengers," then there was a greater issue at hand in the world that must be revealed and uprooted.

Those who put up with and allow this atrocious behavior and deplorable treatment of employees to continue are condoning the disgrace in the workplace by standing in line and allowing it to continue.

Words to Lead By

Q: As a manager, do you herd your people, like cattle and sheep, to a slaughter of pride and confidence, or do you lead people to a better way of life, both personally and professionally?

Q: Are you willing to risk being blackballed by standing up, speaking up, maybe walking away from the toxicity and mindless management, in order to make the positive changes necessary to improve the workplace, your life, and your career?

[D]ecision makers at the top of the food chain spend billions of
dollars every year on everything but hiring the right managers.
They'll buy miserable employees latte machines for their offices,
give them free lunch and sodas, or even worse—just let them all
work at home, hailing an "enlightened" policy of telecommuting.
—Jim Clifton, Gallup CEO

In healthy companies, people debate issues. They know that smart people won't always agree. They expect dissent around any big management decision, and they keep the lines of communication open. They don't silence people who disagree with them because they know that healthy debate is good for them and bad for their competitors.

—Liz Ryan

The single biggest decision you make in your job—bigger than all the rest—is who you name manager. When you name the wrong person manager, nothing fixes that bad decision. Not compensation, not benefits—nothing.

—Jim Clifton, Gallup CEO

Jumping Back into the Toxic Soup

You're a piece of lumber to them now, and you'll
stay a piece of lumber once you begin the job.

—*Liz Ryan*

It was a warm spring day toward the end of April 2019. Wayne was doing some work at his favorite coffee shop, Burlap and Bean.

On this day, his friend Gary was going to meet him for one of their regular "masterminds" as Gary liked to refer to their get-togethers. Gary walked in and greeted Wayne with a handshake and a hug. "Sorry, it took me a little longer to get here than I expected."

"No worries. I was just getting some work done. Glad you could make it!" Wayne exclaimed. "How are Gabby and the kids?"

"Paula is doing great in school, and Gary Junior is deciding which college he wants to attend. Things are great! How about you? What's the latest in your world?"

"Do you remember back in February when I applied for a job with Magma Insurance Company?"

"Yeah, what ever happened with that?" Gary asked.

"How much time to you have?"

"As much as you need," Gary happily responded.

"When I first saw the job posted on LinkedIn, I immediately sent an InMail to the head of the sales division, requesting an opportunity to introduce myself."

"Good idea."

"I put on a full-court press by contacting everyone I knew who worked for Magma Insurance Company to ask for references. After that, I reached out to several industry colleagues and contacts, asking if they would make a call to the hiring manager and put in a good word for me."

"Impressive!"

"Thanks, but I wasn't done. Once I found out who the hiring manager was, I reached out to his ex-boss, who I happened to have a good relationship with. I made sure there wouldn't be any opportunities for them to overlook me for the role. By the time I secured my first interview, I felt very confident about landing the job."

"Wow!"

"It certainly was a strange interview process."

"How so?"

"I expected the interview process to be more thorough and professional. I didn't even have an in-person interview."

"That's surprising."

"The first interview was a thirty-minute phone call on Valentine's Day. The hiring manager, Phillip, opened up the conversation, commenting about how surprised he was by the number of people who reached out to him, recommending me for the job."

"That was a result of your tenacity and past success."

"Three weeks after the first interview, I had a second one. This was another thirty-minute phone interview with the hiring manager's business associate, Danny. This guy was clearly not a seasoned interviewer. At the outset of the interview, he made a comment that he needed only five minutes for our interview. I used the entire thirty minutes though to make sure he knew I was the right guy for the job."

"That is a strange interview process, especially considering Magma Insurance Company is one of the world's largest insurance and investment companies. I would never open an interview making a comment like that. It sounds very unprofessional and amateurish," Gary stated.

"Toward the end of March, I received a voice mail message from the human resources recruiter asking me to call her back so she could provide me with an update regarding my candidacy for the position.

Let me tell you how much I abhor HR recruiters. They speak in these generalities that drive me crazy!

"The interview process is so stressful for most job applicants, and emotions are high. Having to deal with the HR recruiters adds to the stress. They typically use the same jargon. The 'candidate' who is interviewing for the job is expected to act with the utmost professionalism, yet these recruiters seem so callous, sucking the life out of you with an impersonal and far-from-uplifting email or phone call."

"I believe they are either trained to be emotionless, or after years of crushing people's hopes and dreams, they themselves become emotionless and dull," Gary interjected.

"What's worse is when the company recruiter goes silent. They've been ghosting job candidates for decades. I don't think they give a shit about how awful it feels to be left in the lurch. Apparently, somewhere along the line, it became acceptable for recruiters and companies to ghost job candidates without giving it a second thought. Now the tide has turned, and candidates are ghosting employers. After all these years of treating job candidates like shit, the moment they get a taste of their own medicine, they bitch and moan about how unprofessional this sort of behavior is. Assholes!"

A guy sitting a few tables away glanced over at them upon hearing the profanity spew from Wayne's mouth. "Sorry," Wayne voiced to the stranger.

"I recently read an article that mentioned people will even accept job offers and then ghost on their first day of work," Gary interjected.

Wayne laughed. "In a way, many of these employers got what was coming to them. But I digress. So, the HR recruiter at Magma Insurance immediately followed up the phone call with an email. Although I was anxious and wanted to call back right away, I realized I shouldn't be, and there was no sense of urgency on my behalf. Especially if it was bad news, why would I want to call back in such a hurry to be rejected? So, I decided to wait it out and send an email reply later that evening."

"I guess that makes sense. But why did you wait?"

"Stay with me. I thought the recruiter would have left the office for the day and therefore would not see my email until Friday morning, meaning she wouldn't have time to speak with me on Friday, so she would end up scheduling a call with me on Monday or Tuesday of the following week."

"Okay?" Gary responded not exactly sure why Wayne was handling it the way he did. "I'm not sure why you were delaying the inevitable. You should have pulled the Band-Aid off with one quick tug."

"Yeah, yeah. I'm sure you're right, but I was tired of hearing 'no' after 'no.' Especially after responding in a professional and courteous manner to be told they decided to pursue more qualified candidates or some other bullshit line."

"Yeah, I get it. So, what happened?"

"Of course, she replied to my email that evening and offered to call me the following morning at ten o'clock. My master plan failed!"

"That's funny!" Gary let out a laugh.

"Yeah, in hindsight, it is pretty funny!" Wayne laughed along with Gary. "Friday morning comes around, and ten o'clock was quickly approaching. You know, come to think of it, it was March 29, the day after my daughter's birthday and two days before my wedding anniversary. I had a lot to celebrate and be happy for."

"Yes, you do. Whose birthday was it, Kylie's?" Gary asked.

"Yep. She turned ten."

"That's awesome! So, what anniversary was it, twentieth?"

"Eighteenth. The twentieth is right around the corner."

"Congrats!"

Wayne recollected his phone call with the recruiter. He tried to remain cool before the recruiter called. Time dragged on, making it feel like an eternity. Wayne looked at the time on his iPhone practically every thirty seconds as he anxiously awaited the call. Ten o'clock came and went, but his phone did not ring.

He looked at his phone again to make sure it was not in airplane mode. It was not. He checked to make sure he had reception. He did. He checked to make sure it was not in do not disturb mode. It was not. Finally, about ten minutes past the hour, his phone rang.

Having gone through these sorts of conversations with recruiters, he learned to become emotionally detached from the entire encounter.

"Hello, this is Wayne," he answered in a monotone voice.

"Hi, Wayne. This is Maria. How are you today?"

"Good," came his curt reply.

"Is this still a good time?"

"Yes," he replied with no inflection in his voice.

"I wanted to speak with you to give you an update on your candidacy for the sales role ..." She droned on, using the same damn same script every human resources recruiter uses. He wanted her to forgo the meaningless formalities and get to the damn point!

"Okay."

"We would like to extend you an offer ..."

Everything went silent. Wayne hit the mute button on his phone and mumbled, "What the fuck just happened? I wrote this damn job off after they went silent for two weeks."

<hr />

After hearing Wayne's version of events, Gary exclaimed, "Oh my god! I can't believe you got the job!"

"Me too. Especially after taking the personality assessment which was followed by two weeks of silence."

"Oh boy! You didn't tell me about that."

"After my second interview, they asked me to complete a Myers-Briggs personality profiling questionnaire. I can't stand those things. Another automated and impersonal approach to hiring. Once I completed it, I heard nothing from them for more than two weeks, so I figured I lost the job."

"I can't believe you got the offer!" Gary repeated himself.

"Yep. But, you know, I really wasn't that excited about it. Deep down, I wasn't ready to work for another large insurance company, at least not yet. Even though it had been nearly a year since my resignation, I was still recovering from the trauma of working at Pigeon Financial."

"Well, either way, I'm impressed by the way you handled yourself, Wayne. I am even more impressed by your persistence and resourcefulness. You really know how to go after something when you want it, even if it is for the wrong reasons. I am sorry you experienced all that bullshit at Pigeon Financial. I never could have fathomed how bad it was."

"Thanks, Gary, but I think I did it to myself. I worked my ass off from the day I walked through the doors." Wayne described the situation to Gary.

He likened it to running a race, but in this race, he was running for his life. "You put your head down and start sprinting as fast as you can, just running and running for your life, never looking up. You just keep running because that is all you know. You keep running because you're afraid that if you stop, you will fail or die. Although it seems to be working, you keep running until one day, you stop out of exhaustion and finally take a moment to look up to see what's around you. You don't recognize the person you have become, and you don't even know where you are. Although you are running for your life, at the same time, you are running from it and feel more lost than ever before. Having no idea what happened, where you are, and who you've become, you get to a point at which you don't think you will ever be able to go back."

"I know the feeling, and it sucks," Gary added. "I did the same thing, but I'd like to think I did an okay job of looking up often enough to take inventory of my life. It takes a lot of work to establish a career. You sacrifice so much, especially with family. It's a slippery slope."

"And I finally got a job," Wayne commented. "One that I didn't want and wasn't ready for."

"No offense, but anyone else would have killed to have a job like that. You better get your shit together."

"Come on, Gary. Are you going to start in on me now?" Wayne replied in an angry tone, although he knew Gary was not necessarily wrong.

"I don't mean to give you a hard time, Wayne, but I am concerned. Aren't you?"

"Yes, I am. Thank you for asking. Pigeon Financial drove the morale of employees into the dirt. My morale and confidence were destroyed, as well. I needed to take inventory of my life. There are some unresolved things I need to remedy before I'm able to move forward. Although it feels as though I'm taking a hundred steps backward, I believe I will be catapulted forward a million more steps. But right now, I'm lost.

"In the meantime, I got a job because I was supposed to," Wayne continued. "I got a job based on everyone else's fucking expectations."

"And it was with Magma Insurance Company! I still don't know how you did it."

Once Wayne verbally accepted the offer, the formalities began: the background check commenced, and fingerprints and a drug test were scheduled among other prerequisites. In the meantime, the human resources team advised that he give notice to his current employer before moving forward. Regardless, this was one of those things Wayne never felt comfortable with. Resigning before a new job offer was finalized did not make sense.

Then, to his surprise, Phillip, his new boss, invited Wayne to attend an upcoming team dinner at El Vez restaurant in downtown Philadelphia. This was yet another strange move, considering the hiring process had not been fully completed. He was perplexed by the way they handled the interview process, and jumping so quickly into things before the background checks and formalities were finalized.

He decided to go to the team dinner, despite having second thoughts about the job. He had grown tired of being among people who were always putting on a facade, acting as though they were more important than they really were.

Having experienced the atrocious leadership at Doe Financial, which ruined Three Friends Financial before eventually failing, to then endure the tragedy at Pigeon Financial, Wayne had grown tired of these big corporations, the disconnect between upper management and the growing neglect of their employees. He feared that eventually the layers of the onion would be peeled back to reveal yet another shit show hidden behind the curtain of "core values" and "guiding principles."

These people were pretending to be someone they were not, talking a big game and using fancy words to sound important. Deep down, Wayne knew this was not who he truly was, but he went along with it.

Upon his arrival, he was introduced to the team and sat down at the table for some idle chitchat. A few minutes into it, he looked up to see someone approaching the table. This guy looked familiar, but Wayne couldn't quite put a name with the face. As he got closer, Wayne stood up from his seat to extend his hand in greeting, and then his heart sank.

It was a wholesaler he had worked with while at Pigeon Financial. The guy's name was Bud Garner, and he was an obnoxious and overbearing salesman. Wayne put on a bullshit smile, greeting him and acting as though it was great to see him.

He sat through dinner wondering what the fuck he was doing there. It was surreal. He was still trying to reconcile his past with Pigeon Financial and found himself about to jump back into the bullshit again, sitting across the dinner table from this joker, Bud. Of all the people he could have ended up working with, why in the hell was it this guy? It must have been a sign.

Wayne continued, "At the end of the evening, I sat down with the head of the sales division. She suggested we schedule time to meet in the coming week to begin planning."

"Wow!" Gary gasped. "That sounds a little strange to me. I mean they invited you to meet with the team, and wanted to schedule a planning meeting even before your employment was finalized. That is a big no-no from an HR perspective! Asking you to attend a team dinner when you weren't officially hired? You said you didn't even complete the background check, right?"

"Yep! They never should have invited me to that dinner. The head of the sales division should not have allowed it, nor should she have scheduled a meeting with me until the hiring process was officially complete. Even that goofball Bud was still working at Pigeon Financial and his background check wasn't even started. He still had to be fingerprinted and piss in a cup for a drug screen. He even said that he wasn't going to resign from his job with Pigeon Financial until his first day of work with Magma Insurance Company. Even though he acted line an ass, he wasn't an idiot."

"Well, that was a smart move on his part."

"Yep! Then I received my office equipment the following week: iPhone, laptop, hotspot, projector, printer, everything."

"They really did a bang-up job, didn't they?" Gary gasped. "They violated so many rules of the hiring process!"

Words to Lead By

If the entire job interview process was punctuated by periods of deafening silence from the employer, you've been warned! You were expected to sit patiently until they stooped to contact you or until Hell froze over, whichever happened first.

A job offer from people like that is not a good thing. Get on the bus, Gus, and find a better class of people to hang out with.
— Liz Ryan

 # I'm a Frog

"What is 'pre-tend-ing'?"
"Pretending is when you act like something you are not."
"Wow ... And you can just do that?! You can just go
out and pretend to be something you are not!?"
"Sure. Everyone pretends."
"Even grown-up people?"
"All the time."

—*I'm a Frog (Mo Willems 2013)*

Wayne continued sharing the news about his job offer from Magma Insurance Company with his friend Gary, "Well, it gets even worse. A couple of weeks later, I received a message from the human resources recruiter."

"Oh, no! About what?" Gary asked in surprise.

"They rescinded the job offer!" Wayne exclaimed.

"Are you kidding me?" Gary gasped in utter surprise. "How? Why? What happened?"

"They rescinded the offer because I misrepresented myself on the application," Wayne responded.

"No way! You are messing with me, right? Aren't you? Wayne, please tell me you are messing with me."

"Gary, I wish I was, but I'm not." He sighed.

"Okay, so how did you misrepresent yourself?"

Wayne relived the phone call with Gary.

"Hello, this is Wayne," he answered.

"Hi, Wayne, this is Katrina from recruiting. How are you today?"

309

"Good, thanks."

"Is this a good time?"

"Yes."

"I wanted to speak with you regarding your candidacy for the regional sales director position. We received the completed background check from our background adjudicator, and we are rescinding the offer for the regional sales director role."

"Really? Why?" His heart sank.

"It says here that you misrepresented yourself on your application."

"Okay," Wayne responded, wanting to know more, although deep down, he knew why.

"If you believe this is not accurate, you will have five business days to contest the ruling. You will receive an email from your contact, Rasheeda, regarding the decision. In the email, you will be provided with a link in which you can contest the decision if you choose to do so."

"Okay, thank you for the information, Katrina. Can you provide a little more detail as to why the offer is being rescinded and how I misrepresented myself?" Wayne asked. Especially if he only had five days to contest the decision, he needed more information.

"All we know from the report is that you misrepresented yourself. The email Rasheeda is sending you will give you an opportunity to contest the decision."

"Okay, that makes sense. Thank you. Although, if I am allowed five business days to contest the decision, it would be helpful to know how I misrepresented myself so I can effectively file my appeal." Wayne was slowly becoming annoyed by her vague responses.

"Well, it appears you falsified your college information," she replied.

"Oh, yes. I mentioned that to Rasheeda. I apologized out of embarrassment and explained my reasoning to her. I did it out of convenience. It was just easier to put down one school, and I did not see the necessity of putting all the information on the application. After more than twenty years of success in my career, I did not see the importance of listing that any longer, just like not listing my employers from over twenty years ago."

"Sorry, Wayne, we will send you the email in the next couple business days."

"Wow! That's unfortunate and sad. I will await the email," Wayne concluded.

"Thanks, Wayne. Bye."

Wayne continued to explain the situation to Gary, "It was my college education history."

"Really?"

"Yes. I apologized and explained that I did it out of convenience."

"Okay. But did you say you graduated?" Gary posed the difficult question.

Wayne paused. "Yes."

"Oh no!" Gary paused with a sigh. "Wayne, why did you do that?"

"Well, no one ever asked before. Plus, the job description indicated a college degree or similar experience. I clearly have the experience and proven track record, which is just as good if not better than a degree."

"Yeah, but you indicated that you graduated. Wayne, that's not good. You can't do that," Gary moaned.

"I know. You're right. But it doesn't matter. I'm qualified for the job and have consistently proven myself. In all honesty, I didn't put it down because I was embarrassed for not completing college, and I shouldn't be."

"I agree with you, and it shouldn't matter, but it does," Gary pleaded.

"Yes, thanks for the reminder," Wayne responded with a tone of annoyance in his voice. "Well, as I said before, I really didn't want the job anyway. Plus, I think it was a sign that it was not meant to be when I saw that I'd be working with that goofball Bud."

"But, get this, the day after I had the job offer rescinded, my six-year-old daughter was reading the Mo Willems book *I Am a Frog.* Do you remember that book?"

"Nope. Not that one at least. I've read some of his other books to my kids when they were younger, but that was a long time ago. Why? What does that have to do with the job being rescinded?" Gary asked.

"*Everything!*" Wayne enthusiastically replied and proceeded to tell Gary about *his revelation.*

<hr />

The following morning after his job offer was rescinded, Wayne was getting his daughter Chloe ready for school. While he was putting on her socks and sneakers, she read one of her favorite books, *I Am a Frog!* by Mo Willems, aloud.

Wayne didn't hear a single word his daughter read from the book because he was completely lost replaying everything from the day before in his mind. His emotions were high—a mix of relief sprinkled with anger, a tinge of regret, the warmth of happiness, and utter confusion. He was becoming increasingly agitated. Though he was physically there with his daughter, his mind was somewhere else entirely.

She clearly enunciated the words, "'It is pretend!'"

He knelt to put her socks on, first the right foot, then the left. Sitting at the kitchen table, she cheerfully continued reading the story as Wayne grabbed her right shoe and placed it on her foot, "'*It is the end!*'"

Grabbing the left shoe, he remained lost in his thoughts.

"'No, Gerald. Pre-tend. I am pretending.'" His daughters voice chirped in the background.

Still intensely focused, he slid the left shoe on his daughter's foot. "'Pretending is when you act like something you are not.'"

Like a sledgehammer, the words finally came crashing down, breaking through his clouded mind. "'Wow … And you can just do that? You can just go out and pretend to be something you are not? ... Sure. Everyone pretends ... Even grown-up people?'" She continued reading the book as though on some sort of mission, trying to break through and connect with her father.

Looking up, Wayne asked Chloe if he could read the book. With a cheerful grin, she handed the book to her father and ran off to play in her room for a few minutes before it was time to leave for school. Wayne sat in silence, reading the book.

"It is okay, Gerald. It is pretend."

"It is the end!?!"

"No, Gerald. *Pre-tend*. I am pretending."

"What is 'pre-tend-ing'?"

"Pretending is when you act like something you are not."

"Wow ... And you can just *do* that?! You can just go out and *pretend* to be something you are not!?"

"Sure. Everyone pretends."

"Even grown-up people?"

"All the time."

"Holy crap!" Wayne mumbled to himself. "Are you kidding me? Everyone pretends! Everyone fucking pretends!" He looked up to make sure his daughter didn't hear him.

—◆—

Wayne finished sharing his encounter with Gary. "I lost my fucking job because I misrepresented myself! Or should I say pretended?"

"Very interesting and true! I would have never tied the two together. I often tell my kids to pretend, to dream, to use their imagination."

"Yep, that's pretending, or should I say misrepresentation? Kids pretend they are someone else all the time, dreaming about who they want to be when they grow up. Exactly! Somewhere along the line, after all of these loving lessons, envisioning who you want to be and what you want becomes a bad behavior."

"That's so true," Gary said in astonishment. "The story is about pretending. It's about using our imagination. It's about dreaming—"

"Yes!" Wayne interjected. "And I just lost my job because I knew that I was more than what was on a goddamn piece of paper. If I 'misrepresented' myself because after more than twenty years of forging a successful career path I believed my experience to be just as good as, if not better than, having graduated college, I will not apologize for that! The crazy thing is that I excelled at everything I did without a fucking college degree."

"Dude, that is strange, interesting, and powerful all at once," Gary stated.

"We become who we are in life through learning, using our imagination, and dreaming, or pretending. Have you ever pretended to be someone you are not?"

"Uhm, I don't think so?" Gary answered.

"Really? Okay, so when you were dating, did you ever dress up, so you looked better than you normally dressed? Did you ever embellish your accomplishments? Have you ever bragged or boasted about yourself, about your job, about anything?"

"I guess so."

"You guess so? Of course, you have! We all do it. When we pursue the woman or man of our dreams, we do our best to sell ourselves, sometimes acting or pretending as though we are someone we really are *not* so we can catch their eye. We misrepresent ourselves by pretending to be a success when we wear a new suit to a job interview. Then we sell ourselves, touting our accomplishments, even embellishing our past work history and schooling to get the attention of a hiring manager. Many people misrepresent themselves by driving a car they cannot afford, pretending they are wealthier than they truly are. Putting on these misrepresentative displays, or pretending, often works, and we end up getting the attention we wanted, the job we desired, the man or woman of our dreams. Even better, we become who we pretended to be."

"Okay, I get your point. But you lied on your applica—"

"*Really?*" Wayne interrupted Gary before he could finish his sentence. "Are you really going to go there? Don't be an asshole!"

"Well, you—"

"It doesn't mean a damn thing! Now, if I were twenty-six years old and I did this, then I would fire myself! Are you going to tell me that a college degree fucking matters more than on-the-job experience twenty-five years later? You would prefer a college degree over more than two decades of experience and a proven track record? Seriously? I am not making light of college, but isn't college basically a way to teach us things in a condensed time frame so we can get a jump-start on life and career? The things which normally take a lifetime to learn?"

"Yeah, but it—"

"But, what?" Wayne interrupted, becoming increasingly annoyed by Gary's comments.

Gary didn't back down. "But it also shows how someone is able to see something through to completion. Don't forget about the experience of building friendships and relationships."

"Yes, I agree with you," Wayne stated. "But my point still stands. I have built friendships and relationships throughout my career. I have followed things through to completion and have proven successful throughout. How in the world could I be responsible for a one-and-a-half-million-dollar budget? How in the world could I have excelled in catapulting sales at Chariot Horse Advisors from thirty-eight million dollars to seven hundred million? Did I need a college degree to accomplish that? Fuck no! It was grit, determination, a deep desire to succeed, and belief in myself! All I'm saying is that we shouldn't put the weight of the world on a college degree. There is a point at which it doesn't carry as much weight. And this is when career experience, gaining industry knowledge, relationships, and a proven track record of success to back it up is just as powerful as a college degree, if not more so. And employers should honor that. How the fuck did I get highly respected college graduates and business professionals in my field to vouch for me? Are you telling me my track record, knowledge, experience, and relationships don't mean shit without having graduated college?"

"Uh, no."

"I know plenty of people who cheated their way through college. Does having a college degree carry much weight if you cheated? How many people do you know who had someone else write their research paper for them? Or even had a roommate take a final exam for them?"

"No one does that."

"Oh yes they do. Don't fucking kid yourself. What rock have you been living under? No offense, but *you* would never do that. Although I never did it, I know plenty of people who did," Wayne replied in frustration with Gary's logical manner and ignorance. "Take the college admissions scandal! There's fucking cheating and lying all over the place. How pathetic are these ultra-successful millionaires and billionaires who feel the need to lie and cheat to get their kids into college? What really pisses me off is that I am willing to bet my hiring manager read *I Am a Frog!* to his fucking kids! He probably read it to his son and laughed his goddamn head off, enjoying little Piggie lying and misrepresenting herself. I am sure that the human resources manager read that same book to her kids, laughing and urging her children to misrepresent themselves. Who doesn't teach their kids to believe in themselves and use their imagination to pretend who they want to be? Who doesn't do that? Everyone does because that is how life works. Our thoughts become things. We think about who we want to become, and although we may not be that person quite yet, because we pretend, or misrepresent ourselves, our imagination allows us to accomplish it. I checked the box on the damn application because of how much emphasis companies place on a goddamn college degree! I pretended to have a degree because I was embarrassed to say that I didn't have one. But my belief in myself is stronger than any fucking college degree. You can't teach persistence; you can't teach tenacity. You can't teach a deep, deep belief in oneself. What kind of fucked-up society judges someone because they don't have a fucking piece of paper? Oh yeah, our society does! And there are so many college graduates who are fucking miserable drowning in tens of thousands of dollars in college debt and in a career that they did not major in." Wayne paused and took a deep breath. "I take ownership that I did this to myself. Unfortunately, I was one of those individuals who allowed this illusion to be created that I was not good enough because I did not have a degree."

"You make valid points, Wayne, but you got caught," Gary pressed him.

"Yes, I did. And I believe that's the moral of this story, although an awful one."

"What's that, Wayne? Don't get caught?" Gary smirked.

"Yep! If you don't get caught, lying is perfectly fine, except for the fact that you have to live with your lie. You know, in sales, there's a saying that has been said hundreds, if not thousands, of times repeatedly."

"What's that?"

"Fake it till you make it. When I entered the financial services business in my late twenties, I, along with my peers, was advised to dress and appear older than I was."

"Really?"

"Uh, yeah!"

"Why?"

"Because we needed to appear as though we were older and more experienced than we actually were."

"Seriously?"

"Yes, seriously!"

"Did you do that?" Wayne's friend asked.

"Of course, I did. I even wore a wedding band even though I wasn't married. I worked with guys who wore glasses to look older even though they didn't need them. They even had hairstyles that made them look older. Some even got gray highlights in their hair so they would look older."

"I never knew you did that."

"Oh yeah! We totally misrepresented ourselves because that was what we were told to do by executives! The national sales manager at Three Friends Financial used to boast, 'Fake it till you make it!' Sales managers would say the same thing, 'Fake it till you make it. Act like you know what you're doing when meeting with an advisor or a client.' These managers and executives were teaching us to bullshit and lie our way through it."

"Now, that is flat-out lying," Gary said. "Are you pulling my leg?"

"Nope! Do you now understand why I am so pissed off about losing my job because of something as minor as my bullshit college experience over twenty years ago?"

"Now that you put it in that perspective, yes, I see why you might be a little upset," Gary finally came around to see the light.

"Think about it, Gary. Everyone misrepresents themselves. We persuade people to buy our product because it's the 'best in the business,' the 'top-selling' product with the 'greatest' rates, investments, and guarantees. How the fuck can every company have the greatest product, the greatest rates, and the best performance? Everyone misrepresents themselves!

"We have been taught to misrepresent our confidence, our knowledge, and our product to get the sale, and it worked! Speaking persuasively and using our words strategically is an important skill to learn in life, because simply being honest and stating the truth doesn't always work. Even animals fake it or misrepresent themselves when looking for a mate, or they simply kill the competitor to win their mate.

"Pigeon Financial was purchased by a huge Japanese insurance company about a year before I resigned."

"I didn't know that. Did you tell me that?"

"I may have. I don't recall. The reason I bring this up is when there is mergers and acquisitions activity, the company being bought puts lipstick on the pig."

"Huh?"

"They fabricated, misrepresented, inflated the numbers, and so on in order to impress the buyer."

"Ahh, that makes sense. That happens all the time in business."

"Are you saying that it's okay, Gary?"

"Yeah, why?"

"So, you are saying I deserved to have my job offer rescinded because I lied about my education, but it's okay to lie about the numbers, to create extra activity and pad the numbers to make the company look a little better than they truly are?"

"Uh ... yeah?" Gary replied.

"Okay, please explain to me how that's okay, Gary."

"That's a part of doing business."

"Oh, it's that simple, huh? It's a part of doing business. Are you fucking serious?"

"Well ..." Gary was at a loss for words.

"That was going on at Pigeon Financial. Corey and Carl were misrepresenting the numbers to impress their Japanese suitors. They were loving the numbers because they needed to fatten the pig for the feast. This is okay, and I am all for making money, but when it comes with a price tag of fucking with people's lives and careers, that's when it becomes a crime. I understand that this shit happens all the time. But I had a job offer rescinded despite being highly recommended for the job, with an excellent work history and track record of success. All for what? Because most companies won't consider someone who didn't graduate college, and I felt I had to misrepresent myself in order to get noticed. I call bullshit! Gary, I am willing to wager that you have most likely misrepresented yourself your entire life. It's human nature. And don't think for a moment you haven't. Look at your résumé. I'd be willing to bet you that your opening statement is an inflated, egotistical misrepresentation about how much of an 'expert' you are, that you are a 'seasoned professional' with 'years of experience' who is a 'transformational leader' and a 'savvy' 'go getter' blah, blah, blah, blah. And this is in your opening statement. Wait until we get into your previous employment history. Can you say embellishment?"

"Funny, Wayne, I think you made your point."

"I am not so sure. People are so afraid to be honest about who they are. Because if we are open and honest, we will be ridiculed, turned down, or not even acknowledged. So, we create all these inflated misrepresentations of who we apparently are to get the attention of others. Even when reading my résumé, I'm nauseated by the elaborate words and how much I embellish. We're all fucking liars. We lie to ourselves and hide behind a veil of lies because we are afraid of being honest. We are afraid of being less; we are afraid of being insignificant or not enough, so we inflate our egos and misrepresent who we truly are. We even teach our kids practically from birth to pretend or misrepresent themselves. Why? Because we're afraid they might not be good enough? We're afraid we aren't good enough and project it onto our kids. There is nothing like the thrill of competition, but we tend to be competitive in a very unhealthy way with a 'win at all costs' mentality.

"Don't believe me? Do you recognize the following and what they were known for? Lance Armstrong, Tonya Harding, Barry Bonds, Mark McGwire, Sammy Sosa, Ben Johnson, Rosie Ruiz, Bill Belichick, Spy Gate, the Houston Astros sign stealing, and hundreds more. Just google 'infamous sports cheaters.' My daughter's kindergarten classmates are all liars. Each one of them misrepresents themselves because we teach them to pretend and sometimes push them to be something *we* want them to be instead of allowing their true colors to shine. Because deep down we fear that we are not enough, we are making up for our perceived flaws by pushing our kids based on our fears and shortcomings, wanting them to *not* be like us.

"Research has even been conducted proving that a college degree was ineffectual after twenty years because the knowledge a college graduate acquires in twenty years post–college graduation has drastically evolved, which in effect makes their knowledge from college outdated. The individual's knowledge and experience gained over twenty years of career experience, being an active participant in the continual evolving workplace and embracing the latest knowledge technically means this new knowledge is far beyond what was learned in college coursework over a lifetime ago. I misrepresented myself because of the amount of weight companies put on having a goddamn college degree. That is like asking a college student where they went to preschool and then asking for their fucking transcript! Do you get my fucking point now?" Wayne paused.

"Yep, you certainly made your point."

Wayne was more upset about how inhumane and impersonal the human resource recruiters were. Wayne made an honest mistake, or misrepresentation, because he felt as though his lack of a college degree would be held against him. And he was probably right.

He worked so hard to earn the job. He worked with trusted colleagues and peers who raced out to the hiring manager to recommend Wayne for the job. This was not something illegal, but when it comes to these big companies, the human aspect of human resources is nonexistent.

Words to Lead By

Everyone pretends, and there is fine line between believing in oneself to improve one's life and career versus misrepresenting oneself in a malicious manner in order to get ahead, causing harm to others.

Q: Can you decipher the difference between those who misrepresent themselves by lying and cheating to mislead and deceive others versus those who misrepresent themselves because they know the value they bring to the marketplace based on their experience and track history of success?

We become who we are in life through learning and dreaming or pretending. Sometimes we pretend to be someone other than who we are to get things we desire. When we pursue the woman or man of our dreams, we do our best to sell ourselves, sometimes acting or pretending as though we are someone we are not in order to catch their eye.

We may pretend to be a success by wearing a new suit to a job interview and sell ourselves, touting our accomplishments, even embellishing our past work history and schooling to get the attention of a hiring manager. Many people drive a car they cannot afford, pretending to be wealthier than they truly are. Putting on these displays, or pretending, often works, and we end up getting the attention we wanted, the job we dreamed of, the man or woman who caught our eye.

The Mo Willems story is a very intriguing story because it teaches children to use their imagination and set their sights on what they want in life and who they want to become. This story is such a powerful one, indirectly speaking to the power of the mind to manifest things in our lives. And he is spot on! This is truly how life happens and unfolds. Our thoughts create all the things around us. If our belief is strong enough, our pretending becomes our reality.

Without our imagination and our ability to pretend, we would have never landed on the moon. We would not have been able to fly on a Boeing 737 aircraft across the country or the world. The iPhone never would have been created. The hundreds of thousands of miraculous accomplishments and achievements in the world would never have manifested.

Consider the moon landing in 1969. The Apollo 11 team performed thousands of hours of simulations to ensure the entire mission would be a success. What is interesting is the following words are synonyms for simulate: *fake*, *pretend*, and *imitate*. NASA needed to pretend they landed on the moon to actually land on the moon.

Conveyed in Mo Willems's book, as with hundreds of other children's books, pretending is taught at a young age. Pretending is good. Pretending allows our imaginations to grow. Pretending allows us to visualize who we want to become. It is a good thing for children to pretend, but apparently there comes a time in our lives when pretending becomes an inappropriate behavior. Instead of a behavior that is celebrated and promoted, it is something to be abhorred because we must grow up and deal with the apparent real world.

The real world? This real world we exist in is one of fear and mindlessness. We teach our children to be polite, to love, to use their imagination, and even to pretend. Then when they are a little older, in their tweens and teens, fear gradually enters the scene, and suddenly they learn to behave differently; they are taught to compete, to fight, to win at all costs, shifting their mind-set away from being loving, angelic beings. They are supposed to be number one, because anything else is a loser. If stepping on and over others is necessary to their success, this apparent real world teaches them to do just that.

Always dream big and believe in yourself.

 # Final

I would behold the proof that what has been done
through me has enabled love to replace fear, laughter
to replace tears, and abundance to replace loss.
I would look upon the real world, and let it teach
me that my will and the Will of God are one.

—*A Course in Miracles*

The year was 2014. "Hey, Daddy!" Wayne's seven-year-old daughter lovingly chirped upon his entrance into her room.

"Hey, sweetie. Come here," Wayne said with a smile as he sat on the edge of her bed.

"Okay." She did her best to listen to her father but was barely able to sit still.

"Hey, can I see your beautiful eyes?" he asked. She looked at her father. "Thank you. You have such pretty eyes. I have a surprise I'd like to share with you."

"Really?" she replied. "What is it, Daddy?" She was so excited that he worried she was thinking the surprise was a new toy or a puppy.

He slowly brought the book he had been holding behind his back forward and handed it to his daughter. "I would like you to have this."

"Really? What is it?" she said in excitement.

"Well, it's a book called *List Your Goals, Live Your Goals!* It's about this little girl named Jenna."

Abby studied the book, staring intently at the characters on the cover. "Hey, it says W. T. Renroc." She paused. "Is that you, Daddy, W. T. Renroc?" she asked with excitement in her voice.

"Yes, sweetie! That's me. My initials W. T., Wayne Thomas."

"Wow!" she exclaimed. Turning the book over, she let out a gasp of excitement and directed her gaze toward her father and then back at the cover and back at her father again.

When their eyes met, he was astounded by his daughter's look of excitement. The look on her face was like that of a proud parent gazing at his or her child in amazement at the child's accomplishments. But this was a real reversal of sorts. He tried to fight back tears.

"Wow! How did you print it? How did you get your picture on the cover? Where did the drawings come from?" Her questions emanated from a place of curiosity and wonder.

He proceeded to answer her questions. "Well, sweetie, I had someone help me print the book, and I worked with an artist who helped me to make the drawings. Pretty cool, huh?"

"Yes, Daddy!"

On that day, Wayne accomplished several things. The most rewarding part was making his daughter proud. Typically, it is the child who makes the parent proud.

Second, he accomplished something that he never thought possible, publishing his first book. His determination was stronger than his doubt, which paved the way for several more books, opening him up to an entirely different world. He speaks and interacts with people who share his vision, people who believe a change of perspective is necessary.

And it all started with a thought. His struggles all started with a thought, as well. But his ability to understand that pain is a wrong perspective allowed him to make a shift in how he saw the world, his career, and his experiences. Knowing this, he will go on to accomplish even greater things in his life, things he never thought were possible, because he changed his perspective.

Lastly, he wrote books from a place of love. All his books have emanated from love, which is more difficult than writing from fear and anger.

But this book, *Assholes to Angels*, emanated from a place of fear and anger, something he once idolized in the workplace. This book was written to bring to the surface a frustration felt by thousands of people who go to work every day, working for assholes who are responsible for a toxic and demoralizing workplace. This can only lead to more fear and anger. This foundation of fear had crumbled upon his realization that love is, and always has been, his strength. Love is your strength.

Wayne truly believed Albert Einstein intended to say, "Fuck success!" We do a shitty job of teaching our children that it is okay to be at ease and to allow life to flow and to look at our suffering, or failure, as a tremendous teacher. Our pursuit of success is flawed, as is the definition of success.

It is important to understand that we will always experience fear. But what is more important is how we perceive these fears. When we turn fear into an ally and consider it a sign that our perspective could use an adjustment, we can learn from it rather than fight and go to war. This can also be applied to our health and how we approach disease. On the other side of fear is love, because what is not love is always fear and nothing else.

About forgiveness—as Jesus said, "Father, forgive them, for they know not what they do." Wayne is doing his best to forgive himself and forgive those who trespassed against him in life and work. He is doing his best to forgive the bird for pecking his eye out, and he is doing his best to forgive himself for allowing it to happen.

Perhaps you've heard the story of the little bird.
He had his wing over his eye, and he was crying.
The owl said to the bird, "You are crying."

"Yes," said the little bird, and he pulled
his wing away from his eye.

"Oh, I see," said the owl. "You're crying because
the big bird pecked out your eye."

And the little bird said, "No, I'm not crying because the big
bird pecked out my eye. I'm crying because I let him."
—Jim Rohn

For all the angels Wayne has met in his life, he is grateful, and
he loves them. They were honest, they were true, and they believed.
For some people, this love was not immediately felt or received.
Many, including Wayne, learned to build an outer shell (a chrysalis)
on a belief that it would keep them safe. But, unbeknownst to them,
this was the handiwork of the ego, and they were becoming assholes
and very well may have been spinning their very own sarcophagus.

Together, we can allow our angels to shine through. We are all
angels born into a world in which we all too often become assholes
because of the pull of the ego. We become assholes by attacking
people, with both physical and verbal force. There are those who
attack by attempting to prove that they are the smartest one in the
room by making others around them feel inferior and less intelligent.

The following words are worth revisiting:

You have a lot of facts but very little wisdom. Information
is knowing that water is H_2O. Wisdom is knowing
how to make it rain. Information is being able to
make a diagnosis. Wisdom is being able to heal.
—Robert Wright

There are others who attack with sarcasm or humor. Wayne once
learned from Dr. Wayne Dyer the root meaning of sarcasm originates
from the Greek word *sarkazein*, which means to "tear flesh." Think
about that the next time you jokingly make a sarcastic remark toward
someone.

Some people simply attack by physically harming another. One
of the worst forms of attack is one that remains unnoticed except
to the victim. This happens in the workplace when an employee is
treated poorly or abused without any proof. Even worse is when that
employee seeks help and his or her words are ignored, or silenced,

by those who are supposed to be there to protect the employee and instead allow the abuser to tally up more victims in the workplace.

All these forms of attack originate from the ego, which is the father of fear. We become assholes because we believe there is no other way, and most people know of no other way. This is prevalent in the working world. It is about time this changed for the better.

It is possible to return to our angelic ways in our work and especially in our personal lives, but we must be aware of our "assholeness." We must be brave enough to make the positive changes in our lives for the better by returning to our angelic ways and learning to love instead of hate. To forgive instead of seek revenge. To accomplish this, a change of perspective is necessary. All of this can still be accomplished while being successful, while having fun, and while being wealthy.

Being angelic does not mean we cannot have the things of this world and enjoy them.

☯ Chrysalis or Sarcophagus?

Nothing is ever lost but time, which
in the end is meaningless.

—*A Course in Miracles*

Time is more valuable than money. You can get
more money, but you cannot get more time.

—Jim Rohn

In a flash, he peacefully transitioned from the light into the darkness of a world never experienced before, like a light switch suddenly flipped to the off position. At least that was how he assumed it would be.

In anticipation of his life ending, he screamed in terror at the thought of his passing, which became a blurry scene from the river of tears surging forth, stinging his eyes. Bloodshot and puffy from decades of seeing life unfold through tired eyes, old age caught up with him. A slow blink of his eyes revealed a tiny map of veins in the delicate skin of his eyelids, charting a path into his eyes.

The taste of salt caressed his taste buds from the tears flowing down his cheeks into the corners of his mouth. Memories of the beach and salt water from the Atlantic Ocean flitted though his mind. If only he had one last opportunity to ride atop a wave. Just as a wave returns home, becoming one with the ocean once again, he knew he would soon return from whence he came long ago.

The bright light in the room glistened off each tear drop like a diamond radiating in the bright sunlight. His head pounded from his incessant shrieks of fear; his body shivered and shuddered from the chill in the air.

All the comforts of the world would soon be left behind upon his transition into the unknown. Although this moment was inevitable and unavoidable for Wayne, as well as every human being, he still was not ready. Most people are never ready for their transition because they cling to the comforts of the material world. They grasp onto life. They fight to keep it. This fear of loss and nothingness scares the shit out of almost everyone.

It was such a shock to his system that his senses were shutting down. He could barely hear the sounds in the room, but he knew loved ones were there with him. He began gasping for air like a fish out of water, flopping and thrusting about, trying to find its way back home. Eyes were dilated, round and dark with fear as panic set in. Gradually, the flopping subsided, while the eyes remained wide open and dark. Its mouth gently opened and closed while the fish gasped for life, giving the appearance as though the fish were speaking in a quiet whisper of despair. Eventually, the fish's breathing slowed to a peaceful pace as it accepted its fate, knowing that soon it would return home.

He feared death as most people do. But he also feared life. Perceiving the world through the eyes of fear and suffering prevented him from truly experiencing the joy and miracle of life. He worked hard over the years. Now tired and weak, he had nothing to show for it, missing the joy in each moment of his life.

Regret is a funny thing. He regretted waiting his entire life for the right moment to live it. We hold on, waiting for the right time to be happy. We hold on, waiting for the right time to say, "I love you." We hold on, waiting for the ideal moment to arrive, yet time waits on no one.

"What if my whole life has been wrong?" He mumbled the words he once read long ago in Leo Tolstoy's book *The Death of Ivan Ilyich*. The question occurred to Ivan Ilych while he was lying on his deathbed full of regret. Those same words plagued his mind. "What if my whole life has been wrong?" he muttered the words once again.

A sense of peace and love flowed over him, replacing terror and regret. His breathing slowed to a peaceful rhythm. He was ready to return home. This feeling of pure bliss and pure positive energy took his breath away, jockeying for position with sadness and despair. All the things he wanted to say to his wife, his daughters, and his brothers that he never found the courage to say, it was too late. There was no turning back.

Why had he waited until a moment before his death to experience this existential high? What if he had another chance, another opportunity to live life rather than fearing it? What if his struggles were simply from a wrong perspective? Instead of seeing his struggles as pain and suffering, what if he saw them for what they really were, moments of learning? He wanted to know why it took so long for him to feel free and to see the world as God intended. Grasping onto a sliver of hope that this too was a dream, he roared, hoping to awaken. His eyelids slid closed, like a veil being pulled down to darken a room, and everything went dark for him.

In a flash, Wayne woke up from the dream. He was drenched in sweat and gasped for air.

<hr />

No one truly knows if this is how death happens. It simply is an interpretation of the death experience, from a fear-based mind. Do we really know? What if there were light and pure positive energy? Would you believe it?

What if you found out that the sun never sets? Would you believe it? The sun never sets or rises. The sun is always there at the center of the solar system, and as the earth rotates, we have a day. As the earth revolves around the sun, we have a year. The realization that the earth rotated on its axis and revolved around the sun was the creation, or measurement, of time. So, the sun neither sets nor rises.

What if, just as the sun never truly sets or rises, we are never born and never die? Would you believe it? Like the sun, we are always shining, lighting up the world with no beginning and no end. This might be a little too deep for you. Maybe unexpected in a story about Wayne's experiences in the corporate world. But it's worth pondering, especially if you are one of those individuals who finds himself or herself or witnessed a loved one on his or her deathbed full of regret for treating people like shit. Ironically, this is very relevant and shares many parallels to the business world.

As far as we perceive it, we leave the world behind for a place unknown, or death, like being in the light and then thrust into darkness. Most people are uncomfortable being in the dark or silence for long periods of time. Therefore, they have a fear of darkness and a fear of death.

Common questions about death in large part include "Where do we go? What's next?" When we are born, we do not seem to fear birth, nor do we seem to be concerned about where we came from. For most people, it is a mystery, and we just accept it; both life and death. No doctor or physicist can tell you where we come from when we are born or where we go when we die.

We can explain the science of conception, but we do not have any clue how life truly happens. On the flip side, we can explain the concept of death but still have no idea what happens when we die. We dismiss this and go about life without question. Death, however, scares the shit out of us. Our fear of death incites us to question it constantly. Many of us spend our lives avoiding death, rather than living life, and it begins at a young age when we are children. Most of us are infatuated with death; we fear it, hate it, run from it, yet we are attracted to it like a stupid moth to a flame.

We fear death because as far as we know, it means the end to our physical existence. The question remains: what's next? When we were born, like the fish out of water, we resisted this unknown world to flop about, screaming and crying in terror. In time, we acclimate to our existence in this world to eventually die and depart once again for the unknown. But do we really die?

Countless studies and a great amount of research have been conducted on finding a deeper understanding of life and death. Even weighing the body before death and immediately after death has been attempted to quantify this life "force." This has been referred to as the "twenty-one gram theory," which was a scientific experiment conducted by Dr. MacDougall in 1901 and published in the *New York Times* in 1907.

There have been countless stories of near-death experiences (NDE), seeing a light, which is dismissed by most because we cannot see it. The medical community explains this away as a part of the brain firing, thus creating bright light. The most empowering story I have heard was from Anita Moorjani, explaining her death and return to life in her memoir *Dying to Be Me*. She apparently died, and upon returning to life, her body was healed of end-stage cancer!

The cancer was gone; mysteriously, it vanished. Yet, the doctors could not accept it. They didn't believe it because at one moment it was there, and the next, it was gone, nowhere to be found!

The doctors were unable to accept that it was gone. Instead, they were determined to rediscover the cancer, so they continued searching, conducting test after test and scan after scan. They kept searching, believing they had to find something so they could administer the chemotherapy. Silly humans!

The following is an excerpt from her book:

> The doctor came into my room with a whole team of hospital personnel, looking concerned. Then he spoke: "We have the results of the bone-marrow biopsy, but it's a little disturbing."
>
> For the first time in days, I felt some anxiety. "Why? What's the problem?"
>
> My family members were in the hospital room with me, and all of them looked worried.
>
> "We can't find the cancer in your bone-marrow biopsy," he said.
>
> "So how is that a problem?" Danny asked. "Doesn't that just mean she doesn't have cancer in her bone marrow?"
>
> "No, that's not possible," the doctor said. "She definitely has cancer in her body—it can't disappear so quickly like that. We simply have to find it; and

until we do, it's a problem, because I'm unable to determine her drug dose."

Human beings are considered intelligent beings, but there are times when this is questionable. Yes, we are highly intelligent in the human realm with five amazing senses that guide us, but at the same time, they greatly limit us. Our own ignorance limits us. Our fear limits us.

Our death introduces the fear of nothingness. The more we perceive our death, the more we grasp to life. We hold on to all the material things that define who we are, which ironically does nothing to help us understand and accept death. In fact, all these things are simply distractions from our truth. We chase things, status, titles, pleasure, money, and all of that crap because of a fear of being nothing and having nothing.

What if we found another way to truly live? Another way to enjoy life, enjoy work, enjoy our career, enjoy the miracle of life? Until we understand fear and know it as the wonderful teacher it truly is, our suffering will continue unabated. If we embrace fear as our greatest teacher and view our world through the eyes of love and forgiveness, then our vantage point of life changes.

Wayne's career changed. His view of the assholes he worked for has changed. They, too, are angels hidden beneath a harsh exterior of the ego that inconspicuously turns many of us into assholes. Once we face our fears, understand them, and embrace them as tools for growth we will find *A Return to Love* (Williamson 1996) and clearly see life as the miracle we were all intended to enjoy.

Like the caterpillar, we humans slowly creep along on life's journey, receiving nourishment and gathering experiences, all of which define who we become. Along the journey, we often weave an outer shell to keep us safe from our perceived fears. The ego is akin to a caterpillar's chrysalis. We spin this outer ego shell, layer upon layer, to keep us safe from harm as we undergo a transformation, a metamorphosis, turning us into fear-based beings who often act like assholes rather than the angels we were intended to be.

Unfortunately, when we spin this outer shell from the ego's foundation of fear, tragic experiences, and negative memories, this shell becomes our burden. Even when we begin to awaken, shedding our past hurts and tragedies proves exceedingly difficult, as we have allowed our past to hold us hostage from real growth and a life of ease. This resistance wraps around us, suffocating us and preventing us from fulfilling our true intention of spreading our wings to soar in the heavens above like a beautiful butterfly.

Our emotions and thoughts are analogous to the tiny threads spun, which create the caterpillar's chrysalis. The chrysalis is intended to surround the caterpillar, keeping it safe from any threats. With the chrysalis properly spun, the caterpillar successfully undergoes a metamorphosis, allowing it to emerge as a beautiful butterfly. When our thoughts and emotions emerge from a place of positivity and love, we are all but guaranteed to live a life of beauty, just like the beautiful butterfly emerging from its chrysalis.

However, if our mind and thoughts are resistant, laden with fear, anger, hatred, self-doubt, ridicule, and judgment, our chrysalis may very well end up becoming our very own sarcophagus.

Our mind—conscious, subconscious, pain body, id, ego, or however you refer to the human mind—spins a chrysalis of experiences intended to keep us safe. If we experience a shift from a place of love, safety, and acceptance to one of fear, anger, defensiveness, or attack, which can be the result of an unloving and unsafe environment or traumatic experiences, we begin to weave what we falsely believe is a protective barrier around ourselves that will keep us safe from future harm. The longer we allow this outer shell to grow, the more unlikely it is that we will emerge to see the light.

Like a beautiful butterfly, we are intended to emerge from the chrysalis and spread our wings after undergoing a miraculous metamorphosis, but not everyone does. Consider for a moment a caterpillar spinning a chrysalis that is paper thin. Because of its inferior construction, threats from the outside world introduce harm and potential disaster, ultimately resulting in the demise of the caterpillar. However, if a caterpillar spins a chrysalis that is too thick, shutting everything out, ultimately the butterfly does not emerge. The intended protection of the chrysalis becomes the butterfly's very own sarcophagus.

The good news is that this scenario of disaster has not been witnessed in nature—although it is intriguing to ponder what would occur if the caterpillar's chrysalis was damaged or flawed because of the negative influences of the environment, which then could ultimately lead to its demise. But, then again, maybe they never make it to the point at which they even have an opportunity to spin a chrysalis.

Even though humans are very resilient, we are all subjects of our environment and our mind-set. Depending on our individual perspective, experiences, and environment, our life or career may never transform into one of beauty. We all have a choice and can change our lives and career for the better if we allow it to happen and believe it can happen.

For many, their suffering is so strong that their lives are spent in a constant struggle to find experiences of enjoyment and fulfillment, which are often fleeting—especially when someone finds it very difficult to "Be Here Now" in the present moment but rather agonizes over their past hurts or future catastrophes. The more we fight to break free, the more suffering it creates. This continual resistance prevents a life of ease and joy from emerging. Deep down, the beautiful butterfly hidden inside is dying, and the world may never experience its true beauty.

Words to Live By / Life Lessons

How many people weave a confident and strong exterior, but deep down, they are suffering and slowly dying?

Wayne's entire life he feared death. He idolized anger and attack, which stem from fear. Wayne spent his entire life trying to avoid death until he had a dream. In this dream he was on his deathbed and he realized he had it all wrong. Most humans have it all wrong.

We fear death (failure, criticism, judgment) so much so that we forget how to live. When we are faced with death, we then fight to save our lives, but for what? To continue living our lives fighting and fearing death rather than learning how to truly live?

Are we afraid that we are not enough? Are we afraid we will lose all our possessions? Are we afraid that we will lose our titles? Are we afraid we will lose our youth and good looks? We are constantly at war with death until one day we awaken to a life of regret on death's door.

What, or who, are you without your possessions? What, or who, are you without your titles and designation? Seriously, think about it.

Wayne grew tired of being afraid. He grew tired of the anger in the workplace. He grew tired of the assholes in positions of leadership who led from a platform of fear.

The pain became so great that he had to make a change of perspective. He made a difficult change that most would never do because of fear. He did it, and eventually he awakened.

After resigning from his well-paying job, he lost practically everything. He had nothing, yet he gained everything. Who was he without his title and well-paying job? The only thing that remained constant was love. Never wavering, never doubting. It was always present, walking beside him on the path he had chosen. This is who we are. This is what we are. This was his awakening.

Most will never awaken. They will never summon the strength and courage to find our truth, their truth. The idea of not having titles, status, and accolades scares the shit out of most everyone. Because, without them, they have no meaning. Their identity is placed in these things, so they fight, go to war to protect their identity and possessions because without them they are lost. They cannot imagine what life would be like in the absence of this apparent validation.

All this worship over their possessions does not matter in the grand scheme of things. Once they are long gone from the physical realm, no one will remember them, their things, their titles, or their accolades. All that will remain is Love.

By shedding his titles and attachment to things, even falling into poverty, he became wealthier than he had ever thought possible. All his fears came true because he brought it upon himself and yes still survived. He survived because he found his truth. Love and support of family and friends awakened him to life's true value.

It is not found in the latest and greatest possession. It is not found in titles, accolades, or degrees. We all have it. We are born with it, but most of us neglect it, destroy it, and never cash it in. Wayne cashed in. He changed his perspective and found that, as Albert Einstein said, "a quiet and modest life brings more joy than a pursuit of success bound with constant unrest."

👍 What's Right?

We are not our bodies, our possessions, or our career.
Who we are is Divine Love and that is Infinite.

—*Dr. Wayne Dyer*

Like the sun, this story never sets nor rises. It does not have an ending or a beginning. It just flows like life. It shines brightly like the sun. Like life, it has its fair share of struggles and suffering in addition to happiness and joy.

So, what happened to Wayne in the end? Well, we do not quite know because the story is still being told.

What we do know is that Chad Wunderlust resigned from Pigeon Financial a year after Wayne resigned. He had no job lined up; he just up and left. The Magma Insurance Company division disbanded less than two years after Wayne's job was rescinded. The team lost their jobs and were on the street looking for new jobs and a new employer. Corey and Carl continued their cancerous and toxic ways of loser leadership leaving a trail of devastation behind them. Ned remained at Pigeon Financial, pushed to the side riding out his years until retirement.

Don't be an asshole. As a manager, as a leader, you can still bring value to the marketplace without being an asshole. Jim Rohn touted that we get paid for bringing value to the marketplace:

> Would any company pay one person two hundred million dollars? The answer is yes. If that person helped a company make four billion dollars, they would be more than happy to give him or her two hundred million dollars a year.

If you feel lost, or stuck, do not believe for a second that you do not have a choice or that you cannot make changes in your life and career for the better. It can be done; it has been done. It all begins with your perspective. Being aware that pain is a wrong perspective (i.e., belief system) is a good start. Next is your willingness to let go and let love guide you. In the workplace, having the right leadership and management who are brave enough to lead with love as well as embrace and support both the names and the numbers will awaken us to the new definition of success.

"A quiet and modest life brings more joy than a pursuit of success bound with constant unrest." As Albert Einstein wrote on hotel stationary a century ago, maybe it is about time we awaken and redefine what *success* should truly look like.

As Arnold Schwarzenegger said, "I am not a self-made person … I rode on the shoulders of giants …" You know you have the right management and leadership when they are strong enough to allow their people ride on their shoulders.

Wayne walked away from a great career while Pigeon Financial allowed a wonderful employee to walk out the door. Who is to blame? No one is to blame. Although, there was a dire need for a change of perspective, both Wayne's and that of the leadership team at Pigeon Financial.

We raise our kids from a platform of love (i.e., angels). We teach them to be kind, to be honest, to be hardworking until fear digs its claws in deep, and we gradually begin to believe we need to lie, cheat, fight, hate, push people down (i.e., become assholes) to become successful.

We raise our kids and employees based on our knowledge and experiences, which are often riddled with fear. Often, our knowledge and experiences are taught from a vantage point of fear, which for all intents and purposes, we believe is intended to keep our family and business safe. But it often infringes on our people's (children and employees) ability to soar because we believe we know what's best and teach from fear rather than love.

As a parent or as a leader if we ask, "What's right?" rather than "What's wrong?" our entire world changes—our perspective changes. For example, when a child, loved one, or even employee appears upset or hurt, we naturally say, "What's wrong?" What happens when we ask, "What's right?" A little change of perspective allows us to see what's right in our lives despite something that appears to be going "wrong."

What we need in the workplace and the world is the determination to love, the determination to succeed without the need to be an asshole. As a leader and manager, do you show your employees the part they play and what it means to the company, their peers, and their clients? Do they truly know how their efforts contribute to the whole and how they contribute to their growth? More important, as a manager or leader, are you willing to show them how to become better? Do you teach them to become more, to become a leader? Or are you just filling a role and expecting them to "hit their numbers"? Do you show them how they can bring value to the marketplace at the risk that they just might achieve more than you have? Are your people able to ride on your shoulders?

Are you willing to allow them to challenge you from a place of love and respect? Are you teaching them to question things, processes, and established norms?

Lastly, give it all away because it was never yours to begin with. Our children are not ours. As parents, our role is to provide a loving environment for our children so they can rise up and lead their own lives. If our view of love is fear based, maybe we need to rethink our approach. This is no different in the workplace. Our work is not ours, and our employees are not ours. So, we must learn to let go. A good leader and manager will be strong enough to love his or her employees and be strong enough to allow them to ride on his or her shoulders.

The following is a list of things Wayne learned during his career and something managers can embrace to become better leaders:

Names before numbers: Throughout his career, Wayne learned a great deal about the corporate world and sales, both from his own research and work experience. He embraced a deep understanding and appreciation of the need for the numbers to work (generate sales and revenue) to take care of (pay) the names (employees). But the numbers are not possible if there are no names to do the work. It is just as important not to neglect the names in favor of the numbers. This is a delicate balance and one that needs to be reset in the workplace and the world.

No spreadsheet coaching: Metrics are an excellent guide, but they are not *the* way. There comes a time at which you must let go of the numbers and trust the process and your people—especially in financial services, where wholesalers are wired to win; they would rather die than fail. Knowing this, as a leader, you can leverage that desire to succeed instead of putting more metrics on their heads—which segues into the next point.

I.T.S. to Succeed. Know your clients better than they know themselves: For those who are in a position of influence or leadership, I truly hope you glean a few nuggets that will make your teams better, make you better. Managing with a hammer fist is a thing of the past. We can learn to love our people while doing the work necessary to be successful. Successful, by the new definition, includes the attainment of a higher awareness.

As a business leader, you must know your clients as well as they know themselves to truly succeed. Wayne adopted this approach after years of witnessing managers pressing their people to work harder and put up more numbers, repeatedly telling the same mindless story.

If leaders put themselves in the shoes of their clients to understand them better than they know themselves in partnership with a healthy balance of activity and metrics, then they will meet with unprecedented success.

Love your people: Remember Rule Number Eight from *The Energy Bus*: "Love your passengers." Remember *Rule Number* Six from Benjamin Zander: "Don't take yourself so goddamn seriously." Emotional intelligence is a stepping-stone toward this.

Fu*k success! Albert Einstein said, "A quiet and modest life brings more joy than a pursuit of success bound with constant unrest." Are you willing to redefine success according to Albert Einstein's words?

Give it away. It was never yours to begin with: Share your knowledge, ideas and insight with your people. Do not hoard it. The best strategies, playbooks, and intelligence are useless in the hands of the competition if they do not know what to do with it. And this is most people.

Smile when the competition tries to steal your employees: If you are a real leader by loving your people, paying your people, and showing them how to become better both professionally and personally they will decline any offer because they value working with you. Even if they do take another job, then it was meant to be, and you can love them and support them through it.

What's right? As an individual, a parent, manager, leader, or employee, are you willing and able to change your perspective from "What's wrong?" when things seem to go awry to a perspective of "What's right?"

If I have a broken finger and am crying because I broke my finger accompanied by a plethora of fearful thoughts that arise when a parent or friend asks, "What's wrong?" I can come up with a laundry list of things in response to what's wrong. But if I am able to ask, "What's right?" I then can see I am blessed to have a body, hand, and finger that can be broken. Instead of fearful thoughts, I can see what's right, that I actually have a finger that can be broken. If I did not have a finger, I would not be able to break it. I am blessed to have a finger. A change of perspective is all that is needed.

We are all angels: We are all angelic beings, but as life's experiences unfold, fear and the ego sink their claws in deep, and we gradually lose sight of our angelic ways. If we take the time to break through the harsh exterior of our ego, we can awaken our angel from deep within once again. This angel has always been there and will remain regardless of our mood, disposition, or chapter in life—no matter how upset or angry we become, no matter how happy and peaceful we are. Our angelic source is the only constant. It keeps us engaged and aligned despite the turmoil, despair, or suffering we experience while on our journey.

Whenever you feel anger, hatred, judgment, jealousy, or any other fear-based emotion toward someone, look closely into that person's eyes. You will see an angel before your very eyes. Next, ask yourself what you are truly upset about. Whenever we feel anger, it is not with the person, event, or thing, but rather our thoughts about the person, event, or thing.

Thank you for taking the journey with me. I write to become better. I write to understand why I made the choices I have made in my life and career. I write to share my experiences with you in the hope that, in some way, it helps you become better while at the same time helping all of us to change our perspective for the better.

> Fear is a guiding light for most people—but not in a good sense. Love is what truly keeps us safe, no matter what decisions we make. Once we release the need to win, we will never lose. When we release our fear of failure, we will always succeed. There are no risks in the absence of fear. Give it all away because it was never yours to begin with.

# Suggested Reading

Business

The Challenger Sale (Dixon & Adamson 2011)
The Energy Bus (Gordon & Blanchard 2010)
Fierce Conversations (Scott 2002)
The Four-Hour Work Week (Ferriss 2007)
Launching a Leadership Revolution (Brady & Woodward 2013)
Leaders Eat Last (Sinek 2014)
Money, How to Master the Game (Robbins 2014)
Outliers (Gladwell 2008)
Start with Why (Sinek 2011)
Tools of Titans (Ferris 2016)
The Wisdom of Failure (Weinzimmer & McConoughey 2012)

Spiritual

Be Here Now (Ram Dass 1971)
The Biology of Belief (Lipton 2005)
I Can See Clearly Now (Dyer 2014)
Change Your Thoughts—Change Your Life (Dyer 2007)
A Course in Miracles (Foundation for Inner Peace 1976)
Dying to Be Me (Moorjani 2014)
Illusions: The Adventures of a Reluctant Messiah (Bach 1989)
Jonathan Livingston Seagull (Bach 1970)
The Power of Intention (Dyer 2005)
The Power of Now (Tolle 1997)
A Return to Love (Williamson 1992)
Wisdom of the Ages (Dyer 2004)
You Can Heal Your Life (Hay 1984)

Children's

I Am a Frog (Willems 2013)

Novels (Fiction)

Lord of the Flies (Golding 1954)
The Sun Also Rises (Hemingway 1926)

Articles

"The Real Reason Great Employees Quit—and Bad Employees Get Promoted," *Forbes*, https://www.forbes.com/sites/lizryan/2018/03/07/the-real-reason-great-employees-quit-and-bad-employees-get-promoted/#1f0ea413880d

"Why Do Most Companies Treat Their Employees Like Garbage?" http://theunderemployedlife.com/companies-treat-employees-garbage/.

"Five Ways Employees Both Get Mad and Get Even," https://managementisajourney.com/five-ways-employees-both-get-mad-and-get-even/

"Why Are Your Employees Quitting? A Study Says It Comes Down to Any of These 6 Reasons," https://www.inc.com/marcel-schwantes/why-are-your-employees-quitting-a-study-says-it-comes-down-to-any-of-these-6-reasons.html

"Why Do People Quit Their Jobs, Exactly? Here's the Entire Reason, Summed Up in 1 Sentence," https://www.inc.com/marcel-schwantes/why-do-people-really-quit-their-jobs-heres-the-entire-reason-summed-up-in-1-sent.html

Website

Inner MBA (https://innermba.soundstrue.com)

About the Author

'Recognizing the shared nature of my thoughts, I am determined to see. I would look upon the witnesses that show me the thinking of the world has been changed. I would behold the proof that what has been done through me has enabled love to replace fear, laughter to replace tears, and abundance to replace loss.' (A Course in Miracles, Foundation for Inner Peace, 2007 ACIM, W-54.5:2-4)

Inspirational author T.E. Corner continues his amazing journey uncovering life's mysteries and identifying the underlying reason why true happiness and satisfaction with life seems to elude many people. Fear and ego are often the culprits.

Assholes to Angels chronicles his experiences working for mindless and self-serving executives over a twenty year career in the financial services industry.

His work and writing approach has been strongly influenced by the likes of Steve Jobs, Seth Godin and Malcolm Gladwell. His desire for a better workplace and world has been motivated by Dr. Wayne Dyer, Eckhart Tolle, Simon Sinek, Jim Rohn and Zig Ziglar.